SPACE
DOMINO

Kai M.F.S.

Paperback: 978-1-7355031-0-3
Hardback: 978-1-7355031-1-0
E-book: 978-1-7355031-2-7

Cover art, book design, map, and written by Kai M.F.S.
Developmental edits by Aaron Beal.
Line & Copy edits by Briana Morgan.
Quote in the front matter by Carl Sagan.

Printed by Amazon.com, Inc.

First printing edition 2020.

Published by Kai M.F.S.
kaimfs.com

I dedicate this book to my mother, who has always been there with support, wisdom, and honesty. She worked hard and sacrificed to raise us alone and if not for her, this book may have been published years from now, if at all.

I am forever grateful.

I love you, Mom

Acknowledgments

Once upon a time, Spacecrime was a tiny, ridiculously simple text-based web game with a vibrant, fun, vulgar community. I ran the game for years, but unfortunately had to shutter it. Some characters in the story are nods to those players in name or in jest but are not based on them. Most other players I have never met, and some are no longer with us. However, without the fun I had with this ridiculous group, I would not have desired to create this universe in my head years after the game was long gone, and this story would not have blossomed from it. I hope you're all well.

- Kai

I would like to thank…

… my developmental editor and best friend of 20+ years, *Aaron Beal*. He pointed out all the dumb stuff I was doing and his critiques & advice helped me push the story to its fullest potential.

… my line and copy editor *Briana Morgan*, who is as talented as she is sweet. A writer herself, she is a skilled editor and a wonderful human being.

… my friend *Julia Scott* for her formatting feedback and supportively harassing me to finish.

… my beta readers, *Christopher "Crash" Reed, Jane Reed, Daniel Hererra, Tanya Gomez, Michael Corpuz, Gilda Reyes, Polina Kurko, Lannee Nguyen, Chelton Perry, Charles Cervas, Cindy Truong, Amy Garcia, Andreas Rodriguez,* and *Kimberly Hooper*. Their feedback helped me better structure and organize my novel, polish off the story, and find the little errors that go unnoticed while editing.

… various digital content creators including *Jenna Moreci* mostly for marketing but also good writing tips, *Answers With Joe* for his fun science videos, *Hello Future Me,* who volunteers his time to a suicide hotline, for his in-depth character and story breakdowns, *Merphy Napier* for her entertaining book reviews & talks, *Shadaversity* for his magnificent machicolations & righteous medieval content, and The Fandom Menace for being such a diverse, welcoming, friendly, and fun community committed to honest communication and a love of genre fiction.

Map of Colonized Space

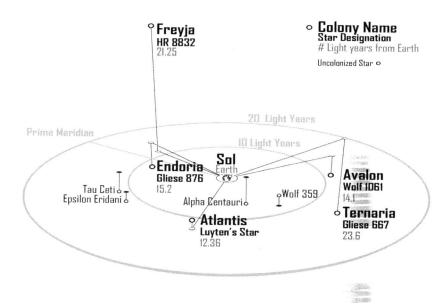

°**Freyja**
HR 8832
21.25

○ **Colony Name**
Star Designation
Light years from Earth

Uncolonized Star ○

20 Light Years

Prime Meridian

10 Light Years

○**Endoria**
Gliese 876
15.2

Sol
Earth

○ **Avalon**
Wolf 1061
14.1

Tau Ceti ○
Epsilon Eridani ○

Alpha Centauri ○

○Wolf 359

○**Ternaria**
Gliese 667
23.6

○**Atlantis**
Luyten's Star
12.36

"You're an interesting species. An interesting mix. You're capable of such beautiful dreams, and such horrible nightmares. You feel so lost, so cut off, so alone, only you're not. See, in all our searching, the only thing we've found that makes the emptiness bearable, is each other."

-Carl Sagan

Prologue

The Concept of Crime

WHAT IS CRIME?

A question not before asked of this pupil, who had already observed a sea of worlds born and die. However, one can gaze upon a single item a thousand times before seeing something new, or something missed. To observe the life of a star, a planet, an insect, or an atom can teach a great many lessons. Yet, for every universe to be experienced, there are infinitely more beyond it, each with their own lessons to teach and wonders to behold. Despite having seen so much, the concept of crime remained elusive.

"Crime." The pupil touched and examined his human body; black skin, five thin fingers, and a nose on his face he could not see without crossing his eyes. "Crime is a byproduct of lawful civilization. Law spontaneously creates a duality, and crime is the inherent counterpart."

What is law?

"Law is a framework for conflicted civilizations that have not yet reached a point of peace and unity."

This one had experienced the wondrous, joyous, and pleasant

facets of physical life. It needed to experience more to blossom into adulthood. Darkness and light dance forever together, perpetuating each other. Without knowing the darkness, one cannot truly know the light, and so the pupil found himself in a craft made for that purpose.

Molded from the aether, the sparkling interior walls buzzed and vibrated. A swirling blue-and-black cloud unfurled from a point and rolled into a large, hovering ring. At its center lay a pale blue dot covered in green and brown landmasses with puffy white clouds and a small, gray moon. Aligned with the planet's terminator, night fell on one of its coasts. Cities illuminated the dark landmasses like nerves in a body, brightest near the water. It was a thriving planet, home to a species at the dawn of a new era.

This one had seen this planet before. It was commonly home to humans, who usually called it Terra, Gaia, or Earth. Resourceful and defiant, human worlds spanned the spectrum of possibilities. Sometimes the world was a utopia, other times a cruel pit of despair or a bloody battleground. In this universe, humans had expanded and colonized other planets, but at the cost of unifying as a species. Dysfunctional as the humans in this universe were, the pupil had seen worse but had always been quick to look away.

Thoughts directed toward the night-laden land below, the pupil watched a young human destined for greatness. Gazing upon the single human's life, everything else faded away. When the ship shook violently and without warning, the pupil's focus was broken, and he was brought back to the present. He looked around the ship to find himself alone. The cloud had disappeared. The walls had become semi-transparent and shined no longer. The ship rattled around him deafeningly, and below, the planet drew closer.

The pupil's human heart raced, a reaction to external stimuli, but his mind remained calm. It was as if his heart wanted to leap out of his chest and leave him behind to crash. He grabbed onto his seat and the ship careened toward the planet. He closed his eyes and fell into the planet's shadow.

Part

1

Chaos and Kismet

Natalie

1

Humble Beginnings

THE ROAR OF A COMBUSTION ENGINE BOOMED IN THE SPACIOUS school garage. It roared repeatedly, louder and longer each time until it wound down to a sputtering hum. The garage full of old cars was brought to a halt as the busy students watched one of the vehicles shake to life.

"Mr. Curtis! We're done!" A dazzling girl with big blue eyes and blonde hair well covered by a bandana leaned out of the passenger window, arm high in the air.

"Yes, Ash, we heard," said a tall, paunchy man with a small tablet and a bushy yellow mustache. He set the tablet down on the rim of the hood and leaned over the engine. "Let's have a look. Natalie, give it another go."

The engine again burst into a roar and shook the car, including the rickety hood propped over his head.

"So, what's up, Mr. C? Good stuff, huh?" Ash leaned hazardously out the window in her class-mandated blue jumpsuit, which stretched from ankles to neck and zipped up in the front.

"Sure is, not that you did the lion's share of the work," Mr. Curtis grumbled.

Ash gasped dramatically. "The lion's share? I did *all* the heavy lifting here. Me and my girl, we're a team, right, Natalie?"

From the driver's seat sprung a lively girl as plain as blank paper with frizzy black hair in a ponytail and a confident smile. Hazel eyes gleaming with pride, she strutted around to the hood of the car. "I couldn't do it without her, Mr. Curtis." Natalie rolled her sleeves back above her elbows, at peace with the swaths of black grease across her forearms. "She's strong for her size and some of the parts were *really* rusted."

"I *literally* do the heavy lifting," Ash chimed in.

"Well, you're on the wrestling team so you'd *better*." Mr. Curtis turned his attention back to the engine. "This looks good to me. Well done, ladies."

He updated their project's status on his tablet while the girls danced in celebration. Natalie kissed her fingers and touched them lovingly to the front of the car. She pranced back around the driver's door and slid inside to turn it off. In contrast, Ash turned her attention to more pressing matters, which for her meant rubbing their success in the adjacent team's face.

"Hah! Suck it, Emilio!"

"Man, this is bullshit," said a boy with a button nose and a thick brow. He sat on a creeper in front of his car, wrench still in hand. "How the hell you finish so fast?"

"My girl's a beast! That's how! You don't want none of this!" Ash taunted.

"Ash, calm down and stop hanging off the door like that. Emilio, no cursing." Mr. Curtis interrupted. Ash obeyed with a heavy, disapproving sigh, but made no fuss. Natalie put the hood down and came around to Ash's side of the car.

"Mr. C." Emilio leaned back against his bumper. "How come we're using combustion engines? Wouldn't working with more modern equipment make us better workers? Nobody even uses these anymore." He elbowed the car behind him.

"Machines all work more or less the same. If you want to learn more, keep going to school. The better your foundation, the better a mechanic you'll be," Mr. Curtis said.

Emilio's eyes drifted to the floor then back up. "Why don't we have less cars, bigger teams, and newer cars?"

"Because we don't have the money for it, Emilio. We only get this stuff because they were going to get scrapped. You're a Delta, Natalie's a Delta, Delta, Delta." Mr. Curtis pointed to Ash and other students around the room, who had all gotten back to work. "Make the most of what you've got. Besides, you can make good money converting and restoring antique cars."

"What if we want to work on flying cars?" Emilio pressed.

"Not even five percent of people even have one of those new fliers, Emilio. They're *new*, you've got some time to learn about 'em." Mr. Curtis walked away.

"Whatever." Emilio leaned back onto his creeper and rolled under his car.

Natalie followed Mr. Curtis back to his station with Ash hot on her heels. "Since we're done, can we clean up and go to lunch early?"

Mr. Curtis gave them an incredulous look. Natalie and Ash offered him big eyes and big smiles, like a begging cat or dog.

He sighed in defeat. "If you can clean yourselves up and pick up your station in time, sure."

The girls ran with excitement to pick up their station. Having kept so covered up, Ash picked up most of the station. The quickest to get clean and fix her makeup, she finished first and stole caramel cubes from Mr. Curtis's desk to keep herself busy while Natalie scrubbed the grease and dirt off her body. The doorway beeped as they left for lunch, illuminating the ancient Greek Delta brands on the left side of their necks.

They got their lunches early and sat at the edge of a high walkway that overlooked the quad. They watched the crowd of hungry students bustle about below. While Natalie fiddled with a chocolate brownie and chatted with Ash, a familiar voice called her from behind.

Natalie spun around. A thin boy with big brown eyes and scruffy light-brown hair smiled back at her. Like Natalie, he was dressed simply in blue jeans and a gaming T-shirt. Lifelong friends, Natalie found him to be rather handsome, with a strong chin and a brown beauty mark under his left eye. Ash, on the other hand, had compared his face to a lazily molded pile of clay.

"Will!" Natalie jumped to her feet. She squeezed him, resting her head on his chest. Sweeping some hair behind her ear, she pulled away.

"What's up, Cooper?" Ash leaned back with a mischievous smile, remaining seated. Will was the starting goalie for the football team, so he and Ash often interacted in sports-related school events, where they were referred to by their last names.

"You know me, living a dangerous life of crime." Will sat next to Natalie.

"*Such* a badass." Ash's big blue eyes widened sarcastically.

"Oh yeah, speaking of, don't you owe me fifty bucks?" Will taunted back with a charming smile.

"I'll have to get you later..." Ash's body shrunk down and she faked a bashful smile at Will.

"That's what I thought." Will slipped the backpack off his shoulder and pulled from it a thin mobile computer with a protective purple case and a shiny, clean glass screen. "For you."

"YES!" Natalie burst, fists in the air. She wrapped her arms around his shoulders and squeezed him again. "Thank you so much." She giddily took back her mobile.

"You're welcome. Next time, just come to me before you brick it," he said.

"I knooooow. I wanted to try to crack it myself. *All* you have to do is follow the instructions, right?" She rolled her eyes. "It's only 'til I turn eighteen and get some AR, anyway. How much do I owe you?" She reached into her backpack.

"Um, we can talk about that later." Will gently grabbed her arm to stop her.

"How about I meet you online tonight, *after* my curfew?" Natalie gave him an exaggerated wink and waved her mobile in the air. With her mobile cracked, she could use it without her parents or officials tracking her every word and move. It was a serious offense, but a law people constantly broke.

"Sure." Will smiled.

"Hey, is there a test in Mr. Anderson's class today?" Ash asked abruptly.

"If your class voted for it, yeah," Natalie said.

"Why… would we vote *for* a test? And, on a Monday?" Ash eyed Natalie with a raised eyebrow and a slack jaw.

"He gave all his classes the option like two weeks ago," Will said. "So his class would be a free period before the break."

"Are you guys messing with me?" Ash leaned back and glared at them. Natalie and Will gawked, amazed at Ash's lack of attention. "Oh *shit*, you're not messing with me." Ash shot up straight with her hand over her mouth.

"You really didn't know?" Natalie asked.

"How come you haven't been studying for it or anything?" Ash smacked Natalie's arm several times whilst Natalie defended herself.

"Oh my god! Do you know how many cool ships were developed for World War Four? I don't need to study for that test, I know that *whole* era. I'm pretty sure I *aced* it this morning," Natalie said.

"Fuck! What the hell, Natalie?" Ash smacked her again. "What the hell?"

Both puzzled and amused, Will leaned around Natalie to address Ash. "How did you *not* know?"

"That – doesn't matter. Shut up, *Pooper*." Ash turned back to her mobile to search for a cheat sheet. Natalie would not have one, so she had to get the answers from someone else before class. Will and Natalie shared a look of bewilderment and giggled.

"Well, *I'm* feeling good about my life," Natalie said. Ash gave her the stink-eye, and then returned to her search.

"I'm feeling pretty good too. But, I've got to go. Meeting up with Dave and the guys. I'll talk to you tonight." Will stood and slung his backpack over his shoulder.

"Yeah. Thanks again for the delivery." Natalie stood with him for a hug. "Have fun with *the guys*," she teased.

"Of course." Will leaned around Natalie. "Later Ash."

"See ya." Ash waved goodbye without looking away from her device. She worked hard to cheat and was not chatty for what remained of lunch.

Without another class together, Natalie and Ash were forced apart until their after-school walk to get smoothies. A little over an hour later they each had a lonely ride home on separate public trams. Natalie watched the massive Rocky Mountains through the windows on her trip to the fringes of town.

After the tram, she still had to walk down a dirt road before she arrived at her family's property and another two-kilometer walk to her house from there. She enjoyed the long, solitary stroll through the woods. Rays of light peeked through the foliage and sprinkled light on the shaded road. Natalie bounced to music playing from her mobile.

A rustle in the wilderness rushed toward her. From behind a thicket of tall bushes leaped Natalie's gigantic mixed chocolate labrador retriever, Gizmo. He was as happy to see her as the day they rescued him.

Gizmo stood on his hind legs in an attempt to lick her face and force himself into a hug. She let him down and wiped her cheek with her sleeve. They traveled the path together almost every day she came back from school. She often found him waiting for her on the path when she returned later than usual.

The tranquil road led Natalie to a cream-colored two-story house with red shingles. It sat in the middle of a clearing at the end of a roundabout that looped around a patch of tall trees. Her father's red truck was parked underneath their shade. To the east, on Natalie's left stretched a vast field of green corn stalks as tall as she. By harvest time, they would be more than twice as tall, dwarfing her small frame. Westward, the colossal and majestic Rocky Mountains extended from the edge of the valley nearby.

The rest of her afternoon she spent with her dad, Bill, taking apart a 2107 Punisher – a classic from the old United States' fifth great muscle car boom. The almost eighty-year-old beauty was in shambles when they found it. They had already done all the prep work, and Natalie was excited to take apart the insides. What started out as Natalie handing her dad the wrong tools when she could barely form sentences turned into an activity they shared to this day.

With the sun setting, the garage's automated lights clicked on. A breeze swept through the garage and nipped at their bones, prompting them to wrap up and go inside. Natalie's mother, Olivia, was ready to call them in for dinner when they entered the kitchen through the back.

The family sat around the dinner table and shared stories while they ate. Bill's mobile buzzed in his pocket. He ignored a cross look from his wife to check it. Natalie's seven-year-old brother, Nathan, took advantage of his dad's distraction to check under the table for easily the tenth time. Usually, Gizmo was there to eat the food he and his sister did not want, but he was again left looking back at his plate with a sigh of disappointment.

"That was an alert from Natalie's school." Bill put away his mobile and halted the conversation. Natalie was sure she was not in trouble, but that was a bad start to a sentence. "Congratulations on acing your history test today," he said proudly.

"That's my girl!" Olivia clapped with a loving tilt of her head. Nathan's cheer was more drawn out and sarcastic.

"Thanks for the good news! Between that and shop class, I'm going to have *so* much free time before the break," Natalie said.

"What about shop class?" Olivia asked.

"Oh." Natalie had not yet updated her mother. "Ash and I got our car running! Anything we get done now just puts us ahead."

"Way to go sweetie!" Olivia beamed. "Ash did her fair share, right?"

"Oh my god." Natalie looked back and forth between her parents. "Dad asked me the same thing. Ash was a *huge* help."

"Well, I'm proud of you." Olivia reached out to grab Bill's hand. "Bill, I don't want to wait anymore," she said sheepishly. Natalie and Nathan glanced at each other and then observed their parents with intrigue.

"You can tell 'em whenever you want," Bill told his wife. Olivia wiggled in her seat, squeezing Bill's hand with an ear-to-ear smile.

"Kids, your father and I have been saving up some money to give you a surprise vacation. We think it *might* be something you two could be interested in. There's this fancy ship they're supposed to finish building later this year. Biggest, *fastest* one ever," Olivia said coyly. She knew they were aware of the ship, which had been news since its concept was put into production.

"The *Felicity*?" Natalie asked, eager for her mother to get to the point.

"That's the one," Olivia said. "Well, the maiden voyage will take a tour through some of the colonies, and we thought it might be a great way to spend a family vacation." She smiled, pleased with herself.

"We're going to space!" Nathan roared, fists in the air.

"We're going on a starship!" Natalie squealed, hands on her head. "Oh my god!" She bounced in her seat and fumbled to get out and run to her parents.

"Now I'm actually happy you did good!" Nathan hugged Natalie as she tried to get around his chair, anchoring her. She returned the hug, then moved along to thank her parents. Nathan followed her example.

"Thank you so much!" she gushed, going from one parent to another.

"Oh, sweetie, thank you two for being so amazing. We're lucky to have such a great pair of kids," Olivia said.

"I can't believe we're going on the *Felicity*! I hear Avalon is magical, and they say that everyone from Avalon has their own ship!" Natalie gushed. "Is this why things have been tight?" Natalie found her seat again with a confirmatory nod from Olivia.

"I knew it!" Nathan said.

"No you didn't," Natalie contested. Nathan shrunk down with a grin.

"Are we still going hiking next week?" Nathan asked.

"Of course, that's free." Bill set his utensils on his plate and stood from the table.

"The cars you and your dad fix up have helped a lot." Olivia stood as well and Bill stacked her dishes atop his. "Thank you, love." Olivia shared a quick kiss on the lips with her husband. "Is everyone finished?"

"Yep." Natalie handed over her empty plate and excused herself.

"Yes!" Nathan jumped out of his seat.

"Mr., that plate does *not* look finished to me. Eat some more of your broccoli. Dip it in the sauce. Natalie, sweetie, can you bring Gizmo inside?" Olivia took Natalie's plate and followed Bill into the kitchen.

"Sure." Happy to comply, Natalie snatched the dog whistle that hung from a lanyard next to the door and skipped outside, down the steps of the patio. She checked over her shoulder before she pulled out her mobile. There was an alert from her school and a pending message from Will. She had to reply with text so as to not be heard. Her parents could still snatch it away if she was within earshot. She stuffed the mobile back in her pocket and her walk turned brisk and upbeat.

The moon looked down on Natalie from the sky, bathing her family's farm in its soft light. The slow dinging of wind chimes on the porch added to the peaceful ambiance.

"Gizmo!" Natalie walked toward the cornfields, blowing the dog whistle. After a moment, barking beckoned far from the east and she headed into the dark sea of waving corn stalks, calling for Gizmo and blowing the whistle.

A pack of clouds rolled in, bringing darkness with them, shrouding the fields in shadow. Natalie's house, on an elevated foundation, grew distant behind her. It peeked over the sea of corn. There was barking, then rustling not far ahead. Gizmo's lovable brown face burst from behind some corn stalks and he jumped onto his hind legs.

"There's my boy! You're out so far tonight," Natalie gushed in her cute, high-pitched dog voice. She hugged him and scratched the sides of his neck. "Come on, it's time to go inside." She grabbed his collar and led him back to the house. Gizmo followed happily alongside Natalie, who checked her mobile as they walked.

After an unexpected tug from Gizmo, Natalie halted. Gizmo had stopped in his tracks. His ears twitched and his head swiveled around. He listened to something she could not hear.

"What is it, boy?" She knelt beside him and lovingly scratched behind his ears. Natalie listened, but there was only the gentle rustle of corn stalks.

Gizmo jumped and switched between barks and nervous whimpers. He looked at Natalie, who held his collar tightly. Unnerved, Gizmo bounced and growled. Natalie gripped his collar and urged him to settle down. She searched for a mysterious figure or animal hidden in the field.

"Is someone out there?" Natalie called out, but there was no response.

She stopped trying to get Gizmo to settle down when rolling thunder rumbled quietly and drew closer. Natalie searched again, but still, there was nothing. The sound seemed to come from the east, but there was nothing out of the ordinary.

Out of thin air, a giant ball of fire exploded into the night sky, barreling toward Natalie, knocking her to the floor in bewildered surprise. "What the hell?" She gripped Gizmo's collar and held her mobile toward the giant fireball. "Record video!" Natalie was quick to get back on her feet.

The inferno appeared to be some sort of ship, red hot from a bad re-entry. It had held together even with a hole through its bow that sparked and crackled with fire. The large silver ship tilted to its side and zoomed not even one hundred meters over her head, close enough for her to break a sweat from the heat. Flat and longer than it was wide, it tapered to a long point in the front and bulged toward the center of the rounded rear half, reminiscent of a giant pumpkin seed. The strange, windowless craft was one large piece of metal with no thrusters. Natalie followed it as it passed; staring in awe, mouth agape.

"Oh... my... god..." she muttered. Her fingers barely clung to Gizmo's collar, but he made no attempt to go anywhere. His growls and barks faded away.

Natalie's favorite picture books as a baby were of spacecraft and cars. She grew up reading everything she could find that pertained to machines. She took great pride in her ability to identify vehicles, as well as knowing obscure details about them whenever possible. She could name the years vehicles were produced, the manufacturers, different types of ships before, during, after the war, and how their designs influenced each other. This craft, however, was a mystery.

The ship missed the house by centimeters and smashed into the roundabout. The house rattled violently and every window shattered. The earth shook with the impact and knocked Natalie back to the ground. Splinters of wood and mangled metal from her dad's truck rained down on the property in streaks of fire. The ship was embedded in the ground like a needle. It stood as tall as her house even half buried and at an angle.

Still recording, she had not noticed that Gizmo had turned back around and was barking at something else.

Three boxy gray and black craft zoomed over her head in pursuit of the crashed ship. Each was as long as a full-sized bus but twice as wide and covered in armor. Isolated cockpits with large round windows maximized the pilot's visibility. Two independently pivoting engines at the tips of the wings gave them a unique profile, which, worryingly, Natalie also did not recognize. The cutting edge crafts sent an eerie chill up Natalie's spine but were at least made of tech she recognized.

The crafts maneuvered easily and their sides opened upward like a car's gull-wing doors. They dropped men down on cables around her house and the crashed ship. Some wore sleeveless outfits and earpieces, while others had tactical helmets and visors. Armor varied from one to another with no uniformity besides their general armament and coordination. In Natalie's life, soldiers were relegated to games, movies, history, and her dad's stories. With the Peaceful Union Act of 2163, armies ceased to exist.

If there were no more soldiers, who were the men storming her house?

"What's going on?" Natalie asked herself, heart racing with panic.

Her father ran onto the porch to see what was happening. The men swarmed him and the house with their weapons drawn. Natalie's father scuffled with them. He kicked one over the railing and quarreled with another. A third jammed the butt of his rifle into his kidneys. They poured into the house while the two men beat him with their rifles until another man stopped them. They stepped on him, yanked his arms back and bound him, then dragged his body into the dirt. Rage sank into the pit of Natalie's stomach and turned to nausea.

Yanked forward, Gizmo's collar slipped from her loose grip and snapped Natalie out of her daze. Gizmo barked and ran into the dark thicket of corn toward the house. He had surely heard the violence and wanted to protect his pack.

Natalie's hands trembled. She helplessly watched her house assaulted and her dog running into a small army of violent, armed men. Gizmo could not help, and neither could she.

Natalie stood there for a moment, speechless until her brain rebooted and a rush of reason swept over her.

"Stop... recording," she said. Her mobile confirmed her order with a beep and the screen turned black. Natalie stuffed it into her pocket and paced backward. Her fists trembled and tears ran down her cheeks. She pressed her quivering lips together. Through deep, stuttered breaths, she looked upon the home where she had grown up.

With clenched fists and a heavy heart, Natalie closed her eyes and turned around. When she opened them again, she walked forward. Her steps quickened to keep pace with her heart. The beating in her chest pressed her forward, faster and faster until she sprinted through the fields. Natalie clenched her teeth and pushed herself to run harder than she ever had before.

Iron Eagle

2

Darkness

An unprecedented event turned a long day for Commander Fuller into an equally long night. The evening had taken a sudden and unexpected twist that required immediate attention. An eerie chill had run down his spine the moment the large, silver ship flew by. There was no room for error on this mission. This gig was the most legitimate work he could find for his crew, and it usually meant less questionable orders. But, this event had Fuller on edge. They hid the foreign ship in a hologram for most of its descent, but it moved faster than they did. Hopefully, nobody saw it.

Commander Fuller slid open a metal panel on the wall to reveal a hidden glass console behind it. With a scar down his left cheek and a lit cigarette dangling from his lips, his rugged reflection scowled back at him. Fuller told himself the cigarettes were to deal with the stress, but he knew it was a bad habit without purpose. When he was honest with himself, he considered it his weakest feature. The war was tough, and he did not smoke before it, but the years since had taxed him greatly.

With the ship's side doors closed, Fuller clicked a small button under the butt of his palm and an interface appeared on his hand. The console screen on the wall flashed while it established a secure connection. A bald, fat man in a brown suit flickered onto the screen. His face seemed to be stuck in a state of unyielding self-importance. The sleazy bureaucrat with small, beady eyes reeked of lies and deceit even through the screen. The man was a government employee named Gregory Deacon, but to whom he answered was a mystery. The main reason Fuller had lived long enough to go gray was because he knew when to play ball.

"Hello, Commander Fuller." Deacon's bright eyes beamed with excitement, but his face made even his genuine smile glow with condescension. "What news do you have for me? Do we have any survivors?"

"Looks like we do," Fuller read the feed of his team's activities on a display in his hand. "The craft has been secured as well. It landed by a house, the civilian family is home." Fuller used his finger as a pen to write on his hand.

"How exciting! How large is the family?" He waited for Fuller to get a response in his feed.

"It's a family of four, three present," Fuller responded as promptly as he could, no intention to speak with or even look at Deacon any longer than necessary.

"Good." Deacon nodded, eyes far away in thought. "This event requires the utmost secrecy, it's a matter of planetary security. There were no civilian witnesses; there was no ship. This was an accident, a terrible tragedy."

Fuller's eyes drifted from his hand to the screen. "You want to run that by me again?" The ship touched down and rattled around him, but Fuller hardly noticed.

"I'm sorry, Commander, which part was unclear?" Deacon asked. "This is a rural area, is it not? I'm sure they have their own power cell. It blew up during dinner or something. Like I said, a terrible tragedy." He interlaced his fingers and smiled grimly.

"Isn't there ah… another way to keep 'em quiet?" Fuller hoped for an alternative to murder. A cigarette dangling from his fingers, he sent a billow of smoke at the screen.

"Commander, we're not taking *any* risks with this. If the Iron Eagle can't do what needs be done, then we can contract someone else for our security needs."

"That won't be necessary. Planetary security comes first. I'll get it done." Fuller clenched his fist off screen, accidentally crushing his cigarette.

"Thank you, Commander, have a splendid night." Deacon's fat cheeks puffed up with a pompous smile and the screen went black. Fuller looked into the eyes of his reflection. This time it looked back at him with judgment.

"Cock sucker!" Fuller slammed the metal panel shut and flipped the nearby switch to open the rear door. He leaned against the wall, closed his eyes, and steadied his breath. The large metal ramp dropped open behind him with a soft churn.

Once he had collected himself, Fuller marched down the rear ramp and lit up a fresh cigarette. Surely he would need many more of them that night. With a drag of his cigarette, he looked over the property. Three members of the family huddled together on the floor with their hands bound and Fuller's men behind them. Not far away from the family knelt a dark-skinned young man with dirt-covered silver clothes that hung loosely from his body.

Fuller re-joined the team's audio channel then headed for Hudson, his second-in-command. Hudson stood by the front door directing those inside when a gut-wrenching scream ripped through the channel.

With a jump, everyone checked their displays. One name, Kaplan, lit up with every cry. Hudson and many of the men stampeded to his position. Two loud gunshots and groans of pain preceded their arrival.

The medic rushed to Kaplan, who lay in the dirt with blood splattered around him. He cradled his left arm, covered in gashes and torn flesh, gushing blood into a puddle beneath him. One man wrapped himself around Kaplan's shoulder to hold him while the medic painted his arm with a clear substance to nullify the pain. Kaplan calmed down and his heavy breaths subsided. With his patient at peace, the medic wrapped organic bonds around injured veins and tendons like tape.

Next to Kaplan an enormous dog whimpered and struggled to breathe, blood pooling around it. One of the men comforted the dog and petted it before he put a bullet in its head to end its suffering.

"How's Kaplan?" Fuller asked.

"Sir." Hudson spun around. "He's all right, they'll have him patched up in a minute. I was about to send the *Arrow* and a team into the fields in case there was someone out there with the dog. I think it could be the teenage girl that's unaccounted for."

"Do it. A word after." Fuller walked away. Hudson called out the orders and followed Fuller. Behind them, one ship hovered toward the cornfields with a half dozen men fanned out beneath it, spread as far across the field as they could.

"Who is that next to the family?" Fuller asked.

"We caught him running from the crashed ship. Looked like he got his bell rung."

"*That's* the survivor?" Fuller asked. Hudson confirmed with a nod, and Fuller looked back in disbelief.

"What were you expecting? An *alien?*" Hudson chuckled.

"He's... young," Fuller tried to provide alternate motivations for his reaction.

"Doesn't look old enough to drink," Hudson scoffed. "Where do you think he got a ship like this? I've never seen anything like it before." He marveled at the silver ship towering over them like an ancient monolith.

"It's experimental, don't ask questions like that. We've got orders I need to fill you in on." Fuller crushed the end of his cigarette under his boot, a new one already in hand. He lit up the fresh smoke then held two fingers over his earpiece to mute his audio.

"What's that, sir?" Hudson followed Fuller's lead and turned off his audio.

Fuller explained their orders, and what they were supposed to do with the family who sat not thirty meters away.

Hudson's excitement about the mission's unique and unexpected turns faded when he realized those twists had taken him somewhere he did not want to be. There was no problem with secrets; they were sometimes necessary to keep people safe. When he joined he told himself he was ready to do what was necessary. What Fuller had explained, however, was never something he thought would someday weigh on his conscience.

"Eyes front, soldier," Fuller got Hudson's attention, which had drifted away in reflection. "This is something you and some of the younger guys here haven't had to do before, but it's part of the job."

"Yes, sir. I understand." Hudson nodded, glancing at the family and the foreboding ship.

Fuller un-muted his audio and turned on his hand display, then tapped around to adjust the channel's settings.

"Everybody listen up," he barked. "The secrecy of this ship and its pilot are a matter of planetary security and maintaining that secrecy is our number one priority. This event, our presence here, none of this ever happened. This house's faulty generator blew up while the family was inside, is that understood?"

"Y-yes, sir," various voices responded in a jumble over the audio channel. The older guys were quicker to respond. Most had already done something dirty in the past.

"All right, let's get to it," Fuller ordered. "Moore, Bowyer, Franklin: take Kaplan and the prisoner back to base."

The two men who guarded the captured survivor helped him to his feet and guided him into Fuller's ship. The men around Kaplan helped him to the ship while the medic, Franklin, bandaged his arm.

Meanwhile, the family found themselves swarmed by the men guarding them. Olivia screamed, Bill tried to push them off and protect her and Nathan, but he had already been too badly beaten to make a difference. They stuck the family with sleepers, small tear-shaped containers with built-in hygienic needles. The family struggled to stay upright, but soon slumped to the floor. Their eyes pulled themselves shut and the world around them faded into darkness.

A drone flew in and delivered a bowling ball-sized aluminium sphere with handlebars. Fuller and Hudson carried it inside and set it down next to the house's battery in the cellar.

When Fuller and Hudson returned upstairs, the family had been laid about the living room and everyone had cleared out. They exited through the back door into a world astir. The last ship set down behind the garage. Once everyone had slipped behind nearby buildings for cover, the night quieted. The silence became absolute.

A rumble shook the ground beneath their feet and rolled like thunder over the fields. The house glowed with a bright light and then exploded. Debris scattered all over the clearing and into the fields nearby. The crashed ship rattled loose, but strangely took no additional damage.

The house sat splintered and in ruin. Its foundation lay shattered with a crater at least twenty meters wide. Only the crackle of fire accompanied the crunch of footsteps over dirt. Nobody spoke as they came out from behind cover.

Fuller lit a fresh cigarette, then took a long drag and looked over the destruction. With his hand on his hip and a long sigh he paced the perimeter of the crater. Others walked around to witness the death they had wrought. Fuller finally broke the unofficial radio silence with an order.

"Let's get back to work."

?

Light

THE WALLS TURNED OPAQUE THE MOMENT THE SHIP HIT THE ground and saturated the room in darkness. To leave the ship meant entering a new reality, but there was nowhere else to go. As long as the pupil remained on the ship, he could never see beyond it. Hand pressed to the wall, a circle of light expanded above him. Before he could exit and get his bearings the ship adopted the alien universe's physics.

The gravity pulled him up to a dirt ceiling with fire that burned downward. With a crunch, he landed in a pile of burning wood. His long silver shirt fell over his face. He received a free crash course on gravity in this universe, but was unable to make sense of space and time. His vision through time was dull and limited. For the first time in his life, he could not see through time. This meant there was no certain future. Somehow, he had become stuck in a linear state of time.

He rolled backward out of the wood pile in a hurried panic and patted his shirt to put out the small fire it had acquired. A failed attempt to stand and run toppled him sideways onto himself.

Time had been easy to figure out, especially when stuck in it, but space was not so intuitive. Using gravity to align himself, he closed his eyes and pulled himself sideways onto his feet like a vampire rising from a coffin. Running to the nearby forest, the world spun in different directions. He tried to focus on the physical space directly in front of him but after a few clumsy steps he fell to one knee, and then it was too late.

A bright light beamed down on him from above and humans in brown, black, and gray armor dropped down around him on cables. The hostile humans pointed weapons at him and yelled in their language. He assimilated the information and raised his hands. The callous humans had firm grips and pulled on him when binding his wrists. They circled around him, then guided him past his crashed ship. He stumbled, but they caught him when he fell, without the same roughness as before. Gradually, he became accustomed to his new, strangely static environment.

It was one thing to have seen millions of species come and go, to see their struggles and their triumphs on a large scale as they sweep across millennia, to see the little details nobody else has the privilege of knowing. It was a gift to know how things connected, what worked and what did not. To watch a species grow from its mistakes and create a better world could be spectacular. But, the terror of being caught in the midst of history as it happened with the knowledge he could damage the natural timeline was all but paralyzing, and clenched his heart in a vise.

The humans did not ask any questions. They meandered about until their commander gave an order and they hooked their arms under his, pulling him to his feet, then escorted him into a nearby craft. Alongside an injured human, a craft flew him away from the crash site flanked at all times by guards.

Amidst a lightly forested mountain range far from civilization, the two guards escorted the pupil, presumed to be a captured pilot, into the underground depths of a large cement structure. They took him down a narrow hall of thick cement cells with gated entrances. Every cell was empty with the exception of the one in the middle. There, an armless man sat on a bench in the back of his cell, obscured by shadows. He watched them escort the mysterious captive past him.

The guards left the captive in the last cell. The humans' footsteps echoed away until the hall's metal door clanked shut. Left in silence, the captive sat on a bench built into the cell's back wall. He had barely enough time to take a breath before a soft voice, inaudible to human ears, broke the silence.

"How did you find yourself a captive?" A bright swirling light appeared in the middle of the small cell. The various tendrils of light grew and extended outward, then its center bulged into a humanoid form. Like a shifting veil it condensed into a human visage with soft features.

The figure floated in place, wings of electric white light open behind it glistening with gold and silver. Its translucent skin shimmered, hands clasped in front of it. The being's silver hair stood upright and swayed like it floated in water. Tiny lights rose from it and drifted away like bubbles before they flickered out of sight. In the being's eyes the young captive saw home. Eternity looked back at him, brilliant like the birth of a universe, the eyes glimmered with light from every spectrum. This being of light was one of the oldest species in existence, able to hide itself even from the young captive's species with a simple adjustment of where it existed in the light spectrum.

"I was disoriented, unable to escape their perception. Your presence is humbling." The young captive bowed. "Rarely are my kind so fortunate as to lay eyes upon yours."

"The only place beyond reach is *your* home. Your presence is equally humbling and puzzling," the brilliant being said. "You could leave through the folds of space to wherever you'd like. Why stay in this cage and play the role of captive?"

"Scholars taught me that if this happens, one should flow with time and allow the universe to heal itself. I am a discrepancy. The universe will mitigate my presence in its own way," he explained.

"So once your presence is felt, you have no option but to move with the choices of this universe." The being's eyes glowed brighter and its gaze intensified. A strange tingle reverberated through the young prisoner's body. "Be calm. All that you are can be seen by the light." The intensity of his eyes faded back to normal.

"What did you see?" the captive asked.

"Your are full of light," the being replied.

"Is that why you're here?"

"No, for the light of others, and here you are found. How is it you came to be stuck in time? That cannot be seen."

"That is something I too strive to understand."

"Unadvisable." The being shook its head. "You came to learn something. When you understand it, you can transcend. Fixate not on what you cannot see, and learn from all you can."

"Thank you for the advice," the young captive said.

"You should be left on your journey." The brilliant being bowed.

"I value our existence together."

"Likewise. Go with love, and your light will shine brightly, easy to find." The brilliant being smiled, light enveloped it, and it blinked out of sight.

With a deep sigh, the captive was relieved to see such a being. Although rarely encountered, their legacy indicated that wherever they were, so too were there beings with tender hearts. Whoever the being was attracted to, he could only hope they would help if he encountered them.

Good can be found on both sides of every mortal conflict.

Natalie

4

Alone

NATALIE SPRINTED THROUGH THE DARK AISLES OF CORN STALKS, teeth clenched, breathing hard through her nose. There had been gunshots some time ago, but her sense of time was distorted. She kept a relentless pace, knees high, her feet barely touching the ground. Her heart pounded in her chest like it wanted to outrun her. Each beat sent a rush of energy coursing through her body. Her lungs were hot coals. The heat rose into her throat and turned every searing breath into a battle to continue. Her legs were melting, but the pain was distant. Concern for her family swirled like a torrent in her mind.

Unfocused, Natalie's attention snapped back to reality when she flew out of the cornfields into an emptiness between the crops and the property's tall, chain-linked fence. Natalie slowed down before she launched herself at the nearest post and scampered up the fence. It rattled with her every movement. She swung herself over and paused at the top, taking a moment to look upon her lifelong home for what may be the last time.

In her moment of peace, the fence shook and rattled and the ground trembled beneath it. What should have been a calm and pleasant goodbye turned into a horrifying spectacle. A bright whirlwind of light consumed her spacious two-story home, then it erupted and launched flaming debris into the night.

Against the bright explosion was a dark shadow.

Natalie gasped, hands clasped over her mouth containing a horrified scream. Her legs turned to gelatin and she collapsed. She tried to grab the fence with one hand and tumbled to the floor. It was as if a spear had been shot through her heart. Her family was inside. She felt them disappear forever.

Her head hung in sorrow, her body frozen in place, her mind stuck in a loop. Tears ran down her cheeks and any glimmer of hope she had was gone. The scene replayed in her mind until she realized that against the light of the explosion there was a silhouette of a ship headed her way. A jolt of energy surged through her, fueled by the urgent need to escape. She wiped her tears, sniffled and gasped for breath. Lungs and throat still ablaze, she looked around to get her bearings. A tidal wave of grief could not be allowed to anchor her in place.

Devoid of strength, Natalie's legs wobbled when she tried to stand. A hand on her knee, she took a deep breath and pushed herself up. Without knowing where she was headed, she meandered into the knee-high creek that ran behind her property. Natalie's feet sunk into the muddy edges of the water with a squish, her hands trembling, her body numb. Completely alone, she could not deny the appeal of staying there to let the cards fall as they might.

Even if she outran the men after her and followed the river into town, nobody there could help her. Who would she ask? What could anyone do? Her only other option was to go south, downstream, which would pass by a few properties before it dumped her in the Rockies.

It hit her like a bolt of lightning.

Will's property ran alongside the creek to the south.

The burst of energy waned. Going to Will could put his life in danger, as well as his family. But if the roles were reversed, she would be angry if Will did not come to her for help. He knew how not to get caught, which was exactly what she needed. Also, her family had probably hoped she would survive, so it was her duty to do so. If she trusted anyone to help her, it was Will.

With the fires of hope stoked inside her, Natalie's heart pumped power back into her veins. She turned around and hurried downstream. She kept to the edge of the creek so it would not slow her down as much. The shallow water splashed around her. It was not long before she found some rocks and patches of grass she could use to hop onto the grassy east bank so as not to leave tracks in her wake since that was how dumb people got caught in movies. She checked behind her and continued her hasty trek under the cover of trees and plants which grew in thickets around the creek. Small animals scurried away and chirping crickets paused when she passed through overgrown foliage.

Natalie wandered around in a haze, lost in thought, and almost passed the bent, overgrown tree her trio of friends used to jump over Will's fence. With her mind withdrawn and distant, the twenty-minute walk to his house was a blur. She found herself at the edge of a large, open patch of dirt covered in tire tracks. Mr. Cooper's truck was parked out front. The porch light beckoned her and someone sat in the family room. She hurried away so as to not be visible from the front and circled around back.

The light from Will's room called Natalie with the promise of safety. Her short, soft paces inched her closer to his room, each one sending shivers down her spine. Heart astir, it beat faster the closer she got to his window.

A cold tremor shot from Natalie's brain to her toes and she paused. There was no reason to be afraid; there was nowhere else to go. She needed to see Will. She needed to tell someone what happened and feel like she wasn't going crazy. Her stomach churned, and the emotions she had bottled up shook her apart from inside. What could be worse than what had already happened?

Natalie closed her eyes, hands together in front of her. Trembling, she took a deep breath and with a determined huff, stood on her toes and knocked on his window. Inside, Will jumped. Sitting on his bed in his pajamas with a game controller in his hands, he stared back at the dark window wide-eyed with shock. After a moment he realized who it was and delightful surprise swept over him. He rushed to the window and the screen on his wall vanished.

"I thought you were going to call me, not show up at my window." Will leaned on the open windowsill in an attempt to mask his joy with a cool smile.

"Can I come in?" Natalie said, clutching her wrist in her other hand.

"Of course." Will reached his arm out. They grabbed each other's wrists and pulled together. The leg Natalie posted against the wall trembled and most of the work fell to Will. She struggled to stand and he had to help her up. Her jeans dripped water onto his carpet. She clung to him for support and pulled herself close to wrap her arms around him.

"What's wrong? Did you fall in the creek?" Will asked.

To Natalie, it was a punch in the gut. A cannonball rose from her stomach and then dropped like an anchor and pulled her heart down with it. She had seen the impossible, witnessed her family assaulted and killed, and then ran herself to exhaustion. Natalie wanted to believe all she had seen and experienced was not real. It was a blissful day followed by a horrible nightmare.

She gripped Will and took deep, stuttered breaths, which devolved into tear-filled gasps. Natalie's knees buckled and her body descended. Will held on so she would not fall unhindered. He lowered himself to the ground with her and she squeezed him harder than she ever had before, digging her fingers into him. He caressed her back to comfort her.

"Th-th-they," Natalie stammered, interrupted by a tear-filled gasp for breath. Her emotions flooded out and her body sank into his arms. She cringed, sniffled, and whimpered, "They're gone."

Natalie and Will

5

Dreams

WILL SAT AT HIS DESK, ONE OF THE SCREENS PROJECTED OVER IT frozen on a frame of Natalie's video. A black eagle in a triangle, its head in line with a flat top was painted onto the sides of the ships. He scoured the internet for military symbols and iconography until he found a match.

Still coming to terms with it all, Will read up on defense contractors. It was unreal that Mr. and Mrs. Owens were dead. And Nathan too – he was playing games with Nathan only a day ago. Natalie muttered something about her house blowing up before she cried herself into an exhausted sleep.

There was no way he could let them down and let Natalie get caught. Will knew his dad would go to the cops, which may get his whole family killed. Will had to help her on his own, which meant getting informed. He could be sad with everyone else in town when they found out, however they found out. What would be the story? He had not considered what things would be like for everyone else, and his mind wandered.

Natalie jolted awake with a gasp and watery eyes. She flailed in panic and scrambled into the corner of Will's bed, leaning into the walls. Her eyes darted around as the memories rolled in like a landslide. Natalie sat upright and wiped a tear from her cheek. Her heavy breaths subsided and she scooted to the edge of Will's bed.

"Hey there," Will greeted.

"Sorry," she mumbled. She checked the window to make sure the blinds were shut. Will had been kind enough to remove her shoes and socks, and roll up her jeans while she slept. The evening was a blur that happened a long time ago.

"You don't need to apologize. Are you okay?"

"Yeah." She rubbed her eyes with her palms. "How long was I asleep?"

"Like two and a half hours, it's almost midnight. There's water there if you're thirsty." Will pointed to a glass of water on a saucer next to her on his night stand. "I thought you might be after what you were running from."

Natalie was quick to grab the water and drink more than half of it. After some big gulps, she regained her composure. "You know who I was running from?" She wiped her mouth, thoughts interrupted by jarring flashes from earlier.

"I watched the video you recorded." Will grabbed her mobile from his desk and held it up. The screens lit up again when he turned to face them. "I zoomed in on the hull of one of the ships and looked up the logo. It's a mercenary group called Iron Eagle. I couldn't really find much more than that."

"Seriously?"

"Yeah," Will said. "They exist pretty much off the books. I did some research and looked up the Peaceful Union Act. It gets vague at parts. I guess they still wanted some firepower since not every country signed on right away, but then never changed it once everyone joined."

"What else did you find?" Natalie inched forward on the bed.

"Everything I found was bad. I think you need to get underground so they can keep hiding your chip," Will said, which left Natalie perplexed.

"*Keep* hiding my chip?"

"Oh, you don't know?" With a hand gesture, he created a new holographic screen and pulled up a list of videos. "I thought that's why you felt safe coming here." Will brushed through the videos then held his hand flat up to it. He plucked the thumbnail off the screen and tossed it onto his wall, then rolled his chair next to his bed, and Natalie.

An anchorwoman with short black hair and a golden flower pin on her burgundy blazer read a story with a disingenuous smile. The timestamp in the corner read eight forty-four that evening.

"A rebel attack has temporarily disabled our local DRC hub. As a result, Southwest Colorado, as well as parts of New Mexico, Arizona, and Utah are off the grid. This will prevent many people in the area from making purchases, but don't worry; officials say it'll be back up by morning. Until then, stick to cold, hard cash cards if you've got 'em."

"I don't know anyone who uses cash cards anymore. You can just wave your hand and everything is taken care of," added her square-jawed male co-anchor with a head of shiny, well-combed hair. *"No cash cards or ID, it's just so convenient. Well, aside from tonight!"* His scripted joke prompted a hearty laugh from both of them. The video continued in the background.

Natalie looked down at her right wrist, where everybody's denizen chip was located. "So, we're invisible right now?"

"Yep. This is the first time in our lives nobody can track us." Will looked down at his own wrist. For him, it may be the only time, ever.

"These occasional hang-ups are such a small price to pay," the female anchor said. *"The United Earth Government has really brought humanity into a bright future."*

"Oh god, shut up." Will slashed his arm in the air at the screen and the video disappeared. "Anyway, you're safe for now," Will turned his focus back to Natalie, who let out a soft, defeated sigh.

"Safe..." Natalie huffed, her eyes fixed on the glass of water between her legs. "The timing is too convenient. Only the government can turn off our chips, and they want to clean this up. If they're involved, they can find me anywhere. Where am I going to be safe?" She beamed a hopeless look at Will. "In the morning, they'll turn them back on, say they fixed the hub, and someone will come to put a black bag over my head, or whatever they do."

"Hey, there's plenty of places you can hide," Will reassured her. He needed her to want to go. It was the only way he could think of that she would survive.

"Like where?"

"You go where you've *always* wanted to go." Will gestured upward. "To space."

"Just like that?"

"Well, we've got to get you underground first. They'll fix up your chip with a new identity, and then you can go to the colonies where there's no UEG." The confidence and enthusiasm in his voice rose as he progressed. "They have *no* presence in the colonies, and you've always wanted to work on ships. The colonies probably don't care about brands, and you're a great mechanic! You could actually do what you've always dreamed of doing!" Will beamed.

"Really?" The word escaped Natalie's lips as a hush.

"Yeah!"

Stunned, Natalie's eyes darted through a menagerie of possibilities. Her chest swelled with a confident breath, but as she let it out all the positive energy inside her escaped with it and she sank back into a sad slouch. Her lips curled into a frown. She cupped a hand over her face and looked away, leaving Will unsure of what to say.

"I'm sorry," she whimpered.

"It's okay," Will reached out and rubbed her shoulder. "This is all pretty shitty."

Natalie nodded and wiped her cheeks. "For the first time, we're invisible." She looked down at her wrist, hand bent back. "And I've never felt more trapped or afraid."

Will sat beside Natalie and wrapped his arms around her. He held her while she tried to stop crying.

"How am I..." she sniffed, "supposed to get to the colonies? How am I even sup–" she was interrupted by a short, stuttered breath, "supposed to even get out of town?" She leaned into Will, who combed hair out of her face and held her.

"I've already got all that figured out," he said.

"Wh-what?"

"While you were asleep I hit up a couple regulars. I figure a regular either breaks their mobile a lot or is an in-between for people who want to stay under the radar. One of them got back to me. I made arrangements to get you to safety..." His voice trailed off.

"But... what?" The words she needed floated out of reach in a cloud of jumbled, abstract thoughts.

"I'm not letting anything bad happen to you, Natty." Will grabbed her hand.

"Okay." She nodded with a faraway look in her eyes.

"We have a rendezvous in four hours. It's a hundred forty-five kilometers southwest in the middle of nowhere. If we leave in the next half hour we should make it there with some time to spare. We just don't want to be late, or they'll be gone."

"Okay. Okay," she murmured.

"Hey," Will lifted her chin to look at him. "You're kind of out of it right now, huh?" he asked. Natalie nodded and combed some hair behind her ear.

"It's just..." Natalie's words escaped her again, like trying to grab a star through a telescope.

"Relax, you've been through a lot tonight. I'll take care of everything, you just take it easy. I'll get you when it's time to go." Will tried to leave but Natalie held him there a moment longer.

"Thank you." She looked up at him, doe-eyed with gratitude.

"You would do the same for me." Will smiled and squeezed her hand then slipped out of his door and closed it behind him.

Despite the gut-rattling fear of reliving the nightmare again, Natalie's body fell into the bed and her eyes shut before she could stop them.

Instead of reliving the tragedy, her dream began in her house, undamaged and pristine, as it had been hours earlier. She sat on the couch, and the world around her shifted to her room. She was sitting on her bed. The sheets beneath her were soft, the feeling of their fibers vivid, not like a dream at all.

"I saw what happened," said a girl's voice behind her.

Natalie whipped around and jumped to her feet. Sitting at the head of her bed was a girl, perhaps a few years younger than her, hugging one of Natalie's plushies. She had thin lips and sparkling blue eyes with wavy blonde hair. She was thin and did not do her nails or makeup. Natalie did not recognize her.

"I'm so sorry," she said, her doe eyes widening, tears welling within them.

"It's not your fault." A tear ran down Natalie's cheek, but it didn't blur her vision. A benefit of dreams. She sat next to the girl. "Who are you?"

"My name is Hope. I don't have a family either."

Natalie turned away, eyes closed. Hearing that she had no family was a figurative stab in the heart, but it caused her real pain. She turned to look at the girl again, but she was gone. The strange subconscious manifestation vanished as suddenly as she appeared.

Natalie and Will

6

All For One

Will woke Natalie as gently as he could and helped her sneak out of his window. She shivered at a bitter chill sweeping through the area. Arms wrapped around herself, she examined the windowless all-terrain vehicle parked next to Will's room.

Built with a sturdy roll cage and a high-density fiber body, it had two side-by-side seats with a small storage area behind them and two windowless doors at waist level. Dark camouflage nets were draped over the mud-covered vehicle. The silver letters which delineated its model, *PROWLER,* were caked in mud. Small fenders protruded over wide, fat tires.

Will leaned over the driver's door into the back and pulled out a black sweater, then handed it to Natalie. Over a white-and-red crest, the sweater read: *WGL – Where Legends Are Made.*

Natalie rejoiced and threw on the sweater, then helped Will push the Prowler to the edge of the property where Will started it up. The Prowler hummed and rumbled to life, its body loose and rickety from being driven through the wilderness. The engine hummed and Will drove them away from his property to the nearby woods with their lights off to avoid detection. He drove slowly. Only the moonlight that shone through the trees lit his way. They were lucky to be so close to the Rocky Mountains, or it could have been more difficult to slip away.

The drive was mostly quiet aside from the occasional directions. Will tried to make conversation. He hoped to keep Natalie's mind occupied, but it did not work.

"How do you think they'll explain it?" Natalie's eyes fixed on the twinkle of lights from her town, which grew farther as they climbed a mountainside.

"I don't know." Will stayed focused on the path ahead. "Whatever fake story they come up with won't totally make sense and everyone is going to have a different explanation for what happened. It'll be a mystery. And, it would have been for me too. I'm glad you came to me."

"I just wanted somewhere safe," Natalie said. "Hey," she perked up. "Will you um, tell Ash? I figure if anyone else should know…"

"Of course," Will agreed. "Ash is tough on the outside, but losing you is going to hurt. Knowing you're alive will help her deal with you being gone."

"I hope so." Natalie swayed with the Prowler from side to side over uneven terrain on its climb to the top of the hill. "This is really the last time I'm ever going to see Belleza." Lovingly, she watched the sparkling lights in the distance. "Am I doing the right thing? I'm going to leave behind Ash, and you, and everyone I've ever known, everyone I grew up with, my whole life." Natalie slouched in her seat. She knew it was goodbye. No matter how hard she tried to squeeze the sweater around her, it brought her little comfort.

"I don't know. I don't think there's any way to know what to do. We've just got to do our best," Will said. "Don't think about the life you're leaving behind, but the whole new life you'll be able to live. You may be leaving behind people that love you, but everywhere you go, when you leave, you'll leave behind new people that love you. You're just that awesome Natty. People will… always love you." They crested a hill and Will turned the lights on, afraid to look at her after what he said.

Natalie looked over her shoulder at Will. "Thank you." She turned back around to stare off into space.

After the chat, Natalie was quiet, so Will focused on driving and made no more attempts to cheer her up. She would talk again if he left her alone for a bit. While she came to terms with reality, he came to terms with the fact that not only was he going to lose Natalie, but he was the one taking her away. He would be the one who drove his best friend and life-long crush into oblivion, soon to let go of her forever.

They drove for more than an hour in silence. Will's mind stayed occupied and awake imagining what Natalie thought. This might be his last chance to ever speak with her, but he had no clue what to say. They rode quickly up the side of a mountain sparse with trees when Natalie broke her long silence.

"Where are all the aliens?"

"What?" Will turned south, uphill to the top of a ridge that turned west and fed into a larger mass of the Rocky Mountains.

"I mean, space is big. We've only colonized a few planets in a tiny part of our galaxy, but you'd figure we'd run into someone, right?" Natalie reasoned.

"My grandpa used to say that when we started going into space, everyone thought we'd meet someone. It was always right around the corner, but it never happened." Will shook his head. "We all know they're out there. Why don't they just say hi?"

"Maybe because of tonight." Natalie stared into the dark wilderness. "If this is what happens when we see them."

"Why are you asking about aliens?"

"Because that's what that ship was. You know you were thinking it. We can't make ships like that." Natalie looked up at the stars through a hole in the clouds, then at the horizon and the hillsides, illuminated by the moon.

"It had crossed my mind." Will weaved through the scattered trees.

Natalie rocked with the Prowler. She inched her head out of her window to look up at the moon through the flickering shadows of the canopy. Moonlight provided most of their illumination until bright lights beamed down on them from above. Natalie jerked back into the Prowler. Both of them jumped, confused.

"What is it?" Will asked in a panic. "Cops?"

Natalie poked her head back out to look. The bright light obscured a large shadow, but a silhouette was all Natalie needed. It had a narrow vertical profile with four whisper-quiet engines stretching out from the body on thin wings.

"It's a Gerridae!" she boomed.

"I don't know what that means!" Will maneuvered them out of the spotlight.

"Giant quadcopter, armed air support," she replied. The Gerridae dropped altitude and maneuvered around them. "Cops don't use these."

"Then who does?"

Natalie kept her eyes on the Gerridae until yellow lights flickered from the sides of its hull. A flurry of thumps and dings showered down around them. She flinched at a violent explosion of cracking tree bark nearby.

"Are they shooting at us?" Will yelled.

"Yes!" Natalie yelled back.

Will zig-zagged around trees. He drove in a straight line then cut sharply to the side. Behind them, a string of bullets thudded against the ground and trees. Some grazing shots dinged against the Prowler.

"What the hell?" Will shrieked. Natalie peeked out to get another look at the ship. Will's focus was shaken when he looked up to see the shadowy ship strafing into their path. He took a deep breath and twisted the steering wheel hard to the right. Yellow lights flashed from the wings and a string of bullets tore through the ground so close they whistled by Will's head.

The Prowler tipped to the left and rolled forward on two wheels. When it lifted off the ground, Natalie was quick to react and hung onto the door grip to lean her body out of the vehicle. The Prowler slammed back down and scraped Natalie's butt against the floor. With a squeal, she pulled herself back inside.

"Hoooooly *shit!*" She buckled her seatbelt then reached over to buckle Will's.

"We can't make the rendezvous like this!" Will swerved around the forested hill and left trails of bullets in their wake.

"Turn off your lights! Try to lose them in the dark!" She pointed at a patch of trees ahead.

Will wasted no time. They zoomed into a patch of trees and careened inside to dart out in another direction. The Gerridae's light shined on their original path, then searched the area for them. Without enough cover to keep them hidden, the ship was on top of them before they could hide again.

A tree next to them exploded with a loud crack and showered them in splintered wood, followed by a string of thuds alongside them. Will zig-zagged toward another patch of trees.

"Hang on!" Will roared as the Gerridae lined itself up again. He turned left then veered right. The windshield cracked, a string of dings and thuds trailed behind them.

Teeth clenched, Natalie gripped her seat. The Prowler's right side lifted, slowing as it reached its peak. It rolled forward on two tires again. It seemed like it would drop back down until it tipped a bit too far and tumbled over its side down the nearby slope. Natalie squeezed her eyes shut and her butt lifted off the seat. The Prowler spun back onto four wheels with a heavy bounce. The slope and momentum rolled it behind a large formation of rocks and trees.

With fast, panicked breaths, Natalie opened her eyes. The Prowler crept forward on its own. There was a hole, head-level in the middle of the windshield with a web of cracks spreading outward from it. The dashboard's glass console was cracked open in front of Will. Wires hung from the twisted metal hole. In front of them, Will slouched in his chair holding his gut, head down, with bloodstain blooming on his shirt.

"Will!" Natalie lunged at him, yanked back by her seatbelt. She unbuckled herself and threw her arms around him, afraid to touch his bloody gut. Will's left hand guided the Prowler until Natalie yanked on the emergency brake. She unbuckled Will and lifted his shirt, gaping at the mosaic of holes gushing blood from his stomach.

"Hurts…" he whimpered, face contorted in pain. Natalie felt around his back but found no exit wounds. She leaned into the back and ripped the medical kit from its mount behind her chair.

Natalie opened the kit and rifled through its contents, but her hands fumbled everything she tried to grab. They would not stop shaking. She found a thin metal tube with a magnetic claw that could protract to pull out bullets. After a quick look around she found the spotlight, which looked elsewhere and moved away. Natalie tried her best to hold the metal instrument still over one of the holes in Will's gut. The shiny metal instrument rattled over a river of blood flowing from him. Natalie slipped it into one of the wounds, and Will whimpered.

"I'm sorry – I'm sorry – I'm sorry!" She felt around for the bullet. "Just, hang on, hang on, I got it!" There was a click against the magnetic base of the clasp. She grabbed the bullet and eased it out. Will clenched his teeth and fist, kicked, and sighed in relief when Natalie finished. He took heavy, labored breaths and remained motionless.

"No! What is this?" Natalie examined the extractor, which held a twisted shard of metal instead of a bullet like she had expected. "Fucking shrapnel?" Natalie yelled in a terrified rage, eyes watery, every passing second drained her of hope. She looked back and forth between the patchwork of bloody cuts and the med kit. He would not survive long enough for her to patch every hole in his gut. It was then Natalie noticed she could no longer see the Gerridae's spotlight.

"That's not enough." Will pushed the med kit away.

"Don't die!" Natalie pulled herself close to hug Will's head, tears streaming down her cheeks. "Not you too. I can't!"

Will grabbed her arm and looked into her eyes, color draining from his skin.

"Run," he whispered. "Run."

A bright light beamed down on them from behind Will. From behind a large gap between trees and rocks the ship descended.

"I'm staying with you like you stayed with me." Natalie sniffled and pulled Will into her, eyes on the silhouette of the enemy ship, its bright light fixed on them. Natalie squeezed Will, ready to embrace their fate together.

Without warning, a concussive boom knocked Natalie back into her seat. The large enemy ship's silhouette burst into flames. She watched in confusion as the gray ship with black markings dropped to the forest floor in a plume of fire and smoke.

Natalie shot to her feet. She wiped away her tears and hurried outside to look over the small valley in the hills before them. In the valley below there was a bright light and a clearing she did not remember being there before.

A shadow zoomed overhead toward the light and swiveled in place. The mysterious ship fired towards the bright light. Another explosion boomed in the valley below. Something fell from the ship, and then the craft dropped altitude and disappeared behind some trees. The bright light flickered in the distance. She sprinted back to the Prowler, where Will slouched over, half-conscious.

"What's going on?" Will muttered, his eyes closed and his breaths slower, weaker. Natalie had seen enough action movies with her dad to know this was not a good injury. Will would not make it back to civilization.

"Our enemies have enemies," Natalie wrapped her arms under his. "This is going to hurt and I'm sorry." She did not finish speaking before she pulled and dragged him into the passenger seat. Will screamed in agony. He gritted his teeth to muffle his screams. He kicked his feet to help, but most of the work fell to Natalie. She leaned his seat back and stuffed bandages over his wounds as quickly as she could before pulling his shirt over them.

After a frantic search for the seatbelt she strapped him in then hurried into the driver's seat and examined the dash. Broken, busted open and riddled with bullet holes, the vehicle and console were fully operational.

That was why they had kept the Prowler for so long. She let down the emergency brake and gripped the wheel with purpose.

"Come on Will, stay awake!" She slammed her foot on the accelerator. "*Neither* of us are dying tonight!"

Ulfberht Crew

7

Trojan Horse

"Aye, Mike," called a bulky red-haired Scotsman with a wild, bushy beard, reminiscent of a rugged young Santa Claus. A gaunt man with sharp cheekbones and small hazel eyes leaned into the cockpit's starboard entryway.

"What's up, Ian? Don't think you can land her?" Mike asked.

"A'course I can land 'er! But we've got a Gerridae flyin' 'round. Yer virus got sum' do with that?" Ian bellowed.

"No, they're supposed to be blindsided. Maybe they're doing a perimeter check. What's it doing?" Mike watched the Gerridae fly over a ridge, spotlight on the ground.

"There's sum' doon there." Ian pointed at a tiny all-terrain vehicle darting from side to side, dipping in and out of the Gerridae's light. "And they're shootin' at 'em."

"What the hell are they doing out in the middle of nowhere?" Mike asked. "They can't *outrun* that thing." The vehicle disappeared from the spotlight and did not reappear. The Gerridae circled the area, its light scanned for the vehicle.

"I guess ye dinnae have t' outrun 'em if ye can hide," Ian chuckled.

"Well, they're a threat and we're already behind schedule. Shoot 'em down." Mike clipped on a small earpiece.

"Aye-aye!" Ian smiled and leaned into the yoke to bring them into firing range. Mike headed back into the cabin with one hand on a rail to stay upright.

"A quick run-through for the newbie." Mike pointed to the only one of three men in the room not on his feet.

"Hey!" hollered the thin man with leathery skin, long gray hair in a ponytail. "It ain't my fault y'all never bring me along." Strapped snugly into one of the wall-mounted seats holding an open flask and a bottle of whiskey, he spoke with a slow country drawl.

"Rick, it's *completely* your fault. You're filling a flask with whiskey *right* now," Mike pointed out. "You're not even wearing the armor I gave you. You just strapped a vest over what I *hope* isn't a greasy T-shirt. Those jeans won't protect you from bullets either." Mike pointed, annoyed he had made Rick protective gray underclothing and layered black sheets of armor like his own only to have it discarded.

"A man needs his whiskey. I thought you said I wouldn't be in any real danger?" Rick screwed the flask lid back on and tucked it into his shirt pocket.

"An alcoholic *needs* whiskey. I still don't want to risk losing my engineer," Mike said. The ship's side-mounted rail-guns boomed outside.

"What was that?" Rick slipped the bottle of whiskey into a narrow compartment next to him that slid out of the wall.

"Nothing, listen up," Mike said. "The facility is on lockdown and we've got the master key. Ian is staying with the ship. Shin is taking point, eliminating inner defenses and locking up non-combat personnel." Mike pointed at the short, thin man a few paces from the cabin's back wall.

A dense, corded suit of white black and red armor covered him from top to bottom, accented by a belt full of small compartments. A sleek white helmet with a black screen, red trim, a large knife, and a massive rifle rounded out his silhouette.

"Rick, you're getting Farouk's arms. Shin will bring you Farouk so you can reconnect them. Once you're done, loot your ass off. This place is going to be full of stuff that's hard to find and easy to sell. Be quick, we don't have a lot of time."

"We're at the L-Z!" Ian called from the cockpit, hovering over the landing zone. Mike slid open a metal wall panel protecting a touch screen and tapped one of the icons. The back wall opened from the top down, creating a ramp.

"Simple plan! You good?" Mike yelled over the wind rushing through the cabin and gave Rick a thumbs-up. He returned the gesture. The ship tilted forward, turning the rear ramp into a flat platform, and Shin hopped onto it. "Stay behind us!"

"Ready!" Ian bellowed after the wind died down.

"Fire!" Mike ordered. Two shots from the rail guns thundered around them and Shin jumped off the ramp.

"You know, I'd jump out of a ship too if I had a fancy supersuit!" Rick cracked.

"You could try squeezing your old ass in there sometime. I'll put down fifty you can't get it over your beer belly," Mike said.

"He's a little Asian guy, comes up to here." Rick held his hand up to his shoulder. "My belly's got nothin' to do with it." His stomach rose in his throat. "Feel like we're fallin' a bit fast?"

The ship slowed harshly. Mike squeezed the handlebar and crouched to keep his balance. They landed with two jarring thuds.

"Ian! Didn't you say you could land it?" Mike asked.

"We dinnae appear t' have crashed, so I's tellin' ye the truth," Ian hollered, then popped the helmet off his head. "I'll take good care o' 'er for ye."

Mike hustled out and Rick hastily threw a tool bag over his shoulder and followed.

With Mike and Rick still in the fighter, Shin crouched when he landed and burst into a dead sprint toward a pair of giant, mangled steel doors. He moved car lengths with each step and threw a cluster of black, golf ball-sized metal spheres at the entrance of the bunker doors, which expelled a cloud of expanding black smoke. He ran in and his suit adjusted to camouflage him in the smoky environment. His helmet's sensors provided tactical data and worked at a frequency that let him see through the smoke, while obscuring the sensors of others.

On the second level of the hangar, men took cover behind the thick cement pillars that encircled the room. Without the Gerridae, only a couple of service trucks and several crates populated the small hangar floor.

The black smoke crept into the room with a hiss and consumed the bottom level. Shin examined the layout and drew a thick black knife from its sheath. Several heat signatures lurked behind cover on his level. He approached the closest one with steady steps. The security contractor peeked out from behind the wall with his visor down, rifle pointed at Shin. Shin stepped to the side but continued his approach. The man searched the cloud for an intruder with Shin close enough to hear him radio in.

"I don't see any hostiles," he said.

Shin circled at arm's length.

"The smoke is messing with our sensors. Withdraw."

"Copy." He raised his visor. The room was still empty. He was briefly confused when a blade slit his throat open. Blood pooled around his body and alarms sounded in the helmets of his comrades.

"I think I see him!" A guard fired into the cloud from above. Shin rolled behind a nearby pillar. The three others on his level rushed to his position. Visors up, their rifles searched for ripples in space or anything out of place.

Like a shadow, Shin moved from one to the next. He was gone before their bodies hit the floor. Once all their comrades were dead, those above sprayed the bottom level with bullets.

Behind cover, Shin drew a black cloth and wiped his blade, then sheathed it. He drew the giant rifle from his back and fired at the guards on the far side of the room. Each shot fired a solid steel alloy bullet that whizzed through the target's armor. He fired almost as fast as the bullets found their targets and launched them into the wall behind them with a bloody splatter.

Shin jumped to the second level walkway. Soaring out of the smoke, his suit's colors shifted back to normal. Shin fired at the two men farthest from him. Their bodies left a trail of blood on the wall as they slid to the floor with a wet grind and a thud.

The startled enemy next to Shin unloaded his clip before he landed. Shin smacked his rifle away and fired point-blank into his chest. The shot blasted him against the back wall with a giant gaping hole in his armor, not meant to withstand a weapon created for space combat. The last two men took cover and fired from around the cement pillars. Clean shots to the chest of each one tore through the pillars and found their targets.

Shin dusted flattened bullets off his armor and let the tiny craters they left in his suit repair themselves. He pressed a button on his rifle and held it in the air above him. Every bullet he had fired whizzed across the room and swirled around the rifle, then reloaded. Once collected, Shin moved on to secure the facility.

With Shin's departure, the hangar quieted for a moment until Mike and Rick hustled into the black cloud Shin had left behind. Mike picked up the black spheres and clicked a button on each, then dropped them back on the ground. A shockwave of blue sparks coursed through the cloud and the smoke receded back into the black spheres.

"Havin' a damn Ranger must make ops easier. Do you fellers just clean up after 'em?" The carnage one man had caused mystified Rick: destruction he had never seen, only heard of. Blood splatters and limp bodies looked like they had been flung against the walls by a tornado. He loved action but was not so fond of blood.

"Depends on the op. We usually have to hit from multiple points but this time we can just follow the bodies." The room clear of the smokescreen, Mike picked the black spheres off the ground.

He led Rick down a bright white hallway. They passed more bodies on their way. The poor guards had no idea what was coming. Soon, they reached the command hub.

Rick took in the room from the second level. In the center of the bottom level stood a round, elevated platform encircled by console tabletops. Narrow staircases sat on either side of the room, perpendicular to Rick and the hallway across from him.

Mike hustled to the center platform and pulled a metal box the size of a playing card and thick as a coin from a pouch on his belt. He touched one of the consoles. Holo-screens and consoles lit up in red access denial alerts. Mike placed the metal box on the console and a yellow bar encircled it. Mike held his thumbs and index fingers in a square and pulled them away from each other. A holographic interface appeared before him and he got to work.

Rick snapped out of his daze and ran downstairs. A hall full of offices encircled the command room. Rick passed a staircase and restrooms, arriving at a four-way crossroads surrounded by spacious labs. In one was a large metal arm suspended upright in an anti-gravity field.

"Bingo." Rick slowed to a stroll once inside and set down his tools. He hunched over the other arm, which lay on the table. "This one's still in one piece." He patted the arm and turned his attention to the one hovering behind him.

Rods of various sizes jutted from the base of the shoulder where it connected to the torso, complete with holes and notches. It had been partially taken apart to reach the access panel. With a grin, Rick pulled a wire connected to a slot in the access panel and tossed it aside. It had been their way in.

After a drink from his flask, Rick pulled out the special tools in his bag and re-assembled the arm's inner panel. He celebrated completion with a drink as well. "That'll do it." He turned around to see Shin and an armless Farouk in front of the glass wall. With a face like a bulldog and round features, even with no arms, Farouk's muscular build was daunting to behold.

"Better not fuck up my arms, you drunk asshole," Farouk said, shirtless and cross. He sat in a nearby chair and rolled to Rick. "Hurry it up, I'm freezin' my ass off."

"Isn't that why you were wearin' a shirt the last time we saw you?" Rick jabbed. Shin unclamped the left arm and held it upright next to Farouk.

"They took my damn shirt off when they took my arms. I don't even know how damn long I've been in that cold-ass cell. Maybe like an *hour* ago my nose started itchin'." Farouk complained while Shin slid the arm into Farouk's empty shoulder socket. "I'll think twice before I let you dicks Trojan Horse my ass again."

"We'll grab a drink when we get to *Oasis* and you'll forget *all* about it." Rick connected the nodes between Farouk's cybernetic arm and torso.

They jumped when the door opened, but it was only the dolly Ian had sent from the ship. The rectangular storage bin with a slanted front end hovered a meter over the ground. It nudged the door open and settled on the ground next to them.

"This one's done." Rick stepped back from the arm and Shin eased the heavy arm into Farouk's torso until it pulled together and locked in with a loud click. Farouk opened and closed his fingers then rotated his shoulder with satisfaction. Rick hooked up Farouk's other arm and Shin locked it into place then took a step back alongside Rick.

"Son of a bitch." Farouk opened and closed his hand into a fist. "It feels like they've been gone so long." Relieved and invigorated, Farouk jumped out of his rolling chair. Feet shoulder-width apart in a boxing stance, he threw some quick jabs, a cross, bobbed and weaved. "Feels good."

"Good. Now, I'm a' get to lootin'. There's some real nice stuff in here." Rick glanced around the room with a nod of approval. "Hell, I might just grab shit that looks expensive. I don't know what some'a this shit is, so it's *really* expensive."

"Do you, Rick. I've got somethin' for Mike. Hey Shin." Farouk held the door open and cocked his head for Shin to follow. He led Shin down the hall back to the command room, where Mike was focused on his screens. Hunched over the console, his fingers danced across the glass. "Hey Mike, I got somethin' important."

"Uh…" Mike kept his eyes on the screens. "How… important…?"

"They brought a guy in earlier. He's downstairs in a cell." Farouk waited for Mike to finish. Once Mike was zoned in, he would break his focus when he felt like it. Mike worked some more before looking over the holographic screens at Farouk.

"Why aren't you wearing a shirt?"

Farouk sighed at Mike. "They cut it off to get my arms, but it's chilly in here, so can we move on already?"

"But, we're underground," Mike said.

"Yeah, but we're in a lab, and you're wearing all that. They keep it frosty in here," Farouk huffed.

"Checks out." Mike nodded, mind preoccupied. "So, who is he? Why is he here?" He glanced down at his screen to check progress.

"I don't know, I just saw 'em bring him in. I was thinkin' we could bust him out too. Runnin' it by you." Farouk gestured at Mike, who pondered the question for a moment with a hum.

"Shin, go with him. Meet the guy. I'll leave it to your judgment. I can talk to him on the ship. Is that it?"

"That's all *I* got." Farouk threw his hands up and Mike got back to work.

Shin and Farouk headed back to the holding area three floors down. They passed the bodies of more guards and Farouk led Shin to the last cell. The stranger sat in the lotus position with perfect posture, eyes closed, hands together in his lap, unbothered by his imprisonment.

"Hey brotha," Farouk greeted. The stranger's eyes opened and looked back at Farouk with a strange innocence and a smile. "What'cha in for?"

The stranger looked back at Farouk in pause before he answered, "Existing."

"You sayin' you're in here because you're black? You're going to have to give me a better answer than *that*. You ain't exactly in county," Farouk joked.

"I am captured here. So, here I wait," the stranger said. Farouk stared back at him, then turned to Shin.

"You want to take this?" Farouk whispered. Shin nodded and Farouk stepped away.

Shin took Farouk's place and examined the young man. "Who are you?"

"I am one," the stranger said.

"Your name is One?" Shin asked.

"I am one. All is one. I am one with all," the stranger said.

Shin paused to examine the unchanging vital signs displayed in his helmet. "You said you were captured for existing. Where was this?"

"A town nearby."

"Which town?" Shin followed up. The stranger's eyes drifted off for a moment before he turned back to Shin.

"Belleza," the young man said with proper Spanish pronunciation.

"How did you arrive there?"

"A crash landing of unknown cause," the stranger said.

Shin pondered his answer and considered which of his many questions to ask and how best to ask it. "Were you committing a crime that would lead to your capture?"

"Crime." The stranger smiled, amused, then shook his head. "No."

"Where was your ship coming from?"

"No place. Every place." The young man's answers turned cryptic again.

Shin's progress waned, and he continued along a different line of inquiry. "Are you a rebel? Or… a monk?"

"Neither."

"Are you loyal to the United Earth Government?"

"I am loyal to no sub-cosmic entity."

"Are you hostile?"

"No." The stranger shook his head, vital signs unwavering. It was as if hostility was a laughable option for him. Shin stood in silence for a moment and pondered the information at hand.

"So?" Farouk got Shin's attention. "Friend or foe?"

"I have one more question. Are you of value to those holding you? Or are you here for punishment?"

"Value," the young stranger said.

Shin pulled a small metal box like Mike's from a pouch on his belt. He placed the box on the glass console next to the cell. A thick red ring appeared around it, blinked, and gave way to a green ring. The cell clicked open.

"That's it? They want him so we're takin' him? What if he's dangerous?"

"He isn't dangerous and he's valuable to them, so we're taking him. The Captain sent me to assess, so I have." Shin opened the gate and stood back.

"Whatever you say," Farouk said.

Farouk took up the rear and the stranger followed Shin back to the command room. There, Mike was still diligently at work. Farouk looked the young stranger over while they waited. There was something off about him he couldn't put his finger on.

"Comin' through," came a voice from behind. The group dispersed and the boxy dolly breezed by with Rick mounted atop it like a horse. His over-packed tool bag rested on the dolly in front of him, partially open. "Who's the new guy?"

"We're bustin' him out," Farouk said.

"All right, see you guys on the ship." Rick waved. The dolly pivoted beneath him.

"Rick, don't leave without us, man." Farouk took small steps to follow.

"Sorry, dolly's on her way, I'm on top of it. Some things are out of our control." Rick patted the side of the dolly.

"We're still in enemy territory, dumbass," Farouk reminded him.

"Now, how's this going to work?" Rick wondered aloud, looking up at the staircase in front of him. "This ain't good."

The dolly lifted upward to climb the stairs and Rick slid off the back of it. He kept his tool bag from sliding off with him and followed the dolly upstairs.

"Now we wait." Mike grabbed the small silver box from the console and tucked it safely in his pocket. The ring on the console disappeared and everything shut down. The bright white lights of the bunker turned off, replaced by dim red emergency lights. Mike ran up the stairs past Rick. "Let's get moving!"

Shin scouted ahead. The others came out of the bunker behind him in line. Shin scanned the perimeter on their way to the ship, fifty meters away.

"Aye Mike," Ian called in the voice channel. *"I'm pickin' up what seems t' be a vehicle comin' this way from the East."*

"Rick," Mike called. "Secure the loot on board and strap in. Farouk, escort our new friend inside and get ready to fly. Ian, switch with Farouk and join me outside," he ordered. Each split up to accomplish their task as soon as it was given.

A small, lightly camouflaged off-road vehicle burst from behind some bushes at the tree line. It turned sharply and continued toward them at high speed. Shin raised his weapon cautiously and they watched the bundle of metal and broken glass bounce toward them, driven wildly over rough dirt. Branches dangled from every nook and cranny. A string of giant crater-like holes across the windshield obscured who was inside.

"Hold on, Shin." Mike raised a hand. "Ian, does that look like the vehicle the Gerridae was shooting at?"

"Aye," Ian said. "Looks like."

"Fan out," Mike ordered. The three men spread out into a semicircle with Ian and Shin on either side of Mike. He held his left hand flat towards the vehicle. "Stop!" The vehicle ground to a stop and kicked up a cloud of dirt ten meters away. The cloud rolled over Mike. Shin and Ian approached from the sides. "Step out of the vehicle!"

Before Mike could finish, a youthful girl kicked open the vehicle's small metal door and tumbled out. "Help!" She tried to stand, but her knees buckled and she collapsed. "Please help me!" The girl yelled through wild, ragged black hair, face peppered with lacerations. She dragged a bloody hand over her forehead to comb away hair and left a swath of red across her face.

"Calm down, kid." Mike lowered his pistol to ease her panic.

"Please! He needs help!" The girl could barely get the words out. She looked to the passenger's seat, where Shin was crouched over a bloody teenager.

"There is an adolescent here, vitals are fading," Shin said.

"You can leave me! But, save him, please!" she pleaded. With a loved one on the brink of death, the time Mike took to consider the request was an eternity.

"Who are you? What's your name?" Mike asked.

"N-Natalie... Owens," she stammered.

"You're in the middle of nowhere. Where are you from?"

"Belleza, Colorado."

"Belleza?"

"That mean something to you, Shin?"

"The man from the cell said he landed in Belleza," Shin said. Across from him, Ian searched the vehicle for weapons.

"I remind ye this lad could die any second, but we could probably save him if we get 'em to the ship," Ian said.

While they spoke, Natalie wilted. "Please, save my friend." She hung her head with a whimper. "I can't let anyone else die tonight."

"Our ship isn't a place for kids," Mike rationalized, but he could not take his eyes off the girl, only a few years older than his own daughter.

"Neither is this." Ian nodded at the mangled bunker doors behind Mike. *"They've n'un on 'em. Just a couple kids caught up in sum' bad."*

"Get them inside." Mike holstered his weapon. "Ian, take her. I'll drive this thing in. Shin, prep the gurney." He marched toward the driver's seat around the puddle of sadness and desperation who had driven it there. Before Natalie could process what was going on, Mike had thrown the Prowler into reverse and driven away.

"Come on, lass." Ian reached an arm out. Natalie took his hand and he pulled her up. Her legs quaked and did little to help her stand.

"Thank you." Natalie sniffled, relieved to finally catch a break. She wiped her tears and held onto Ian's arm for balance. He guided her in, sat her down by Rick and strapped her in. Natalie watched Mike hook Will up to a bag of artificial blood dangling from a hook above him. He was strapped to a gurney against the wall opposite her. With a foot, Mike closed a small drawer emanating a cold white fog while he fiddled with the plugs. Next to Natalie, Shin strapped the Prowler to the ground.

"Farouk, Get us out of here!" Mike yelled. The dropship jolted off the ground. In a mad dash, Mike pulled a chair down from the wall next to Will and strapped in. Shin sat next to him and examined the worried young girl they picked up.

Across the narrow room, Natalie stared at Will in fear the worst could still happen. "Please, Will," she whispered, eyes puffy. She stared at her friend's limp, pale body and a tear ran down her cheek. "Hang on."

The craft rocketed into the sky, to the starship that awaited them.

Ulfberht Crew

8

Connected

AT THE CENTER OF A SPACIOUS ROOM WITH A DARK BLUE CARPET rested a large oval table with a thick, wooden rim encircling a large glass console. Around it, a half dozen empty chairs. Mike and Shin sat in the middle of one of the table's long sides. Shin's helmet rested on the table next to Natalie's mobile. The video of his conversation with the stranger back at the bunker disappeared.

Shin's face was sharp, but his skin looked soft to the touch. He had a scar across his cheekbone from under his left eye toward his ear, but otherwise had an unassuming look about him.

"That was interesting. I see why you wanted to sit in on my questioning Natalie." Mike tapped on the rim of the table.

"I'm glad I did. Her video corroborates what this guy said." Shin was moved by Natalie's story and glad he encouraged Mike to bring them along. He believed coincidences in life were the universe's way of speaking to us. Following those connections before had led him into the Ranger force, this crew, and other defining moments in his life.

"What did he say his name was? One?" The video of the other

teenager they had picked up raised more questions than answers. He scrubbed through Natalie's video with the audio off.

"I think he meant that philosophically. I asked who he is, not for his name."

"Well, let's call him One for now, to keep things easy," Mike proposed.

"Works for me."

"Did you notice he doesn't have a brand?"

"Yes, but he's not old, and I don't think he's from the colonies." Shin excluded the most common reasons he might not have a brand.

"So this guy comes from who knows where and crashes by Natalie's house in a weird-looking ship. She runs away and ends up in the same place as him in the middle of nowhere. Not only in the middle of nowhere, at a *secret* Ministry-UEG bunker, and in the tiny window of time we happened to be there too. The chances of that are astronomical." Mike shook his head, trying to connect elements which did not neatly fit together. "Something feels really weird about this."

"I like when the universe lines things up for us," Shin said. "Think about it. We were delayed. Had we been delayed more, they die, but our attack goes normally. Earlier, they pass through without a problem. Now they can actually get somewhere safe."

"That's the other thing, where the hell were they going? They could have been walking into a trap. They could have been turned right over to the feds for a reward. They don't know who they were meeting or what they were walking into. It was a total shot in the dark," Mike retorted. "Didn't Natalie say the other hacker in her town disappeared? Maybe it was because of that contact."

"What else are they going to do? Maybe their parents trust the UEG. They might go to the cops and get her caught. So, they roll the dice. It's what I'd do. Isn't that how we met?" Shin pointed out. "You asked for someone reliable and got me. I'm still here."

"I guess there are exceptions," Mike said.

"Come on, Mike. Do you really think these kids are spies?" Shin asked.

"I don't know, but until I can rule out that possibility I'm not assuming they *aren't* spies just because they're kids. Hell, what girl her age knows what a Gerridae is? Or cares? This is all too strange. I'm missing something, so let's talk to this other guy and put it all together."

"I'm ready if you are." Shin put his helmet on the chair next to him and grabbed Natalie's mobile. Mike pressed down on the wooden rim of the table and a rectangular block flipped up to reveal a console on its underside.

Mike pressed a finger to the console. "Farouk, bring him in."

Within a few breaths, Farouk guided the young man into the room and sat him across from Mike. Shin circled to the other side of the table to keep his eye on him from behind. Whether he was a threat or not, security was his job.

"Thanks, Farouk," Mike said. "Could you and Ian unpack the loot?"

"You got it." Farouk gave the visitor a sideways look and strode out.

"Hi there. My friend here brought me up to speed on your chat from earlier," Mike began. "What's your name?"

"I have no name," the young stranger said.

"I'll work with that for now. Do you mind if we call you One? That's how you identified yourself before." Mike could coax a name out of him with some conversation.

"I would like that." One smiled.

"So, One," Mike said "How is it you came to crash on Earth?"

"Our ship was struck by an unknown force." One's voice was calm but lively.

"*Our* ship? Who else is with you?" Mike asked with concern.

"I am only in *your* company."

"So, you don't have anyone traveling with you?" Mike checked the young man's response. After an agreeable nod, Mike continued. "Where are you from?"

"Home," One said without a hint of sarcasm.

"*Where* is home?" Mike's tone and a roll of his eyes hinted at his budding frustration. He hoped it would not be like pulling teeth the whole time.

"Home is not a place, places are a part of my home," One said.

Mike's head turned to Shin with a raised eyebrow. Shin shrugged and shook his head.

"Can you relate to me geospatially where you're from?" Mike attempted.

"No."

"Why not?" Mike threw his hands in the air.

"There is no place to relate. There are no words in any of your languages to express a world for which you have no context." The young man's serenity was steadfast. He appeared too young to have such calm in a stressful situation. Mike was still convinced he was laying on the bullshit and was not trying to make sense. He gave nothing more than abstract obfuscations.

"How is there no place to relate? Everyone is from somewhere." Logic was the ultimate equalizer. With it, he would inevitably figure out who One was.

"All time and space you know are but a small bubble in the infinite expanse of the greater reality." One looked off into space. Mike and Shin stared at him and considered the implications of his sentence.

"Really?" Mike asked. "What are you trying to say? You're from *outside* the boundaries of time and space?"

"Yes," One said. Mike was amazed at the nerve One had to make such a ridiculous claim, albeit airtight if he could stick with it.

"Okay, let's go with that." Mike humored the unlikely story. Surely, One would continue to dig himself a deeper hole. "So from outside the boundaries of time and space, you came *here*, to *Earth*, and *crashed?*"

"I did not choose to crash." The stranger shook his head.

"But the *other* two things are true?" Mike said.

"Truth is all I speak."

"You do realize this seems… far fetched?" Mike still attempted to be polite.

One nodded. "Likelihood does not dictate truth."

Mike sighed at the response, already practiced in hearing indirect but airtight answers when seeking simple ones. The next step was to ask for proof, which he surely could not provide. "Can you prove to me you are what you're saying you are? Because you look *completely* human."

"It is one of the few things I am allowed to do when asked." One raised his hands from his lap and placed them palms-up on the table between them.

Mike glanced at Shin, who looked back equally as surprised by the gesture. One sat quietly, patient and serene. Mike reached a hand out. The look in One's eyes was not of deceit or deception. Instead, he looked warm and hopeful. He even had a subtle, tender smile. Mike hovered a hand over One's. It might somehow be a trick, but there was only one way to find out. What was the worst that could happen? He touched a finger to One's palm.

On contact, an intense static jolt shot up his arm and consumed Mike's body. The resonance of the buzz intensified and drowned out the world. Every molecule in his body vibrated and lightened until he dematerialized.

The outside world ceased to exist, leaving only a void. There were flashes of the silver ship with no discernible parts, entrance, or engines. With the images came innocuous knowledge about the ship and its function. The darkness disappeared and he saw through One's eyes in every direction at once. He careened toward the Earth in an unlit ship with transparent walls. Outside, the planet grew larger.

Next to Mike was an iridescent being with a human silhouette. The being was luminous, but the sun was the only light source. Despite a lack of distinct features, it was as if the being was smiling not at One in his memory, but at Mike. Mike waved, and the being waved back. As the Earth's shadow overcame the sunlight, the being dissolved with the light from the feet-up. Little specks of light floated away like ash from a fire until the last sliver of sunlight vanished.

The ship rattled and shook. Mike soared over mountaintops and into a valley. Below, Natalie held on to a large dog and her mobile in the middle of a field. Like strings being plucked inside him, he experienced her fear and excitement as if it were his own. There were lights, sounds, forms and shimmers around him he could not comprehend. While he soared by the house, time slowed until the entire scene ground to a halt as Mike focused on a single item. The world frozen in place, he stared wide-eyed at a fountain of fluffy, radiant white light emanating from Natalie's house.

A tug in his gut pulled him toward it. Unable to deter his gaze, Mike floated through the ship and the house, which faded away the closer he got to the source of the warm, comforting light. It was strangely familiar like he had been there before but could not recall. At peace and consumed by the amorphous light, Mike closed his eyes and basked in the familiar feeling until he remembered what used to make him feel this way.

In a flash Mike's eyes were open and he looked into the big blue eyes of a beautiful blonde woman with fair skin and full lips. Her long eyelashes, her bashful smile, she was like an angel in human form. His heart raced at the sight of her. With every beat, a ripple passed through his body and into the space around him. Nose to nose, looking into each other's eyes, her heart beat with his.

The beautiful woman caressed the sides of his face and pulled him in for a kiss. Her lips were as soft as he remembered, but when he pulled away, he was on his knees in a dark room, her dead body in his arms and covered in blood. Lights lifted off the ground outside and shined through the shattered windows over an empty toddler-sized crib on the floor, tiny mattress tossed aside.

Mike's heart drummed faster and louder through his body; his head closer to bursting with each beat. A red hot dagger had driven itself through his chest and his heart was still beating. The crippling pain of loss rippled through his soul as if it were happening again. The world pulled itself apart around him. A rising ring in his ears became deafening, and he was like a wine glass ready to shatter. The lights outside flew away.

"Hope…" he moaned, eyes on the crib as he had before. As the world around him broke apart, a young girl's voice shined through the pain.

"Daddy? Dad… is that you?"

"Hope?" There was a warmth nearby, indistinct but familiar. His entire being hovered on the verge of exploding, but her voice helped him hold it together a bit longer.

"Dad! I can feel you! Where are you?"

"Hope! I'm coming for you!" Mike yelled, overwhelmed by the mounting pressure.

Mike shook apart and the world vanished again. He shot backward over his chair as if struck by lightning. Shin rushed to his side. On the floor, Mike's eyes fixed on the ceiling. Stunned, tears escaped the corners of his eyes.

"Are you okay?" Shin asked. He looked at One, who put his hands back in his lap, un-phased by what happened.

"Yeah, he's an alien." Disoriented, Mike took a moment to get his bearings then rolled onto one knee. "How long was I out?"

"You barely touched him and flew out of your chair. You're not hurt?" Shin discounted the possibility Mike had been electrocuted.

"I'm fine. I saw stuff. The kids are in the clear, and this guy is probably going to be with us for a while." Mike did not break eye contact with One. He put his chair upright then sat back down.

"What did you see?" Shin asked.

"A lot. I understand things but have a lot of questions too. I've got a lot to think about." Mike looked both confused and in awe at One. On the trapdoor console, one of the crew quarter icons lit up. Someone was on the general channel, which no one was ever in. It came from the crew quarters on deck five where Natalie was staying while he sorted things out. Mike tapped on the icon to bring up the audio.

"Hello? Can someone please take me to my friend? I want to know if he's okay. I really want to see him, I won't bother anyone," Natalie's shaky voice beckoned. *"Is anyone there?"* Mike tapped the audio off.

"We could leave her in the infirmary with her friend," Shin suggested. "I'm pretty sure she'll sit there until he wakes up."

"I'll send Addie for her. As for you, One," Mike began. He closed the trapdoor console and stood up. One followed his lead and rose to his feet. "I'd like some time to myself, so we'll talk later. Shin will show you to your quarters."

"As you wish." One bowed.

Mike returned the gesture. "Welcome to the *Ulfberht*."

Natalie

9

A Friendly Face

"Excuse me? Is my friend okay? Can anyone hear me?" Natalie smothered the console next to the locked door. After a while, she let her finger off the microphone icon and rested her back against the wall.

The two-deck tall community area connected a honeycomb of ten living quarters with an entrance on the bottom level between two sets of stairs. A two-person couch served as the only furniture in the otherwise empty eggshell-white room, She deduced they were a small crew if the area was unlived in. Nerves frayed, her back slid down the wall and she sat on the floor. She closed her eyes, rested for a moment and wished for Will to be okay.

The doors slid open next to her and startled Natalie back to her feet. In walked a spritely young woman with beautiful milky black skin and bright honey eyes, frizzy hair tied into curls. Short spikes adorned the knuckles of her fingerless leather gloves. Tattered jeans wrapped around wide hips, she wore a brown short-jacket covered in punk rock patches over a violet tank top. A name tag sewn into her jacket read: Firefly. She was short but judging by how she carried herself, she was in her twenties.

"Hi!" Kind eyes and a brilliant smile illuminated the young woman's cherubic face. "I'm Addie."

Addie's heart sank when she beheld the miserable state of the poor girl before her. Natalie's hair was mangled, her face and arms covered in dirt and abrasions, and a swath of dried blood ran across her forehead. She looked exhausted above all.

"Natalie." She went to shake hands but Addie lunged in, wrapped her arms around Natalie and squeezed her. Confused, Natalie froze, then embraced the hug and took solace in it. "Do you know if my friend is okay?" She pulled away and fidgeted in hopes of good news.

"I talked to Nikolai, and your friend is okay," Addie said. Natalie let out a massive sigh of relief and threw herself back into Addie.

"Aw." Addie rubbed her back. "It's okay, you're safe with us."

"I thought he was going to die too." A tear rolled down Natalie's cheek. The relief of good news was like a cold rush of air from opening a freezer on an unbearably hot day. It was everything.

"Oh, honey." Addie squeezed her. "We didn't want you to think the crew was full of big scary guys so I came to take you to the infirmary." Addie was jovial and genuine as if every word she spoke came straight from her heart. "Let's get you cleaned up first. You don't want your boyfriend to see you like this when he wakes up."

"Oh, we're not-" Natalie blushed and pulled away. "He's my best friend."

"My bad, I just figured. Think you'd like a warm shower and fresh clothes?"

Natalie examined her arms and ran her fingers through her tangled hair. Her lips trembled and she nodded. "Thank you." Addie hooked her arm around Natalie's and led her to the showers in the back corner of the common area. Natalie wiped away her tears.

"Don't worry one bit, you got him to us in time. You're safe here, and this is a good crew. I wouldn't fly for them if they weren't the most amazing people in the whole universe," Addie assured her with a magical smile.

A steel countertop ran along the shower room wall adjacent the door with mirrors in front of it. Across the room, five narrow steel stalls spanned the length of the room. Addie pulled a first aid kit and some wash rags from a cabinet under the counter and set them down. While Addie got sorted, Natalie saw herself in the mirror. She ran her shaky fingers through her hair in a futile attempt to tidy it until Addie turned Natalie to examine her arms and face.

"You're not so bad, these are all minor. Let's wash you up." Natalie had a rough night but all she needed was some love and prying was the wrong move.

Natalie washed her face and arms, then Addie rubbed ointment on her wounds. When wiped away a minute later the scratches and abrasions on her arms had vanished.

"You're so nice, thank you," Natalie said, more adjusted to the sense of safety.

"Thanks, sweetie. You're a doll yourself, and once you get to know the rest of the crew you'll see they're all teddy bears on the inside. It is nice to have someone around who is closer to my age, though."

"How old are you?" Natalie asked.

"Twenty-four, but everyone except Farouk is *twice* my age," Addie despaired.

"Your gloves are pretty hardcore, and I love your top," Natalie needed to say something nice after Addie had shown her such kindness. "Purple is my favorite color."

"No way! Me too!" Addie bounced, "and thanks." While she watched Addie rub ointment over a large abrasion on her arm, Natalie realized she had no idea where most of her injuries came from. "Where you from, Natalie?"

"Colorado," Natalie murmured, then cleared her throat. "A town called Belleza. We're a young town. My dad is… w-was one of the founders." Forced to correct herself, a fist squeezed her heart and she hurried the conversation along. "And you?"

"I'm from Avalon," Addie said, realizing her misstep. "A little town called Serenity. I've never heard of Colorado, is that next to Canada?"

"Kind of, it's one of the United States."

"Oh. Sorry, we don't learn that stuff out here." Addie cringed, embarrassed.

"It's okay. All the stuff I know about the colonies is what we learn in school and rumors. Is it true that everyone at Avalon has their own ship?"

"Um…" Addie held for a moment. "*Kind* of. The sooner you've got your own vehicle, the sooner you can get around. Even if you don't live on Avalon prime, most people have at least a small, personal ship."

"That's *so* cool," Natalie gushed. "Is that how you can fly? You said you fly, right?" Natalie searched for Addie's brand, but she had none. It should have come as no surprise. But, she was so young, there was no way she could be the pilot.

"Yep, I'm the pilot of this bad boy." Addie puffed up her chest.

"How?" Natalie said with opaque surprise.

"I used to drag race at Avalon before the Captain gave me a job here. Everyone called me Firefly back then." She motioned to her nametag. "When we're moving between systems there isn't much for me to do, so I have a lot of time to read and play games. It's pretty dope. And, I get to fly one of my dream ships. I just wish we got into a scrap once in a while."

"What ship are we in?" Natalie could not believe she had not already asked. However, if Addie raced ships and was now flying her dream ship, it was surely a gem.

"We're in an old Stinger, from Earth's War." Addie grinned.

"A Stinger?" Natalie gawked. "American Warship? From World War Four?"

"Is that what you guys call it?" Addie asked, but Natalie was too starstruck to hear her.

"Titan Stinger, model AWS-two-fifty-six. That's like a… space unicorn," Natalie said, aghast.

Addie laughed out loud and re-packed the first aid kit. "You know your ships. Yeah, she's a real diamond in the rough. I've been trying to convince the Captain to upgrade our warp system, but there never seems to be any *time* for it," Addie said spitefully. Natalie looked around in silent awe. "There we go, you already look amazing, even without a shower."

"Thanks." Natalie looked bashfully into the mirror. The blood had been washed off her face, her injuries were healed or bandaged up, and she looked much cleaner than she felt. "I'd still like a shower, though."

"I'll go get some clothes for you." Addie hurried to a nearby cabinet and grabbed a towel. She handed the towel to Natalie with a heartwarming smile. "The showers are small but the crew is too so we got no water restrictions. Ring me when you're ready."

With Addie gone, Natalie was alone again, but safe. This was the first peace she had since before her world was turned upside down. She hung the towel on a hook outside a stall door, undressed, and stepped into the small shower.

The dirt-filled water didn't swirl around the drain like it did on Earth. Instead, it was sucked away. The tiny contrast with Earth shook loose an avalanche of emotions that the pressures of survival had kept at bay. She leaned against the wall and bawled, her tears washed away by the downpour of water, forgotten to the world, as she would be too.

Part

2

A Big Universe

Sam

10

The Bloodhound

DEEP UNDER COLORADO'S ROCKY MOUNTAINS, PIER-LIKE CEMENT walkways ran alongside four sets of metal tracks into a spacious room with high ceilings. At the end of the outer track was an empty egg-shaped maglev pod, no longer levitating above the magnetic rail but settled on the ground. On the opposite side of the room, Commander Fuller paced along a walkway with a lit cigarette. He kept a steady gait, thumb hooked on his belt. Two cigarette butts lay discarded nearby.

Another pod emerged from the dark tunnels that fed into the room. It passed by Fuller with a whisper and decelerated into its terminus. Before it crept to a stop, its door hissed open. A youthful dark-haired man in black slacks and a light blue button-up shirt climbed out of the pod, a white lab coat in one hand. His narrow brown eyes found Fuller.

"Fuller, is everyone okay?"

"Evenin', Sam. Your team is fine. Mine," Fuller paused and with a long sigh watched the tip of his cigarette burn, "is half as big as it was an hour ago."

Sam stood speechless for a moment. "I'm... sorry," he said.

Fuller took a long drag off his cigarette, held it in, and then let out a plume of smoke. "It's a soldier's life, don't worry yourself about it. I've got to brief you on the situation before you head up there." He led the way to the lift.

"Why? What's going on?" Sam unfurled his long white coat then swept it around his back and slid into it in one big motion. His last name, Bernard, his rank and the silver shield of the Ministry of Science were attached to the lab coat over the chest pocket.

The Ministry of Science shield consisted of three bulging equilateral triangles. Lines connected the corners of the two innermost triangles to create a swirl effect. The outermost triangle was upside down, with lines connecting its corners to the walls of the center triangle. A bar ran along the top with three embedded letters: M.O.S. The logo represented the depth of truth and the skewing of perspectives necessary to find it. With each stage, the image of truth became clearer. Their motto was, after all, *In Pursuit of Truth, Understanding, and Wisdom*.

"First, what do you know already?" Fuller took a drag off his cigarette.

"I got a call about the incident, which I should have been here for. I was looking forward to examining the ship and meeting the survivor but then I got a call about the attack on my way here." Sam shook his head. "They attacked the *entire* Ministry system, not just here. I hope you don't have more bad news for me."

"They took the survivor." Fuller blew his smoke up into the ventilation.

"Damn it!" Sam burst. "Why? How would they even know?" He combed his fingers through his hair and pulled it in frustration.

"You'll go bald doin' that. But to answer ya, Knight *had* to see 'em brought in, probably figured he's a friend. No way to know short of askin' 'em, but he looks like a regular guy. They might not even know what they've got."

"Goddamn it." Sam groaned. "What else? Give it to me straight." The soft roll of the lift echoed down the shaft.

"Your team plugged in that arm to see if they could crack it open from inside." Fuller took a drag of his cigarette and relished the smoke for a moment. Arms crossed, Sam pinched the bridge of his nose.

"About ten minutes later, the bay doors were blasted open, and a goddamn Ranger tore through this place like a storm. Killed every guy I had here." Fuller held back his rage and crushed the cigarette between his fingers. "The rest of us were a mile away, locked in the main hangar with the ship we picked up. By the time we made it over here, they were long gone. They also raided a few of your labs."

"And with the systems wiped, we can't even figure out how they got in." Sam sighed hopelessly. The softly lit lift touched down and Fuller was the first one on. Sam closed the waist-high gate behind him and Fuller worked the console. The lift rose and soon the light from the lowest level disappeared. "How is the ship?"

"Let's come back around to that later. Did you say they wiped the whole Ministry system?" Fuller pointed at Sam with two fingers.

"They attacked the system's core, through here. It went haywire around the planet. We're restoring from backups at every location," Sam's bewildered face had a stronger impact on Fuller. "I can't believe there's a civilian who can do that. It shouldn't be possible." After a moment, Fuller grunted to regain his attention. "Sorry." Sam shook his head like he shook off a fly. "Does my team have an ETA on a system restore?"

"Nope. They haven't even started yet." Fuller pulled out his pack of cigarettes.

"What?" Sam exclaimed. "Why?"

"Well, that's the last bit o' news. The UEG sent a Special Agent to hunt down whoever attacked us." Fuller put a new cigarette in his lips and tucked the pack away.

"What do you mean, Special Agent?" Sam's brow furrowed with concern.

"That's his official title." The lighter clicked on and Fuller put the flame to his cigarette. He puffed on it and let out a cloud of smoke. "After the Union, the UEG disbanded its militaries but kept a staff of advisors, security, and special agents to investigate situations like this. The one they sent here has a reputation for being vicious. I've heard rumors of people dyin' mysteriously under his command and it gets swept under the rug."

"Why would they send someone like that?" Sam asked.

"This is a joint Ministry *and* UEG bunker. A secret one hidden under a hologram. Someone found it, attacked it, disrupted the Ministry's network, and got out without a scratch," Fuller said. The light from the detention hall shrank to a sliver then disappeared. "Add to that they've got a Ranger and an advanced cyborg, these people are a serious threat. This guy's mission is search and destroy. He's a fuckin' psychopath, but everyone looks the other way because he *always* gets the job done."

There was a brief silence before a crack of light shined above them and brightened the lift. They reached a level of offices and living quarters.

"So, what does this guy have to do with my team?" Sam asked.

"Well, he's interrogatin' 'em," Fuller remarked.

"What?" Before the lift could come to a complete stop, Sam jumped over the gate and sprinted down the hall. "What the *hell*, man?"

"I needed to let you know what you're walkin' into!" Fuller double-timed it into a four-way fork in the hall after Sam, who looked down each path anxiously.

"This way." Fuller turned the corner and led Sam to the plain wooden doors of a conference room. Raised voices were audible from down the hall. Sam ran ahead to open the door, but it was locked. He waved his hand in front of the wall console but nothing happened. He waved again, several times in frustration.

"You're the second highest ranking person here! You know *something*!" The muffled, unfamiliar voice boiled Sam's blood. "Nobody *hacks* the Ministry!"

"System is down, remember?" Fuller scooted Sam out of the way and kicked the door near its handle. The doors splintered and burst open.

"Tell me, you rat!" A lean, clean-cut man with a protruding brow and an angry scowl leaned face to face over a quiet Indian man. He recoiled in fear from the grim stranger who held a long triangular knife to his ear. His dark, sunken eyes bulged, a burning desire to cut the helpless scientist in his seat on display for all to see. His fine charcoal coat and perfect hair were little more than a veneer of civility.

Nearby was a taser stick, often called zappers or t-sticks. The clean-cut man had surely used it before drawing his knife.

Sam's face turned red and like a tidal wave he rushed shoulder-first into the man and sent him flying over a meter, slamming into the back wall.

"Back off!" Sam roared, standing between the agent and the scientist. He snatched and activated the zapper. Its tip erupted in blue sparks. "Who do you think you are? If you want to talk to anyone on my team I'd better be there too or I *will* use you for *unethical* human testing!"

"Woah." The man put his hands up. "I take it you're Chancellor Samuel Bernard." He spoke with decorum, but his slow, methodical speech gave his words a sinister presence. "I didn't think you'd have such fight in you." His empty stare looked through Sam as if he did not see him as a person. Sam was an opponent, a new piece in a game.

The agent tucked his knife into its sheath. A chill ran up Sam's spine, his eyes locked with the ghoulish man, but he dared not look away.

"Dr. Ganesh, please wait for me outside." Without breaking eye contact, Sam pointed behind him at the scientist. Standing by the doorway with his arms crossed, Fuller gave Dr. Ganesh a nod as he hurried out.

"I'm Agent Jones." The stranger reached an arm out to shake hands, dead eyes locked with Sam's.

"I don't give a shit *who* you are. You will not question *anyone else* in this facility without me there. Do you understand?" Sam said with authority. He ignored Jones's outstretched hand and pointed the zapper in his face, sparks erupting wildly from the tip.

"Yes." Jones leaned away from the sparks with gritted teeth. "However, given that the Ministry system has never before been compromised, it is likely that there's a mole in this facility. I would also like to bring up the authority with which I am here." He adjusted his square-buttoned coat as if an unruffled presentation granted him additional authority.

"You're in *my* facility. If you want to talk to *my* people, I *will* be present. I don't give a *damn* who sent you here. You got me, Agent?" Sam inched closer to Jones, who trembled with rage at the perceived disrespect. Fuller stood upright, hand over his pistol and ready to draw.

"Understood," Jones conceded with a bedeviled scowl.

Sam stepped back and gestured to the door. "I'd like you gone sooner than later."

Insulted, his eyes burned a hole through Sam, but he followed his orders.

"The local defense craft was pursuing a vehicle. My time would be better spent looking into it." Jones fixed his tie and blue-charcoal waistcoat. He passed by Sam, who stood ready to jab him with the zapper.

Jones glanced at Fuller, who smirked back at him. He huffed and looked away, nose in the air. He was not worth Jones's time. Fuller followed him into the hall and watched him turn the corner and go upstairs. Fuller strolled back into the room to find Sam in a seat, his hands shaking.

"Doc, that was *impressive*." Fuller gave a nod of approval. "Human testing huh? You guys uh, do that stuff here?" He tried to mask real concern, but when he looked at Sam he was unsure if he had even been heard.

"Do you think that guy's going to kill me?" Sam asked. "You were right. That guy has psycho written all over his face."

"I think you'll be fine," Fuller shook his head. "An upper-level member of the Ministry like you is too risky."

"But, he's an Alpha too," Sam said. "He might–"

"Alpha with a little a, Doc. You're still the big brand around here."

"Jesus, that guy is scary." Sam let free a sigh of relief.

"I warned ya. I'm surprised you came in here guns blazin'. I'm pretty sure people don't usually talk to him like that. Way to keep it together."

"I couldn't let him treat my team like that. But, when I looked into his creepy eyes I knew I had to stand my ground. The way he looks at you, it's like, I don't know. I've never been so unnerved by the look in someone's eyes. How did he get here before me?"

"I asked about that. He said he lives close, probably in one of the nearby states with nobody around, everyone minds their own business," Fuller said.

"Excuse me?" came a voice from outside. "Samuel, may I come in now?"

"Oh, Aman, of course," Sam called Dr. Ganesh by his first name now that Jones had gone. "I'm sorry I left you outside."

"It's okay." Aman entered. "You stared down the devil for me, I believe *I* am the one who owes *you* thanks."

"Were you hurt? Are you okay?"

"He was rather overzealous with his taser, but I was not seriously injured." Aman put Sam's worries at ease.

"Good. I hope you aren't too shaken up because I need to know what happened here," Sam said.

"I can tell you, and I take responsibility for-"

"Hold on," Sam said, "just tell me what happened." Ganesh sighed and stared at the floor for a moment before he mustered up the courage to speak.

"The man with the prosthetics, his cybernetics appeared simple, but were deceptively advanced, and elegantly so. We couldn't figure out how to open them. It neither emitted nor received signals and scans were ineffective. So, we thought there might be an internal mechanism for unlocking it, and that we may be able to open it if we connect to it manually."

"Did you follow procedure?" Sam asked.

"We followed all standard security precautions. We created an isolated sandbox and double-secured the connecting UTB ports before we plugged it in. There was no apparent breach of security until we lost control of the entire bunker." Aman shook his head, still in disbelief.

"So, the whole thing went offline all at once?"

"Yes, we were completely locked out of the system. None of the overrides worked and we were cut off from the other section of the base. Fuller's team rushed by the labs and then we felt the explosion," Ganesh went on. "A few minutes after that, a Ranger led us away at gunpoint and locked us in room one-zero-four. After a while the base switched to back-up power, the doors unlocked, and the attackers were gone."

Sam leaned back and mulled over Doctor Ganesh's story. "How did we lose control of the base?"

"I don't know, but it is unprecedented. The Ministry system is the *most advanced* and unique in existence. To my knowledge, there has not been a breach on record," Aman's voice rattled with apprehension.

"I've never heard of a security breach either, so the team is to keep that to themselves. It doesn't leave our lab except through *me* and who *I* choose to tell, understood?" Sam ordered.

"Yes, I will let the others know to remain silent on the matter." Aman nodded.

"Thank you. How long before we're back online?" Sam focused on what they could fix instead of what they could not.

"One, perhaps two hours," Aman estimated. "The Bunker will be fully operational by Sunrise and we immediately placed temporary emitters. Although, we will still need to make several large physical repairs at a later date, like the bay doors."

"Thank you, Aman." Sam rose to his feet. "Also, please have someone make an inventory of what was stolen. I can't believe we got raided on top of all this."

"I will begin right away." Aman bowed and left to tend to his duties. Once he was gone, Sam and Fuller waited for the echo of his footsteps to disappear up the stairs so they could speak freely.

"This doesn't feel right. It feels fishy," Sam murmured.

"What do you mean?" Fuller raised an eyebrow.

"Aman and Jones were both right. There's never been a breach of the Ministry system. Nobody outside of it has access, much less knows how it works."

"Well, someone had to make the damn thing," Fuller reasoned.

"The guy that made it was on another level, but he died *years* ago. The system is revolutionary. He even created the languages it's built on for the specific purpose of creating the system. It doesn't work like anything in the private sector or anywhere else. It's *completely* unique," Sam realized he had begun to rant nervously, and the troublesome implications of a breach took shape in his mind.

"Then how the hell you keep it runnin'?" Fuller asked. "Don't it need updates?"

"The Ministry put the people he was training to study it in depth after he died. They became the experts. So, the only people who understand our systems on a level capable of doing this are highly ranked members of the Ministry."

"I see what you're gettin' at." Fuller nodded. "So, a pissed-off ex-Ministry bigwig or an inside job. But if it's an inside job, why would they attack their own base?"

"I guess it could be ex-ministry if someone took it upon themselves to secretly learn its inner workings before they left. But, that's a sizable list of rogue scientists and an unlikely scenario." Sam shook his head. "This is a joint base, anyone from either side would be attacking their own base. The Ministry and the UEG don't always see eye-to-eye, but they would both want what you brought in tonight."

"If one of 'em wants it for themselves, they'd have to move it to a private facility and wipe their tracks," Fuller proposed. "But someone from the Ministry would still have to be in on it."

"Well, Knight was the way in, but the Ministry couldn't have planted him. We've studied that anomaly for weeks, but we didn't know it was going to send a ship crashing into our backyard when it terminated. And, he was here hours before it happened." Sam rested his cheek in his palm with a sigh. Nothing fit together as it should. "There wasn't enough time for *anyone* to make a move."

"To be straight with ya, this asshole *ain't* someone you send on a wild goose chase. He's like a samurai sword. If you pull it out, you draw blood."

"It could be a few people who want it for themselves," Sam proposed, to which Fuller nodded. "Then, they sent Jones to get it back at any cost."

"If it's a small group, it would be a cabal of UEG *and* Ministry folk." Fuller scratched his scruffy neck. "A few people with a lot of power doin' whatever they want. Not uncommon if you look at history." Fuller paced away from the wall.

"So it's either deep-seated corruption." Sam held one hand out in front of him. "Or, there's a hacker out there who can get into any digital system they want," Sam took a breath, "*and* they have a high tech cyborg and a Ranger as muscle." Sam held his other hand out in front of him.

"Both pretty disturbin' notions if ya ask me. Still think that asshole is overkill?"

The back of Sam's hand buzzed with a light electrical charge and a hologram appeared over it: Incoming Call.

"I see your point. At least we still have the ship," Sam said optimistically and tapped his hand for details.

"Yeah. Sorry, Sam, the ship disintegrated a few minutes after the attack," Fuller said. Sam's mouth dropped. "Turned into little specks of aluminum." Fuller pointed at Sam's hand.

Sam checked the call and his demeanor changed right away. He gestured for Fuller to hold on and held his fist horizontally in front of him to answer the call. A hologram materialized over his hand. It was the face of an aged man, white hair pulled back into a ponytail.

"High Archon Adison, this is Chief Science Officer Samuel Bernard. How can I help you, sir?" Sam greeted him with a smile. Fuller circled around to stand over his shoulder.

"Good morning, Sam. How's the bunker?"

"She's hurt, but we'll be online within the hour. Fuller's team took heavy losses and we're making an inventory of what was stolen. We'll have to wait 'til nightfall tomorrow to fix the bay doors but we'll be camouflaged again by morning."

"That's a shame." Adison shook his head empathetically. "Fuller, you have my regards," he said. Fuller nodded but said nothing. "And Samuel, I have the utmost faith in your ability to get your house in order."

"Thank you, sir," Sam said.

"With that said, have you met that agent the UEG sent over?" Adison asked.

"Yes," Sam glanced at Fuller, "I met him earlier."

"How did that go?"

"Well, he was *torturing* my team. I had to pull him off Dr. Ganesh and threaten him to get him to comply." Sam tried to downplay the incident.

"Threaten him?" Adison was taken aback. "With what?"

"Threatened to use him for human experimentation. I was impressed," Fuller said. Adison smiled at Sam.

"Impressed?" Adison said. Sam shrugged modestly. "Sam, I've known men with greater egos than yours cower before The Bloodhound."

"The... Bloodhound?"

"That's what they call him." Adison wrote on his desk console. "He can track down anyone and leaves a trail of blood behind him." Sam pinched the bridge of his nose, discomforted by the grim imagery that surrounded the agent he threatened on a whim.

"Don't look so blue. You're a rising star in the Ministry. You're very young to be in your position, and you've worked hard to achieve it."

"Thank you, sir." Sam dropped his hand and smiled.

"Not to mention the bravery, leadership, and compassion you displayed by standing up to that agent. You have the makings of an Archon."

"Th-Thank you, sir. To be compared to an Archon is humbling." Sam's stomach churned with anxiety.

"Would you like to be an Archon someday, Sam?"

"It would be an honor," he gushed.

"Well, this attack happened to the whole Ministry, but it came from *your* base. Even though you weren't there, it doesn't look good. It's a blemish, especially considering what we lost."

Sam's excitement melted away. Before he could say anything, Adison continued.

"We have a bit of a problem that you can solve, and a position as one of the youngest Archons in the Ministry's history *will* be waiting for you if you can do it."

"It's definitely worth considering." Sam tried to contain a mix of excitement and fear that swirled within.

"That agent, he's known for killing, *not* retrieving. Whoever he finds he's going to kill. However, he doesn't know what Fuller brought in earlier. In fact, he *can't* know about it. He doesn't have the clearance, but he can get the job done. I need you to make sure he doesn't *kill* the specimen your security team retrieved. Then, bring it back without telling anyone else about the nature of what you're retrieving." Adison leaned back in his chair while Sam pondered the offer.

"So, I would have to accompany that maniac who wants to kill me – on his manhunt?"

"That's right. You've been on our radar. Now you seem to have what it takes to deal with *him*. If you prove you can handle The Bloodhound and get this mission done, you'll prove yourself more than worthy of the title."

"Thank you, sir." Sam's face paled.

"All right, here's the situation." Adison paused for a breath. "That man is a representative of the UEG. You will represent the Ministry. Let him do his job. Provide support if you have to, but your only job is to retrieve the specimen alive. Nothing else matters. You've shown him you're not a pushover. Stay strong, keep your eyes open, and you'll be fine. Think you can handle it?"

"What about my lab?" Sam asked.

"I'm sure Ganesh can fill in. It's a good opportunity to see if he can do the job. This might take a few months if you have to travel to another system," Adison said. "Do you accept?"

Sam paused, mouth agape. He looked up, as if at Jones. This was the opportunity of a lifetime, and he could not let Jones kill the only extraterrestrial specimen in over a century.

"Yes, sir, thank you. I won't let the Ministry down," he said.

"Sam," Adison leaned in, "keep your eye on that Agent."

"Oh, I will."

"Good luck, Archon Bernard." Adison smiled and winked, then ended the call. Fuller watched Sam go back and forth between surprise, disbelief, excitement, and terror.

"Congratulations." Fuller patted his shoulder. "You're about to be a supreme scientific authority. You just gotta leash yourself a bloodhound and fetch yourself an alien."

"This is going to be a nightmare isn't it?" Sam asked.

Fuller nodded. "Probably."

Ulfberht Crew

11

Oasis

"*Oasis*, this is the *Slap Attack* requesting to dock in slip G-forty-two." Farouk pressed his gloved cybernetic fingers to the console.

A large ship passed behind them and eclipsed the small craft in its shadow. They floated in front of a long row of slips for smaller crafts embedded in a rocky asteroid wall. Home to over fifty thousand people and bustling with at least twice as many visitors, the city-sized space station was built into a cavernous asteroid which orbited between Saturn and Uranus. They had left the *Ulfberht* parked far away from *Oasis* station territory to maintain a low profile.

"*Slap Attack* huh? Big fan of Farouk Knight over there?" The operator sensed a fellow fan on the other side of the audio channel.

"Yeah, you could say that." Farouk smiled, chest swelling with pride.

"*He's one of my favorites too. Top five all time, easy. You're good to go, Slap Attack,*" the operator chirped.

"Thanks, *Oasis*, I appreciate it. God bless, brotha'," Farouk said. He made sure to take down the operator's name from the display.

Farouk set the ship down in the long slip. He placed his helmet on the console and ordered a print of one of his old promotional pictures from a local shop, then joined the others in the cabin. Everyone had changed into civilian clothes. For Shin that meant light blue jeans with a white shirt and an old tan jacket. He put on a beanie and some big black sunglasses. Mike wore jeans with a T-shirt beneath a well-insulated navy pea coat. Rick had taken off the vest Mike loaned him and threw on a sweater, but remained otherwise unchanged in his loose grease-stained clothes.

"Good job patchin' up that lad, Nikolai," Ian complimented the monolithic square-jawed Russian next to Mike. He wore a dark gray and crimson coat open-faced over a dark dress shirt. Once meant for the Russian Spaceforce General, most of its luster was gone. The four stars on the lapel left off-colored shadows on the coat they once called home.

"This was nothing, I just tell computer what to do. You got him to me with enough time. I once performed surgery in the middle of Russian blizzard with only kitchen tools," Nikolai said with a thick Russian accent.

"Did *that* guy make it?" Rick asked. Nearby, Farouk opened the rear ramp.

"No, but not because of surgery. Surgery was good."

"Nikolai and I are going to order supplies and meet you guys back here. We'll let you know when the dollies are ready." The group migrated to the bay, then made their way through winding halls into the station.

"I need a drink after being in that cell for six mothafuckin' hours," Farouk said.

"Shin and I'll join ya. He said he'd grab a drink with me after the thing," Rick said. Farouk looked to Shin, who gave him a confirmatory nod.

"I s'pose we're all goin' t' the pub," Ian said.

They climbed a wide staircase into a crowd of people bustling through the spacious cavern. Large stone and metal buildings protruded from the rocky walls. Walkways for the higher levels over their heads and brightly colored holo-signs for shops and restaurants lined the walls around then. Between the daylight and clouds drifting through the holographic sky, it passed for a nice day on Earth.

"If we did not have so much to discuss, we would join you," Nikolai said.

"See you guys in a couple hours." Mike waved and walked away with Nikolai. They disappeared into the crowd and the other four broke away.

"I can't wait t' get me hands on a pint!" Ian boomed.

"One sec." Farouk jogged into a nearby shop.

The other three waited outside by a two-story tall archway into the next section of the station. It was full of merchants, beggars, and people trying to get through without losing anything. A homeless man sat by the edge with a sign begging for money to buy a ticket home. Underneath the value was an ID number preceded by a credit tag: a letter C styled like an atsine. As such, the digital tag for credit ID's was playfully called a catsine. Next to the homeless man was a faded red line that delineated a pressure door that would be sucked shut if the next compartment breached. A sticker-laden sign nearby advised people to keep a safe distance away, but there had never been a breach and the area got a lot of foot traffic.

"All right, let's go." Farouk was back before they knew it. "Where we goin'? I want some chicken wings and a banana daiquiri." He checked the pubs with the augmented reality in his contacts. The others laughed at his choices. "You guys can drink whatever the hell you want. I ain't got nothin' to prove. I want to eat and drink something I enjoy after being in a cell all night."

"Then get y'self a red or a stout, I know ye like those," Ian suggested.

"I want – a mothafuckin' – banana daiquiri. I *might* have a beer afterward," Farouk insisted. "But if I get one, I want it in a big ass frosted mug." His hands pantomimed a large mug in front of him.

"But, a banana daiquiri and wings?" Ian winced at the potentially disastrous flavor combination.

Shin interrupted the conversation, pointing to their right. "There is a well-rated pub this way called Scraps."

"What's the beer selection like?" Rick asked.

"Vast."

"Yeah! My man Shin stayin' on point." Farouk clapped and led the way with a newfound pep in his step.

"I'd like t' get back t' the banana daiquiri," Ian requested. "Na' ha' could ye pair that with a plate a' wings?"

"I guess you *are* the expert on food," Farouk said with a mixed tone that left Ian unsure of his intention.

"Aye, as the chef that's mah specialty. Which is why I'm pleadin' with ye' not t' do it," Ian jested, hands in front of him like he was praying. "It's downright blasphemy."

"Ian, do you like Banana Daiquiris?" Farouk asked.

"Not really," Ian grumbled.

"Well, *I* do. You may not enjoy a banana daiquiri with wings, but I will."

Soon, they made out the sign for the bar over the heads of the crowd. It stood out, host to steel letters and a robot sculpture made from old ship parts instead of a holo-sign like almost every other business. As they neared the building, a passerby in the crowd stopped them.

"Hey! Farouk!" A scratchy voice called. Farouk looked around in search of the source and spotted a group of swashbuckling Latin men headed their way.

"What's up Nacho!" Farouk greeted with zest.

"Farouk Knight! What's up jéfe?" The short, bald Mexican in a ragged azure pea coat with golden trim clasped hands with Farouk and patted him on the back. A single earring on his left ear twinkled with the various colors of the nearby holo-signs. "See, puto? I told you," he said to one of the other three men with him. They seemed to care little for concealing the guns and blades tucked under their jackets.

"Oh shit, we're big frans. Friends. Fans." His friend in a jacket held out his arm for a handshake. "What happened to your arms?"

"*Que putas?*" Nacho smacked his friend on the back of the head and the others broke into an uproarious protest at the insensitive comment. "*No seas tan shute. Da le respeto, guey,*" Nacho scolded in Spanish so Farouk and his friends could not understand, but their AR closed captioned it in their preferred language.

'*What the fuck? Don't be so nosey. Show him respect, ass.*'

"Their captain is that guy Aries we get our hax from," Nacho said, *hax* being a general term for numerous forms of digital contraband. "I'm sorry, homie," he said to Farouk, then introduced his friends. The one who committed the faux pas was the last to be introduced, and apologized for his transgression.

"It's cool, don't even trip. These are my friends: Shin, Rick, and Ian. Nacho is a friend of mine from Freyja. How you been, Nacho? Last time I saw you was in that scrap with those Dragon Claw dickheads."

"We got a security contract at Endoria, so we're based there now. But yeah, we got in a fight over that card game. Fucker stabbed me." Nacho unbuttoned his shirt and revealed a scar on the lower-left hemisphere of his ribcage.

"Those Dragon Claw are some real assholes." Farouk examined the scar.

"The motherfucker was cheating too," Nacho went on.

"Yeah, dawg, *all* those fools were cheating," one of his friends agreed.

"Poor sports are the worst kind'a bitch," Rick chuckled.

"One time a Dragon Claw dude tried to say I cheated in a beer-chugging contest," another one shared. The group spoke over each other, each agreeing with Rick in their own way. Shin sighed and waited for the clamor to wrap up. He did not care to share anecdotes about unlikable people.

"It's been so chill here since they got banned," Nacho said, which prompted the group to simmer down.

"Banned?" Farouk was shocked.

"Yeah, like a couple months ago." Nacho looked to his friends for confirmation on his time frame, which they gave.

"No shit?" Farouk said in pleasant disbelief.

"I didn't think *Oasis* would actually *ban* anyone," Rick said.

"Yeah, but those fools cause too much trouble for no reason. We're all just trying to live, you know?" Nacho said.

"At least there's finally an *Oasis* where you won't find any Dragon Claw," Farouk joked. Well met with laughter, Farouk moved things along. "But, we're about to grab a drink. You guys want to join us?"

"Aw." Nacho groaned. The group's jaws dropped and their disappointed expressions all converged on Nacho. "Next time, homie. Our captain called us back to the ship. We're about to bounce. Back to work."

"All right, next time. Here, let's link up." Farouk and Nacho exchanged info then said their goodbyes and parted ways. Nacho's group left, star struck after an unexpected encounter with Farouk Knight while Farouk and the crew headed into Scraps.

"You know they only laughed at your shitty pun because you're famous."

"I don't need to be the funniest guy in the world, I just need to be relatable, and most people aren't that funny. So, kiss my ass, Shin."

"Y'know, Shin, I'm glad you came along," Rick said.

The group found a tall round table and were quick to order their first round of food and drinks. They carried on talking trash and shared stories about their time apart.

"Next round is on me." Farouk placed on the glass table a thin card with fat green letters that read CASH CARD and tapped through the menu that appeared next to it. He felt generous after a daiquiri and two beers.

"You guys can really put these away, huh?" An energetic young man arrived with a tray full of pints and set them down around the table.

"What're ye talkin' about?" Ian said. "We're takin' our time t' savor the intricate flavors. Y' should see us when we get pissed." He seized his glass. The young man laughed and excused himself.

Ian raised his pint. "T' the finest crew in space."

"Here-here!" The group banged their pints together and took a hefty swig. While some glasses came down softly, others slammed on the table with a clink.

"Did we put alcohol on 'er shoppin' list?" Ian asked with overt concern.

"I took care of it," Rick said.

"Aye. We dinnae know ha'long we're gun' be out, and it'd be a damned tragedy t' embark on a long journey without a pint." Ian grunted and took another drink.

"Especially if we're draggin' kids with us," Farouk huffed.

"I don't think they're stayin'." Rick sipped some head off his beer.

"It's too dangerous. Mike will probably drop 'em off somewhere," Shin proposed.

"Aye, but we dinnae have time t' make arrangements for 'em. We cannae dump 'em somewhere and wish 'em luck," Ian said.

"Yeah we can," Farouk countered.

"In the colonies, they're already adults," Shin said.

"And we can give 'em some money before we send 'em off. That'd be nice of us, right?" Farouk looked around for approval. He got a mix of grunts and a positive reception. Farouk nodded, pleased with himself, then paused. "Hey, what do you guys think about the other guy?"

"I'm sure Mike and Nikolai are talkin' about him now," Ian said.

"Did you ever get his name?" Farouk asked Shin directly.

"His name is One."

"One?" Farouk put his beer down.

"You're pullin' our legs." Rick chuckled.

"Who names their kid One?" Farouk said.

"In Japanese, my name means truth. The strangeness of names is culturally relevant," Shin said.

"Aye, that's a good point there, lads. The first thing used t' come t' mind when I heard *shin* was a bone. Now, I think a' Shin." He motioned. "We'll get used to One. That is if he's stayin'?"

"For the foreseeable future," Shin said.

"It might be nice to have some new blood around," Rick added.

"We've been runnin' on a skeleton crew for a while now. I kind'a miss havin' a team."

"That's true. I *have* been gettin' pretty tired of you assholes," Farouk said.

"Welcome to my world." Shin grinned.

"Why do you assholes think I drink so much?" Rick said.

"Bah, ye missed us in that cell didn't ye?" Ian gave him a playful punch.

"I missed my arms more."

"For all the teasing." Shin slid his tall glass to the center of the table. The group quieted down to listen. "These moments remind me there was a time I didn't think I would find a home again. This crew has reminded me that life will always prove you wrong. Farouk, I'm glad we got you back safely." Shin held his pint in the air.

"Aye!" Ian said. All four glasses bashed together. "Last one done buys the next round," he said before chugging his beer.

"Hey, that's not fair." Farouk had the most beer. The other three did not stop and poured beer down their throats. "Shit." He tipped his pint back and raced to finish first with no desire to pay for the second round in a row.

Ian was the first one to put his pint down with a clink. "Amateurs," he managed to say before a long, overwhelming belch. He pounded his chest while Rick put down his glass and wiped his chin. He let out his own hardy burp and they watched Farouk and Shin race to the end of their glasses. It came down to the wire, with a sliver of beer swirling out of the glass until they both slammed them on the table. Farouk's glass touched down a hair before Shin's to the praise of the others.

"Who needs kids around when we have Ian?" Shin muffled a burp. He set down his empty beer and placed his own cash card on the table. While everyone ordered their drinks, Shin checked his messages.

"Message from the captain. We don't have time for a fourth round."

"Bullshit!" Farouk burst. "That's real convenient, Shin. Real convenient."

"*I* had four," Rick boasted. "Slowpokes."

"Hey, I had four too."

"Well." Rick cringed. "You had three and a banana daiquiri." The crack earned him a middle finger from Farouk and a chuckle from Ian.

"All right lads, let's call it." Ian stood and scooted his seat in.

"We've still got more than a half hour." Rick pointed at the clock on the table.

"Whatever man, the dollies with are waitin' for us to load up our supplies. We pay per minute," Farouk said.

With a groan from Rick, the group slipped out of the bar. They did not notice the raggedy white-haired man who sat against a wall at the edge of a nearby alley. He held a crude cardboard sign. As soon they stepped into the quad, the wrinkled man dropped his sign. Before they knew what was going on he had hurried in front of them.

"Sinner!" The energetic and animated man yelled. "You desecrate your body with machines! You're a sinner in the eyes of God!" He jabbed his index finger at Farouk. The man's pants bottoms were in tatters and written in messy black marker his dirty shirt read: *Dogs go to Heaven — Cyborgs go to Hell.*

"His shirt ain't even clever." Rick shook his head.

"Just ignore him," Shin said.

"He looks like he's on a good one," Rick commented on the man's bloodshot eyes and dilated pupils. Whatever drug cocktail he was on, it really brought out the bigotry.

"If God wanted you to have arms, he'd *give* you arms!" The man yelled and hustled to stay ahead of the group, hunched over with one fist balled up.

"I *had* arms, dumbass," Farouk barked. He tried to move around the man and diverted his eyes. "God has nothing to do with my prosthetics."

"No, he doesn't! God works in mysterious ways! Remove the Devil's limbs and be the way God intended you to be!"

"Fuck off, old man," Farouk said, looking away.

"You defy God! You don't know his plan!" He demanded their

attention, as well as that of those around them. The group tried to continue to their ship, but the old man persisted.

"Mothafucka', *I'm* Christian. I've read the Bible. God doesn't say a damn thing about cybernetics." Farouk's tone became deep growl. He took an aggressive stance then continued on his way. The old man recoiled, and then followed again.

"Aye. Move along there, old man." Ian tried to get between them and put his hand on the man's chest to keep him from advancing.

He would not be denied and lunged at Farouk. "Take off the Devil's limbs!"

The old man yelled and pulled at Farouk's arm. Ian tried to pull him away. Farouk again tried to ignore him and yanked his arm away. The old man threw a wild kick at Farouk, who had reached the limits of his patience.

Farouk shoved the man away. A normal person would have pushed him to the floor, but Farouk's enhanced strength sent him flying. He crashed into a wall and flipped backward over it, then fell onto a stairway. Rick chuckled to himself.

"Aye, well, I tried," Ian said. The outburst granted them a moment of peace, but the world had no desire to leave them alone.

"Hey!" From behind, a much younger voice called out. The group stopped and turned around to find a tall young man headed their way with a half dozen friends behind him. The tall pirate was clean-cut wearing a gold eagle on his blue jacket and an angry scowl. His friends were all dressed alike. "What's your problem, man?"

"The hell you talkin' about?" Farouk asked.

"You go around pushing people over staircases? You broke that guy's leg!" He pointed behind him. His friends gathered around and spread into a semi-circle.

"Good. He won't be able to harass anyone for a few days," Farouk replied.

"Dickheads like you give people with prosthetics a bad name," the guy said, his threatening posture delivering a clear statement of intent.

"Dickheads like *him* give Christians a bad name. What's your point?" Farouk retorted, appalled at the representation of his religion the old man portrayed.

"That guy's got about the same chances against you as a little kid. Would you shove a little kid?" the man yelled.

"No, but I'd smack 'em upside the head." Farouk pantomimed a smack.

"You come to us angrily, making assumptions," Shin spoke up. "Picking fights for others when you don't even know if they deserve your help."

"*This* guy fighting *that* guy back there isn't cool. I don't need to know anything else," the instigator insisted.

"Well, we cannae stop ye from bein' a dobber."

"Probably not a smart move there, sport." Rick gave them one last chance to change their minds.

"What, because he's a cyborg?" The man scoffed. "Unless your face is made of metal, I'm about to teach you a lesson in respect."

"Oh yeah?" Farouk's smirk gave away the amusement he had tried to hide. "Let's see what you got. First one's free." Farouk tapped on his chin.

"Today, you're going to regret being an asshole." The brash young man charged in with a big right hook. As promised, Farouk let the punch connect. The impact shattered most of the bones in the man's fist. He roared and cradled his trembling hand.

"Not bad," Farouk said with a sly grin. The angry instigator's friends pulled out brass knuckles and knives. Farouk's attacker drew a switchblade with his good hand. Committed, he lunged at Farouk blade-first.

It was not a smart move.

Sam

12

Manhunt

THE SUN'S FAINT TANGERINE LIGHT BLED INTO THE EDGES OF A deep blue sky when Sam stepped out of the Bunker's mangled hangar doors. He stirred a cup of coffee and blew on its steamy surface. Parked out front was a small transport craft the size of a compact two-story house. Troopers, low-ranking Earth Orbit Security personnel in blue uniforms, pushed hover platforms loaded with crates and boxes.

"How you doin' doc?" Fuller's voice beckoned. He and Dr. Ganesh approached alongside a trooper with a box-filled platform.

"I'm *not* looking forward to this," Sam said. The trooper took the cart of Sam's belongings to the ship while Fuller and Ganesh stayed with Sam.

"Ever been off-planet?" After two years, Fuller knew little of Sam's personal life.

"No, I've always been so busy I never got the chance to." Sam took a cautious drink of his coffee.

"Well, I guess this ain't all bad, huh?"

"Chancellor Bernard!" Agent Jones yelled from the edge of the craft's ramp. "We leave in two minutes!" He held up two fingers in case he was not heard. Sam gave him a thumbs-up and Jones headed back inside.

"Well, I guess I should get going." Sam shook Dr. Ganesh's hand. "Aman, you've been a great Lieutenant Director."

"You as well, Samuel. I couldn't have asked for a better boss. I have some big shoes to fill."

"You're going to do great." Sam patted him on the shoulder. Ganesh opened his arms, to which Sam leaned in for a hug and held his coffee at a distance as a precaution. "I want to see her in better shape than how I left her." He pointed at the hangar doors. The ship's engines hummed to life behind him.

"I don't think that will be difficult." Ganesh pointed to Sam's coffee, offering to take it for him. Sam thanked him and took one last sip, then handed it off.

"Hugs are a bit excessive don't you think?" Fuller scoffed.

"Do you want a hug? I'm going to miss you too, Fuller." Sam veiled his honesty with a mocking tone.

"Ah, shove it. I just wanted to make sure you're really out of my hair ya little nerd." Fuller kept his affection restricted to a handshake.

"Thanks, man," Sam said. He had acquired a sense of safety with Fuller around, confident he could handle anything. Henceforth, he would be on his own.

"Be careful." He squeezed Sam's hand and pulled him close. "Watch your back, don't show weakness, and *don't* trust that guy." Sam looked back into Fuller's eyes, which beamed with concern deeper than Fuller could manage with words.

"Thanks for the advice. You guys take care of yourselves." He headed for the ramp and looked back at his friends one last time. Fuller saluted. Sam returned the gesture, then departed.

The ramp closed behind Sam and he ran up a short, narrow stairway from the supply-stuffed loading bay into the cabin. The cabin seats were arranged in two rows of three. It was filled with almost a dozen troopers who chatted and joked amongst themselves. Two men in the front row stood out, dressed in jeans and T-shirts.

Sam shuffled to a seat in the middle of an empty back row. The craft lifted off and hovered over the platform. The walls turned transparent to reveal the world outside. Sam buckled himself in. The craft's nose tilted skyward. He turned to see his friends again, but some commotion in the front row caught his attention.

A tall, square-jawed man had noticed Sam come in. He whispered something to the shorter man with spiky black hair who looked over his shoulder at Sam. The number five appeared on the walls and counted down by one each second. The two men in the front row unbuckled themselves and darted to the back. The beefy guy almost two meters tall sat to Sam's right. The shorter man, who reached the tall one's chin, sat on Sam's left. Startled, Sam watched them buckle in.

"How ya doin' Doc?" The tall man grinned. The counter reached zero and they rocketed into the sky. Sam's stomach churned from the sustained kick of inertia that pressed them into their seats. The two strangers laughed. "Ya face!" the tall one blurted. The hurricane in Sam's gut settled, easier to deal with.

"You eva' been in space befo'e?" the tall man asked with a thick Boston accent.

"First time!" Sam's chest heaved, eyes straight ahead.

"Then you should check *that* out." The tall man pointed to Sam's left.

Sam looked eastward. The Sun's rays beamed over the horizon and exploded in brilliant white light that cascaded off the clouds and land below. The blue sky on the walls faded into a menagerie of stars. No longer viewed through the atmosphere they were perfect spheres that did not twinkle. The walls displayed spectrums of light humans normally could not see, expressed as vibrant colors which created the cloudy arm of the Milky Way Galaxy. The tiny home Sam had never left was juxtaposed with the unbelievable vastness of the universe.

"Whoa," Sam muttered, overwhelmed by a universe singing with the radiance of its stars.

"I'm James," the tall guy said. Sam peeled his attention away from the view to shake his hand.

"Sam." He turned around to introduce himself to the shorter, blue-eyed man, who went by Matt. They were both high betas.

"You guys from Boston?" Sam asked.

"Yeah, we grew up togetha', joined up togetha'. Turns out we're a great team," James said. "How about you?"

"I'm from Washington." Still captivated by the view, Sam managed a casual chat.

"Washington, huh?" James said. "You said you've nevah been to space?"

"Yeah, I work a lot. Like, always."

"Well, we're going to teach you to have some fun. But, we were kinda wonderin' why you're taggin' along," he pried.

Sam contemplated for a moment. "I'm here to protect Ministry interests."

"Ah, it's one a' those, huh?" James gave him an exaggerated nod. "We were on the West coast when we got the call. We neva' heard a' no Ministry offica' comin' on one a' *these*. It's weird, ya know?"

"What's one of *these*?" Sam inquired.

"You know, one a' these," James whispered. He checked the troopers around them and leaned in to whisper. "Don't know what the mission is yet, but if they wake ya up in the middle a' the night and tell ya to gear up, it's probably because they want someone dead."

"I'm not here to kill anyone." Sam put his hands up.

"A' course not." James chuckled. "That's probably our job, which is why we wonderin' about *you*."

"I see." Sam grasped the roots of their curiosity. "I only need to retrieve something, but it should offer an interesting break from the norm."

Ahead, a solitary gray and blue ship grew larger. The armored, triangular bow looked like a hammerhead shark with thrusters on the sides. On the aft, four short, thick wings tapered from the keel, lined with massive rail guns. The wings were above and below the main body so shots could clear the obtuse bow. A grid of four thrusters propelled it from behind. Once close, it became clear the ship was massive, twice as long as the Golden Gate Bridge is tall.

Their craft pulled into a docking bay on the ship's belly. The craft's bay door opened behind them and a new source of light flooded the room. The troopers were quick to shuffle into the bay. Jones entered from another room and passed the trio with a puzzled look, then hummed and marched off.

"Briefing in five minutes, pick up a hitch for the location," Jones bellowed. The loud stomp of his boots echoed on the bay's metal floor. Troopers followed him out and unloaded the crates.

"Troopers will take ya stuff to ya room fo' ya. Betta' hurry, don't wanna be late," Matt patted Sam on the shoulder and followed James out. A trooper handed each of them a hitch, a small wrist-mounted device that links them to the ship.

The three men took a maglev pod to the war room where the meeting was to take place. On the way, Sam synced the hitch to the mobile implanted in his hand so he would not have to wear it. When they arrived, they sat at a rectangular aluminum table in the center of the room. At the head of the table, Agent Jones read from a sleek silver tablet inscribed with the leafed-globe emblem of the United Earth Government.

Sam sat with Matt and James on the long side of the table across from two intimidating strangers. One was a lean Ranger with perfect posture. His sleek, bug-like helmet laid on the table and he was covered from neck to toe in white and blue armor with *K.R.A.* embossed on the chest plate. The back and arms housed mechanisms within armored shells. He had dirty blonde hair and small eyes with a pronounced jaw and nose. Cauliflower ear and a short haircut made his already large ears stand out. He wore a grim look on his face.

Slouched in his seat, the other light-skinned stranger pulled headphones from his ears and stuffed them into his pocket. His hair was cut short and a sleeve of tattoos covered a brawny left arm. His T-shirt, stretched to the limit by his muscles, barely maintained structural integrity. Unlike the intense Ranger, his honey eyes oozed boredom.

"Welcome, gentlemen." Jones put down his tablet. "I'll begin with introductions. The names of the men to my right are classified, so you'll refer to them by codenames. I'm sure some of you have heard of the Kraken. Call him Ken." Jones introduced the Ranger to his immediate right. "And next to him, Samson." He gestured to the muscle man, who gave a casual nod. "To my left, James Coleman and Matthew Akers, a two-man strike team with an exemplary record in the field."

"How's it goin', guys?" James greeted amiably. Matt sufficed with a nod.

"And lastly, this is Samuel Bernard, a consultant from the Ministry," Jones said.

"Hey." Sam waved.

"A consultant?" Ken asked in nonchalant astonishment. "That's a first."

"Yes, it was a joint facility, they are sending their own man along to complicate our lives," Jones said. "If there aren't any more questions, I'll begin. A secret UEG–Ministry bunker was attacked early this morning." He tapped on his tablet. The footage and dossier on the attack projected as holograms over the table. "The base's local RAD, a Gerridae, was lured out by a small ATV, the owners of which have been tracked to a small town in a nearby valley. They've been detained while *we* follow another lead."

Fuller had always called the ship by its name, so Sam discretely looked up RAD: Recon And Defense.

"I don't see a vehicle picked up from the attack." Matt flipped through the holograms in front of him.

"Aside from the tracks it left, we retrieved that information from the Gerridae's black box, as well as the lead we're following. Are there any full contact fighting fans here?" Jones asked with an undertone of disdain. Everyone except Sam and Jones raised their hands, but one did not need to be a fan to know the name. "The attackers broke out a prisoner with advanced weaponized cybernetics that was captured yesterday. That prisoner was Farouk Knight." He brought up a picture of Farouk on the holo-screen.

Samson's body language came to life and a fire burned in his eyes. His posture straightened and he leaned in with a big smile. "Farouk Knight?" he boomed, eyes fixed on the picture. "The motherfuckin' Slapdaddy himself?"

"That's right," Jones said, voice bereft of amusement.

Samson held his hands up as if to thank a higher power and balled them into fists. "Thank you for picking me for this."

"I knew you would appreciate the opportunity to fight the former heavyweight champion," Jones said.

"If he can go blow for blow, I can't wait." Samson shook his balled fists in excitement at the notion of fighting a legend and prove himself against the best.

"Moving on, then. It was reported that the sole attacking force at the bunker was a rogue Ranger. So, I've brought a newer, better version for us."

"So, what are us normal guys here fa'?" James pointed at Matt and himself.

"I assume they have a ground force, even if the Ranger is the tip of their spear," Jones explained. "You two are here to deal with them, be it offensively or defensively. You'll be working with me. We also have the *Rampart's* troopers, shuttles, and fighters at our disposal."

"Gotcha," James drummed on the table.

"The lead we're following is promising. It appears the ship that shot down the bunker's Gerridae was an old DC 15 series Armadillo. Approximately a half hour after the attack, an Armadillo named *Slap Attack* docked at the *Oasis* space station," Jones went on. "We're headed there now. *Oasis* is known for harboring pirates and other unsavory characters, as well as having little regard for Earth law. We requested the transcripts for the ship but received no response, so it looks like we might have to *take* it."

"Armadillos are short range, they had to have a ship in orbit or somewhere nearby," Samson said.

"I have no idea how they got by Earth Orbit Security, but we need to eliminate the threat and ensure there are no others," Jones said. "So, we're going to try *capturing* them first in hopes of procuring whatever information they may have. If that doesn't work, the gloves are off." He tapped a blinking icon. "Yes, Captain Slater?"

"We're arriving at *Oasis Station* in less than ten minutes," a deep, mighty voice boomed from the speaker.

"Thank you, Captain. Please send the Commander to the war room and try to get a hold of the station one more time before we arrive," Jones requested.

"Roger that." The call ended.

"Gentlemen, be prepared to kick down the front gate. We assemble in the docking bay in nine minutes. Dismissed," Jones ordered. The four men stood from the table at once and headed for the door.

"See ya later, Doc." James patted Sam on the shoulder.

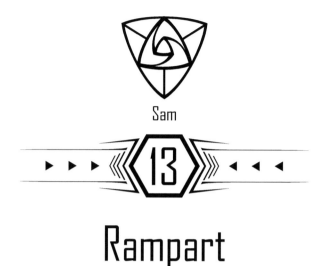

Sam

13

Rampart

James was the last one out and in his wake entered an immaculately dressed officer without a hair out of place. His navy uniform with white and gray trim could have been brand new, and the light glistened off three pips on his collar. Shined daily, they maintain their luster. He stood at the end of the table, opposite Jones.

"This is Commander Haynes, second in command of the *USS Rampart*," Jones introduced the picturesque man with a strong brow. "Commander Haynes, this is Chancellor Samuel Bernard from the Ministry of Science. He'll be joining us on our search but not on the ground. Could he observe from the bridge or something?"

"I don't think that'll be a problem at all. Right this way, Chancellor." Haynes gestured to the door, wedding band twinkling.

"You can call me Sam. A pleasure to meet you, Commander."

"The pleasure's mine, I've never met a Chancellor before. Welcome to the *Rampart*." Haynes led him out and sent a message on his hitch.

"Thanks. This is a good looking ship you've got here." Sam glanced back at Jones, whose sinister eyes followed Sam until the doors closed.

Sam hoped to make new friends on the ship, and commanding officers were a good start.

"Thank you," Haynes said. "She's a beauty. Sluggish, but tough as hell. You're lucky. A lot of people don't get to see, much less ride in one of these."

"Why's that?" Sam asked.

"There aren't a lot of them. They've only been able to build a few lately to meet increased pirate activity in the system, and they don't get much attention because of de-weaponization." Haynes referenced the Peaceful Union Act from two decades earlier.

"We don't really have to deal with pirates very much on Earth, do we?" Sam could not recall any direct incidents with pirates in Earth space.

"That won't last long if we don't have anything to fight with, and they attack sub-light transports sometimes. My husband always worries." Haynes waved his hand over a glass console on the wall. The double doors before them slid open with a whisper.

The bridge was a large, circular room with a tall ceiling. Across the front wall was a gorgeous display covered in streaks of light that bent as if through a fisheye lens. At the foot of it were three workstations embedded into the floor. A curved, chest-level wall encircled the back of a round platform in the middle of the room with three chairs, which separated it from the workstations that lined the walkway behind it.

A man with a face like weathered stone sat in the front and center chair of the command platform. The brawny man wore his coat open-faced and without a belt. He rose from his chair like an ancient guardian and stepped down from the platform. Even once he was on the same level, Sam still had to look up to see his face. "Captain Franklin Slater." His giant hand reached out for Sam's.

"Nice to meet you. Chancellor Samuel Bernard, Sam is fine though." Sam tried to match the pressure in the Captain's handshake to prevent his hand from being crushed.

"Pleasure to have an officer from the Ministry aboard," Captain Slater said. "Have you been on the bridge of a battleship before?"

"Nope. First time in *space*." Sam flashed a nervous smile.

"I'll show ya around." Captain Slater waved and Sam followed him around the front of the elevated central platform. "This is the command platform. Commander Haynes and my CCO sit up there with me." He noted the two empty chairs behind his. The Chief Communications Officer was not present. "These two spots here are for my DSO and my pilot." He referred to the Digital Security Officer and pointed at the oval workstations embedded into the floor. A half dome covered the front of the pilot station to encompass peripherals. The ships were so slow they did not have a yoke and instead, a glass console extended in a semi-circle around the pilot. The puffy chairs looked like one could sink into it and sleep forever.

"These are cool." Sam knelt to peek inside the pilot's embedded cockpit with childlike excitement, then got back up to follow Captain Slater.

"That one is weapons command." The Captain pointed to the last embedded workstation. "And that there's my navigator," Slater pointed at an officer at a console against the wall. Slater guided Sam around the other side of the command platform to its thin back wall. The nearby bridge doors opened and a female officer entered, blonde hair pulled back in a ponytail.

"Speaking of security." Captain Slater wrapped his arm around Sam's neck and pulled him close. "You and that Agent are technically my superiors in all this, but I'm still in command of my crew and I've *heard* of that Agent. He's got a reputation."

"I've been warned." Sam nodded beneath the clench of the Captain's massive arm. The female officer approached and waited for the Captain to finish.

"Any chance you could whip me up some way to keep tabs on him? Know where he is; hear what he's saying? This is my ship, I want to stay a step ahead of him if I can."

"You can count on me, Captain," Sam assured him, happy to find allies.

"I appreciate that, Chancellor. And, to show you my appreciation, I'd like to bring you into the loop on something." Captain Slater leaned in to speak softly.

"Sure. About what?" Sam asked, intrigued and perplexed.

"You said it's your first time in space, and talkin' to you here has given me a lot of information about you. That said, you haven't thought about what happens when you and that agent find your target, have you?"

"Uh." Sam looked away. "No, I guess I haven't. It's all been kind of sudden."

"Can I ask what your mission is?"

"To protect Ministry interests and retrieve something that was stolen," Sam said, practiced from his conversation with Matt and James.

"Sounds like you can't tell him what you're after. Even if you could, would you trust 'em? You might have to get your hands dirty. Feel free to grab a suit of armor for yourself." Slater patted Sam on the back and turned to the patient officer. "Wells."

"Sir, I tried on every channel, *still* no response from *Oasis*," she said. Captain Slater looked over his shoulder at the timer next to the *Oasis* ETA on the front screen. There were less than two minutes left before they arrived.

"I guess it doesn't matter anymore." Slater headed back to his chair.

"Sam, this is Lieutenant Commander Amber Wells, our Chief Communications Officer," Commander Haynes introduced. "And, this is Chancellor Samuel Bernard."

"Chancellor, huh? You're pretty young to be a big shot." She shook his hand, her chin held high. The athletic alpha with a firm grip had sharp features, intense blue eyes, and held herself like a proud warrior despite being Sam's height. Most of the tall women Sam knew tried to make themselves look shorter, but not this one.

"Thanks, I was going to say something to the same extent, Lieutenant Commander. You can call me Sam." He smiled.

"It's a pleasure. Call me Amber." She grinned and returned to her duties with focus.

"Agent Jones, we arrive at *Oasis* in less than a minute. We were unable to open a channel," Captain Slater called in. Amber and Haynes took their seats on the platform.

"We'll see if they ignore another hail from a UEG ship again." Jones's voice boomed through the speaker. *"My team and I will depart as soon as we arrive."* Sam repositioned himself next to the platform, arm's length from Amber and the navigators.

"Roger that, Slater out." The Captain swiped down on his chair arm to end the call. The interface projected in front of his chair disappeared.

"Arriving at the *Oasis* station in thirty seconds." The pilot's flat voice broadcast throughout the ship. At ten seconds, the timer centered itself on the front screen and counted down until the pilot announced: "We've arrived at the *Oasis Sta...tion.*"

Warped by an oscillating field of energy, the lights that flowed by the front screen coalesced into stars when the ship came out of warp and a clear, crisp picture overtook the screen. Captain Slater eased to his feet, followed by Commander Haynes. Amber covered her mouth, agape in shock. Sam's knees turned to jelly, and he leaned on the platform's back wall for support. The room looked on in disbelief.

"Oh my god." Amber's soft voice broke the absolute silence that had taken over.

Oasis was a bustling city built into a cavernous asteroid once mined for its resources. They expected a lively space station. Instead, scraps of ships floated by and bumped into chunks of rock and steel. Twisted debris blanketed the area and the station appeared to have been torn open. Most horrifying were the lifeless bodies that drifted alongside the debris. Many ships, as battered as the station, hung together by threads. Pirate ships with open bounties, civilian ships, and shuttles provided aid. The bridge crew could only stare, horror-struck at the remains of what was once one of mankind's greatest accomplishments.

"This is why we couldn't open a channel." Amber watched pieces of people, rock, and metal float by. Captain Slater could not turn away and walked backward into his seat to pull up his holo-screen. He opened a channel to Jones.

"Agent Jones, report to the bridge," Slater said, his words bereft of life.

"Did they finally answer? It's too late, tell them we're coming."

"You're going to want to come to the bridge, see this for yourself," Captain Slater responded.

"I'll be there in a minute," Jones huffed and ended the call.

Captain Slater looked upon the destruction that had preceded their arrival. The room looked on in silence for a moment until the Captain paced toward the screen and uttered what everyone was thinking: "What the hell happened here?"

Ulfberht Crew

14

Dragon Claw

"I<small>T WAS LIKE</small> I <small>TRANSCENDED TIME AND SPACE.</small> I <small>FELT HER IN</small> front of me. I spoke to her. For that split second, we were together." Mike sat atop a bar balcony with a half-empty beer overlooking a bustling crowd below that flowed through the plaza like blood through veins. Across from him, Nikolai's vodka neared its end. After a brief pause for reflection, Mike continued. "And the memory, it's like I was there again. I could feel the weight of Faith in my arms. It was real. Even my nightmares never felt like that."

Nikolai tapped his chin with a finger. "You should take him to the wissard." His thick Russian accent skewed words. "It would be the wisest decision. They will be friends."

"He and Al would get along, but I can't. I've got too many questions." Mike could not articulate the whirlwind of anxiety, curiosity, and a void in his perception which had caught him unaware.

"Such as?"

"I want to know how I made contact with her, and if I can do it again," Mike said. "Can he hear thoughts or something? If he's psychic, why does he need to touch me to show me stuff?"

"You *know* it was her?" Nikolai placed his cash card on the table.

"It was her. I've haven't heard her voice since she was a baby, but I could *feel* her." Mike balled up his fist, eyes distant and watery.

"Another drink?" Nikolai asked. Mike sighed and examined his beer.

"Definitely." He gulped down what remained of his drink and Nikolai tapped on their table to order them another round. Mike watched the crowd below, each person on their own journey through life. "The whole world feels different."

"Everything is the same, comrade," Nikolai boomed. "It is *you* who is different." He pointed at Mike.

A young server with a low-cut shirt arrived with their drinks. She set them down and picked up their empty glasses with a smile. They waited until she left to continue.

"Michael, tonight has been a plan for years, yes? Your plan, it is working. We infiltrate Ministry bunker, you install virus, then we drink to celebrate." Nikolai held up his glass. "Now, this *visitor* is dropped in your lap, and you learn your daughter is safe and waiting for you? What more could you want? Leave him on Elysium where he will be safe. Albert already understands universe. He will have friend that is not robot."

"But, maybe there is some way he can help me contact her, or," Mike stammered, "or something I can learn that could help me."

"You say you felt his purpose. He is here to observe. You will not find cooperation in him," Nikolai pointed out.

"I have to try, though."

"Then try, but remember some things. You have confirmation that Hope is alive and you installed special software in Ministry systems. If you focus and follow plan, you will have her back soon. This stranger is unknown factor, and valuable to UEG and Ministry. They will send people after him. To keep him could bring danger."

"We've been flying under the radar for years. How is anyone going to find us?" Mike dismissed Nikolai's concerns. "Once we pick up Maya, we'll know our heading. Then we do like you said, stick to the plan.

Until then, we've got some time to burn, why not spend it talking to someone who shouldn't exist? We can take him to Elysium later."

"It *is* a unique opportunity," Nikolai submitted. "But you should ask to understand, not for what you seek. If you let this change mood, confidence, choices, you could lose everything you have worked for all these years. If you take him to the wissard, you can focus on your objective."

"Ask to understand, you got it. Thank you, Nikolai, for all your help getting me this far," Mike said.

"I leave my clan for noble cause: to rescue my goddaughter and help a loyal friend. I require no thanks." Nikolai raised his stein in the air. "*Nostrovia.*"

"*Nostrovia,*" Mike said. Their glasses slammed together and splashed alcohol on the table. "It's nice to get a breather like this. We might be on the ship for a while."

"Once you have your daughter, take nice long vacation," Nikolai said. "She will enjoy the outside as well."

"That'd be nice. We should have the guys head back and load up the supplies." Mike tapped on the back of his hand to access his implant and found a new message from Shin. Nikolai put two fingers to his black bracelet for a holo-screen, but an outburst from Mike distracted him

"No way!"

Nikolai hummed in inquiry.

"*Oasis banned* the Dragon Claw a couple months ago," Mike clarified.

"Banned?"

"Yeah, banned. The ordinance goes: No Dragon Claw ships or personnel allowed at the *Oasis Space Station*. They are to be denied service and berth," Mike read on. "And, there's an open bounty for any Dragon Claw member found on the premises."

"Even Ternarians have not been banned!" Nikolai smacked the table in laughter.

"Well, Dragon Claw was started by Ternarians." Mike set his beer down to send Shin a message. "And, you can't *ban* a whole colony. A pirate clan is more feasible."

"If any colony is going to be banned from a place, it would be Ternaria." Nikolai chuckled and eyed the crowd. "But, it does seem more quiet."

"Yeah, that's true, seems pretty calm all around. Some assholes out there are probably getting in a fight, but I'm sure people are happier without any Dragon Claw around." Mike tapped the stein icon on the table for the beer menu, his drink already half empty. "Ready for another?"

"Da," Nikolai agreed.

They enjoyed the last off-ship time they would have for months to come. A couple drinks later, the back of Mike's hand buzzed to alert him it was time to go.

On their way out the fast tempo of a rowdy live band welcomed them to the first floor. Nikolai examined a holo-map of the station emitted from his bracelet. He stopped Mike and spun to his left. "Shortcut this way."

Mike followed Nikolai through the restaurant and into the kitchen. "Uh... Nikolai?" Service staff watched them pass. Some paused, processed the situation and decided not to care. The cooks cared the least and continued cooking. A manager complained that they weren't allowed there.

"It's okay, we are leaving." Nikolai waved without looking back.

"Oh, god." The manager rolled her eyes and let them go out the back door.

Mike and Nikolai strolled into a brown rock-walled alley that cut straight to the side entrance of their dock and avoided the bustle of the quad. Storage rooms and a large garbage chute nearby jutted from the rock. The alley was mostly empty but peppered with trash and large items like couches left by the local homeless.

Behind them, the door closed, and they found themselves staring down a trio of unfriendly men. A large, bald man facing away put on a newsboy cap, but not before they noticed the tattoo of a dragon in the shape of a spiky circle with wings and claws on the back of his head: the insignia of the Dragon Claw.

The other tall, burly Latin man sported a handlebar mustache with a leather jacket and a bandana. The third guy was average sized but looked small next to the others. They fiddled with a device and hastily concealed it when their lookout noticed the duo.

Mike and Nikolai shared a look, then turned back to the pirates.

"What you lookin' at?" The bald man with the newsboy cap postured up and puffed his chest to intimidate them. He tilted his hat down and his chin up.

Nikolai smiled, amused by the tall, muscular oaf.

"What's that you guys got there?" Mike asked.

"None a' your business," growled the bald brute. "Why don't you old timers get the hell out of here before you get hurt?"

"It's okay, we have great healing machine on our ship. Can you say the same?" Nikolai taunted.

The shorter man in the sweater stood on his toes to whisper to the bald man.

"We hear there's an open bounty for Dragon Claw members on *Oasis*." Mike cracked his knuckles.

"We can not refuse such an easy bounty," Nikolai added.

"Easy bounty?" The bald man looked to his friends, then slowly drew a large knife from a hidden sheath. "This asshole says we're an easy bounty."

"You guys must really want to die." The man with the mustache strapped on a pair of brass knuckles. The shorter man put down the device and circled around to enclose Mike and Nikolai in a semicircle with their backs to the wall.

Nikolai pulled his coat off behind him to reveal a full upper-arm tattoo of a tiger on his right side. Muscular and burly, Nikolai hung his coat on the restaurant's door handle. "You can have the small one."

"We don't have a lot a' time so let's make this quick. No screwin' around." The bald oaf tossed his hat on the floor with his coat.

He charged at Nikolai knife-first. Nikolai intercepted with a hard jab to the nose, caught his arm, wrapped around his shoulder and then threw his body the other way. In one swift motion, Nikolai slammed him onto the graffiti-covered rock floor and rolled back to his feet with the man's knife aimed at his second opponent.

Panicked, the other thug punched at Nikolai, who dodged and lunged in with an elbow to his face. Nikolai twisted and flung him over his shoulder onto the floor then tossed the knife away.

The bald oaf shook his head and got back on his feet. He assaulted Nikolai with a flurry of powerful punches. Nikolai covered up and dodged, charging into him. He lifted the oaf off the ground and slammed him to the floor. The pirate's head bounced with a loud crack that echoed down the empty chamber.

The other man cursed Nikolai and attacked. He easily dodged and wrapped up his neck and arm, then slammed him to the floor. He gasped for breath, but as everything faded away Nikolai let go and knocked him out with a heavy right fist.

Nikolai strode over to Mike, who had not fared as well against his opponent. They were still fighting, his opponent was still armed, and Mike had a shallow gash across his chest and blood under his nose. His opponent had a bloody lip and squinted one eye. Mike took advantage of the impaired vision and avoided a determined flurry from his opponent. He slammed a knee into the enemy's gut and grabbed his knife-wielding arm, held it straight, then dragged him to the ground. Mike pinned him to the floor with a knee to his back and pried the knife from his hand.

With his face on the ground and his arm locked up behind him, the young pirate helplessly watched Nikolai lumber towards him.

"Wait, wait! Let me go! Please!" he cried.

"Why would we give up half our bounty?" Mike laughed, then wiped his bloody nose with his palm.

"There ain't going to be anyone to pay your bounty! This station is about to get blown to hell. Please!" he pleaded. "Let me go and we can all make it out of here alive. We thought we'd beat the shit out of you real quick. We don't have a lot of time!"

Nikolai's towering silhouette stopped within arm's reach, then a giant fist slammed the pirate's head against the cold rock floor and knocked him unconscious.

"Yeah right, dick." Mike let go of the guy's arm and stood up, pinching his nose.

"Okay, comrade?"

"I'm fine." Mike wiggled his jaw. He picked up his coat and donned it triumphantly.

"You did not do well." Nikolai searched for the device they had tucked away. "I will arrange for you to train with me, Farouk, and Maya."

"Come on, that's not necessary." Mike brought Nikolai his coat.

"If you want to succeed in your mission, you must improve hand to hand combat skills." Nikolai examined the device.

It turned out to be a mobile ansible communicator. The screen and buttons were unresponsive, so Nikolai cracked open the metal box and examined its contents. He shuffled through its tangled patchwork of internal mechanisms. In a moment of realization, he held the device away in bewilderment. "No…"

"What is it?" Mike asked. Nikolai snatched his coat and looked him in the eye.

"We must go!" He sprinted away.

"Wait, what about the reward?" Mike held his nostril shut and chased Nikolai down the long, spacious back alley.

"He was telling ze truth! Run!" Nikolai tapped on his bracelet. "Shin."

"Copy," Shin responded.

"We are leaving. Prepare to depart immediately!" Nikolai huffed. They cut through a cargo-sized doorway to their dock, where they encountered people again. Nikolai attempted to move politely through the crowd, but his large frame and sense of urgency led him to charge through pedestrians. He cut a clear path for Mike, who received many dirty looks.

When they arrived at their slip, the last of the coffin-length delivery drones floated out through a dedicated hatch. They rushed onto the ship, where the rest of the crew had already gathered and prepared to go.

In the cockpit, Farouk followed departure protocol. "*Oasis Station*, this is *Slap Attack* in slip G-forty-two requesting permission to depart." The graphic of an open ramp on his console turned off and Nikolai burst into the cockpit.

"Farouk! Let's go, now!"

"We've got to get cleared man, calm down." Farouk put a hand up to calm him.

"I don't care. Blast the doors open if you must!" Nikolai pointed at the console.

"Mothafucka', I–" Farouk paused and held a finger in the air, then nodded. "Copy that, thanks *Oasis*." Farouk put his hand down and looked back at Nikolai. "We're clear. Why we in such a hurry?"

"Because the station is about to be attacked!" Nikolai held up the device he took from the pirates, which was host to a blinking green light.

"Oh, shit!" Farouk jumped in his seat, eyes transfixed. "Is that a bomb?"

"What? No. It is old Russian beacon."

"What the hell, man? Get it out of here!"

"It is already disarmed, just fly!" Nikolai sat down in the co-pilot's seat next to Farouk and buckled up. He opened the device and unplugged a wire inside to disarm it then closed the lid and slipped it back in his pocket.

Farouk grabbed a hold of the yoke and spun the ship around. When the lethargic doors to the slip opened, Farouk rocketed out with a jolt and barely missed a passenger ship. Nikolai made the walls transparent and looked out for hazards while Farouk flew by the seat of his pants. Flying recklessly through station traffic, he practically skimmed the paint off a half dozen ships and ignored repeated hails from the station.

No sooner had the *Slap Attack* cleared *Oasis Station* space than a series of bright flashes of light peppered the sky. From each appeared a massive ship, intimidating and patch-worked together from different ships.

There was a moment of terrifying awe before collision sensors blared and streaks of light zoomed past them. Every ship opened fire the moment it dropped out of warp. Massive slugs and beams of energy bombarded *Oasis* and the surrounding ships.

Farouk banked and barely avoided a hail of enemy fire, which could tear them to pieces with one direct hit. The *Slap Attack* handled clumsily in space, but Farouk's experience with his ship allowed him to pilot the vehicle with finesse. He leaned into the yoke and headed through the middle of the two nearest ships.

One ship's automated defenses kicked in and opened fire. Slugs that dinged off its thick armor rattled the *Slap Attack*. They flew closer to the attacking ship and Farouk fired on the turret to give them some breathing room. The lights on the ship illuminated a large, blood red Dragon painted on the hull. They flew out of enemy turret range and it disengaged.

The crew unbuckled themselves and watched in shock as the Dragon Claw shredded passenger ships alongside *Oasis*. Pieces of the station broke off, ships splintered apart, and the station crumbled before them with all its inhabitants trapped inside.

"What the *hell* is this?" Ian asked in slack-jawed disbelief.

"This is a massacre," Shin said through gritted teeth. "Why would they do this?"

As suddenly as the attack had begun, they stopped firing and bright flashes of light consumed each ship. The Dragon Claw fleet vanished and left in their wake a shredded mass that was moments prior a busy and popular space station.

None of them had ever experienced a silence as absolute as the one that fell upon the cabin at that moment.

"Farouk," Mike muttered, almost in a whisper.

"Yeah?" Farouk's voice was distant and soft. His eyes had not left the unprovoked slaughter before him and a tear ran down his cheek.

Mike swallowed hard. "We might need to make repairs. Get us back to the ship. Tell Addie to call Leo and set course for Ganymede."

"Aren't we going to try to help?" Farouk's voice cracked.

"Aye, we can't… leave all these people like this," Ian added.

"We're a crew of not even ten, what are we supposed to do? We have to keep a low profile and we can't bring the ship in close. People will show up asking questions, maybe even the UEG." Mike cleared his throat. Their skills would be helpful in rescue efforts but put them in jeopardy. If only the situation were different.

"I'm not drunk enough for this shit." Rick rested his face in his hands.

"We do not have the supplies, or time, or manpower to help. Maya will be waiting for us." Nikolai backed Mike's call.

"Does the Red Storm have ships nearby? Maybe they could help," Mike said.

"I will inform Iskra." Nikolai took in the ruined station, mourning the loss of life. "Farouk."

"Yeah." Farouk nodded, and after lingering for a moment, returned to the cockpit.

Jones

15

Floating Ruins

THE *RAMPART* SENT EVERY SHUTTLE TO THE *OASIS* PACKED WITH aid. Agent Jones led Commander Haynes and Sam to find someone who could get each of them where they needed to be. Behind them, a flood of troopers poured out of the shuttle unloading supplies. The three officers bumped their way through loud, bustling halls. People rushed by hauling the injured on hover carts instead of gurneys. Gruff pirates paid them suspicious glances then returned to relief efforts.

A short brunette with scattered white hairs was the first station employee they found. She directed people at a junction, a hologram projected from her thick blue bracelet. She wore one of the station's rugged black uniforms with blue trim.

"You, woman," Jones called to her.

"What?" she asked curtly, adjusting a satchel slung over her shoulder.

"I'm Commander Haynes." He rushed past Jones in an attempt to start things off on a better foot. "This is Chancellor Samuel Bernard from the Ministry of Science and Agent Jones. We've come from the *USS Rampart* with ten shuttles full of supplies and we need to know where to put them."

The woman gasped, a hand clasped over her mouth. "Oh my god. Thank you so much." She shook Haynes's hand. "I'm Theresa. Thank you, we need anything we can get. Could I please see the inventory list?"

"Of course." Haynes pulled back his sleeve to access his hitch. "Also, our CCO has offered to help coordinate any communication and rescue efforts remotely while we get your systems back up. But, we have something of a time limit."

"Whatever help you can offer is amazing. Thank you *so* much," Theresa gushed. "What's your time limit?"

Jones stepped forward. They had wasted enough time exchanging pleasantries with this meaningless peon, so he got to the point. "I'm looking for someone I believe was here prior to the attack. I'd like to speak with communications and station security."

"Okay." Theresa looked to Sam and Haynes. "Please, come this way." She led them out of the busy halls and into the nearby quad.

What should have been an open, lively space was filled with the cries and moans of the injured. The copper scent of blood permeated the stale air. People sorted bodies into rows for identification while others helped the wounded. Nearby, some cried for their loved ones. The howling echoes of misery closed in around them.

Unshaken, Jones eyed the lights bolted into the cavern's craggy rock ceiling. The holographic sky was gone but the lights and holo-signs on the ground level still worked, most converted to red crosses. "Everything in this sector seems to be operational."

"G sector took some light damage but no direct hits," Theresa explained. "It's become the center of our rescue efforts. We'd have nothing without this place."

"It's strange that every sector took massive damage yet *this* one remains untouched," Jones commented as they reached the top of the stairs. There was no way into the next section. The metal pressure panel at the foot of the archway had been sucked shut when the compartment next door breached, leaving a deep indent in the ground where it once rested. "How many sections are sealed off like that?"

"There are sealed sections all over the station. We're re-sealing and evacuating as fast as we can, but we don't think we'll get to everyone. There's people trapped in bars, shops, living quarters, all with limited or no access to essential systems. Some will run out of air before we can get to them." She took a deep breath to steel herself and press on.

Theresa led them up a small flight of stairs into an unassuming steel building. The inside crawled with station personnel coordinating rescue efforts; most injured themselves, wrapped in blood-soaked bandages, broken arms in slings. Theresa guided them away from the busy lobby into a back room with a half dozen engineers.

"You two with me. You can wait here, I'll be right back with everything you need," Theresa said, turning to Jones, then into the room.

Jones crossed his arms and leaned against the wall, listening to Chief Engineer O'Neil, a boisterous sap, gush over meeting a Ministry Chancellor as if Doctor Bernard had ever risked his life for Earth. Thankfully, Theresa returned with fingers dancing across a rubber-backed tablet before the conversation in the room became insufferable.

"You said you needed to speak with communications and security?"

"The sooner the better," Jones said.

"I set up this tablet so you can find anyone that's accounted for." She handed it to him. "I've bookmarked Carlos, our Chief of Security and Phillip Palmer, the station's Chief Operator. Please leave this with any station personnel when you've finished."

"Thank you. You should get back to whatever you're supposed to be doing. The clock is ticking." Jones strolled away.

"Please, take your time." Theresa held back her spite.

Jones's first stop was a hotel turned clinic, where Phillip Palmer had been checked in after the attack. Every room Jones passed was packed with injured. On the third floor, he found the room he was looking for. With more than half his face in bandages, a broken arm and leg, and tightly bandaged ribs, the man laid immobile in bed, eyes half open.

"Hello, Mr. Palmer," Jones said.

"Hey." Phillip's gentle voice barely managed a whisper.

"I'm Agent Jones. I'm after a very dangerous group that was at this station before the attack." Jones clasped his hands behind his back.

"They... Dragon Claw?" Phillip struggled to speak, words long and drawn out, broken up by strained breaths.

"I don't believe so," Jones said, pondering the root of the question. Phillip looked away, disillusioned. "I'm wondering if you or one of your co-workers might have cleared an old Armadillo named *Slap Attack*."

"Frankie cleared that ship." Phillip grunted and took a moment to regain his breath. "It was the real deal. Sent an autographed picture. Made his day. Wouldn't shut up about it." Tears welled in the corners of his eyes.

"He died in the attack?"

"Yeah." Phillip's eyes drifted, still in shock. Jones sighed in disappointment. Speaking to someone who made contact with his quarry would have been more useful.

"Do you know if that ship departed the station?"

"Before the attack, we got..." Phillip's eyes drifted shut then opened again as if he had woken up. "Sorry, meds kicking in. We got complaints about that ship almost crashing into people on the way out."

"That will suffice, thank you." Jones left the room. Phillip was already asleep.

Jones followed the directions deep into the innards of the station to speak to the Chief of Security. To avoid traffic, he strapped into a suit to pass through a breached compartment shrouded in darkness and without gravity. People trapped in buildings knocked on the glass for help as he passed. After a tedious half hour journey, he reached a sector illuminated by dim red emergency lights and found the Chief in his office.

"Security Chief Carlos Ortiz?" Jones called a short bald man with a goatee, floating next to a desk bolted to the floor. He gripped the side of it to stay in place, holding down a tablet that projected a hologram of information about the Dragon Claw.

"That's right. Who are you?" Carlos shut down the hologram.

"I'm Agent Jones. I represent the UEG and I have some questions."

"Can I see some identification?" Carlos held his hand in a fist in front of him and pressed a finger down on his black glove.

"Of course." Jones tapped on his hitch and sent over his credentials. Carlos looked it over then terminated the interface.

"How can I help you?"

"I'm in search of one Farouk Knight, former full contact fighter now fitted with cybernetic arms. I was wondering if you had any information that might help me find him," Jones asked.

"Sounds like a guy from an incident that was reported about a half hour before the attack," Carlos said. "They described a muscular guy with cybernetic arms and three friends. They got in a fight with some Blue Eagle guys."

"A pirate clan?" Jones asked.

"Blue Eagle? Yeah. Started by old American vets."

"The others in his group, can you describe them?" Jones hoped to get a lead on anyone else in the group.

Carlos gestured above his head. "Tall guy, description puts him about here. One point eight meters, one eight and a half. White, wiry, middle-aged. Fat guy, same height, bushy red beard." He brought his hand down to his height and rocked his hand in the air. "Asian guy around my height, one-seven, one six-and-a-half, scar on his face."

Jones hummed and smiled. "Interesting. Were they traveling with anyone else?"

"Nah, we don't really keep track of that," Carlos said. "And, all our recent security footage is gone."

With a sigh of disappointment, Jones took a moment to think. "Do you know if the cyborg and his group may have belonged to a pirate clan? Perhaps the Dragon Claw?"

"No. Sounded like freelancers. *Definitely* not Dragon Claw."

"How can you be sure?"

"Aside from the recent ban on the Dragon Claw and the open bounty on 'em, we believe the Dragon Claw attacked the station," Carlos said, unable to bridle his anger.

"What leads you to believe the Dragon Claw were responsible?" Jones asked, curious about how they knew who attacked while trying to figure out which way was up.

"We detained some of their guys in a back alley in G sector after the attack. Their big guy was dead, skull was cracked like a peanut." Carlos turned his tablet back on and showed Jones the images of the dead pirate. "The other two were out cold and beat up. They weren't shocked by the attack, so I'd put my money on 'em knowing something."

The red lights lining the corners of the ceiling blinked and white lights turned back on. From around them came the hum of power returning to the consoles and machinery. After that, they fell to the ground slowly, then quickly as the gravity kicked in. Objects fell to the ground throughout the rooms and halls, followed by the brief celebrations of nearby personnel.

"The only thing they've told me is they got in a fight with some guys." Carlos picked the conversation back up.

"Would it be possible for me to question them?" Jones asked.

"We haven't got much out of 'em but we've kind of got our hands full. You can give it a shot if you want." Carlos closed the projections and wrote some orders on the tablet, then handed it to Jones. "Our system won't be back up for a bit, this'll get you in."

"Thank you."

"Rough 'em up if you have to." Carlos winked, unaware of Jones's reputation.

Jones grinned. "Oh, I plan on it."

Natalie

16

Space Unicorn

After a foggy eternity in the medical bay next to Will, Natalie followed Addie out of the infirmary to the elevators across from it. Earlier, her attention had been fixed on seeing Will, but now she looked around to take in the ship.

The steel floor was separated into large panels, many of which were pressure panels that would be sucked up to close off sections in the event of a breach. Their red delineations had faded, barely visible. Once a brilliant eggshell white, the paint on the walls had faded and the gray metal behind them bled through, more toward the vertical center of the wall where people would lean or bump into it. They had a full crew at some point. Instead of handrails, there were intermittent inlets in the walls and most corners were chamfered, a signature of Titan Starships, the main contractor for the United States during World War Four.

"You know what? Let's walk. It'll be good for you to walk around a little." Addie took Natalie's mind out of the clouds.

Natalie nodded. "Sure."

"It helps to think about other things with so much going on." Addie carefully avoided any explicit mention of Natalie's various troubles. She led her to their right, toward the aft port staircase next to a cargo lift for moving equipment.

Twelve hours earlier an avalanche of questions about the ship would have spilled from Natalie's lips, but try as she might, she drew a blank. "Like what?"

"I don't know. Is there anything in the colonies you've always wanted to see?" They passed a long hallway that led down the length of the ship, mirrored on the starboard side.

"I've always wanted to visit Avalon," Natalie said.

"I'll show you around. You can meet my old crew," Addie said.

"What's life like in the colonies?" Natalie followed Addie up a wide staircase.

"It's great! I mean, it's probably not as glamorous as life on Earth, but I love it. There's freedom, adventure, and it feels like the whole universe is your playground. I used to love watching the sunrise from low orbit." Addie's whole body lifted as if she could drift away at the thought.

"That sounds amazing. Earth isn't really *glamorous*. At least not where I'm from. I couldn't wait to move to Denver for college next year. *That* was going to be my adventure. I didn't think I'd make it to a starship."

"Is working on a ship your dream job?" They turned the corner onto deck three.

"Machines are my *life*, and ships are the biggest most awesome machines ever," Natalie said, then wilted. "My dad used to say... If we can dream it we can achieve it." She cleared her throat, her voice cracking.

"That's a good lesson to hold on to," Addie said. "I never stopped believing in what I could do, and I ended up here. I was kind of a troublemaker back home." She tried to move the conversation away from Natalie's parents and their wisdom. "How long have you loved ships?"

"Since I was a baby. I'm kind of a gear-head, been fixing up cars my whole life. I love machines, but working on a starship is my ultimate dream."

"The colonies don't really care about your brand as long as you can do your job, so you could live your dream," Addie said with an optimistic smile.

They passed the port hall on level three and the elevators on the right while they talked. Where the medical bay was on the deck below there was a short hall which led to the Bridge. The room on the left led to the armory. On the right were Logistics and the War Room, the latter of which was their destination. Addie waved her hand over the wall console to open the thick double doors.

"Natalie, please, come in," Mike greeted.

Natalie checked with Addie, who smiled and motioned for her to enter. She eased into the room where she had been questioned early that day. This time Mike sat with two new faces on either side of him. Natalie sat opposite them and Addie found a seat next to her.

"This is Nikolai." Mike introduced a monolithic Russian to his left with a large brow, blue eyes, and a chiseled face accented by a strong, round chin. Punching it would hurt the hand more than his face. Nikolai nodded, stoic, but with a glint of charm. "He's our first officer and the one that patched up your friend."

"Nice to meet you." Natalie bowed her head. "Thank you for saving Will."

"It was the right thing. No thanks necessary." He humbly waved her off.

"And this is Maya," Mike introduced the athletic olive-skinned woman to his right with big, powerful brown eyes. Maya wore simple make-up and did not bother to paint her nails. The youthful woman flashed a welcoming smile that put Natalie at ease.

"Nice to meet you, Natalie. Mike filled me in about how you ran into our crew. It's been a hell of a night, but you're some brave kids," Maya said.

"Thank you." Natalie blushed at the beautiful woman's praise.

"Sorry to drag you away from your friend, but we've got some stuff we need to figure out and it can't wait for him to wake up." Mike got straight to the point.

"Okay. What is it?" Natalie's face twisted with anticipation.

"We've got places to be, and we need to figure out what to do with you and your friend down there," he said.

"Wh-what do you mean?" Natalie asked.

"In the colonies you two are adults, you can make your own choices. So, we're willing to get you a ride somewhere. We'll deactivate your chips and give you new identities and some money to get you started. From there you guys can find jobs and start new lives in the colonies," Mike explained.

"Really? Like we can use AR and vote and stuff?" In disbelief, Natalie looked to the others and was met with various nods. "So like, we start new lives *now?*"

"Augmented reality, voting, responsibility, stress, all yours." Mike nodded.

"What about Will? We haven't talked about this." Natalie looked down at her lap. What would Will want? Would it be possible to send him home? There was no telling how long they had been gone. All her time had been spent in a chair next to Will. A whole day could have passed.

"If you're thinking that he might want to go home, I'm sorry to say that won't be possible," Maya said. "Mike asked me to stop by the Cooper residence on my way. The house was under surveillance. There seemed to have been a struggle, his room was sacked and his parents are missing. A story has already been planted in your region about an accident that destroyed your house." She transitioned into a direct, all business attitude.

"So, Will is stuck out here with me," Natalie summarized absently. The fear that whoever she went to for help might be put at risk had come true, and now Will and his family shared the same fate as Natalie and hers.

"At least you both have the luck of being stuck with a comrade," Nikolai said.

"I did bring a bag of personal effects from his house. Caramel bars, some snacks, games, controllers. Stuff to keep you entertained on your downtime," Maya explained.

"Thank you, Miss Maya," Natalie said, Maya's kindness causing a shudder in Natalie's brittle heart.

"Just Maya is fine."

"Your friend will be okay within a couple days," Mike said, "but our next trip will take some time and we need to leave as soon as possible. I know this might be sudden, so we can give you a couple hours to do some research on the colonies if you'd like. We could also offer suggestions if you're not sure where to go or what your options are."

"Um…" Natalie thought for a moment.

For Natalie, research on the colonies was not necessary. If she went anywhere, it would be Avalon. Surely Will would follow since he knew nothing about the colonies. However, Natalie found herself with the opportunity of a lifetime. She could work on a Stinger, which was in production only near the end of the war. Few Stingers were made or even saw battle, and most were recycled after the Peaceful Union Act. It was an amazing ship, and this was possibly the only one of its kind still flying. She could learn a lot by working on it. The crew seemed like good people despite their shady appearances. They had treated them with kindness and asked for nothing in return. They even went so far as to offer them money.

"I don't need to do research on the colonies, but I've got an idea for at least, like, something temporary, maybe?" Natalie struggled to speak her mind.

"What's that?" Mike asked.

"Can I have a job on your ship?" Her heart trembled as the words left her lips.

"A job?" Mike asked.

"Yeah, well, I guess Will would need a job too. But, I'd like to uh," Natalie glanced at Addie, who smiled and nodded. Natalie straightened up and made her request, "I'd like to be an engineer."

A hum of intrigue bubbled from Mike's throat. Chin in one hand, his other hand sequentially tapped the table. "Sorry kid, I can't tell if you're being serious. You're seventeen, this isn't a high school art project."

Addie shot Mike an angry look that burned with such intensity she could have melted a block of steel.

"Oh, She's serious," Maya grinned.

"I'm *totally* serious," Natalie countered. "I've worked on cars my whole life, I love machines, I've read about every ship *ever*. There probably isn't another Stinger flying *anywhere* and this ship is *awesome*. I've always dreamed of working on a starship. On Earth, I never could have because I'm a Delta. But I thought, maybe here?" Her shoulders perked into a light shrug. "You guys seem cool, and working on this ship would be a dream come true. Please?"

"Natalie does seem to be a good judge of character," Maya said. "We are pretty cool."

"Since you're not qualified to be an engineer, I could give you a paid apprenticeship. You'd work under our mechanic, Rick. He'll assess you and see if you've got what it takes. If you don't, we'll show you where you can get started."

"That would be amazing." Natalie's voice was almost a whisper. She trembled, eyes beaming at Mike's response.

"Good with you two?" Mike asked.

"Why not? At seventeen, I was already master of Systema. With Rick teaching, she will be excellent engineer," Nikolai said.

"Maya?" Mike swiveled his chair to face her.

"I like her." Maya grinned. "It'll be nice to have some fresh faces around here, and *you* could use some practice relating to teenagers." Maya turned to Mike with an incredulous look. Mike grunted, looking away.

"I guess that's that. Natalie, welcome to the crew, at least for now," Mike said.

Natalie's face lit up. She took a moment to process the news and then spoke up again. "I have another request."

"Oh?" Maya was amused by Natalie's boldness. "What's that?"

"So, you said we could have a couple hours to do research on the colonies before you dropped us off somewhere. That means you've got a couple hours to spare, right?" Natalie impressed the officers with her keen deduction.

"Right…" Mike looked back at Natalie.

"I was wondering if I could see the ship. Like, from outside." Natalie pointed up. She absolutely *had* to see the ship from space in all its glory.

"Yes!" Maya smacked the table with both hands, answering for Mike, who supported it with a wave of his hand. He had no problem with the request. "I'll join you. I haven't gone on a spacewalk in a while."

"Okay!" Natalie's response was a reflex.

"Don't worry, I'll take care of her." Maya patted Mike on the shoulder and hopped out of her seat. She had the physique of a super hero, muscles and all.

"As long as you bring both suits back I'm happy," Mike teased as Natalie and Maya left the room.

"Come on, airlock is around the corner," Maya led Natalie out of the War Room and around the corner to the port hall airlock, located past a short hall of offices.

The airlock had shallow lockers with space suits which conformed to fit each occupant, within reason, and comfortably over their clothing. When Maya slipped an arm into her suit, Natalie noticed the tattoo of a raven on her shoulder blade.

"Cool tattoo. Do you have any others?"

Maya glanced over her shoulder, "No, that's my only one."

"Why do you only have one?" Most people get more.

"I had more, once," Maya closed up her suit and picked up her gloves. "But I got rid of them. They're personal identifiers, not good for my line of work."

"What's your line of work?" Natalie inquired innocently.

"Oh, I do a lot of things. I have to look professional. I tend to travel from time to time," Maya snickered to herself then focused on her suit. "I mean, not like *through* time. I help people with their security. Like a consultant."

"Is that what you do on the ship?" Natalie asked curiously.

"Yes, I'm the ship's Chief of Security." She donned and secured her helmet. Natalie mirrored her to ensure it was properly fastened. Maya tapped on a small arm console to bring up a holographic interface. Natalie copied and turned on the suit's audio.

"All set?" With a thumbs-up, Maya's voice buzzed in Natalie's helmet.

Natalie returned the gesture. "Fueled up, ready to go!"

Maya depressurized the airlock. Natalie looked around until the lights in the room changed from yellow to blue and the circular door opened into space. Maya grabbed a handlebar on the wall and flung herself out.

With the ship's gravity still on, the weightlessness did not kick in until Natalie followed Maya out, although not as fluidly. She gripped an interior handlebar with her body outside and let go with a gentle push away from the ship.

Maya giggled. "Come on, don't be afraid. You have thrusters, you're not going to get stranded out here."

An interface inside Natalie's helmet pointed in Maya's direction like a game. She turned around to search for her against the sparkling black expanse. Natalie moved clumsily at first, but quickly got the hang of the thrusters and soon flew merrily through space.

"Let me know when we're a good distance away from the ship," Natalie said.

Maya looked over her shoulder and stopped not far ahead. She spun in place to watch Natalie fly toward her. After a long haze of time spent in sadness, her mind had been taken off her loss and she was smiling, happy. Maya held out her hand when Natalie got close. She slowed down but awkwardly crashed into Maya.

Maya helped her turn around. "There she is: the *Ulfberht.*"

Before Natalie with every hull light on, the *Ulfberht* was an absolute splendor to behold. Awe-struck, she took in the eight-story-tall, three hundred forty meter-wide, five hundred and eighteen meter-long wonder.

The long, sleek ship resembled the blade and hand guard of a sword.

The bow tapered to a point and it had four armored thrusters on the stern with two wing-like extensions from the sides. At the tips of the wings were armored thrusters with massive railguns above and below them. Built for maneuverability, the ship had two pairs of concave forward-facing thrusters on its bow. There was a trio of vertically oriented circular thrusters on the aft as well and Natalie knew there to be a matching set on the keel, not visible from their vantage. The hull was also host to railgun turrets and a large cannon, which guarded the docking bay on the stern of the ship.

"We've made some modifications," Maya said. "You'll get to know them working with Rick, but keep it within the crew. Understood?"

"Yeah." Natalie nodded absently and floated in place like a statue. Heart pounding, time had frozen the instant she laid eyes upon the ship. She could stay in that moment forever.

"What do you think?" Maya asked after a while.

"She's... so beautiful." Tears broke off into bubbles in her helmet, awestruck by the ship's beauty, heartbroken that she could never share the experience with her family.

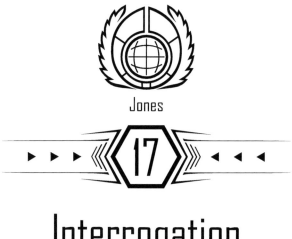

Jones

17

Interrogation

Jones had the prisoners taken into an interrogation room and cuffed to their seats with their hands behind them. He escorted the guards out and made sure the cameras were off, then cuffed their ankles to the chair legs so they could not lash out.

The two men watched Jones slide the table in front of them against the wall. The larger one tried to look tough. The smaller man could not feign toughness.

"I'm Agent Jones." From his coat he pulled his double-edged knife, placing it on the table. "I'm going to give you an opportunity to leave alive, it's up to you if you take it." He placed his zapper down parallel the knife. "You see, I've heard a series of coincidences that don't quite *feel* right. I'm not one for *feelings*, but when you get one in your gut, I believe you should follow it. Don't you think so?"

The larger pirate raised his chin in the air, resolute to not give him an inch.

"Right." Jones left the table and paced to the center of the room in front of them. "Your attack on this station is of no concern to me. I *only* care about what *I'm* after. Give me the information I seek, and I'll leave you here for the authorities and be on my way. If not, I'll be forced to partake in a very dirty part of my job. It is, however, a part I take great pleasure in. So, it matters little to me which path you choose." He stopped a meter away. No response from either man left the room silent, and Jones in the wake of his own condescending monologue.

"Because you're so quiet, I'll assume you're excellent listeners and have no questions. My compliments to you both." Jones paced back and forth in front of the two men. "Immediately before the attack, the ship I'm looking for was reported to be leaving in a hurry, and you two were thoroughly beaten."

The two men scowled at Jones, who pivoted on his heel to walk the other way.

"With an open bounty on Dragon Claw and you two found in a back alley beaten up just before the attack, I have this sneaky suspicion that bounty hunters, or someone, caught you two before you finished whatever you were supposed to do. These clever individuals figured out what you were doing and ran to escape the oncoming attack instead of collecting the bounty. Does that seem like a possibility to you?"

The smaller man could not hide his guilt. The beefy guy with a handlebar mustache kept a tough disposition.

Jones stepped closer and crouched between them. "There's *no* way it can be a coincidence. The alternative is the people I'm after were *in* on the attack. Because, why would the ship I'm looking for be fleeing in such a hurry unless they knew an attack was imminent? Either way, you have information for me." Jones put his hands on their shoulders and smiled. "What do you think?"

The two men looked at each other. The large man took a deep breath, a gargle bubbled in his throat and he spat at Jones. Looking down at the mucus on his chest, Jones scoffed at the man's foolishness and shook his head in disbelief.

"Fuck you, you don't scare us, cop." The pirate puffed up his chest.

Jones chuckled on his casual stroll back to the table and pulled a handkerchief from his coat to wipe off the snot. He grabbed his knife and returned in slow, unrushed steps, stopping an arm's length from the large man, who looked back at him smugly. Jones eyed the pirate for a moment then looked to the smaller man.

"Learn from his mistakes." Jones pointed his knife and circled the large pirate. Examining the brute, he stopped at his right side. He took a moment to examine a sleeve of tattoos that had caught his attention.

"You're some sort of officer." He pointed at one of the tattoos with his knife. "These are your ranks and accomplishments. Am I right?" He examined the trail of dragon images on his arm. "To a criminal, tattoos are power. These tattoos represent *all* the power you've accumulated. This is your resume, your value." Jones pinched the dragon shield tattoo on his upper arm and dug his knife into the skin above it. The pirate screamed in agony as Jones filleted a long strip of skin off his arm.

"There." Jones tossed the skin behind him. The bloody slab landed on the other man's face. He jerked away and screamed at the sudden and unexpected brutality. "I've taken what little power you've struggled to acquire. Your brethren will now see you for being as worthless as you really are. You're a criminal, and thusly you have no value." Jones walked between the two men and basked in their panic and screams.

"You son of a bitch!" The man's voice cracked. "You can't do this! I know my rights! You're a fuckin' psycho!" Jones let him writhe in pain for a moment. Even once he had calmed down, he huffed and groaned through clenched teeth.

"Hardly." Jones looked down his nose at the brute with a smile. "I take the world for what it is, like you. Everyone has a part to play. Everyone was born to do *something*. I'm doing what I was born to do because I am part of life's plan." Jones lunged at him and stabbed between his ribs twice, once on each side. The man gurgled and gasped for breath. "But you, with your collapsing lungs, do not *appear* destined to be a part of that plan. Life's story goes on, yours ends here."

"Stop! Please stop! Help! Chief! Security! Someone help! He's killing him! He's killing him!" The other prisoner could not look away from his friend's pained face warped in terror. Each of his quick breaths filled his punctured lungs with blood. The young pirate tried to squirm free.

"Yell all you want, it won't help." Jones looked him in the eye and lunged to bash him in the mouth with the butt of his knife. "Your clan very recently attacked the station and killed thousands. I was *overjoyed* to hear they had prisoners. That means I can do *whatever* I want." He held his knife under his jaw. "And, everyone will look the other way because, in times of crisis and tragedy, the weak do away with their morals."

"Please." The corners of the young prisoner's eyes rolled tears down his cheeks and he shook his head. "Please, don't."

"Don't what?" Jones stepped away. "I haven't given *you* a chance to answer my questions."

"I'll answer anything, just stop hurting him, please!"

"In that case, I assume I have your complete cooperation?" Jones twirled his knife and stepped in front of his dying prisoner. Hunched over, the dying prisoner's head hung limp, taking short, gargled breaths.

"What do you want to know?"

"Does the Dragon Claw recognize Farouk Knight as one of its members?"

"The fighter? I-I don't think so," he stammered.

"Could the men who assaulted you be associated with Farouk Knight?"

"I don't know any of them, I-I don't know. I've never met Farouk Knight. I don't know who he rolls with." He avoided eye contact with Jones.

"Describe the men from the alley."

"A big Russian guy with tattoos. Miguel said he's from the Red Storm." He motioned to the man next to him. "He didn't recognize him before."

"Do you know his name?"

"I don't know who he is."

"And the other assailants?" Jones moved on.

"It was just him and one other guy. He was about your height, thin, with like a pointy nose. I sliced him with my knife." The man was quick to describe Mike.

"Oh? You cut him?" Jones asked. The young prisoner nodded. "See?" Jones relaxed his posture. "As I suspect the ones I'm after are from Earth, that *is* useful information. I assume security has the knife?"

"I don't know." The young man checked on his friend. "Can you get him some help? Please."

Jones looked the dying man up and down. Blood dripped onto the floor. "I think your energy would be better spent thinking about your own future. He'll be dead soon. It wouldn't be prudent for you to be uncooperative."

"Please. I'll do whatever you want, just help him."

"You'll do whatever I want anyway. Think logically. All the doctors are a half hour away helping the injured from the attack. They haven't the time or resources to help *him*. He'll survive a while longer, but it'll be painful. You really want me to help him?"

"Yes, please!"

Jones shoved his blade into the pirate's jugular and yanked it downward.

"No!" The young man's voice cracked, eyes pouring.

A crimson waterfall gushed down the man's shirt. Jones wiped the knife on the flailing man's jeans, then took a step back.

"You're a fuckin' psycho, man." The young prisoner watched his friend die in front of him. Jones bashed him with the butt of his knife, then sheathed it.

"Thank you for your cooperation. I think you may still be useful, so I'm bringing you with me for further questioning." Jones circled around behind him. "But, I don't want you getting any ideas, so..."

Jones kicked his hands, still cuffed together behind him. The young man wailed in pain. Unsatisfied, Jones swung his boot again and broke several fingers between the two kicks.

"There we go. You should be quite well behaved." Jones un-cuffed the prisoner and re-cuffed him with his hands in front of him. He cradled his trembling, mangled fingers while Jones un-cuffed his feet. "Come on now, don't dawdle." Jones grabbed the prisoner by his arm and stopped at the table to grab his zapper.

"You didn't need to break my fingers, man," the prisoner blubbered.

"It's better than you stabbing me in the back and trying to escape. Now, you can't hold a weapon." Jones led him out and through the halls.

It was not long before muffled conversation echoed down the hall. He peeked around the corner of the doorway into security's central hub. In the center of the room, Carlos stood before a hologram of the station over a table. With him were two security guards and two engineers with tool belts.

Jones gripped his prisoner's arm and stared at him. "You're not going to say a word about what happened in there. Understood?"

Eyes diverted, the prisoner nodded and Jones dragged him into the room. The room paused. Every eye burned a hole through the injured pirate, who looked down in shame. Some took delight in his condition.

"Any luck?" Carlos asked.

"A bit, yes," Jones said. "I was wondering if you happened to have recovered any bloodied weapons at the scene of their altercation?"

"Just one," Carlos said.

"Would it be possible for me to take that weapon with me? I believe it could be a lead," Jones asked.

"Sure. John, go grab that knife out of evidence. Victor, take that other dickhead back to his cell," Carlos ordered. Both left without giving it a second thought.

"That's not necessary. Let's let him stew for a while," Jones said. Carlos chuckled but did not rescind his order. Jones groaned to himself, anticipating complications.

"Looks like you went a little overboard." Carlos eyed the broken pirate.

"That's... an opinion." Jones backed away. A moment later, the guard ran back into the room and aimed his taser pistol at Jones.

"He *killed* the other prisoner," he said. Carlos drew his pistol and took aim. Unarmed, the engineers shared an unsure look. The one closest to Jones pulled out a screwdriver and aimed it at him.

"What are you going to do with *that?*" Jones asked with opaque amusement.

"I'll put it through your eye if you get near me," the engineer jabbed.

"You're under arrest," Carlos said. "Hands in the air!"

The other guard returned with the bloodied knife in a plastic bag. He looked around in confusion, then drew his pistol and took a defensive stance.

"Please. These *criminals* attacked the station, killing thousands," Jones contested.

"I don't give a shit. That doesn't justify killing in cold blood. That isn't *justice.*"

"Justice?" Jones scoffed. "I don't have time for this." He reached his left arm out in front of him and tapped his hitch. "Call Commander Haynes."

"Agent Jones," Haynes answered. *"How can I help you?"*

"I've made progress on my end. I was wondering about your progress with the relief efforts." Jones's selfless tone had an undercurrent of callous sarcasm.

"Things are going well. We've dispatched our shuttles to evacuate people in the sections they couldn't get to in time. Sam helped get power on across the station ahead of schedule. The print labs here were destroyed so we're making them some industrial 3d printers on the ship so they can make parts, but it'll be an hour until the first batch is done. We've already requested a materials refill from Earth."

Jones stared down Carlos while Haynes updated him and watched the resolve drain from his face as he listened to the contributions the UEG ship made.

"An hour? An ambitious decision since we don't know how long we're going to be here." Jones did not take his eyes off Carlos, who now wavered despite his anger.

"Yes, well... since it's hard to get around the station, we figured we would be here a while. Will we have time to finish them or should I recycle the

materials we've used?" Haynes did not conceal his disgust at the prospect, a crack in his professional demeanor.

"I don't think there's a need for that quite yet. Thank you for the update, you'll hear from me again in a half hour. Jones out."

The call ended. Carlos and his guards lowered their weapons. Jones was not going to draw a weapon because he did not need one.

"One hour before those printers are complete. It would be a shame if I had to leave before then."

"What do you want?" Carlos said.

"The knife, please. Also, the UEG is taking custody of this man." Jones pulled on his prisoner's arm, who looked to Carlos and shook his head in desperate protest.

Carlos took note and considered the proposal. If he kept a level head, he could benefit from the exchange. He could not hold him there since his crew expected to hear from him in thirty minutes. Negotiation was his best option. "That's two things."

"Oh?" Jones recoiled. "Well, I want both, so what do you propose?"

"Make it two hours and you can take him with you," Carlos said.

"Hey, no. No. Don't do this, man," the prisoner pleaded with Carlos. "Please."

"Two hours?" Jones grimaced. "Seems a bit much. An hour and a half."

"If either him or the knife are worth an hour, then its two hours for both," Carlos argued. Jones smiled and nodded at the straightforward negotiation.

"Right you are. Two hours it is. I'm glad we could come to an agreement." Jones conceded, giving Carlos the semblance of a victory. He could use the extra time to figure out his next move and do some research on pirates.

"Stop talking." Carlos scowled. "John, give me the knife." Carlos put away his pistol. John handed the knife to Carlos, who kept his eyes locked on Jones. He approached with the knife and reached out to hand it off.

"Thank you, Chief," Jones said.

Carlos did not respond. Instead, he turned to the prisoner. "Sorry, man."

Jones left the station and took the prisoner's shuttle back to the *Rampart*. He stayed true to his word and called for a meeting as soon as they departed two hours later.

In the War Room, Jones waited with his team and the Captain. Sam was the last to arrive. To Jones's surprise, he was early. "How was your humanitarian mission?" Jones patronized. Sam sat next to James, who looked at Jones with his hands up as if to ask, *What the hell? Matt and I were down there too.*

"We saved thousands of lives. How was whatever *you* were doing?" Sam asked, aggravating Jones which in turn amused Captain Slater.

"I uncovered who attacked the station, procured a prisoner and new information on our targets."

"Who attacked the station?" Captain Slater asked.

"The Dragon Claw pirate clan. Their motives are unknown, but one of their men and his shuttle are in our custody. It seems our Armadillo rushed away before the attack as if they knew it was coming. If they were trying to escape, they could have had a run-in with a Dragon Claw ship. A stretch, but a possibility."

From his coat, Jones pulled out a plastic bag with a switchblade and passed it down the table. "Our prisoner slashed one of our targets. However, the results were protected by the Ministry," he said with a sarcastic delight. "By some ironic miracle, you're actually useful to me on this mission, Chancellor."

"I'll check it out." Sam examined the mystery in his hands.

"I also have a lead on the Ranger." Jones typed on the table. Ken stepped forward with interest. "A man matching Knight's description was involved in a fight. I suspect one of the men with him was this man." A hardy-looking Japanese man with a scar over a large stretch of his face appeared over the table.

"How do I know that name?" Captain Slater looked over Shin's profile.

"Shin Morikawa, a Japanese Ranger," Jones said. "He disappeared *during* the war after unlawfully exposing controversial decisions in Alliance governments and military."

"You mean exposing war crimes?" Captain Slater clarified.

"He was *rightfully* branded a traitor for violating national security, but evaded arrest." Jones glowered at the Captain. "He's also been a ghost until now. Of the five rogue Rangers, two fit the height of the attacker and only one is Asian. I haven't identified anyone else, but after further questioning, I've learned the Dragon Claw on *Oasis* were supposed to make a rendezvous after the attack." Jones turned to face the Captain next to him and smiled. "I say we help him make his appointment."

Natalie

18

Gear Head

THE ENGINEERING ROOM WHERE NATALIE REPORTED FOR HER
first day spanned decks four and five in the rear central mass of the ship,
across the hall from the docking bay. From there, Rick escorted her to
the center door of a short hall on deck three toward the bow of the ship.
It was a long room with gray walls lined with a dozen fake rifles. Cords
with hooks dangled from the ceiling meant to latch onto a body harness.

"Whoa. Is this the gunner room?" Natalie spun to take in the room,
awestruck by the simple space she knew to be so much more.

"Yep," Rick huffed, perturbed that he had to drag some kid along
to work on the ship with him. He reached the back of the room and
dropped his duffle bag to the floor, then pulled a panel off the wall to
reveal an access port to the maintenance shafts.

"It's a lot plainer than I thought it would be." Natalie ran her hand
over one of the rifles. "I thought the guns would look like turrets. Can
I pick one up?"

"Go ahead." Rick motioned to one. "Just don't pull the trigger."

Natalie pulled the nearest rifle from its mount. It was light, like a toy. Upon removal, the dull gray walls and ceiling lit up, blanketed with sparkling stars.

"Wow!" Natalie burst, eyes wide, mouth agape like her jaw had come unhinged.

"You know why we got gunner rooms?" Rick adjusted his battered, old tool belt.

"Because of scramblers," Natalie said, taking in the view. She pointed the rifle as if shooting at enemies. Somewhere on the ship, a turret aimed where she did, but she did not grasp that in the moment.

"This is so cool." Natalie placed the rifle in its mount. "How can we see outside the warp bubble?" Alcubierre warp drives had evolved since their creation, but the restrictions that accompanied creating a bubble in spacetime remained the same.

"When Mike was 'bout your age he created a mappin' program. Ships would drop to sub-light, record a piece and add it to a public map."

"The Captain? No way. Shouldn't he be famous?"

"Yep." Rick slung the duffel bag over his shoulder and headed into the maintenance shaft. "Come on, we've got work to do."

Natalie followed him into a narrow hall that ran behind the gunner room, security, and the library. On either end was a ladder up into a maintenance level that ran between decks two and three. There was a similar level between decks four and five. They were traversable via a network of shafts tall enough for an adult to crawl through on their hands and knees.

They crept to the end of the tunnel over the port access hatch for the main water reservoir. The shaft turned left into a short junction then left again, spanning the length of the port hall.

Rick turned into the next shaft and spun around, then opened the grated floor. He reached past fuses and wires then unclipped a thick, half-meter long silver rod from the roof of the ventilation shaft that ran below the electrical access. The rods were filled with algae that produced most of the oxygen for the ship.

He showed Natalie how to unclip the rods, which would later be cleaned and reused. She was tasked with the next one, but it was stuck. Instead of asking for help she examined the rod Rick had pulled out and tried again. This time she had a more calculated approach and yanked it loose after a couple of hard pats and a firm tug. They continued down the corridor replacing algae rods. As simple a task as it may be, Natalie took pride in her work, learned quickly, and was no stranger to labor. Rick had been presumptuous and was put at ease by her work ethic.

"Y'know, workin' with you may not be so bad," Rick admitted after a couple of hours. "You look like you've been doin' it for a while."

"Thanks. I've always wanted to work on a starship, but I never thought I'd be able to because of my brand." Natalie scooted away with a used rod, ends crusted with algae. She stuffed it into a sack in the duffle bag while Rick dropped the grated floor panel back into place with a clank that echoed down the tunnel.

"Never liked those damn things. You know they started off as a *fad?*" His tone oozed contempt.

"Really? A fad?"

"Yeah, when genetics started gettin' real advanced, people put their status on their resumes, on their datin' profiles." With a disapproving grunt, he dragged the duffel bag behind him and led them down the tunnel. "Course, that was mostly Alphas and Betas showin' off. But, people liked it; said it helped 'em distinguish who the best candidates were. People started gettin' tattoos of it. I thought it would go away 'til people started passin' legislation after the war."

"Why did they make it law?" Natalie was fascinated to hear about how the world she knew had come to be.

"You want to know the truth? People are cowards. They need someone to blame for things. Some sum' bitch, a senator... Greene! That was it. Senator Greene said that it was stupid people with power and influence makin' stupid decisions that led to the war," Rick explained. "So, if you're branded based on your genetic capacities the world would be a *safer* place, corruption would disappear. Bunch a' horse shit. God damn Greenes. Been one in the Senate for like a hundred years."

"So, can I ask about *your* brand?" Natalie asked.

"What about it?"

"I don't, um, see it?" Natalie said.

"That's 'cuz I never got one," Rick chuckled.

"But, how did you like, get a job and function in society?"

"How the sam hell you think I ended up out here? I ain't gettin' no tattoo sayin' I'm better than someone else. I left Earth. Most people in the colonies don't have brands." Rick led them to an access panel on deck three behind the stairs, but it required a transition through a vertical shaft to exit.

Natalie's mind wandered while she helped Rick move the heavy duffel bag into the hall. She and Will's risky choices had led them to such an unlikely life. Then a memory from that night flashed in her mind.

"Hey." Natalie ended the brief silence. "The night you guys rescued us, there was someone else there I haven't seen around the ship. Is he part of the crew or something? I thought we met everyone."

"I don't know. You're going to have to ask the Captain about that. I just take care of the ship." Rick brushed off the question since he was a poor improviser. A message had gone out to the crew two days prior. Mike and Maya had thought it best to keep One a secret from Natalie and Will since he was tied to their families' deaths.

Rick's evasiveness struck Natalie as odd given his open nature and it lingered in her mind. When the clock struck: lunch, Rick grabbed a tablet and told her to meet again in ninety minutes. She messaged Will to join her for the meal. Arms and shirt peppered with green algae, she meandered into the mess hall with a twist of her body to stretch her muscles. She grabbed a juice box and turned to find a seat, but jumped in surprise when she realized the quiet room was not as empty as it seemed.

Maya sat alone in the corner of the room adjacent the entrance. She had been eating lunch with a cup of tea, reading from a holo-screen when Natalie arrived and walked right past her. Maya's hand in the shape of a gun, she had Natalie in her sights.

"Bang."

"Oh my god!" Natalie clutched her chest. "Have you been there the whole time?"

Maya cracked a smile. "If I were an assassin, you'd be dead. You should mind your environment."

"You scared the crap out of me." Natalie sat across from Maya. "Lucky for me you're not an assassin."

"At least one you haven't charmed. Lunchtime? I see you like to hunt your own food." With bridled amusement, Maya watched Natalie jam a straw into her juice box, succeeding after four wild stabs.

"I hate these things. But yeah, waiting for Will." Natalie took a sip from her juice.

"How's your first day going? Rick isn't giving you too hard of a time is he?"

"It's really cool," Natalie said honestly but short on enthusiasm, still reeling from her recent tragedy. "I've read about air reclamation rods but I've never *held* one before. They can be hard to unclip. My friend Ash used to do all the heavy stuff in shop class, like when parts were all rusted. I can handle it though." Natalie hoped to reassure Maya they had made a good choice hiring her.

"Sounds like you're knee deep in the exciting life of a starship engineer," Maya deadpanned.

"I know, right? It's the dream. What are you reading?" Natalie nodded at the hologram over the table. Without a visible headline, there was only text.

"The UEG defense contract is expiring this year, so everyone is bidding for that sweet government payday," Maya said.

"Earth hasn't had any pirate problems. They'll probably go for the cheapest option that doesn't suck. My money is on Korea Aerospace or IST," Natalie said.

"Why IST?"

"IST is reliable, affordable, and their modular designs would be useful."

"Not a bad deduction," Maya said, pleased with Natalie's effortless response.

"Oh hey, so I was just curious, I've met everyone in the crew, right?" Natalie asked.

"Nikolai and I were the last ones you met?" Maya asked. With a nod, Natalie pictured the towering Russian with a jolly disposition. "Then yes, you've met the whole crew. Why do you ask?"

"Because the night you guys rescued us I remember someone else there. I was wondering why I haven't seen him around."

"That was a rescue mission you stumbled into," Maya said. "We dropped him off before we left for Freyja."

"Oh, okay. I asked Rick and he said he didn't know anything." Natalie took another drink from her juice box.

"Rick was mostly there to loot."

"Thanks for giving me a straight answer. That's been bugging me for hours," Natalie said. Will walked through the entryway and stole Natalie's attention.

"See ya later, alligator." Maya tipped her teacup at Natalie with a wink.

"Nice talking to you." Natalie hopped out of her seat with a smile.

Eager to work, Natalie was early to return from her lunch and put her nose to the grindstone until the end of the day. Rick admitted that they worked a longer day than usual, but he wanted to see what she could handle. He was pleased with her work but could see the strain it put on her, so he gave her the next day off. After that, they would start normal shifts again and ease her into more strenuous work.

On her day off she idled in bed and got a late start. When she arrived in the mess hall for breakfast, it was empty of people but filled with the delicious scent of food. The opening between the galley and the mess hall had trays of food ready to serve with plates on the far end. There were biscuits, potatoes, strawberries, watermelon slices, bananas, eggs with spinach, bacon, ham, more food than Natalie could eat despite wanting it all. While she served herself, the rumble of someone lumbering down the hall echoed into the room. She turned to see Farouk strut into the mess hall.

"Morning."

"Good morning," Natalie said. Farouk grabbed a plate and helped himself to the breakfast Ian had cooked, moving at a faster pace than her.

"You got the day off?" Farouk asked. "Usually I'm the only one gettin' breakfast this late."

"Yeah, being a ship's engineer is hard work. My arms and back are killing me." Natalie drooped into an exaggerated slouch and grabbed a fork, then plopped into the nearest seat. Farouk took the spot across from her. "If Rick works this hard every day, why isn't he all buff like you?"

Farouk let loose a hearty laugh and pointed at Natalie with his fork. "He's a wiry guy. That's how his body is. You havin' fun?"

"You know it. Rick is super cool, too. I like talking to him, it feels normal," she looked down at her food with a nod.

"Well, he loves machines, you love machines, it makes sense." Farouk sensed Natalie's heavy heart and hoped to move her mind along. "I thought he'd be a dick on your first day. He doesn't really like kids."

"I think he was trying to be, but I know my stuff," Natalie said, chin high.

"That's what's up. How's your boy?"

"Good. He's a deckhand, so he mostly cleans, but he's healed up and Nikolai says he'll have feeling back in a couple days," she said. Will had been given cleaning duty since he had little else to offer. "Hey wait, what's your job?"

Farouk took a moment to finish chewing. "I'm the gardener."

"Seriously?" Natalie asked.

"Yeah, and? I'm damn good too. All these fresh fruits and veggies are because of *me*." Farouk pointed to the strawberries on her plate.

"I didn't know you're a gardener," Natalie gushed with a mix of joy and surprise.

"I learned it from my momma when I was a kid." Farouk smiled for a moment then looked away sadly. Natalie realized that they had more in common than she realized, but that was as far as that topic would go for the time being. Neither of them wanted to dig any deeper. The conversation stalled and they ate quietly.

"Ian is a great cook." The awkward silence proved too much for Natalie.

"Chef. He's Nikolai's personal *chef*," Farouk corrected. "Nikolai leaves the ship for months at a time, though. So when he's gone, we fend for ourselves."

"They leave? I guess there are things *not* to look forward to," Natalie cringed.

"Yeah, Nikolai has responsibilities. It ain't that bad, we just change up our shopping list." Farouk shrugged off losing their chef for months at a time.

"If Ian's the chef, why was he there the night you picked us up?"

"He was flying my ship. He joins us sometimes, mostly on the easy stuff." Farouk gathered the last of his food into a small pile on his plate.

"Why weren't *you* flying your ship?" The practical question was quick to leave Natalie's lips without much thought behind it.

"Because I was in the bunker until these guys picked me up."

"So, they were there to rescue *you*?"

"I wouldn't say *rescue*. I was there on purpose, like a Trojan horse," Farouk clarified. "Who'd you think they were there for?"

"I thought you guys were there to rescue that other guy."

"You mean One? Nah, he just happened to be there. They brought him in while I was waitin' for my ride," he said.

"His name is One?" Natalie's asked.

"Yeah. Weird name, but he's an alien or some shit, so whatever." Farouk finished what was left on his plate.

Natalie stared wide-eyed at Farouk. He had said it so offhandedly that she was caught off guard. If he was an alien, it had to be the one that crashed in her yard.

"Or whatever? If you're an alien, you're an alien." Natalie played it cool. She had stumbled into the right person.

"True that. Rick was tryin' to explain it. He said he wasn't from our universe or somethin'." Farouk pondered for a moment. "Not like it matters. He's always in his room. Got to go check on the plants. See ya."

Farouk departed with his plate and left Natalie alone and stunned, the gears in her mind spinning with new information. While Rick sidestepped the question and Maya tried to throw her off the trail, Farouk either did not care or was out of the loop. She spoke of it with no one else but counted the seconds until she could tell Will.

A few hours later, Natalie got her chance when they sat down for lunch in the gunner room. As soon as they were alone, Natalie cut to the chase.

"So, I was talking to Rick and I asked him about this guy who was at the place where they rescued us, but we haven't seen him on the ship, and he said he doesn't know anything. Then, I talked to Maya and she was like, 'oh, we rescued that guy and dropped him off.' But then today I talked to Farouk and he said that they were actually there to rescue *him,* not the *other* guy!" Words spilled from Natalie like a waterfall.

"Okay…" Will gave her a bewildered look.

"Do you remember how we were talking about the ship that crashed at my house and how it was probably alien?" She spoke quickly, unable to get it out fast enough.

"Yeah." Will took a bite of his sandwich.

"He's on the ship," Natalie hissed. "That's the guy."

It took a few seconds for Will to recoil with surprise and shake his head. "Wait, what?"

"You were knocked out but there was this other guy with them that night. I think they picked him up from my house and took him to that bunker," Natalie explained.

"No way. What are the chances of that?"

Natalie had a lot to say and could talk enough for them both. Questions were the path of least resistance.

"We were in the middle of nowhere. Where would they take the survivor of a crash like that? Probably to the nearest *secret* government base in the middle of *nowhere*," Natalie said giddily.

"Good point. But, these guys, us, and him, in the same place, at the same time? That's crazy," Will contested, still doubtful of how events had unraveled.

"Okay yeah, these guys being there in time to save us was pretty lucky," Natalie admitted. "But, this alien isn't even from our universe. He could have landed anywhere, any *time* in the whole universe and he landed at my friggin' house. I want to know why."

"Oh." Chewing, Will took a moment to consider what she said then gulped down his food, "But, if the crew is trying to keep us away from him, we're going to have to meet him without them noticing."

"I thought we could start with checking out the other crew quarters first, then the guest quarters. If I don't find him, I'll ask Addie where he is."

"So, once we find out where he is, when could we sneak around to meet him?" Will submitted to Natalie's hours of preparation. She already had a plan and would undoubtedly talk him into going along with it.

"Addie told me there's going to be a birthday party in a couple weeks for Farouk, Nikolai, and Rick. I think that'll be our chance. You in?"

"I'm not letting you be the only one who meets an alien." Will grinned. "I'm in."

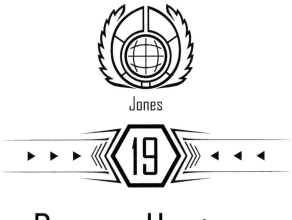

Jones

19

Dragon Hunters

"*Oblivion*, this is the *Bearded Dragon*, do you copy?" The tired voice of a beaten and broken prisoner called into empty space. Agent Jones loomed over him in the cockpit of the shuttle to ensure his cooperation. Samson and Ken waited in the cabin.

"*Bearded Dragon, this is Oblivion. Where the hell have you been?*" boomed a growling, angry voice.

"Captain!" The prisoner recoiled. "We uh, ran into some trouble. We need medical attention. I'll fill you in on the ship."

"*I'll see you when you land,*" the Captain growled. The prisoner hung his head in dismay and a location beacon appeared on his console, blinking steadily. With a heavy sigh of regret, he set the ship's autopilot.

At the center of the spherical holo-map over the console, a large ship appeared and crept toward them. Jones looked outside at the star-filled sky, but there was no ship. The starscape did not seem to change until growing void became apparent. The shadow grew and consumed the stars in front of them.

A series of lights illuminated the void to reveal a large ship, bay doors opening at its center. Jones weaved his head around to examine the large black ship on their approach. What appeared to be large spikes jettisoned from the hull of the vertically oriented ship. Illuminated above the bay doors leered the painting of a red dragon's head, which breathed fire and looked down upon them.

The shuttle slipped into the bay, faced its bow toward the doors and touched down. A roguish mix of men and women waited on the first and second levels with their rifles ready. Six heavy bruisers scattered around the first level behind the shuttle. They aimed their hefty rifles at the shuttle's double-layered doors.

From the second level, the scowling Captain joined the welcome party and suspiciously eyed the vessel. In his late thirties, a large black lotus tattoo on his lower neck covered the intimidating man's brand.

Like a mouth, the shuttle doors hinged open from the floor and ceiling. Unlit inside, ambient light from the cargo bay should have illuminated the interior of the shuttle, but it was pitch black.

Samson and Ken burst from the ship, crashing into the nearby bruisers. The room exploded with the thunderous boom of rifles. However, the crew was not armed with railguns as they had expected. Bright bursts of crackling, concentrated balls of energy erupted from the pirates' rifles.

With only a light suit of armor, Samson was caught by surprise and hit in the arm after he tried to smack what he thought would be a bullet out of the air. He was scorched up to his shoulder and cracks ripped through his armor. An intense shock ran through his body from head to toe and back. Every muscle ready to cramp, he pushed through the pain. Unable to hold still amidst enemy fire, he jumped to his side, zig-zagged and rolled to avoid the crackling spheres of energy. Sparks and streaks of electricity scattered across the floor and singed the ground behind him, then dissipated.

Samson made a mad dash for the nearest pirate. He snatched the bulky rifle from his hands and threw him into the wall. Moving on as swiftly as possible, he was grazed only twice more. He crushed enemy weapons and threw the soldiers into each other, careful not to strike them. There was no need to kill people for no reason, especially given his obscene physical advantage.

Ken had fewer reservations. Every enemy he encountered was injured or killed with the exception of a few lucky enough to have a comrade thrown into them by Samson before Ken arrived. Unlike Samson, he was covered in armor, ran on walls and darted about so quickly they could only fire at his shadow. A blade jutted from a compartment on his right arm and glowed red. It cut clean through enemy weapons as easily as it did their bodies. He leaped to the second level and fired thick composite-alloy nails from a compartment on his left arm.

The Captain faced off against Samson, who ducked and darted from side to side to avoid his shots. The clever Captain managed to anticipate Samson and shoot him in the leg. He trembled in place, paralyzed by the shot. Two more shots got him in the stomach and collarbone before a dead body slammed into the Captain and knocked the rifle away. Samson collapsed in pain with a cringe and tried to contain his trembling body. A trickle of blood ran down from his nose.

Ken charged the Captain, grabbed him by the neck, and kicked his knees out from under him. He slammed him to the ground and held his thick arm-blade to the Captain's face. The Captain tried to stab him in the ribs, but the knife dinged against Ken's armor. Ken took the Captain's knife, held it up and discarded the useless knife. Again, he held his arm-blade to the Captain's face.

It became clear that resistance was futile and he stopped fighting, baring his teeth at the Ranger. Some of his crew were still conscious and took aim, but nobody dared fire and risk hitting their Captain.

"Hold your fire." An unfamiliar voice came from the staircase.

The attackers and pirates held steady, fingers on their triggers. Jones's face emerged, then his body. He dragged a bloody, battered prisoner up the stairs and tossed the wounded pirate on the floor.

"I'm Agent Jones. Thank you for saving me the trouble of doing this all the way to the bridge." He gestured around the room of battered, dead, and dying pirates.

With a wave from Jones, Ken dropped the Captain and backed away. Arm in the air above him, he closed his hand into a fist. The needles he had fired into enemy pirates wiggled free of their corpses. They flew toward a glowing blue disc on the back of his forearm and slid inside.

The Captain gaped at the attackers and rose to his feet. Jones pointed at the pirates in the room who had not lowered their weapons. He looked around at his crew and held his hand out flat. The pirates lowered their weapons but stayed alert and ready to attack at a moment's notice.

"What do you want?" The athletic Captain stared Jones down with cold, steely blue eyes. He had stylish black hair and was surprisingly clean cut.

"I thought I'd start things off on the right foot and introduce myself." Jones motioned for the Captain to do as he had done.

"Captain Skinner. What the hell do you *want?*" Skinner's patience for the unlikeable attacker wore thin.

"Ridley Skinner. I've been reading up on the pirate clans since they came up earlier. You've got quite a reputation. You go by Black Lotus, don't you?" Jones paced by the railing a few meters away.

"Did you want an autograph? It'd be my first."

"Simply a trade. I picked up your crewman from *Oasis* and thought I'd bring him back to you in exchange for a little information." Jones looked to his injured prisoner.

"He got himself caught, and he looks pretty banged up, but I'll hear you out." Skinner crossed his arms and glowered at Jones.

"I'm after a ship that I believe was leaving in quite a hurry at the time of the attack. I was wondering if there was a chance you might have seen an old Armadillo fleeing the scene?" Jones asked, chest out, chin high.

Captain Skinner scratched at his chin and took a few steady paces. "The only reason you'd come here is if that's the only lead you've got, and I'm the only one left to ask. That makes me mission critical for you. He's not compensation enough for the information you're looking for." Captain Skinner gestured toward the prisoner Jones had brought. "So, how about you throw me a bone?"

With a grimace, Jones accessed his hitch. "I could kill him, and you, and everyone on your ship. Even if your weapon suppressors only allow your weapons to fire, we don't need guns to turn this into a ghost ship," he said coldly.

A beep in Skinner's ear demanded his attention, "What is it?"

"A UEG ship just came out of warp, they're right on top of us," his radio buzzed. Skinner closed his eyes and let out a long sigh.

"Are you realizing how outmatched you are?" Jones taunted.

Nearby, Samson had gotten to his feet and examined one of the pirate rifles. He wiped some blood from under his nose and leaned against the rails.

Skinner looked around at his crew whilst he contemplated the dilemma. Their faces told him they were ready to fight and die for the Dragon Claw. Skinner realized, however, this was not the time for that. He was not cornered yet.

"You think we're alone out here?" Skinner replied. "As a single ship you've got us by the balls, but we're a rendezvous for all the ships that hit *Oasis*. We've got a lot of friends at warp around us. We break radio contact, your one ship will be blown to shit, and then you won't have anything to run away with. They won't board this ship to take it back; they'll blow it up to get all of you. Mutually assured destruction. But, you seem like a reasonable guy. I'm sure you can think of a *better* outcome."

Jones nodded. "You're not as stupid as you look."

"UEG ships carry a bunch of extra food for relief efforts. We'll take that for the information you want." Skinner did not let Jones's jab bother him. "You can just ask for more and the UEG will send you a refill."

Jones paced toward Skinner, stalwart. He stopped a few steps away to examine the Captain. Without a word, Jones pulled out his mobile and opened a channel. "*Rampart*, prepare a shuttle's worth of food rations in the docking bay."

"Roger that," Amber responded.

"When we take your shuttle back to our ship, we'll load it full of supplies," Jones said. "Send a pilot along to fly the shuttle back. But the information I want, I get now."

With a grunt and a nod, Skinner looked to one of his nearby crew. "You go with 'em. And you," he said to Jones, "you'd better keep your word."

"I always do," Jones replied.

Captain Skinner examined Jones. He was straightforward and cocky. Jones thought he had all the cards, despite Skinner's argument to the contrary. Dominance was what he wanted, and he achieved it. Jones would keep this word because he took great pride in himself.

"One of our ships had a run-in with an Armadillo during the attack. They exchanged fire, both took damage," Skinner shared.

"So the craft we're looking for took damage? That's useful, but it leaves me a lot of places to look. What else can you offer?" Jones inquired further.

"Well, that's the information you were looking for. We *could* make you a short list of shops in the area they might go to for parts or repairs, but we've got our own repairs to take care of, and you never asked for that." Captain Skinner said.

"I see." Jones paced away. "I'll pay for those repairs if you'll give me something I can *use*," he said with some contempt.

"Let me see a cash card or something." Skinner held his hand out. "For all I know you don't have the funds to back up that big talk."

Jones smirked, pleased with the Captain's boldness despite the mortal danger. He wanted to make that little bit of information as profitable as possible. Jones reached into his pocket and pulled out a thin box. He inserted a cash card and a holographic interface appeared over it. Jones tapped around then pulled out the card and tossed it to Captain Skinner. It slid across the floor and stopped at his feet.

Sneering, Skinner looking down at the clear card. He glared at Jones, who smiled and turned away. Without a need to be prompted, one of Skinner's crew ran to pick up the card then handed it to his Captain.

Skinner nodded in thanks then tapped on the card to reveal the quantity on it. The numbers appeared. Content with the payment, he slipped the card into his pocket.

"There ain't many places around here you can get parts for an Armadillo, you can count 'em on one hand. But, you've got to know where to look." He pulled back his sleeve and touched a finger to his wristband for a holo-screen then made a list for Jones. Jones's hitch dinged when the exchange was complete. "I know your type. There's no need to hurt any of the people you meet at those shops."

"I'm sure you do. Thank you for the information, I'll use only as much force as I find to be necessary." Jones headed for the staircase. Samson stopped him and leaned in to whisper in his ear then showed him the rifle.

Skinner glanced around the room. Confident as he may have been earlier, doubt crept in that Jones might go back on his word.

"We'll be taking one of these as a souvenir," Jones said. "Strange that pirates would have such advanced weaponry. I don't suppose you would tell us where you acquired it?"

"I don't know where it comes from, I just know how to use it," Skinner said.

"I'll have our *tech* guy take a look at it." Jones and Samson walked back down the stairs with Skinner's pilot while Ken kept watch on the pirates. Once they reached the shuttle ramp, Ken stepped onto the handrail and dropped down to the first floor. He stood aside Jones at the foot of the shuttle.

Skinner and his crew rushed to the edge of the second level and looked down at the attackers. Samson and the pilot were already inside. Jones stood next to Ken and looked up at the pirates.

"Don't forget the balance of power here, *Black Lotus.*" Jones chuckled and entered the shuttle, as if despite all Skinner's power and reputation he was a joke. "I won't leave the comfort of my ship if we meet again."

"You can *count* on it," Skinner growled.

A segmented wall rolled down from the ceiling and closed off the bay from the shuttle. The other compartment depressurized and the pirates watched the shuttle depart through the partially transparent walls.

Skinner gripped the rails, trembling with rage.

"You all right, Captain?" somebody asked.

"I'm going to *kill* that son of a bitch," Skinner growled. "Make sure we flag that ship as an enemy of the Dragon Claw. Any Dragon Claw ship crosses paths with them again, they're getting blown out of the goddamn sky."

"Yes, sir."

"You okay, Pete?" Plunder asked the prisoner Jones had brought in. His broken fingers were set and bandaged but left unhealed.

"Yeah," he nodded. "That asshole tortured and killed Miguel."

"I'm sorry you had to go through all this." Skinner took a deep breath, let go of the handrail and helped him off the floor. "Don't worry, we'll get this all sorted out and we won't have to keep doing these attacks. Let's get you to sickbay."

Natalie and Will

Party Time!

FOR OVER TWO WEEKS NATALIE SEARCHED THE *ULFBERHT* FOR THE alien, whose existence she increasingly doubted the longer she failed to find him. All forty of the living quarters and the guest quarters on decks five and six were empty, as were the two unused living areas on decks one and two. The only living area of the ship where she dared not tread was the officer's quarters.

The search helped to keep her mind off the loss of her family. By day, she kept herself distracted from the painful thoughts and her nights, while full of nightmares and flashbacks at first, had become more peaceful. Increasingly frequent dreams of Hope were like a soothing balm, taking away the pain.

By the time the triple birthday party came around in late August, she had not found the alien anywhere. Natalie had reached the date of their single opportunity to sneak into the alien's room. If he was in the officer's quarters, they would surely need a code to get in.

The crew elected to have the party in the lounge, located above the mess hall. They were connected by a staircase and each had an opening to the galley. The officers had fixed up the lounge and scattered drinking games around the spacious room, already furnished with comfortable couches, tables, and an arcade machine. Music boomed down the hall the night of the party, welcoming Natalie and Will to a group of drinking, dancing, and laughing people they now considered friends.

They had fun, despite the age difference with most of the crew. Over the weeks they had gotten to know everyone better and had been treated as adults. Maya seemed to be everywhere and Natalie loved talking to her about the colonies. Shin was reserved and quiet but he and Will got along well. Natalie often caught them talking in the mess hall, and the party was no different. They even teamed up for beer pong, matching up against Natalie and Rick in the final, who ultimately won. Addie insisted on taking pictures all night, culminating in a group picture with the birthday cake.

After they cut the cake Addie got some space from everyone and plopped herself into a semi-circular couch. She put her empty frosting-smeared plate on a table and laid her head back, snuggling a glass of red wine. Her legs crossed, she bounced a foot to the beat of the music. Natalie and Will seized their opportunity and dropped in on either side of her. Addie's eyes opened and her face lit up.

"Hey, guys!" she swirled the wine in her glass. "Do you like wine?" Will shook his head with an uninterested frown.

"I've never tried it," Natalie said. Without responding, Addie handed over her glass. Natalie examined it, sniffed it, and took a sip.

"Wow, that's really good." She handed it back.

"It's my favorite. It goes great with cheese and crackers." Addie pointed behind her at the snack table. "They're so good. I kind of want some right now." Addie began to get up, but Will jumped off the couch.

"I'll get some for us," he said.

"Oh, Will, you're such a sweetheart," Addie fawned.

"Don't mention it." Will excused himself, flashing Natalie a smile as he departed.

Addie waited until he was beyond earshot then poked Natalie in her ribs, to which she bounced in her seat with a yelp. "So, are you guys a thing yet?"

"*What?* No." Natalie shook her head, her cheeks bright red. "It isn't like that."

Addie smirked. "Well, until we upgrade the warp system on this baby, it's a thirty-nine day trip to Freyja. Why don't you guys just drink a little tonight and see what happens?"

"You know, you and my friend Ash would get along *really* well," Natalie deflected, arms crossed.

A mischievous giggle escaped Addie's lips. She took a sip of her drink and uncrossed her legs. Her eyes glazed over, face an equal balance of sleepy and happy, she pivoted her body to face Natalie. "Honey, you saved each other's lives. I'm surprised you haven't rode that white knight like a roller coaster." Addie wiggled her hips and tickled her. With a laugh, Natalie jumped and jammed her elbow back.

"Stop! Oh my god." Her heart aflutter, Natalie peeked over her shoulder at Will, who was assembling a plate of cheese and crackers with his back to them. If she didn't cut to the chase, it was no doubt that someone would show up and ruin her opportunity. "I wanted to talk to you about something."

"What's up, buttercup?"

Natalie glanced back at Will then around the room and leaned in close to whisper, "I know the alien who crashed at my house is on the ship. I want to talk to it."

Too drunk to conceal her reactions, Addie's eyes bulged and she squirmed in her seat, wiggling into a more attentive posture. She checked the room and eyed Natalie, then leaned in. "How do you know about that?"

"Farouk mentioned it."

"Oh my god, Farouk," Addie whispered through gritted teeth, eyes squeezed shut, "check your god damn messages." She glanced at Will, whom she now knew had only offered to get cheese and crackers to keep her there with Natalie, the sneaky bastard. "Let's go somewhere else so I can explain."

"I'll get Will." Natalie shuffled to hop out of her seat but Addie clutched her arm.

"No," she whispered. "Just you and me, right now, let's go." Addie's hand slid down to hold Natalie's and pulled her out of her seat. She scampered into the hall with her drink in one hand and Natalie in the other.

A moment later, Will returned with a plate of crackers and cheese to a vacant couch. "Seriously?"

Addie pulled Natalie around the corner of the dimly lit starboard hall to the gunner room, her brisk pace tugged on Natalie's arm. There, she commanded the computer to start one of her playlists. A punk rock song's angry drums and guitar filled the air and Addie pulled Natalie to the back of the room. The volume was loud enough so they could hold a conversation without being heard from outside.

"Okay." Addie looked Natalie in the eye and examined her while she sipped on her wine. "Why do you want to talk to him?"

Natalie teetered from side to side, considering her response. "He landed on my house and destroyed my life. I want to know how, or why, or something. I just… *feel* like I need to talk to him."

"Aw." Addie drooped, then squeezed Natalie with a sympathetic hug. "You're looking for closure."

"I guess?" Natalie patted Addie's back. She did not know what to call the strange tug in her gut that pulled her toward the alien.

"Okay, well…" Addie pulled away and ran her hand down Natalie's arm. "You should know he isn't an alien, like how you might think."

"Farouk said something about that, but he said he didn't get it," Natalie recalled.

"Usually when people say alien they mean extra-terrestrial, which means from another planet. Alien means foreign, so technically he's an alien, but he's not from another planet." Addie took her time to enunciate.

"He's from another universe." Natalie had spent weeks thinking about everything Addie was drunkenly explaining and was sure of her conclusions. "Right?"

"Not exactly." Addie put her hands out as if she held an invisible ball. "If you imagine the whole universe as this ship, then he's from outer space. He's not from another ship, and we can't perceive that reality."

"Woah." Like her mind, Natalie's eyes drifted, imagining the possibilities of the alien's origin. He may even know what happens to people after they die.

"But, if you think he can answer any questions you have," Addie sliced her free hand through the air and teetered forward, "forget about it."

"Why?"

"So, the alien's name is One. It's easier if I tell you that now." Addie tilted her head back and finished what was left in her glass. "The Captain has tried talking to him a few times since we picked him up. He says One can have a bad effect on our universe so he gives really cryptic answers if he answers at all."

Natalie let Addie's advice roll around in her head. Addie was drunk, but she wanted the best for her.

"I understand. Thanks for the advice, but this has been eating at me. I need to do this." Natalie balled her hands into determined fists and straightened. "I just need you to get me into the officer's quarters."

"You don't need my help you can walk right in. You'll find One in the officer quarters, room one," Addie said.

"I thought it would be restricted like the officer's lounge. And, wouldn't the Captain be in room one?" Natalie asked.

Addie shook her head. "It's like a whole extra step to get into our quarters with restrictions on so Mike removed them when we became a skeleton screw. And everyone picked their lucky numbers, nobody ended up in room one. Funny how things work out, right?" Natalie was still confused, but Addie tilted back and got her balance, then spun around to make for the door. "Music off. Let's go!" The punk music in the background faded away.

Natalie followed Addie out but stopped at the corner of the hall. "Wait, could you have Will join me? We're supposed to do it together."

"*Yeah* you are," Addie winked and gyrated her hips.

"Oh my god." Natalie squeezed her eyes shut and covered her glowing red face.

"I'll get Will, you wait here." Addie walked away, swaying from side to side along her path. She returned to find Will at a table playing a card game with Farouk, Ian, and Shin. She leaned over to whisper in his ear, "Natalie needs to get something from her room but doesn't want to go alone. Could you go with her?"

"Why didn't you guys go right now?"

Addie shot him a serious, annoyed look. "I'll take your spot, just go."

"Okay. Thanks for teaching me the game, it was fun." Will hustled out of the room slightly off balance. In the dark hall, Natalie waved from around the corner. She signaled for him to follow and quietly led him to the officer quarters one deck up.

The officer quarters were in the block next to theirs, both opened into the single hall that ran down the length of the habitation levels. Tablets and gaming controllers littered the otherwise neat living area. There were even paper books, an uncommon sight. Natalie picked one up and flipped through its pages, a burst of vanilla filled her nostrils.

Near the entrance was a steel door with a red number one painted on it. It was slightly ajar, like they were expected. Standing in the middle of the living area, Natalie eyed the door anxiously. She put the book back on the table and moved to the door, Will following closely. She stood in front of it, eyes fixed on the slender opening.

Hand pressed against the cold steel, a tremble ran through her body and all the possibilities that lie ahead anchored her in place. The anticipation was paralyzing until a hand grabbed hers and she jumped in surprise.

"You can do this," Will whispered.

With a smile, Natalie squeezed his hand, took a deep breath, and gently pushed the door open. Their hands entwined, Will followed her in.

Designed for one person as opposed to bunks, the officer quarters were more spacious than the normal rooms. A bed rested against the back wall but the room was otherwise empty of furnishings. In the lotus position atop the bed was a thin young man with black skin, no hair, and a content look on his face. Wrapped in a robe like a monk, he looked their age, like someone with whom they could have gone to school. She recognized him as the one from that night but was at a loss of words. Pondering where to begin, a blank stare was all she could manage at first.

"Hi, my name is Natalie, this is Will," she said. Manners always came first.

"I know," One replied.

"Addie says you're not from our universe." She drew an astonished look from Will, whom she had not made privy to that information.

"Correct."

"If you're not from our universe, does time exist where you're from?" She hoped to get her bearings so she could find a course in the conversation.

"As a concept, a tool," he said.

"So when you came into our universe, you could have shown up anywhere, any time, right?" Natalie prodded.

"Correct."

"So, why did you land at my house? Thirty years ago there wouldn't have been a house there. Why didn't you land back then?" her voice rose in intensity as she went on.

One looked back at her without saying a word.

"Addie said it would be difficult to get answers, but you answered my other questions," Natalie said. "Why?"

"Answering your other questions does not affect your universe," One said. Simple and logical, it gave Natalie an easy framework to formulate her questions. There were so many questions she had wanted to ask him, and most of them he would not answer.

"Why do you look human?" Will asked while Natalie deliberated.

"When observing, we take the form of the species we are watching, so we can experience the world as they do," One explained.

"You said observing," Natalie said. "But, you crash-landed. How?"

"I do not know."

"So, you don't know why you ruined our lives?" Natalie asked.

For the first time, One paused and looked away. "The crash is a mystery to me."

"Well then," Natalie began.

"Wait." Will grabbed Natalie's shoulder. "He didn't say no. He doesn't know why he crashed, but he knows why he ruined our lives."

"Is he right?" Natalie asked One.

"The question is flawed."

"Okay." Natalie crossed her arms and pondered her next question. "What can you tell us about why you crashed at my house when you could have landed anywhere else?"

One paused again. His subtle expressions hinted at contemplation. "I arrived where your universe chose to place me."

Natalie and Will shared a perplexed look. "What do you mean, *chose?*" Their voices overlapped. One did not answer. They stared, waiting for him to speak, but he did not waver.

"So, if he's not answering, that means his answer affects our universe," Will reasoned. "Because the answer will affect how we see the universe, which is important."

"So, if the universe is alive, what are we?" Natalie asked, but got no response.

"Aren't our cells alive? And the bacteria in our stomachs?" Will said, a dead look in his eyes as his perspective zoomed far out into the deep cosmos where he was little more than an insignificant speck. "Maybe that's what we are to our universe."

"Okay, to you, is there any difference between us and the cells in our bodies?"

One looked at Natalie, then Will and back. "No, and yes."

"Have you ever taken the form of a cell?" Natalie asked curiously.

"Yes." One bowed his head in a single, firm nod. The two teenagers pondered his responses for a moment and imagined themselves as cells in a body.

"So a universe can make decisions?" Natalie asked explicitly.

"The question is flawed."

"If we're like cells, are we doing things the universe wants us to do, or are we making our own choices?" she adjusted her question.

"The things you do are what the universe wills, but you do not do as the universe wills," One said.

"That's comforting." Natalie breathed a sigh of relief.

"So we have free will, but if we're as insignificant as cells what difference does it make?" Will asked. "What does it matter what we decide to do with our lives?"

One looked back and forth between them. "Does it not matter if a cell in your body turns cancerous?"

"But, we can't *kill* the universe," Will argued.

"There are restrictions to my words and interactions because the decisions you make, matter. If they did not, I could tell you anything," One explained. Will narrowed his eyes at him, annoyed at being proven wrong without being given an answer.

"So, we can't kill the universe and our choices matter," Natalie said. "But, we didn't want to know that stuff. All we wanted to know was why you crashed at my house."

"Why does anything happen to anyone?" One asked. "To understand that would be to understand the meaning of life."

"Is that what we're asking?" Natalie received only a blank look from One. She pondered her questions until Will caught her attention.

"Can you see the future?" Will asked.

"Not since I arrived," for the first time, One looked insecure. A silence swept over the room. The two teenagers shared a hopeless look, unsure of how to proceed. While Natalie wondered if she had sought a fruitless goal, One awaited their next question.

"I just wanted to know why we were the ones that got pulled into all this," Natalie slouched, drained and defeated.

"Why—is the most important question. But, you should pose it to yourself. You have all the answers you need."

Natalie locked eyes with One, whose compassionate gaze touched her soul. A tear rolled down her cheek. She wiped it away in hopes Will had not noticed it.

"Do you have anything you want to ask him?" she said.

"I guess…" Will looked curiously at One. "Are you like… God?"

One looked at him for a moment. They could now tell he was not declining to answer, but contemplating his response.

"A universe is a habitat, as is my home. If you perceive God to be all things in the universe, then *you* are God, and I am of a foreign god. If you believe God to be one with all things in existence, then we are equals."

Natalie and Will contemplated his response for a moment. It led Will to another question, and when it popped into his head, he perked up.

"Why *were* you watching our universe?" he asked. "Why are *you* here?"

"That seems to be the question *I* must answer before I can leave," he said, receiving a frown from Will.

"That's all for me." Will got to his feet and helped Natalie up.

With a gulp, Natalie nodded and followed Will to the door. She turned back to the serene alien on her way out. "Thank you for talking to us."

One bowed to them with a smile and Natalie closed the door behind them. They left the officer's quarters and strolled quietly into the hall. The tempest in Natalie's mind drowned her senses. The questions she wanted to ask broke down to asking the meaning of life. Why does anything happen to anyone? What is the meaning of those events?

Natalie had asked her father a similar question once as a child. Lamenting her grandmother's death, she asked why she had been taken instead of someone else, somewhere else. Why not someone bad instead of someone so full of love?

"There's no such thing as bad people, Natty," she relived the memory, the warmth of his arm wrapped around her as real as it was then. "Everyone is good and bad. Good and bad things happen to everyone. What matters is what we do with our lives after something happens to us. Be gracious in victory, learn from your defeats, and appreciate what you have, because nothing is forever. Now, we live lives that grandma would be proud of."

After the initial shock of what happened the night One landed, Natalie tried to push everything as far back in her mind as she could. She tried to pretend it happened long ago to someone else and immerse herself in a new life, but she had neither properly dealt with the pain nor fully embraced her new life. The circumstances of her life were completely different than before, but she spent most of her time obsessing over the past and searching for One.

"Natty?" She jumped, yanked from her daze. A hand on her shoulder, Will was there, and she was back on the *Ulfberht*. "You okay?" he asked with loving concern.

"Yeah, why?" Natalie bit her nail. Will wiped a tear from her cheek.

"No reason," he shook his head. Natalie giggled awkwardly and pulled away.

Looking into Will's eyes, she could see the boy she had grown up with and the man he would grow up to be. All the times he had been there for her, and she had been there for him. She had ended up there because Will was willing to sacrifice everything for her, as she was for him. The reason she was okay stood right in front of her. He had been her pillar through it all. Natalie's eyes bloomed in wondrous recognition. Will loved her, and she loved him, but she had been too busy pretending to be okay to realize it. She would surely cry herself to sleep that night, but soul-crushing revelations are not without their silver lining.

"What is it?" Will noted her sudden change in demeanor.

Natalie stepped toward him with purpose and clutched his shirt. She grabbed his face and pulled it into hers. The moment before their lips touched, time slowed, a shock ran between them. Lips pressed together, their bodies pulled closer to one another, enveloped in a swirling deluge of passion. After a moment, she pulled away with a sigh of satisfaction.

With a trembling breath, she ran her fingers down his cheek. "I realized, maybe the universe is huge and we don't matter, but we matter to other people. That's why we're both still alive. We don't know how much our choices will affect the world, but they affect the world around us. Our lives are whatever we want them to be. So, I'm going to make it good."

Jones

The Goblin's Burrow

"Welcome to the Goblin's Burrow! I'm Leo. If you're looking for rare parts, I've got what *you* need. How can I help you?" The short, stocky man with a ring of frazzled graying hair and a plump belly pushed a pair of thin round glasses up his bulbous nose. He headed for Jones, Samson, and Ken with a spirited pep in his step.

The Goblin's Burrow was a single round room with an area Jones approximated to be one hundred square meters with a high ceiling and a second-floor walkway that encircled the room with no visible staircase. A meter-tall screen ran along the walls at a comfortable viewing level displaying parts and deals. Leo's service desk was against the wall opposite the entrance with a path connecting the two. In the middle of each hemisphere of the room were large ornamental pieces of old warships. The mangled chunks of towering metal jutted from short platforms.

"What beautifully morbid reminders of the Fourth World War." Jones stood in the center of the room and complimented the monoliths on either side of him. He and Samson were dressed in their normal attire, but Ken had thrown a long coat over a hooded sweater and some loose pants over his armor to blend in on Ganymede. He carried a backpack with his helmet, in case it became necessary.

Samson leaned against the wall by the door with his arms crossed. He watched the outside for possible customers or anyone who might interrupt. Ken circled the room.

"Yeah. The First Galactic War." Leo's chest swelled at the sight of his decorations, unaware of the roll in Jones's eyes.

Jones did not care for Leo's phrasing as it assumed the colonies mattered and were anything more than extensions of the countries which founded them.

"They're some real beauties," Leo went on. "From the Kurko and the Washington." He pointed at each. "Even my decorative scraps are the best there is. Every part I've got is top of the line. I inspect each one personally."

"My engineer tells me that he can't print *everything* I need," Jones said. "So I have to actually get out and find the parts. I feel like a caveman."

"Oh yeah, there's only so much you can print," Leo said. "Some parts require special engineering or materials a printer can't work with. Some of those parts aren't even made anymore, but I'm the guy that can get 'em."

"Would you happened to have parts for an old Armadillo?" Jones asked.

"Those things aren't too common. There's a lot of other armored dropships that fly better in space, Armadilloes aren't too practical anymore. What model you lookin' for?" Leo knew his inventory by heart.

"Fifteen series." Jones paced toward Leo.

With a cringe, Leo looked away. "Well, I've got all the standard Armadillo parts. Exclusive fifteen series pieces, a couple gyros, landing gear, a cooling system, and thrusters. I've actually modified the thrusters, so even if you don't need 'em, your ship will fly better in space. It's a solid upgrade."

"Thank you, I'll consider it. I've been to two other shops already and I'm yet to find what I'm looking for. I'm surprised you have all the standard pieces. When was the last time someone even came by for Armadillo parts?"

"Oh, it's been a while. At least three months." Leo's first lie. At that moment, Jones found the shop he was looking for. "Like I said, there's more practical ships these days. So, the parts aren't flyin' out the door. What part are you lookin' for?"

"I'm not entirely sure." Jones shot Ken a commanding look, prompting him to circle around behind Leo. "But, you're going to help me find it."

Leo jumped at Ken's looming silhouette behind him. He looked to Samson, who locked the door and turned the window opaque. Leo shuffled away from Ken.

"You're the third shop I've visited. Mad Mack was the first." Jones accessed his hitch and pulled up a hologram. It was the picture of a pudgy man in a blood-soaked bathtub, his face frozen in a mix of terror and pain.

"Mack…" Leo mumbled as he looked upon his friend's picture.

"Yes. He had quite a mouth on him. Very bold. *Too* bold." Jones pointed to Mack's severed thumb. "We used his thumb to get access to his records after he refused to cooperate. He didn't have what we were looking for. Daniel at the Elephant's Graveyard was very cooperative after I showed him this. I would even say he was *eager* to help. I know you sign a confidentiality agreement with your customers, but can I count on you for the same level of cooperation?"

"What are you looking for?" Leo grumbled, surrendering to the misfortune that had walked through his door.

Jones swiped his finger over the hologram and switched it to the pictures of Farouk and Shin. "Has anyone come in looking for Armadillo parts? Or, have you seen either of these men?" Jones watched Leo, examining where he looked and the subtle expressions and body language that would betray any deception. While technology could assist him, unused skills become rusty, and Jones would not tolerate such a thing.

Leo took a moment to examine the pictures then shook his head. "No, sorry. Is that it?" He looked to the floor.

"It would be, Mr. DeLuca, but I happened to be exceptionally good at spotting a liar." Jones stepped toward Leo, who backed away in fear. Ken dashed to flank him between them.

Leo put his hands up in front of him. "Ho-hold on." He turned ninety degrees and put his back to one of the twisted corkscrews of scrap metal.

Ken pulled back the sleeve of his civilian clothing to reveal his armor. His thick blade shot out from his forearm.

"Since you seem to have the information we require, you won't end up like *Mad* Mack," Jones said. "But, you don't have to remain in one piece to help us." He showed Leo the headshots again. "Have either of these men been to your shop?"

Hands up and pinned against his own decor, Leo took rapid, fearful breaths. There was no way out of the situation. "I sell rare parts, I've got to retain every customer I get," he mumbled and put his hands down, eyes on the floor.

"I won't tell anyone if you don't," Jones said. "So, answer my question."

Leo nodded, unable to bring himself to speak.

"I love it when questioning goes this easily, don't you?" Jones asked Ken, who shook his head with a grin, eyes glued to Leo. "So, Mr. Goblin, although I must say you look more like a troll to me; were you able to deliver on your promise? Did you have what they needed?"

Leo sighed with regret before he gathered the courage to answer, "Mostly."

"Most? Not as good of a shop as you claim to be, I see?" Jones crossed his arms.

"I can *get* what you need. Found the part, but it'll take some time to get here."

"Oh? So, they'll be back?" Jones threw his hands in the air and walked in a circle. Leo nodded his head with a solemn sigh. "Wonderful! We just have to wait for them to come back. When will that be?"

"They said they didn't know," Leo said. "Said they'd call me when they're back in town. The part will be here in a few weeks." Leo kept his answers vague, but true, since Jones was missing information.

"Thank you for your cooperation," Jones said.

"Don't mention it," Leo grumbled, disappointed in himself.

"Oh, I won't. But, we'll be around for a while. I think we'll dock here until our targets return. We'll be keeping a *very* close eye on you. Don't even *think* about trying to warn them, or we *will* gut you and plant you atop your decorative trash." Jones shoved Leo against the scrap metal.

"I understand." Leo held his hands in the air, defeated.

"Good." Jones stepped back and headed for the exit. "Good day."

Ken retracted his blade and followed Jones out. After they left his establishment, Leo sat down on the ground feeling helpless, demeaned, angry and used.

The door slammed behind them. The city's industrial district flowed with locals and travelers. Some bartered or haggled over prices, others watched robots load their crates onto trucks. All of them peeked out of the corner of their eyes at the trio.

"So, we're just going to wait for them to come back?" Samson asked.

"Absolutely. You couldn't ask for anything better than to know where your prey is going to be. You have to maintain the element of surprise," Jones accessed his hitch. "Hail Captain Slater." A moment later, a hologram of Slater's face appeared.

"Agent Jones, what can I do ya for?" Slater's voice rang with apathy.

"I need surveillance on Leo DeLuca, owner of the Goblin's Burrow. Intercept all his transmissions and put a tail on him at all times, as well as surveillance at his work and residence," Jones ordered. "We need to ensure he doesn't warn our targets."

"Roger."

"And, secure the cooperation of the local authorities. We're going to be here a while and we require autonomy."

"How long is a while?" Slater asked, attention piqued.

"Unknown, possibly months. Jones out." He ended the transmission.

"So, now we wait around? Train up?" Samson asked.

"Not quite. Do you see the faces of the people around us?" Jones stared straight ahead while Samson snuck glances at the inhabitants of Ganymede city. Some watched them walk by with intrigue, but most were suspicious or had the look of an enemy in their eyes. In a port full of travelers, they were outsiders.

"This area is teeming with people who hate the UEG," Jones pointed out. "If we're to remain here, we must remain vigilant."

Ulfberht Crew

22

Coming Clean

MIKE APPROACHED THE GUNNER ROOM AND REACHED OUT FOR the console, but stopped short. From inside he heard giggling. Natalie and Will had started dating, so he thought a wiser course of action would be to knock.

Three firm taps on the metal door halted the giggling from inside and Natalie called out, "Come in!"

To his relief, they were fully clothed, sitting next to each other on several layers of blankets holding game controllers. A game screen hovering over the wall was covered in a black screen with big yellow letters: PAUSED.

"Am I interrupting anything?" Mike asked.

"No," they both answered together.

It was hard to tell if they were lying, so he moved along and walked inside.

"Good, good. Sorry to interrupt your game. Do you two have a few minutes to talk?" They looked at each other and he held a hand out to ease their concern. "It's okay, you're not in trouble."

"Okay," Will said.

"Yeah, we can talk," Natalie followed up. But, neither their rigid postures nor their ghastly faces could hide their tension.

"Ugh." Mike sighed, looking around the floor. He took a seat in front of them and crossed his legs. Will reached behind him and handed him a large pillow. "Thanks." Mike stuffed the pillow beneath him and relaxed into a more comfortable pose. But, when he looked up, Natalie and Will were still staring wide-eyed at him, waiting for him to speak.

"So, I'm going to get straight to it so you two can relax, because you're making *me* tense. I'm not upset, but I'm curious and I want to talk about it. So, I know you two spoke to One."

The two teenagers turned to one another, sharing a nervous look, then turned back to Mike.

"How do you know we *supposedly* spoke to One?" Will said in an attempt not to incriminate them.

"Besides the fact that Maya knows everything that happens on this ship, you're not even supposed to know who One is, so the way you phrased that question gives you away," Mike said.

Will's eyes darted away as he contemplated what Mike said, then he shook his head in defeat. "Damn."

"But, we're *not* in trouble?" Natalie asked.

"That's right."

They breathed a sigh of relief then nodded their heads.

"Well, that's a relief. Why aren't you mad?" Natalie asked.

"Because I've had a few conversations with One, if you can call them that, and I never get anywhere. Did you guys get anything from your conversation? Because I notice your moods have changed since then."

"Um." Will raised an eyebrow then looked to Natalie, who shrugged. They exchanged looks and hand gestures until Mike urged one of them to speak with a stern clearing of his throat, his eyes darting between them.

"We didn't get any of the answers we were looking for," Natalie said.

"Yeah, and some of his answers were really annoying," Will added.

"I can understand that." Mike nodded in agreement, eyes wide. "But, did you get anything out of him?"

"We asked him if he was God and he said that depends on what you think God is," Will began.

"And we asked him if there's any difference between us and a cell and he said no," Natalie said.

"Oh yeah." Will pointed at Natalie. "When we asked him if we have free will, he said if our choices didn't matter, then he could tell us anything, which makes sense, but it was still an annoying answer."

"Wow, you guys asked him some pretty deep questions. Did you make a list of questions to ask or something?"

"No," Natalie said with a casual shake of her head. "I wanted to know why he crashed at my house and ruined my life. We ended up in weird places. He said we were asking for the meaning of life, and I have all the answers I need."

"Do you?" Mike asked.

"Yeah, it turns out I did." She smiled, then paid Will a loving glance.

Will returned the fond look, then turned to Mike. "What do you ask him about?"

"Mostly about my daughter."

"You have a daughter?" The two teenagers shot up in their seats, eager for details. "Where is she?" Natalie asked.

"I, uh… don't know."

"What?" Will's question rode on the back of a soft breath, almost inaudible.

"My daughter was kidnapped a long time ago. I'm trying to get her back. That's why I'm here, with this ship, this crew, that's why I attacked the bunker where I found you two. I'm trying to rescue my daughter, and the crew is here to help me."

"Oh my god, that's so sad," Natalie cupped her hands over her mouth.

"I'm sorry, Captain. We didn't know," Will said.

"It's okay, I've never told you two about any of that. You kind of ended up flying with us out of circumstance." The question was not hurtful, and easy to brush off.

"So the rest of the crew knows everything, but not us? That's messed up," Will teased, shaking his head.

"Yeah, Captain! And, Rick told me you made the star mapping program that ships use. Shouldn't you be famous or something?"

"I *was* famous. I was also kind of an entitled dick back then."

"How did you end up out here?" Will asked.

"You guys really want to know?"

"Yes!" Natalie and Will said, almost in tandem.

Mike adjusted in his seat. "Okay then. I'm sorry if I get emotional. It can be hard to talk about. Where should I start?" he asked himself.

Over the next thirty minutes, Mike shared his story with Natalie and Will.

Mike

23

Hope

Twenty years ago, an old friend tried to convince Mike to help establish the Ministry of Science. He was an affable man with a joke for every occasion and a genuine desire to help others. Mike had witnessed impractical acts of selflessness, so he could be sure his intent to better the world was genuine. He asked Mike to create a unique system to protect the scientific work being done within the Ministry. Mike declined, despite his friend's insistence on the contributions he could make. Soon after, he died in an accident. In his mourning, Mike accepted his friend's request.

He threw himself into the founding of the Ministry and worked with a minimum of sleep to adapt his private projects and create a computer system the likes of which nobody had ever seen. The Ministry system's unique nature and construction precluded it from being compatible with public software and rendered it impossible to breach. It was soon touted as the most advanced and secure digital system in history.

Following high praises, Mike became one of the first High Archons, the highest rank of all Ministry officials. Brash and arrogant with a reckless curiosity, he saw eye to eye with a number of high-ranking

Ministry officials that were more comfortable wading into questionable waters for the sake of scientific discovery and progress.

Mike's brain was challenged like never before, and the thrill of the job grew with every new challenge he overcame. Within a few years, Mike was involved in several off-the-books projects that needed unique software development. Charged with the programming and algorithms, Mike had no concern or idea of what he created.

His heavy involvement with the ministry led to meeting another founder, Albertus Schulze. Many called him the Wizard because of his otherworldly understanding of the universe. He and Mike were both masters of their fields in ways that others could never hope to be, and the two visionary Archons got along splendidly.

After five years of friendship, they figured out they were on the same project, which was segmented for secrecy. Mike took the opportunity to work alongside Albert, mostly for the good company. In the underground bunker where they worked together it was rumored there were gardens in one of the floors below, and one day he was struck with an urge to explore. Instead of eating in the cafeteria, he went for a stroll to find them. A garden would be a relaxing place to eat and work.

The rumored garden was indeed on one of the lower levels and was as beautiful as rumored. Spacious and colorful, it was lush with exotic flowers from around the world. The entire floor was thick with the invigorating aromas of the garden. A bench with a small round table was an inviting place to eat in serene silence.

"Hello." A soft voice startled Mike and he looked up to see a stunning woman with flowing blonde hair and big blue eyes a few paces away. Hands together, she clutched a box and paperback book instead of a tablet. Without a shred of makeup, she had a radiant glow about her. Taken aback, Mike cleared his throat.

"Hi."

"I usually have my lunch on this bench," she said.

"Oh." Mike was in the center of the bench with no room on either side of him.

"It's okay, I can find another." She turned to leave, but Mike stopped her.

"No, no, please." He scooted over. "Have a seat."

"I don't want to be a bother."

"Not at all. You're—it's beautiful here." Face flushed, Mike could hardly look away. Her kind eyes and a sweet melody in her voice were captivating. Then, she smiled at him and his heart melted.

"Thank you." She took a seat on the bench next to him.

"I'm Mike."

"Faith," she said, their eyes locked.

For months they met and got to know one another. Her opinions were deep and well developed. She was a goofball who yearned to get into the minds of the characters in her stories and live in their worlds. Her talks about themes got Mike to re-read books he had not read in years. Even her opinions on cultures and customs were informed and compassionate. Most refreshing of all, she never talked about work. She was a fountain of thoughtful insight who quickly became the highlight of his day. Mike looked forward to lunch and spent more time at the bunker where she was stationed.

Then came a day when she did not show. Mike ate lunch on their bench alone for a week. When Friday came and she had not appeared he looked up the Bunker's personnel, but could not find her. He feared she had been transferred until the following Monday when he arrived for lunch, and there she was. But, she was unwell. Quiet and distracted, she cradled and massaged her head.

"Are you all right?" Mike asked with concern.

"I've just got a terrible headache." She rested her head in her hands.

"Oh, let me get you something for that." Mike went to jump off the bench but she grabbed his hand to stop him.

"No," she said, atypically fragile. "No, it's okay. It's not like that."

"What do you mean? A headache is a headache. Unless it's a migraine. Is it a migraine?" He spoke quickly, wanting nothing more than to make her feel better after not seeing her for a week.

"No, not quite."

"What's the problem, then?"

"I don't want to talk about it, I just want to enjoy our time here." She squeezed his hand and forced a weak smile. Mike was not about to let go of her hand, so he stayed, but the incident troubled him. For the rest of the day he was distracted.

"Michael!"

Mike jumped at the sound after staring into a screen of code. "Al, Jesus Christ, what the hell, man?" Al was leaning over his shoulder, *deep* in his personal space.

"I called your name three times," Al said, to his surprise. "You seem so different lately. What is wrong?" he asked, fidgeting with a helmet.

"Oh, nothing. Just a girl."

"You? Distracted by a woman?" Albert laughed. "I don't believe you."

"That makes sense, but I can't seem to get this girl out of my head. I think about her when I wake up, I think about her when I fall asleep. While I work, even."

"My friend, is this the first time you know love?"

"Love? No," Mike scoffed at the idea. "I don't—there's no such thing as romantic love. It's not a thing. So, not a valid hypothesis."

"Love is love, romance is optional. You are in love, I can *see* it. Many things make sense now." Al smiled slyly.

"I—what? What… what are you working on over there? What is that thing? It looks like you're trying to make a helmet to keep aliens from reading your thoughts."

"There is not enough aluminum foil for that." Al chuckled. "This is for my part of the project."

"What *is* your part of the project?"

"We are not supposed to talk about it, but we are both High Archons. Who will scold us?" Al laughed. "It is a helmet for translating brain waves. I believe it is an interface for an artificial brain and intelligence."

"Should I be creating countermeasures in case we're messing with an illegal Ai?"

"I do not believe so. This sort of device means they are creating an artificial brain that can not interact with technology without the interface."

"So, that part is meant for the human?"

"I would imagine. It is a helmet, after all. Would you like to try it on?"

"Sure, why not?" Mike rolled his chair over. Al strapped the helmet onto him and jiggled it to ensure it was secure.

"Perfect fit." Albert patted the top of the helmet and there was a light poke at several points on his head. It was then that the troublesome feeling he had been living with coalesced into understanding.

"Wait a sec," Mike said as Albert unbuckled the helmet. "Is this being tested?"

"Not unless artificial brain is complete, I imagine." Albert shook his head. "It is not yet calibrated for testing, and your algorithms are incomplete. If we test on people, it would cause them immense pain." Albert removed the helmet from Mike's head, but the little pricks on his scalp sent Faith's words running through his head in a loop. *I've just got a terrible headache. It's not like that. I don't want to talk about it.*

The next day, he found Faith waiting for him at one of the benches. "Hi!" She welcomed him with a smile. Instead of greeting her he sat down, grabbed her hand, and leaned in close. He opened his mouth, but she cut him off. "Yes."

"What?"

The answer to your question, her voice chimed, but her lips did not move. He looked around, and then into her eyes. "Yes, I'm single."

Mike looked back in confusion. "I—wait, what?"

Faith put a finger over his lips. *I know what you want. You can't ask me that question here. They'll hear you.* "I'm a woman, I know things." She winked.

Mike's body trembled, heart sinking. With a distant gaze, he sat shaken to his core.

You should kiss me, so they aren't suspicious.

Mike leaned in and when their lips met, an energizing shock ran through his body. Lightheaded, his heart raced and his body tingled from head to toe.

Oh, shit, Al was right, an involuntary thought rushed through his mind. Faith blushed and looked away.

"Where's your lunch?" she asked.

"Huh?" Mike looked around. He was so focused on his question that he forgot to grab lunch. "I guess I was so nervous about talking to you today, I forgot it."

"How long have you been psyching yourself up to ask me that?" Faith played along with the make-believe story.

"It's hard to say."

"Let's share." She handed him half of her sandwich, already cut diagonally.

"Thanks for lunch." Mike smiled. *This is even worse than an illegal AI. I'm so stupid.* Mike chewed a bite of his sandwich. All the pieces had come together.

"You're welcome," she said. *Don't be so hard on yourself.*

They're experimenting on you, and I'm helping. You didn't volunteer, did you?

No, but you didn't know.

Now I do.

There's nothing we can do about it. They'll kill you. Let's enjoy our time together.

I intend to, but I'm not letting you stay here as a guinea pig. I... I can't.

I've been in one dungeon or another my whole life. It's nice to form a physical connection with somebody, not just watch them from afar, hearing their thoughts but unable to talk to them.

Why can I communicate with you? Am I...?

No, Faith cleared her throat, bringing Mike's attention out of his head and back into the physical world. *I can hear your thoughts and project mine.*

"So, I realized yesterday that I never asked where you were born," Mike said, reminded they needed to maintain a surface-level conversation.

"Canada." Faith smiled at him. "My mother was from the Netherlands." She eased Mike out of his discomfort.

When you hear me, you can respond and I'll hear. So, we can have conversations like this without being on our lunches.

Her smile burst into his mind like a scent reviving a memory. It was a dagger through his heart. All the months they had been talking, she knew who he was and what he was doing but treated him with nothing but kindness.

A week later, Mike brought up his concerns with Al at a convention and they devised a plan. Two weeks later Faith turned up missing while Mike and Albert were reported to have been involved in a terrible accident. Most in the ministry mourned the loss of two great prodigies, but some were sure something was amiss.

Mike and Al went on the run with Faith and traveled through the colonies as discreetly as possible. A year and a half after their escape, on July 4, 2170, Mike and Faith had a beautiful baby girl. Neither of them had ever before felt such a joy that they were brought to tears. Mike wanted to name her after her mother, but she refused. A compromise led to her being named Hope.

Hope was one and a half when Al went off on his own, vowing to get a hold of Mike when he had secured the safest possible place for them to live. He did not want them raising a child on the run, and so he disappeared.

Mike had made friends in his time on the run, all of whom proved instrumental in their survival. His past became a secret. He was another veteran shat on by the system who decided to take his future into his own hands. Veterans in the colonies gave them aid without question. He had fought in the war but had not seen as much combat, not to mention his service was followed by a successful career in the Ministry.

Always scouting their exits ahead of time, Mike never stayed still, always careful and prepared. Once, while scouting a way out, Faith screamed and called out to him in his mind. He sprinted back to their shelter but was not fast enough.

Kicking open the back door, rifle tucked into his shoulder, Mike burst into the hideout. He scanned the room but there was nobody there. There were only bodies. Two friends died defending his family. Then his heart shattered into a million pieces, never to be the same again.

Lying next to a broken child's bed and broken glass was Faith. Blood pooled around her, eyes staring straight ahead. Mike dropped his rifle and ran to her, kneeling in a pool of blood. Bawling, he pulled her close. There was no way to know how they got around her telepathy or knew where they were, but it did not matter anymore.

"Faith," he croaked, holding her to his chest, petting her soft hair. "I'm sorry. I'm so sorry." Mike held her tight as lights ran over his face. He pulled his head up to see through the broken windows, floodlights rising from the ground. "Hope," he whimpered, watching the lights disappear, leaving him alone in the darkness.

Ulfberht Crew

24

Bonding

Natalie and Will stared at Mike, wide-eyed and their mouths ajar. Natalie wiped away tears from the corners of her eyes and took a deep breath.

"That's so sad," she said.

"So, you haven't seen her since she was two?"

"That's right. I took it really hard at first, that's when I met Maya. She helped me get back on my feet, and that's when I got this ship, started recruiting, started figuring out how to find her. My whole life revolves around trying to get her back, and this crew has vowed to help me, each for one reason or another."

"How did you find this ship?" Natalie asked.

"Luck."

Natalie rolled not only her eyes but her head and torso as well. "Okay, but like, what's the story?"

"I'm not telling you guys *another* story right now."

"Aw." Natalie's shoulders dropped and she pouted, but it had no effect on Mike.

"Sorry about your wife," Will said, thinking back to the night he rescued Natalie. The thought of losing her propelling him to do whatever he needed to get her to safety. He could relate to Mike's story, except without the massive success and riches. Still, he empathized with Mike's absolute dedication. Until then, Mike's skills and history had been a mystery to him.

"It was tough, but I've been lucky to have this crew to help me put myself back together. How are you guys holding up?"

"We're okay, I guess," Will said, sharing a look with Natalie, who nodded, squeezing his hand. "I guess things were kind of weird for a minute, but this is… life now. And, you guys are cool."

Natalie nodded in agreement. "Is it okay if we ask about your daughter?"

"Sure." Mike shrugged. "What do you want to know?"

"What was she like?" Natalie asked, thinking of the girl in her dreams.

"She was playful, and she always wanted to snuggle." Mike's eyes became distant and a smile crept upon his face. "She used to love it when I would do that cheap magic trick with the ball in a cup. You know what I'm talking about?"

"Yeah." The teenagers nodded.

"You did that to entertain her?" Natalie asked with a raised eyebrow.

"Well, she was watching a magician do it on a show once and was so captivated, I tried it, and she loved it. So, I kept doing it." Mike put his hands up with a smirk.

Natalie's mind rushed to her childhood, playing with her dad, fixing cars with him, and while she tried to hold it in and take her mind elsewhere, she could not. She wilted, a tear running down her cheeks. Will quickly scooted toward her, wrapping an arm around her. She fell into his chest, wiping her tears, settling her emotional breakdown in Will's comforting arms.

"You know, everyone in this crew has lost someone or everyone we care about. If you ever need to talk to any of us, we're here for you guys," Mike said.

"Thanks, Captain." Will rubbed Natalie's back. "If we can help you get your daughter back somehow, let us know."

"Yeah! Totally," Natalie said with a brilliant smile, straightening up, wiping her face clean of tears. "We really appreciate you guys taking us in."

"I appreciate the offer. I don't know what you could offer but you've been great, so you're welcome here." With a groan, Mike pushed off one of his knees and rose to his feet. "I guess I'll leave you guys to your games. Thanks for the chat, and for being honest about talking to One."

"This was nice. But, before you go…" Natalie raised an arm to stop him as if she was in class, a habit so engrained she did not even think about it. Mike stopped and faced the teenagers again, looking to Natalie. "It was cool hanging out, and I like hearing your guys' stories. Will and I were wondering if the crew would want to do like a board game night once a week? With the print lab, we can print whatever game we want to play."

Mike smiled and nodded, rocking his head from side to side. "Yeah, that sounds fun. We don't really have a lot of communal activities like that. How about Thursday?"

"Thursday is perfect! Any day is perfect, really, but yeah! Thursday! Will and I will print some games."

"Looking forward to it."

Part

3

Threads of Destiny

Ulfberht Crew

25

Freyja Fly-By

Traveling twenty-one and a quarter light-years from Earth at two hundred times light speed, the *Ulfberht* took thirty-nine days to reach the second-farthest colony from Earth. As HR-8832 was not a catchy name for a colony, the star was long ago renamed Freyja.

The planet Freyja Four rested on the outer edge of the star's habitable zone, filled with rocks, oceans, plants and animals big and small like on Earth. The teal sky, full of fluffy white clouds, turned dark green and orange with the sunset. The flowery aromas and fresh air offered a revitalizing change of pace from the stale, metallic smells on the *Ulfberht*.

"Perimeter security is down. Let's move in close," Mike ordered. He, Shin, and Farouk approached a large, solitary house on a hill surrounded by tall trees with red leaves. Shin stood ready behind cover near the back door and Farouk waited by the kitchen entrance. Maya kept watch from the top of a nearby hill to cover their backs. Inside, the view from the security cameras looked normal.

Hidden in the wilderness near the front door, Mike typed away on a tablet so he could work discreetly without holograms revealing his position. He slid the small tablet into an armored compartment on his leg and drew his taser-pistol.

"Okay team," he whispered. "House is unlocked and scramblers are down. Shin, find our guy."

Shin eased out from behind a tree and scanned the house for their target's location. "He's in his study. First floor, in the back."

"Breach positions, ready check." Mike hustled to the front door and greased the joints.

"Ready by the back door," Shin answered first.

"By the kitchen, ready when you are," Farouk said.

"Move in."

The three of them opened their doors and slinked inside, taser-pistols in hand. There was nobody in the house except them and their target. If they could get him by surprise, it would be a quick and easy abduction.

Using thermal vision, Shin watched their target work at a desk. He approached slowly with careful, quiet steps. A meter away from the study's door, a floorboard creaked beneath Shin's feet. He stopped dead in his tracks and watched the red and orange figure in the study for a reaction. The figure looked up toward Shin, then after a pause, rushed to grab something from under his desk.

Shin hurried to the door and kicked it open, but was forced to take cover before he could fire a shot. The target, a balding, pudgy man with big ears and fat cheeks, fired at Shin with a short-barreled rail gun and blasted a hole through two walls. Shin fired around the doorway. The target flipped his desk onto its side and blasted holes in the wall to force Shin back.

"Careful," Shin warned, "he's got a railgun." Even though Shin would survive a railgun shot, it would leave him bruised and hurt more than he cared to deal with. Rushing through a wall would make him an easy target. All options considered, his best bet was to wait for his team.

"Hey Shin, remember when I said you could borrow my shoes and you said you'd lose mobility?" Maya said on the audio channel.

"Thanks for the reminder. Super helpful." Another shot whizzed by Shin.

"Yeah, my sound-cancelling shoes would be super helpful. I was thinking the same thing just now."

Shin fired around the corner to keep the pressure on while he waited for his team to flank. There was a sudden burst of shattering glass. He peeked around the corner and caught a glimpse of the study's window busted open. Their target fired a shot at the door. Shin jumped back and the doorframe exploded into splinters. The target stepped on his chair and leapt through the broken glass.

"He's outside." Shin turned on his thermal vision again. He ran to the front. "Coming to you, Mike."

Mike rushed back down the hall to the front door, which he had left open. The man ran by in a full sprint. His belly bounced with every step, puffy cheeks jiggling.

"Heya, Brad," Mike yelled. The chubby man turned, eyes wide like he had seen a ghost. He tried to fire at Mike, but was too slow.

Three shots stabbed into him, sending a massive shock through his body. He twitched and shook, momentum carried his body through the air. His rifle tumbled out of his hands and he hit the floor with a thud, dirt grinding beneath him. While he was still twitching and disoriented, Mike injected him with a sedative.

"Cat's in the bag. Let's get back to the ship. It's about damn time I found you." Mike rolled the fat man onto his back and blurred into a silhouette.

*"Technically, **I** found him. You guys turned an easy snatch-and-grab into a shoot-out. Way to go!"* Maya chirped with peppy sarcasm.

"I'll take the blame for that." Shin heaved the fat man over his shoulder. They tossed their cargo into Will's Prowler and hauled him back to the *Slap Attack*, which was cloaked in a clearing nearby.

When they arrived, Maya had the *Slap Attack* ready to go. They tried to strap him into a seat, but the straps were too short, so they tied him down with rope like a piece of furniture. Once finished, they left the remote property behind and within a minute they pulled out of Freyja Four's upper atmosphere and were headed back to the *Ulfberht*.

"Hey Mike!" Farouk called from the cockpit. Mike joined him a moment later. "The ship's really low on power. With that regulator out after *Oasis*, I think keeping her cloaked this whole time drained her. She's running real sluggish. Until we get that part from Leo we should only use it when we need to."

Mike eyed the stars. "I don't know, there's a lot of bandits out here."

"We didn't see any on the way in."

"Get us out of security range first. We don't want anyone picking us up coming out of cloak." Mike returned to the cabin.

"Roger that."

In the cabin, Maya broke the silence that followed takeoff. "That went well."

Mike nodded. "It felt good to take him down."

"I would imagine. It would have gone smoother if I would have gone in alone."

"Probably true. But, I wanted to do it myself, and *you* don't like working with people. Nothing I can do about that." Mike gave her an exaggerated shrug.

"You just wanted to pump him full of electricity," Maya contested.

"True, but now we have to get him to talk." Mike crossed his arms, staring at Bradley, incapacitated across from him. "That won't be easy."

"You should probably keep the kids away from him," she suggested. "You don't want to scare them."

"Good idea. I'll try avoid them even knowing he's here." Mike sent Rick a message to ensure Natalie and Will would be nowhere near them while they transferred Bradley to the brig.

"Don't think you're getting out of training today, by the way." Maya said.

"But, we bagged our guy. We should celebrate, take a load off."

"Nikolai said you about got your ass kicked on *Oasis*. But, today *was* a success," she confessed. "So how about only one hour instead of two? Spend the other celebrating."

Mike gave Maya a sidelong look. "It wasn't that bad, but I'll take it."

Although his hand-to-hand training alternated between Maya, Nikolai, and Farouk, Maya kept them all in order and maintained Mike's training schedule.

"Oh yeah, I figured out how Natalie and Will found out about One," Maya said.

"How?" Mike perked up in his seat.

"Someone didn't check their messages and spilled the beans."

"Farouk." Mike sighed, eyes closed.

"Got it in one. It all worked out, though. Hell, we even got a game night out of it."

"That *was* fun. Remember when I wondered if Hope would like board games, and Natalie said she had a dream with a girl named Hope who loves board games? Do you think that could be her?"

"Probably an imaginary manifestation Natalie made in a dream after talking to you about her," Maya reasoned.

Shaking his head, Mike crossed his arms, slouching in his seat. "I thought it was a possibility. I asked One about it, but he didn't say anything."

"How out of the norm," Maya dragged out the sentence to emphasize her utter lack of surprise.

Mike changed the subject to the upcoming game night and they carried on for a while. Without any sign of trouble, the cabin livened up.

"Mike! Get over here," Farouk called from the cockpit.

Mike unbuckled himself and hurried out of the cabin. Farouk pointed at the hologram over the console with their ship in the middle, represented by a green fighter. Behind them were six red dots at the edge of the map. "A pack of ships cruised by us, then they turned around. They're following us."

He shot an irritated look at Farouk for suggesting they travel uncloaked, even though he had been right.

"What? What were the chances? Besides, we're *really* low on power."

"Have they tried hailing us?"

"Nah, they're just creepin'." A call appeared on the console. On the long green hexagonal holo-button, *Ulfberht* was written in black. When Mike tapped the floating button a video of Nikolai appeared on a new screen.

"I see you have suitors pursuing you," Nikolai said.

"You know our good looks get us into trouble," Mike said. "Addie on her way?"

"Coming in the *Dragonfly*. ETA, less than one minute." Nikolai checked the console.

"Mike, they're gaining." Farouk brought Mike's attention to the hologram. The pack of ships accelerated toward them.

"Step on it!" Mike grabbed a hold of the nearest handlebar and braced himself for a burst of speed that never came. The ship accelerated, but not with enough force to knock anyone off balance. The enemies continued to advance, but not as quickly.

"Seriously?"

"If I hadn't turned off the cloak, we'd be adrift right now," Farouk said.

"I will provide you with cover fire when you are in range." Nikolai's hands were at work on the console.

The red lights in the cockpit flashed to alert them of incoming fire, which rattled the ship. Farouk leaned hard into the yoke and rocked the ship from side to side to avoid enemy fire. Three of the ships raced to cut them off and surround them. They swooped in together and opened fire in Farouk's path while the other two applied pressure from behind. Farouk swerved to avoid attacks. Mike was too busy hanging on to notice the green dot zooming toward them on the map.

"Let's have some fun!" Addie's voice boomed over the speaker.

The small Razorback model fighter—named *Dragonfly*—flew past them and engaged the enemy ships. Her opening shots sent one of the ships spinning away. She circled around and three enemy ships broke off their pursuit to fight her.

Addie proved to be more than they could handle. *Dragonfly* was a fast and incredibly maneuverable fighter with no shortage of directional thrusters. In Addie's hands it was practically impossible to hit, which made the dogfight one-sided. Addie was never in their sights for long and always found a way behind them. She would cut left, cut right, up and around, spinning to fire as she passed with uncanny precision.

The bandits quickly turned back. Some laid down cover fire while others fired tow-cables at their disabled allies and dashed away.

Addie caught up with the *Slap Attack* and pulled alongside them on their glide back to the *Ulfberht*. The image of her glowing, exuberant face appeared on a screen next to Nikolai.

"Is everyone okay?" she asked.

"We're good here, Addie, how about you?" Mike let out a sigh of relief.

"Hah!" Addie let loose an adorable cackle. "They didn't stand a chance!"

"I'm glad I decided to play it safe after that Dragon Claw attack. Thanks for the backup." Mike said.

"Of course! You should have me be ready to go any time you guys are off ship. I'll jump at any chance to take my baby out for a spin."

"Let's do that. We're going to cruise in at this speed. Go ahead and dock first."

"See ya back on the ship!"

Rebels

Resistance

"CALVIN, THIS IRISH RED IS DELICIOUS," LEO TOLD HIS BARTENDER, a slender light-skinned man with dark hair, a well-groomed beard, and tattoos down his left arm.

Hearthstein was one of Leo's favorite local bars, but he had not visited since before the arrival of the UEG almost a month ago. The unnerving man that commanded the UEG troops always had eyes on him. Leo had lived in paranoia until he became accustomed to their methods and was confident enough to return.

"I *knew* you'd like it. It's from a Martian brewery I found, Red Knight. I ordered some of their other beers. If they're as good as these we might have a bunch of new stuff coming in." Calvin wiped down a freshly poured pint and set it on a coaster in front of another customer at the bar then returned to Leo.

"I'd say that's a good call." Leo set his glass down, looking up at a nearby screen. The hologram displayed horrific wreckage of a shipyard after an attack. The banner at the bottom read: Pirates Attack Endorian Shipyard. Beneath it: 24 August 2184.

"Just like the *Oasis* attack last month. The world is messed up, man. I hope that kind of thing doesn't come to *us*." Calvin swirled a rag through a glass.

"Yeah…" Leo grumbled, far more aware of the dangers around them than Calvin. "Do they know who is behind the attacks yet?"

"Nah, they have no idea." Calvin leaned on the bar and glanced around the sparsely populated room to check if anyone would need another drink soon. "So, where you been, Leo? We miss you around here, man."

"You know, busy." Leo shook his head. Two dings rang behind the bar.

"You need to come around more. You used to be down here every Wednesday. Now I feel like there might be someone else, another bar, maybe? I've been feeling pretty jealous." Calvin feigned sadness. He tapped on a console hidden behind the bar and grabbed two empty glasses, moving back to the taps.

"Hah! You got me. The bar down the street stole my heart. What can I say, Cal? You're not puttin' out. Daddy's got to get his rocks off *somewhere*."

"I knew it! Breakin' my heart, Leo. Breakin' my heart. I thought you were different. I thought you cared."

Leo chuckled, swirling his beer. "Nah, nothin' like that. It's been a little hard to get out. Been so damn tired after work. You know what I mean?"

"I feel ya, buddy." Calvin set the beers down on a round tray for a server and tapped on the hidden console again. He grabbed a small glass and filled it halfway. "I pick up so many hours here I miss out on stuff *I* want to do." He brought the sample to Leo and set it on a new coaster in front of him. "This is another new one we've got."

"Thanks." Leo smiled and sat up straight. "Maybe you guys need some new people around here."

"Yeah, people who don't call out so much. Maybe we should invest in robots like practical business-folk," Calvin said.

"Nah, no robots. I like people."

"You're lookin' kind of down. You all right?" Calvin leaned on the bar.

"Yeah, I'm good." Leo tasted the sample. "Jesus." He looked at the empty glass in his hand. "I like this one even better."

"Told ya, we're getting some new stuff around here. You want one of these after you finish up that one?" Calvin took the empty glass from Leo.

"Nah, I've got to get going," Leo chugged the last of his beer and set down the glass. He placed his cash card on the glass bar top. Calvin paid little attention to Leo paying his bill until he hopped off the barstool.

"Woah." Calvin stopped him, noticing the massive tip Leo had left. "Leo, hey…"

"Don't worry about it. You're always *lookin' out for me*, you deserve it." Leo waved off Calvin's concern.

Calvin leaned in to whisper, "Leo, come on man. This is too much."

"If it makes you feel better, you can stare while I shake my ass on the way out." Leo winked, waving as he walked away.

Confused and in disbelief, Calvin watched Leo exaggeratedly shake his ass on his way out of the bar. Calvin looked down at the transaction to make sure he had read it correctly, then back at the front door. A well-dressed man in a booth on the other side of the room got up and left the bar, abandoning a full cocktail, the ice melted, condensation visible from afar. He watched the video feed from outside. The shady character mumbled to himself and followed Leo down the street.

"What the hell?" Calvin wondered aloud. Four subtle dings rang from the console behind the bar, but Calvin ignored the new orders. He glanced at them in passing on his way to the back.

"Cindy," he called to the thin blonde with a pixie cut slicing limes and pointed behind him with his thumb. "Could you cover the bar for a minute?"

Calvin took a staircase to the staff area and burst into the owner's office following a quick knock. The owner of the bar was a tall man with a large nose, dark hair and a purposefully scruffy face. Laid back and personable, he was dressed in casual attire. He had been speaking with a shorter beady-eyed man in slacks and a button-up shirt.

"Excuse me." He closed the door behind him.

"Hi, Cal, come on in whenever you want," his boss greeted sarcastically with a wave of his hand. "I was just thinking how much I'd love it if you barged in right now, or any time."

"Hey Dan," Cal greeted the beady-eyed man sitting across from his boss. "Chris, sorry to interrupt, but I think we need to talk, like right now." A nod from Chris dismissed Dan. Calvin gave him an awkward wave and made sure the door was closed.

"This better be good, Cal," Chris said as Calvin took Dan's seat.

Calvin scooted the chair in and leaned over the desk to whisper, "I think Leo's in trouble."

"What makes you think that?"

"Well, you know how we've been wondering what the hell this UEG ship is doing here? Well, Leo hasn't really been around. Then today he comes by, tips me *stupid-fat* and then some guy in a suit followed him out of the bar," Calvin explained. "The guy was here the whole time Leo was and didn't even touch his drink."

"I see." Chris leaned forward in his chair, hands together on his desk. "Most of the UEG presence we've been tracking is in Leo's area."

"Why are they watching Leo?"

"I don't know, but whatever those Earthers are up to, we can't trust 'em. Leo is the best damn go-to guy in the area. We need to figure out what he's dealing with. Let's keep our distance and study up before we reach out."

Ulfberht Crew

27

The Machine

IN THE *ULFBERHT'S* DIMLY LIT INTERROGATION ROOM, BRADLEY was an emaciated pile of flesh that would tip out of his chair if not for his hands being cuffed behind him, as his feet were to the chair's legs. In the month since he had been picked up, he had endured physical torture, barely slept, was questioned daily and had been fed intravenously; deprived of food and water. His attitude gave him a punchable face, and a desire to cause him further discomfort led to a busted nose and a swollen eye.

Bradley had little to offer. Maya headed up the interrogation and got a name: Donovan Fletcher. He had been put in charge of the project after Bradley. Even with the parameters of his malware updated, it was still a waiting game, and Mike was done waiting.

The door swung open and light flooded into the room. In a delirious daze, he pulled his head up to see his visitor. He forced his good eye open and expected Maya as it had been every time before, but this time Mike stood at the threshold, fiery eyes burning a hole through him. Since they day he was picked up, Bradley had waited for Mike to show himself.

"It's about time," he said, worn down to his core.

Mike stepped inside and closed the door behind him. Bradley watched Mike grab the nearby chair and sit across from him without saying a word. The two men stared at each other, each gritting their teeth at the presence of the other.

"How you doin', Brad?" Mike asked.

Bradley let out a pained chuckle. "Fuck you."

"Brad, I've got a problem." Mike closed the door behind him.

"The hell do I care?" To Bradley, problems for Mike were cause to celebrate.

"My problem is you, Brad. You're not giving me what I need."

"That rogue agent already got what I know," Bradley grumbled. "Put a bullet in me and get it over with."

"You recognized Maya?" Mike asked.

"I recognize everybody I've seen." Bradley was unimpressed, or feigned it.

"You wouldn't have got a chance to recognize Al, then, since you haven't seen him," Mike said.

"Is the old wizard still alive? I'll be a son of a bitch." He shook his head. "How does an arrogant cock sucker like you make so many powerful friends?"

"Everyone needs a computer guy," Mike joked. "And, I may have been a cocky in my youth, but I wouldn't say arrogant."

"You don't think you were arrogant?" Bradley asked. "I s'pose you think you haven't tortured me for the last few weeks, you've just politely asked me some questions."

"I do think I heard Maya say *please* once or twice. I'm not like I used to be, though. I've been through a lot, learned a lot since then."

"Bullshit. You've always been a prick." Bradley's words slurred. He leaned over to spit a wad of blood on the floor. "You get everythin' handed to you."

"I've worked hard for everything I accomplished in my life, and I left it all behind for *her*," Mike growled.

"So, you just stole her! 'Cuz the goddamn child prodigy thinks he can take whatever he wants. Even back then you walked around like you owned everything." Bradley snarled, his ancient hatred for Mike alive as it was when they worked together.

"I didn't *steal* her, I *rescued* her!" Mike leaned in, enraged by Bradley's twisted perspective. "She was held captive her whole *life*. Nobody *belongs* to anyone!"

"Bullshit! You think you can have whatever you want. I had to work for every millimeter. You were *offered* that High Archon position. You didn't even care about the Ministry. You were part of it for the glory; to add to your legacy. How'd that work out?"

"Selling your soul to the devil isn't the same as working for what you have," Mike countered. Bradley was no stranger to bribes, cover-ups, and moral ambiguity. "You got in bed with the most inhuman shit that's ever walked the Earth and you think *I'm* the asshole? You're telling me that fathers and daughters should be torn apart? That people should be held captive forever because they're great science experiments?"

"If it's *your* daughter, hell yeah!" Bradley said spitefully. Mike shot to his feet and smashed a fist into Bradley's face, wrapped it around his neck, his other fist cocked back.

"What if it was *your* daughter? Could you go on living your life knowing what they're doing to her?" Mike roared.

Bradley choked and struggled to breathe until Mike let go. He paced away, running his hands through his hair. Bradley coughed and caught his breath while Mike collected himself. After a minute, the room remained silent, but both men were composed. Mike sat down and took a deep breath.

"Brad, I have two things I need to say. First, I know you're hiding something, and I'm going to find out what that is."

"Good luck with that." Bradley huffed and looked away, sure of himself.

"And second... Well, the second part is more of a question. Do you remember that machine Al and I built?" Mike coaxed a worried look from Bradley, who nodded. "We built another one and modified it a little to work with a *normal* human brain."

Bradley trembled in his seat. His stomach churned and his heart tried to beat a path out of his chest.

"Why?" he said, shaking. "Why would you do that?"

"That brings me back to the beginning of this conversation. You're not giving me what I need." Mike looked into Bradley's eyes and watched fear set in. Before Bradley could accept it, he took a journey down the five stages of grief. First, came denial.

"Bullshit." He shook his head. "You wouldn't. You're an ass, but you're not... no. You wouldn't do that."

"There's nothing I won't do to get my daughter back," Mike said intensely, looking him in the eye so Bradley could see his absolute resolve.

"No." Bradley shook his head again. "No. Nope. I don't believe you."

"Farouk," Mike boomed. "Bring it in."

Mike stared Bradley down without a word, contemplating one last time the line he was about to cross. Unbeknownst to him, his face melted into a regretful, apologetic grimace. "I'm sorry, Brad, but this is how you seem to want it."

Glowering at Mike, the boom of heavy footsteps in the hall drew closer. The door swung open and banged against the doorstop. Bradley's eyes widened with horror. In the doorway loomed a hovering platform with a steel box at the base. A pole jutted up from it and sprouted into wires which plugged into a headset that hung from a hook. Farouk pushed the benign-looking machine inside while Mike moved to give him space.

After denial, came anger.

"Fuck you, Mike! Stop! You son of a bitch!" Bradley struggled. "Don't do this!"

Mike stood over the withered, broken man and pitied him. Bradley's life decisions had led him to that moment, from which he had given himself no way out. Farouk positioned the device behind him. Mike pulled the helmet from the hook and placed it on Bradley's head.

Bradley bargained as Farouk slipped out, door closed behind him.

"Come on, please. I'll tell you whatever you want to know."

"You're hiding something. Tell me what it is." Mike strapped on the helmet with no expectation that Bradley would tell him anything.

"I told you everything I know about your daughter. I swear."

"That's not the right answer," Mike said. If Bradley knew something that could help him but did not pertain to his daughter, he could be telling the truth while keeping Mike from his goal.

"I don't… I don't want to go out like this." Bradley shook his head. Depression came quickly.

"You know, back then, when I got the hunch you were testing the stuff we were making and asked you about it, you said no. But, it seems to me you know exactly what this could do to someone," Mike deduced. "Consider it karma."

Bradley had no response. The assessment was impeccable. The commitment in Mike's eyes confirmed there was nothing he could say. Even if he survived, parts of his brain would be deduced to goop. If he relaxed, he might survive to live a miserable life, but Mike would get everything he was trying to hide. If he resisted he would die, but might be able to withhold information from Mike. Bradley accepted his fate. He took a deep breath, held it in, then let out a long sigh.

"Anything you want to say before we get started?" Mike asked.

"You going to flip that damn switch or you goin' to make me listen to you talk?" Bradley said boldly.

Mike reached for a switch on the box but hesitated. "Are those your last words?"

"Last words." Bradley pondered for a moment. "Yeah. Get off your high horse. We have different standards, we cross different lines, that's all." Bradley stared straight ahead. "You're about to cross one you wouldn't have crossed before, right? As we get older we become more of who we are. Think about it."

"I realized that when I built this thing. Goodbye, Brad." Mike flipped the switch.

A series of lights on the helmet lit up to indicate that all nodes were operational. Bradley's mouth gaped with pain and he hunched over. An eerie croak escaped his throat then his body contorted as the pain shot from his head to his toes. Teeth clenched, he convulsed violently. His heavy breathing steadied and he moved less but continued to twitch and cringe with the occasional horrifying groan.

A screen appeared on the wall next to them, opposite the observation room. It was a video of an older memory. Through Bradley's eyes, he opened a beer and took in the view of his new home on Freyja.

"I don't care about your life." Mike faced the video. "Let's see if you're holding back. What do you know about my daughter?"

The image swirled and morphed into a new memory. Bradley let out a harrowing groan from the pit of his soul. In the new memory, Bradley sat at a wooden table outside his house with a man across from him.

The thin, handsome man had genetically modified red eyes. His vulturous, pointy nose and chin, well-combed black hair and condescending demeanor were familiar. Mike immediately recognized him as the man to whom Bradley used to report. He had not aged a day in the sixteen years since they last met.

A cold chill ran up Mike's spine. Fists clenched, he whispered, "Lazarus…"

"*What a quaint home you've made for yourself. How is life in the colonies?*" Every word was soaked in velvety disdain. Polite small talk came off as a blatant formality. Most importantly, the memory was from within the last four years, as that was when Bradley moved to Freyja.

"*It's not Earth, but I've got a nice place thanks to the Ministry's retirement plan. I can get pretty much anything I want out here, no hassles,*" Bradley said.

"*No prying eyes. Must be nice,*" Lazarus said.

"*I do miss some of the work I used to do for the Ministry. I like a challenge. Oh!*" Bradley perked up. "*I heard the UEG caught up with that dickhead a few years ago. What happened? Is he dead? Is the project running again? I've been anxious to find out but I haven't spoken to anyone who would know.*"

"Smith was reported dead. The subject..." Lazarus gave him a dejected groan.

"No..." Bradley was shattered. He set down his drink and put a hand over his forehead, covering part of his vision.

"Not to worry. The project is up and running with the subject's daughter and Donnovan Fletcher at the helm. She is still, unfortunately, too young. In about fifteen years she'll be a viable asset. We've begun designing her a permanent home."

This was good news. It meant she was somewhere temporary and easier to breach. Also, they would be moving her at some point, which would be the perfect time to strike. Bradley had indeed been holding back.

Mike glared at the real Bradley, noting his bloodshot, bulging eyes. He said nothing, in order to not disturb the memory. From time to time, Bradley grunted through clenched teeth, breathing rapidly. It became white noise to Mike.

"They had a daughter?" Bradley's memory laughed. *"I was always recommending they move the subject somewhere made just for her. Where did they decide to make her permanent home?"*

"Oh, don't worry about that. It's a little something we were imagining before Smith's vanishing act. I was actually hoping you might be able to help us with something," Lazarus said.

By all appearances, that had been all the information Bradley had to give. However, Lazarus in a recent memory gave Mike the chills. He let the memory continue, with hopes to learn what they were up to.

"Whatever you need." Bradley sat up. It did not matter what Lazarus had to offer, Bradley wanted to be a part of it.

"After you said you missed the old days I knew you would be interested. You've noticed the pirate problem around here, haven't you?" Lazarus asked.

Blood oozing from his ears, the real Bradley let loose a haunting moan.

"They're a nuisance around here. I can't believe the colonies are so lawless."

"The colonies have been trouble since they seceded from Earth," Lazarus said. *"That lawlessness is a problem, especially if the UEG ever hopes to extend their influence into the colonies."*

"No..." Mike said to himself, eyes welded to the screen. Fixated on the memory, he no longer paid Bradley any attention and did not notice that his eyes, nose, ears and mouth were turning into rivers of blood.

"That would be a dream come true. The people out here don't even realize how much they need the UEG," Bradley said with a blend of disgust and concern.

"Fact of the matter is we've noticed these pirates have got some real firepower lately, stuff we don't have at home. Haven't been able to get our hands on any of it yet, but if you could find out where the weapons are coming from..."

"Say no more." Bradley put his hand up. *"I'll find out where these pirates are getting their weapons and take care of it."*

"Actually." Lazarus held up a finger. *"These weapons pack quite a punch. We would like their designer alive."*

"Alive? I thought this was going to be fun?" Bradley chuckled. *"Besides, I'm sure if I purchased one, I could figure out how it works."*

"Perhaps, but if the designer is who I think, we want to use him. He's a clever fellow, as you'll see if you manage to purchase one of the weapons," Lazarus said.

"Whatever you say. So, what's keeping the UEG from moving into the colonies? It can't be a single rogue weapons designer."

"No, de-weaponization and public opinion are to blame for that. But, we have plans to change those as well," Lazarus said.

"Oh?" Bradley leaned in. *"Do share."*

"Th-The old f-f-fashioned way, of c-course." Lazarus grinned. *"Just keep y-y-y-y-your eyes op-p-e-e—n-n-n-n-n..."*

The image fluctuated between shapes and cloudy blobs of color, with voices that cut in and out like a skipping audio track, then it disappeared.

Bags under his eyes, mouth agape, Bradley's face was melted wax. Thick trails of blood streamed from his eyes, nose, ears, and mouth. He was dead in his chair.

Mike smacked the wall hard enough to rattle the room. Disappointed and at a loss, he clenched a fist and closed his eyes, trying to calm the tempest of anger, fear, and frustration brewing in his chest.

The door burst open and slammed against the doorstop. Farouk stormed in, eyes fixed on Bradley. He paced back and forth, fists balled up and anxious to hit something. Finally, he gestured with both arms at Bradley and yelled, "What the *hell*, Mike? What the hell is *this*? This shit ain't cool!" Farouk's booming voice trembled, angry but tempered, even if only by a hair.

Still deep in thought and focused on his own emotions, Mike paid little attention to Farouk. He took a deep breath then let it out.

"Say somethin'!" Farouk demanded.

"Oh my god, quit your whining." Mike pounded the wall with his fist.

"What the fuck did you say?" Farouk leaned back in surprise.

"I know what I did, okay? I knew when we built this thing." Mike turned around and pointed at Bradley. "This guy was a piece of shit. He did this to people. This is fuckin' karma or ironic justice, but it's what he deserves! You signed on to help me get my daughter back, not tell me how to do it."

The two men stared each other down in front of Bradley's corpse. Farouk huffed and flared his nostrils, still trying to calm himself. As angry as he was, he was unwilling to break his word. There were greater concerns to deal with.

"Gentlemen, let's not cry over spilled milk." Maya's cut in, her hands pressing against their chests to push them apart.

"I wasn't fuckin' crying. I was protesting immoral actions, as is my duty as a human fuckin' being," Farouk said.

"What did you think, Farouk?" Maya raised an eyebrow, a hand on her hip, giving him a look that told him he was the only one on the wrong page. "Did you think we were going to send him home when we got what we needed? Or, turn him in to the police? Maybe he could have been a new crewmate? This was his destiny the moment we picked him up." She chopped an arm in the air at Bradley.

Farouk's eyes drifted away in consideration of Maya's logic. He had never considered what would happen to Bradley.

"This, though?" Farouk pointed at Bradley. "This is fucked up. Don't we have the technology to, like, see people's dreams and thoughts? We've had that shit for more than a hundred years. Why didn't we use that?"

"It's not the same," Mike shook his head. "Those can be blocked with genetic or cybernetic modifications. This can't. You also can't control and force them to give you what you want, like I can with this."

"Why didn't you make it, you know, not a damn nightmare machine?" Farouk's anger waned.

"Because he did this to other people," Mike said again.

Farouk gave Bradley a pitied look. "Everyone deserves a chance at redemption."

"Gave it to him. He didn't take it, so I brought this thing out."

"Have you used this on anyone else?" Farouk probed to see if his moral conflict was greater than this one incident.

"No." Mike shook his head. "This was meant for *him*."

Farouk looked back and forth between Mike and Maya, then down at Bradley. "All right. If you use this again in the future, though," Farouk began, but Mike finished his sentence for him.

"We'll make sure it doesn't do this."

"All right." Farouk nodded. "All right, cool." They shook hands and moved along.

"Well that's settled, let's get on to business," Maya said with a clap.

"Yeah, who was that creepy demon-lookin' motha'fucka'?" Farouk asked.

"The exact same question I had, in fact, practically verbatim," Maya chuckled. "Actually Mike, did you catch what he said about a weapons designer?"

"Yeah, I had the same thought. We should check on our friend."

"I sent him a message while Farouk was on a rampage, I'll let you know when I hear back."

"Let's hope he's okay. As for your question, Farouk, I met that demon-looking motherfucker back in our Ministry days. The project Al and I worked on together, he would come around sometimes. Brad here would kiss his ass and bring him up to speed. He'd give us the run around when I asked about his clearance and who he reported to. I knew he wasn't Ministry, and I didn't find him in the UEG systems either. He introduces himself as Lazarus."

"His name is Lazarus?" Farouk said in dumbfounded amazement.

"He's really letting it all hang out isn't he?" Maya joked.

"The hell kind of name is that? Why doesn't he just walk up to people like, 'hey, I'm the Devil, 'sup.' He ain't even trying to hide."

"He *wants* you to know you're talking to the devil," Maya said.

"Thing is, he hates the colonies." Mike kept the conversation on track. "He's one of those people that thinks they should be offshoots of Earth, so that's where the majority of their resources should go."

Farouk and Maya rolled their eyes and scoffed. "The worst," Maya said.

"Brad was one too," Mike nodded at Bradley. "I'll call the *Yellow Shark* and have Tony's crew turn Brad's place upside down. Let's find out what he was doing."

Lazarus

28

Man of Virtue

"Mr. Donald Brown? Do you mind if I join you?" asked a tall man in a fine black suit that contrasted with his pale skin. From behind an empty chair at a white table, he stared at Brown with haunting red eyes. Alone on the balcony of a café surrounded by treetops, there were not even cameras to protect him.

A tall, muscular man in sunglasses blocked the entrance to the empty balcony. Hands together in front of him, the stoic man was bulky with cybernetic prosthetics hidden beneath a gray suit with a matching fedora. It seemed to Brown that it was in his best interest to hear the stranger out.

"If you'll tell me about those eyes." The thin black man with sharp cheekbones set down his tablet and ran his fingers through his grizzled hair. He had been reading a book and drinking coffee in his own expensive but flashier navy suit with a gold chain that dangled from his belt. Brown grabbed his coffee and eyed the bodyguard.

"Genetic manipulation makes for some *interesting* possibilities. This," the man motioned to his eyes, "is simply a novelty," he lied. In actuality, he could see infrared, ultraviolet, and a broader spectrum of light than most humans. The red tinge his eyes acquired was an unexpected consequence of repeated manipulation.

"And your friend there?" Brown nodded to the hulking man. "Looks like he's got his fair share of prosthetics."

"You've got a good eye, Mr. Brown. Lenny there is my bodyguard. His cybernetics are top of the line, all custom," he bragged. Brown nodded and examined the bodyguard.

"You've got to be careful with those *cyborgs*," Brown said loud enough to offend the nearby bodyguard, but he did not flinch. "People say with too many implants, replacements, modifications, you lose your personality, your empathy, your humanity. You become a mindless golem, and you can't trust someone who has lost their humanity." Brown checked the bodyguard for a reaction.

"That golem follows my every command. I've had it for years." The man smiled. In disbelief, Brown looked back and forth between them. "Surprised?"

Brown squirmed in his seat to get comfortable again. "Golems are as illegal as it gets. The human rights and cybernetic restrictions broken to create one are staggering."

"But they can stop *anyone* who dares attack you if you equip them with weapons-grade cybernetics, and they have no moral hang-ups about following any order. There really is *no* competition. I can show you how to make one if you'd like. Men like us could always use a good bodyguard."

"I tried doing it without breaking any laws, but I started with his body instead of his brain," Brown cringed. "My cyberneticist wasn't very good with brain work."

"That was your mistake. You need to break their humanity away piece by piece, replacing it as you see fit. It takes some manipulation, but you can *coerce* someone with no prosthetics at all into becoming your golem."

"I thought I could use more emotional and psychological approach. I appreciate the offer. I'll think it over. I didn't get your name." Brown's right hand reached out.

"My name is Lazarus." He shook Brown's hand.

"Is that your birth name?" Brown leaned back and crossed his legs. His shoes were as lavish as the rest of his outfit, complete with a gold buckle to match his chain.

"It's the name you know me by." Lazarus folded his hands together, symbolically closing the door on the topic.

"I suppose I can live with that." Brown took a sip of his coffee then set his cup down on a saucer next to a half-eaten coffee cake. Anyone familiar with shady characters like Lazarus knows it is unwise to waste their time. "What can I help you with?"

"Help me? You misunderstand. I've come on behalf of a mutual friend, and I'm here to help *you*." He placed a clear business card with a red devil-tailed L on the table and slid it to Brown. The card synced with his contact lens and revealed its information.

Intrigued and uneasy, Brown nodded his head and scooted his chair forward, clearing his throat. "I may not be in need of help but if this is who is offering, who am I to turn it down? How do you intend to help me?"

"Your great-grandfather was a very smart man. He invested in all the right industries before he left the church life. His good decisions now put you in a fortuitous position. Under the right circumstances, you could become one of the richest, most powerful men in the world."

"My father, my grandfather before him, and my great-grandfather before him were all men of God, as am I. I only seek to amount riches so I can help others, like the good book says." Brown cracked a disingenuous smirk at the comment. He believed in the concept of what he was saying, but not the physical expression of it. His altruistic nature did not normally extend beyond those who could help him in some way.

"Please, Mr. Brown." Lazarus held in a laugh, his hand in the air for Brown to stop talking. "The disingenuous man of God has been done to death. I believe, actually, since the very advent of religion. Don't try to act like a holy man when your great-grandfather was an evangelical pastor who used the money from his congregation to live an extravagant life and later invested his riches into Babylon Mining, which is what now affords you a private balcony at this expensive café. We need not put on airs here, Mr. Brown, not between us." Lazarus gestured at himself and Brown, who was taken aback by Lazarus's frankness and knowledge of his family history.

"There's more to me than a caricature, Mr. Lazarus. I may have grown up rich but my father would leave me with my cousins every summer, and they had no money. I learned to scrap, I learned to hustle, to scam, to cheat. I learned how to get my way. Don't think me some simple rich boy. I bring much more to the table than that," Brown said with a confident sway in his body and a sparkling, toothy grin.

"That's quite the pitch, but unnecessary. Babylon Mining makes ship-building for Arc Industries much cheaper. Your grandfather was sharp to establish a starship company on the shoulders of what his father had built. XJB is expensive. The UEG has been shopping around, but no other company would be more cost-efficient in terms of quality and price than Arc Industries." Lazarus pointed to Brown.

"As I'm sure you know, my grandfather didn't start Arc alone. His partner and his descendants have always been against making weapon ships. No fighters, patrol ships, battleships, nothing; like we're goddamn SpaceX." He shook his head with a frown.

"Well, let us speak hypothetically for a moment," Lazarus proposed, to which Brown agreed. "If you *were* to build a battleship, let's say the size of that cruise ship you're building." He motioned, the name floating out of reach.

"The *Felicity*," Brown said.

"That's the one. A battleship that size, not custom-built but made on an assembly line and without the fancy amenities, how many ships of that magnitude do you think Arc could produce in a year?"

Brown examined Lazarus for a moment and ran the question through his mind several times before he responded. There was something larger at play.

"The extent of UEG weapons is restricted to Earth Orbit Security. Why would the UEG need so many battleships?" Brown asked.

"Please, Mr. Brown. We're speaking hypothetically," Lazarus said with an unnerving, sinister playfulness.

A dark cloud rolled over Brown, followed by an eerie churn in his gut. Something dreadful was afoot. Lazarus had a dangerous question to ask him, but he had not asked it yet. When he did, Brown needed to answer correctly.

Brown gulped and squirmed in his seat. He took a drink of his coffee and set it down, then clasped his hands together. "If I were to estimate, one factory could produce a ship like that in about eight to twelve weeks. So, that's four to six per factory, per year, but production times increase over time. I own twenty-eight factories throughout the system, most of which just build parts. So, to fully answer your question, Arc could make forty to sixty large ships per year if I devote all of Arc Industries' resources to the task."

"Well, Mr. Brown, the UEG's fifteen-year contract with XJB expires this year and the UEG hasn't settled on a replacement. I think Arc Industries should have that contract. I know your partner is against it, but I'm sure an intrepid businessman like yourself can figure something out." Lazarus grinned.

"I… do have something I've been working on," Brown admitted. "He's old, he's smart, but I think I can work over the family."

"It sounds like you already have it well in hand," Lazarus smiled. "You've got a good head on your shoulders, Mr. Brown. I feel that with the unexpected nature of life, if a tragedy were to strike, the people would need someone like you, a man of *virtue* to help them find the *right* path amidst the chaos of a changing world. I get the feeling that role would fit you well."

"Is that so?" A cold tremble rattled his insides. Whatever was going on, this was his chance to get ahead of it. A once in a lifetime opportunity was being presented to him on a platter. This was about more than a contract, about more than money or the UEG. This was about power. "And, what *is* the right path?"

"When our lives, our very freedoms are threatened; the people must rally behind the state." Lazarus leaned on the table, closer to Brown. "It may require sacrifice, but law and order are clearly the way. We can't have crime and chaos running amok in our society when our survival requires *everybody's* cooperation."

"Who would I be not to answer such a divine calling?" Brown said, to which Lazarus smiled. "If God requires, I too shall be a shepherd to the people like my great grandfather once was."

"Excellent!" Lazarus clapped his hands. "Then I shall report to our mutual acquaintance that you'll be pursuing the contract with the UEG. I'll leave you to figure out your business." Lazarus pulled from his pocket a small, flat metal square slightly thicker than a coin. "This should help you smooth things out."

Brown held his hand out flat and Lazarus dropped the small square into it. Brown drew a circle around it and a credit value projected over his hand: one hundred million.

"More than I need," Brown huffed.

"Think of it as a welcoming gift. As long as you show me faith, devotion, and discretion, you'll be well taken care of. But if you go the way of Lucifer, we shan't cast you out. You'll be turned to salt," Lazarus said gravely.

"Mr. Lazarus, I believe we understand each other perfectly," Brown's voice did not tremble, but his insides crumbled in fear.

"Good." Lazarus stood from the table, and Brown with him. "I should leave you to your work."

"I've got quite a bit of it ahead of me. It's been a pleasure, Mr. Lazarus."

"Naturally." Lazarus turned in one quick motion and walked away with a confident strut. The man Brown had been led to believe was a golem stepped aside to let Lazarus pass and then followed him out.

Brown eased back into his seat then clutched his chest and let out a long, deep breath. "Oh my Lord. That was terrifying." He collected himself, then returned to his reading and coffee.

Rampart Crew

29

Pre-Gaming

"SAM, YOU SACK A' SHIT. YOU TOOK MAH GOD DAMN QUEEN?" JAMES threw his arms in the air. Their spectators, Matt and Amber, laughed as Sam placed James's queen alongside six other pieces he had taken, as opposed to James's two. The four of them sat in the *Rampart's* mess hall, still in orbit over Ganymede, awaiting their target's return.

"He's got ya in four moves," Matt pointed out. As time went on, he became more talkative. The group hung out regularly once they had settled in orbit over Ganymede.

"Three," Sam corrected him.

"Three moves my ass, Sammy boy. What do ya think about this?" James took Sam's knight with his rook.

"Check." Sam moved a bishop from across the board and took James's knight.

"Ya dirty cock suckin' bishop." James held back a rant, shaking his fist at the holographic chessboard. "I forgot he was there." To Matt's amusement, James had got too worked up and no longer saw things that were right in front of him. James sighed and ran a hand through his uncharacteristically messy hair. "I was gonna try get ya queen."

235

"I know, I baited you into it. That's why you're in check now," Sam said.

"All right, this ain't ova'." James scanned the board. "Shit." He scratched his forehead, bewildered by his dwindling options. After an upset sigh, he moved his king behind a pawn.

"Check." Sam moved the same bishop over a few spaces, in line with the king.

James growled at the board and moved his king again. To the reception of amused snickers, Sam moved his queen into place.

"Checkmate."

"Fuck you, Sam!" James shot out of his seat and tipped over his king. "Ya dirty... basta'd." With a shake of his head, James headed for the galley.

"You got wasted again, bro!" Matt hollered at James as he paced away.

The volume in the *Rampart's* lounge became louder now that their entertainment was done. Clusters of the crew littered the lounge enjoying their off time. People tended to enjoy their leisure time in the colony, but the *Rampart's* lounges were still lively with the buzz of the crew.

"Can't take a loss, can he?" Sam noted while they chuckled at James.

"Oh yeah! That guy's a shitty looza'. That's why I told 'em he should play ya. I told 'em I thought he could beat ya." Matt laughed and smacked the table. "Now I gotta hear 'em cry like a little bitch, but it was worth it."

"I want to watch James lose more. That was exactly what I needed before my shift. Thank you, Matt," Amber said.

"Doesn't night shift get boring? With everyone asleep and nothing going on?" Sam asked.

"Gives me a chance to read. I've been on my own since I was eleven, I don't do bored. But, this was fun." She gestured to the game.

"Yeah, we been here two months and I didn't know you guys played chess," Sam said. "Why didn't you start talking sooner? We could have been playing all this time."

"I leave most a' the talkin' to James. But, I think we'd a' been gettin' ah asses kicked fa' two months if you knew. You're good, Sammy. I'd ratha' do zero-grav patrols every day than play chess with you."

"Why? Is that a pain in the ass?" Sam asked.

"It's the *worst*," Amber groaned. "But I've got to get going, guys. Thanks for the entertainment." She slid out of her seat and the men stood chivalrously. "Lunch tomorrow, Sam?" She walked backward, pointing at Sam with a smile.

"Wouldn't miss it." He smiled back, watching her go.

"You move like a turtle, Sam." Matt sat back down.

"Shut up. I haven't dated in a really long time. It's scary. What's so bad about the patrols?" Sam eagerly changed the subject.

James returned with four open beers and placed one in front of each of them. "Where the hell did Amba' go?"

"Work. You hear this guy, James? He wants to know if zero-grav patrols are a pain in the ass."

"Sammy, they're like if every time you made a move in chess, you also got to kick me in the balls. Zero-grav patrols can suck ma' cock. Oh yeah, P.S. Fuck you, Matty, y' lyin' bitch." James gave Matt the finger then took a drink of his beer.

"Why is it so bad?" Sam asked.

"Because, gravity gea' is nice, but not nice enough to walk around in it for a few hours. It's all floaty," James explained. "We've had a'tificial gravity fa' what? Thi'ty, fo'ty years? Why ain't they made 'em betta' yet?"

"Well, we've only been able to adapt artificial gravity into space suits for a little over a decade, but it does sound like they should be better."

"It's 'cuz there ain't no demand," Matt said. "Same reason we still use the same arma we did at the end of the war."

"I bet you could fix 'em up with that big brain a' yours." James pointed at Sam's head. "Think ya could make 'em betta'? You've been workin' on that custom arma, right? You gonna give ya'self all the sick gear and leave us with standard issue? Some friend." James shook his head with a look of disgust.

"Maybe." Sam smiled. "I could try. I've never actually played with gravity gear."

"I'm sure you'll figure it out," Matt encouraged him.

"And if ya do, we have our own suits we brought with us. Fix 'em up in case we eva' get caught up doin' some bullshit mission in space." James gestured around him.

"All right, all right, I'll give it a shot."

"Yeah! That's what we wanna hea'!" James smacked Sam on the shoulder.

"Hey, why don't ya come out drinkin' with us tonight?" Matt offered.

"There's a massive gamin' event and a football game tonight, so the bar is goin' a' be *packed*," James added.

"Thanks for the offer, but you guys know I don't really like big crowds. Too many people makes me feel anxious." Sam shuddered.

"Well, since ya got totally shit-faced last time, ya off the hook. But, that means you're buyin' the first and last round next weekend, all right?" James was quick to ditch Sam, with no desire to be reminded the whole night of his three straight losses.

"Screw that." Sam scoffed. "I'll buy the first round and an appetizer."

"That's a deal, buddy." James and Sam shook on it. James took a big drink from his beer. "Well, I know you're always sad to see us go, but we've got to get dolled up for the ladies." James stood and stroked his face. "Finish Amba's beer, will ya? See ya." James and Matt walked away.

"See you guys later, good luck tonight." Sam waved goodbye.

"With a mug like this, who needs luck?" James smacked his grinning face.

Sam smiled and watched his friends finish their beers before they left. He had worked so much in recent years that he had missed out on hanging out with friends and having a social life.

"I think tomorrow. Tomorrow I'll ask her out." Sam pulled Amber's beer closer. "Or I'm going to keep missing out."

"Hey, Coleman!" A crewman yelled from across the lounge. "You guys going out for Smash International tonight?"

"We don't need a reason to go out and drink like you pussies," James taunted. They threw insults back and forth, then James and Matt tossed their bottles in the trash, and they were gone.

Rebels

30

Wasted

IN A GANYMEDE CITY APARTMENT BUILDING, CALVIN, A bartender at the Hearthstein Pub, shuffled through his closet in search of the perfect shirt to wear before going out. A small pile of shirts lay on his bed, all of them wrong. He needed to look cool, but friendly. He threw off a blue shirt and put on a black one with a giant steel scorpion on the front. That was the winner: the perfect shirt.

A loud knock on his door broke his train of thought and he hustled to answer.

"Chris!" Calvin greeted. His friend and boss stood in his doorway, hands in his coat pockets. He was dressed better than usual, but it had nothing to do with what lie ahead that night.

"Hey, Cal. You ready to go?"

"I think so, how do I look?" Calvin posed, highlighting his shirt.

"Fine? This isn't a date." Chris shook his head.

"I'm still *nervous* like it's a date. I'm kind of trying to do the same thing, right?" Calvin hurried into his room and returned jamming his wallet into his pants pocket.

"You trying to bang someone tonight?"

"No." Calvin shook his head, locking the door behind him. "I mean, you know, trying to make a good impression, trying to get someone to like you."

"You try?" Chris gave Calvin a sidelong look. After a groan from Calvin, the two walked all the way to the street without saying a word. The quiet only exacerbated Calvin's frayed nerves.

"How's Leo doing?" Calvin whispered, anxiety heightened by the silence. Conversation would help him relax.

"Not yet. Wait 'til we get there," Chris whispered.

With his mind a torrent of fear, excitement, and concern, Calvin looked into the sky. His eyes rested on the Ganymede Ring; a massive ring built around the moon that protected it from radiation and boosted its atmosphere. To accomplish this it increased the moon's spin by running an electric current through the ring to pull on the core. Mars and other moons had similar rings. Over time, some rings became megacities that wrapped around their respective celestial bodies.

The grandeur and majesty of it, the massive feat that it was to create such a thing always gave Calvin a sense of wonder, which in this instance helped calm his nerves. Jupiter was larger in the sky than a pen held in one hand toward the horizon, but it was not as impressive as the ring of lights stretched across the sky, the massive structure a testament to human potential.

The prolonged silence had taken its toll on Chris, so he talked about work. Specifically, the success of the new Martian beers they had recently brought in. It helped boost Calvin's confidence as well as do away with any lingering anxiety.

They arrived at a short metal building a few blocks away from the city's bar-filled downtown district. The pair turned a corner into an alley and walked in the darkness alongside the abandoned building. They entered through an emergency exit and continued down two stories into the building's dark, empty basement. Their mobile devices provided light to avoid piles of trash left by squatters.

The basement walls were lined with bricks made from the rock excavated to create the space. Certain walls were accented with wood panels. Chris pressed along the wall and shined his light around until he found what he was looking for. From the wall, he withdrew a loose brick and reached inside. There was a shallow click from the nearby wood-paneled wall. Chris returned the brick and led Calvin to the wall, then pressed against it. A hidden door in the wall swung open effortlessly.

"Watch your step." Chris led the way and Calvin closed the door behind them.

A rickety spiral staircase made of old grated metal clanked with each step. They descended into Ganymede City's original colony; a vast and cavernous underground city that had been abandoned for a ground level city once Ganymede's atmosphere could support support human life.

"Hey!" Leo called out, already waiting for them nearby. He hurried to swallow what was left of his hot dog. "You ready, Cal?"

"I think so." Calvin patted himself down. "This is scary and awesome. You join up with the underground thinking there's going to be super spy stuff, but there isn't, like ever. All we do is smuggle people away from Earth. We've finally got some excitement around here!"

"Don't ever wish for excitement, kid." Leo covered his mouth. He finished chewing and swallowed his food before he continued. "You weren't here for the war. You haven't seen what people will do when they're desperate. Whatever you think you've seen, war is worse. You don't want it; trust me on that one. You shouldn't be as psyched about this. Take it seriously." Leo pointed a stern finger at Calvin's face.

"You got it." Calvin nodded, drained of his excitement.

"Good. Is there anything we can get you? You look a little freaked out."

"Gee, Leo, I wonder why. I'll take a hot dog," Calvin said.

"Sorry," Chris answered for Leo. "We got a couple for him since he can't go out right now." Leo's presence there was under the radar. "We can't let them think Leo's up to something."

"Let's go over the plan. You know the plan, right?" Leo asked.

"Yeah. I go in there, make friends, leave with them," Calvin said.

"There's one thing you've got to know." Leo made sure to get Calvin's attention. "There's cameras at that bar. So, tomorrow someone's going to come looking for you. They're going to ask you some questions. You just need to relax and tell the truth."

"The truth?" Calvin exclaimed.

"The *truth*. Obviously, don't tell 'em it was a plan," Leo clarified. "Tell them about the night, hanging out with the guys, whatever you guys talked about, what you remember, the usual stuff."

"Okay." Calvin rubbed his hands together with a nod. "I got this."

"You can do this." Chris patted him on the back.

"What are their names again?"

"We didn't tell you. Get their names when you meet them. Everything's got to be totally natural," Chris said. "You want a shot before you go?"

"How about two?" Calvin said with faux jubilation.

Two shots of tequila were exactly what he needed, but one of them had worn off by the time they arrived at High Borne Pub. Ganymede City's downtown district had seen some new regulars in the last few months, but that night it was packed from wall to wall with a rowdy mob of drunk patrons. The room was hot and thick with the scent of alcohol, peanuts, and joint smoke. Calvin entered more relaxed than he had been when Chris picked him up. He needed to act natural, so he went straight to the bar to greet friends. On the wall was a long row of beer taps, each with a unique, decorative handle.

"Hey Tina," Calvin greeted the short-haired blonde with a nose ring and a sleeve of colorful tattoos down her left arm. A few screens showed an exciting football tournament on Atlantis, where it was daylight. The players were returning to their start positions after a goal. The rest of the screens hosted an action-packed gaming tournament on Earth.

"How you doing Cal!" Tina greeted. "The usual?"

"Damn straight," Calvin said. Another patron who was there first heckled Tina for pouring Calvin a drink right away.

"We've got a special going on right now. Buy a pitcher, get a joint half price," she offered. The bubbly head of the beer ran down the side of the glass. She poured some out, wiped it with a towel, and set it on a coaster in front of Calvin.

"I think I'm good without this tonight. Hold onto it for me, will ya?" Calvin slid his cash card over the bar, trading it for the full glass in front of him, filled to the brim with a dark yellow beer. Other bartenders and servers rushed by around them, many briefly greeted Calvin when they passed.

"What you been up to, Cal?" Tina asked while she worked to fill a never-ending chain of orders.

"Drinking! I found a couple prime breweries on Mars. Got Chris to start importing their stuff. People love 'em. They're our highest sellers," Calvin bragged.

"Congratulations! I'll have to swing by. It's been a while."

"Thanks!" Calvin said. The crowd erupted behind them, then simmered. "Smash International is out of control." Calvin checked the tournament which had stirred up the crowd. People on the edge of their seats watched the fast-paced three-axis fighting game.

"True, but Rogue and TUF didn't get invited for being too green. So, it's not *too* distracting." Tina looked for the bright side.

"TUF?"

"The Unstoppable Force. People callin' him TUF now. At least until he takes Jester's name." Tina nodded with a grin.

"Ah, TheRealJester. That cocky shit talker guy." Calvin was all caught up.

"You mean the *undefeated* shit talker guy with gorgeous eyes," Tina corrected.

"Just 'cuz he hasn't lost doesn't mean he *can't* lose." Calvin took a moment to watch the fighting game.

"Hey, Tina!" bellowed a tall, muscular man with well-combed brown hair, slick and shiny. "Let me get two mo'e." Tina nodded and pointed at the man.

"What'cha drinkin'?" Calvin asked the towering giant, arms as big as his head.

"Space Dolphin Stout." He placed two empty glasses on the bar for Tina.

"Not bad, you should try the Warrior Stout," Calvin recommended.

"Yeah? Hey-o Tina, can I get a Warria' Stout instead?" he asked. About to pour his drink, she scooted over to the correct tap.

"Here you go." Tina set the drinks down on the table and hurried back.

"If I don't like it, it's yours, bill and all." The man took a sip of the dark beer and nodded in approval. "That's a damn good beer! Kinda smoky. I'm James." He reached out to shake Calvin's hand. His grip was crushing, but it was clear he wasn't trying to be rough, he was simply strong as hell.

"Calvin, I'm a bartender at the Hearthstein Pub," he introduced himself.

"Nice to meet ya, Calvin. I haven't been to your ba', I'll have to check it out. Thanks fa' the suggestion." James took another drink and raised his glass. "Good stuff."

"That's from a Freyjan brewery. They make the best damn stouts in the colonies." Calvin pointed at James's drink.

"That's good to know. What else you recommend?" James leaned in to listen.

"If you're looking for stouts, Skull Rock is another good one, on par with what you're drinking now I'd say, a little more coffee-flavored. After that, Rebel and Big Stick are the best ones they've got here. They've got some good dark lagers and IPAs too."

"That Skull Rock sounds like my kind 'a drink. Can you drink that whole thing in one go?" James pointed at Calvin's full beer.

"Can *you* keep up?" Calvin challenged. James laughed then bumped his glass into Calvin's. The two chugged their beers and slammed them down on the bar at the same time. "Not bad."

"Not bad yaself, let me get ya next one. Hey Tina! Let me get three Skull Rocks!" James raised three fingers high in the air and Tina gave him a thumbs-up.

"You're going to drink two?" Calvin asked.

"Nah, the other one's for ma' buddy, I know he'll like it. Nice shirt. I *love* Steel Sco'pion," James said.

"Steel Scorpion is like beer. What would life be without it?" Calvin pointed at his shirt. "I've got everything they've done. I even have a secret track that's data-locked to the stick it's on."

"You gotta be shittin' me! I'd love to hear it!" James boomed over the noisy crowd. A moment later Tina arrived with a pitcher, three mugs, and a joint instead of three beers like James had asked for. James thanked her and tucked the joint in his ear. "Hey, why don't you join my friend and I?" He handed Calvin the glasses.

"I'd love to hang out with some Scorpion-heads." Calvin took the glasses. "So, where are you from? I don't recognize your accent." He followed James back to his table.

"I'm from Boston, Earth," James said over his shoulder.

"Awesome. I've never been to Earth." Calvin followed closely behind James, who effortlessly pushed through the dense crowd, making the journey easy for him.

"You gotta go, man. It's the human homeland!"

"I'm so busy all the time, and I don't have a chip!" Calvin spoke loudly so James could hear.

"Oh yeah, I fo'get you don't all get chipped." James set down the pitcher on a small round table and Calvin placed the mugs next to it. "Calvin, this is Matt, my best friend in the whole damn universe, known 'em since we were shittin' our daipa's." James patted the leaner, more reasonably sized man on the shoulder.

"Hey, Calvin," Calvin shook hands with Matt as he pulled up a chair. The crowd went wild again and an announcer from the gaming event called the match.

"Nice to meet you." Matt raised his voice to be heard. He was less talkative and jovial than James.

"This guy knows his beer." James poured a drink for Matt, who took in the aroma before he drank.

"Damn. That's a good one." Matt nodded.

"On Calvin's recommendation." James poured a drink for Calvin and himself, then held his glass up in the middle of the table. "Cheers, fellas!"

Their glasses dinged like a bell in a fight and they spent the rest of the night getting so drunk that none of them could stand. Calvin introduced them to all his favorite beers, and somewhere along the line, they started doing shots. They outlasted the events as well as most of the patrons who came to watch them.

"How are you guys doing?" A cute server with a captivating smile removed three empty glasses from the table.

"We're—*hic*—good." James waved.

"Okay, we're closing up in a few. You guys all settled up? Need us to get you a ride or something?" she offered.

"S'okay, we're walkie," James slurred.

"Just paid, too," Matt murmured. The young woman smiled, wished them well, and was on her way.

"We," Calvin paused to burp, "we gotta finish these."

"See? James, we too jrunk," Matt said. "We… nah, less get a ride."

"Too 'spensive," James protested.

"We have spents accounts, dummy."

"S'principle," James stabbed the table with his finger. "Shouldn't coss s'mush."

"Where you guys at?" Calvin asked.

"Like, six blocks, uh…" James held a finger in the air, then tapped on his hitch. "Where's the ship?" A holographic arrow appeared over the hitch, pointing behind him.

"I'll walk with you guys," Calvin offered. "Thizz my city. I know shorecuts."

"Cool." James nodded.

"Thanks, man." Matt rested his head in his hand.

"We still gotta drink these." Calvin sighed, staring at the half-full beer that still awaited him.

"Lez do it!" James smacked the table, causing Calvin and Matt to jump. The three men grabbed their drinks and bashed them together, then chugged them down in one go. Calvin slammed his glass down first, with James and Matt close behind. "You, sir." James pointed at Calvin. "You can drink."

"You guys too." Calvin pointed back with a smile, teetering in place.

"You good?" Matt asked.

"I'm good!" Calvin leaned on the table to keep his balance as he got to his feet.

Matt and James also struggled to stand up straight. Matt stumbled into Calvin in their attempt to navigate through the sea of chairs between them and the exit. They said their goodbyes to Tina and left as a group. All three men leaned on one another to stay upright. None of them could walk by themselves. Still loud and rowdy, the boisterous trio marched three blocks through streets and alleys.

"Cal. You gotta come jrink with us again. You're awesome." James put Calvin in a loving headlock. With Calvin on one side of James and Matt on the other, eyes half closed, the three of them walked in a cluster, leaning on each other for support.

They entered another alley, there was a sudden and brief screech of tires behind them and a van door slid open. Calvin turned enough to see two masked men with bats rush out of the van. Before any of them could react, the back of their heads were bludgeoned and they were knocked unconscious.

James and Matt's bodies were dragged into the van, their hitches tossed away, and Calvin was left alone in the alley to sleep off the night.

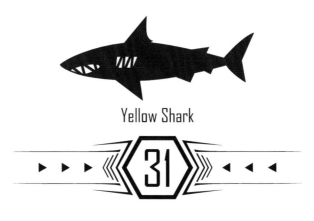

Yellow Shark

31

Blood in the Water

ANTHONY FRANKLIN, CAPTAIN OF THE *YELLOW SHARK*, PREFERRED to go by Tony for the name's perceived fun and personable nature. He was a tall, lean man with a waterfall of wavy shoulder-length black hair and eyes as deep and dark as a black hole. Tony kept his face mildly scruffy but dressed stylishly; vests, slacks, and nice shoes.

Tony knocked on walls and felt his way around Bradley's house in search of slicks; false walls and accessible but well-hidden compartments where spies hide important items. All around him the house was alive with the shuffling and banging of his crew performing a thorough search.

Tony stepped around a hole in the floor, which revealed a steel-alloy sheet under the wooden panels. Even with the power off, it was still operational and obscured their tech from seeing beneath the house. The entrance to the secret area could be anywhere.

"Come on, tear down the walls if you have to." Tony's British accent echoed through the house as he paced from room to room and directed two dozen of his crew in their search. Some salvaged valuables while the rest cracked open walls and took knives to furniture after the salvagers did their pass, in case anything else was shielded.

"Captain," called a petite woman with short red hair and a pierced lip.

"Yes, Deanna my dear, how can I help you?" Tony pivoted to address her.

"We found a stash of cash cards. Looks like a few *million*." Deanna tried to contain her excitement.

"Fantastic! I'll have to let Mike know this one's on the house. Thank you for the good news." With a joyous cackle, he headed for the study.

"Any time, captain." Deanna returned to her duties.

Tony paused at the threshold of the study and took in the room, its window burst open and holes in the walls from Mike's attack. There were only two crew members there, a man and a woman on a salvage pass. Tony paced around the room looking for slicks. He passed by the overturned desk and the wooden floor creaked beneath his boot. Stopped in his tracks, he stomped the floor, then ran his fingers along the cracks between the long wooden panels, offset from one another. Tony stepped to the side and stomped again, drawing the attention of the salvagers.

"Oi, I think we may have something here." Tony checked against the wall but found no switches or hidden buttons. The salvagers joined him in his search.

"I can't find anything," one of them said. The other concurred.

"Check the desk," Tony checked the overturned desk. With nothing on the bottom, he stood to open the drawers and feel around inside.

"Think I found it," the female crew member said, her hand stuffed in a drawer.

"Well? Let's see it," Tony ordered.

She pressed the button hidden against the roof of the drawer and there was a click, then a segment of the wood panels popped up. Tony pulled up the hidden door that hinged near the wall. The entrance was located behind the desk so it could be easily accessed without it being moved. Beneath the hidden doorway was a steep staircase.

Without being asked, the male crewmember drew his rifle and crept downstairs to check the room. "All clear, captain. I think we found it."

Tony hurried down the hidden stairs with his other crew member close behind.

In the middle of the room was a large metal table with a thick steel tube longer than a person, surrounded by a menagerie of smaller machined metal parts, wires, circuit cards, bolts and screws, all holo-labeled and organized around the long central tube. There were doors into other rooms, but they had found what they were after.

"Bloody hell." Tony paced around the table and reached a holo-panel. There, he toyed with the interface and slid a timeline backward. Holograms of the parts reassembled themselves into a giant cannon. "This is for a ship," Tony muttered. He searched through the menus and found something labeled *Logo*. It was a simple insignia which resembled a W in a rectangle.

"Hey, boss, I think this is one of those new weapons we've been hearing about," the nearby crew woman said.

"I'm inclined to agree with you. This doesn't look like any piece of hardware I've ever seen before." Tony nodded. "I've *wanted* one of these. Get Deanna and a team down here to run a security sweep and catalog all this. We're taking it with us. Actually, I want this entire room." The man by the door was quick to follow his orders and ran upstairs.

Tony examined the countertops, tools, and consoles along the walls, taking in every detail. He shuffled folders and flipped through well-organized papers and containers. Almost unnoticed was a clear business card with a red devil-tailed L.

He held the card up to the light. Since there was no printed information, the card surely had a digital element to it. "I'd better take precautions. You've surely got teeth."

Tony returned to the ship with the card and left his crew to dissect the room. Two days later he had assembled everything he found and called Mike with the news.

"Hey, Tony. Got any good news for me?" Mike greeted.

"A few good bits, actually. First, there was a lot more money here than I was going to charge you, so this job's on the house!" Tony said.

"Thanks! How about everything else?"

"I found this little bugger in a secret room under his study." Tony held up the card, and Mike's eyes widened.

"Lazarus. I knew he'd leave something," Mike growled.

"Is that what this stands for?" Tony placed the card on the table in front of him. "We didn't want to peek inside. Pretty sure it's got some *nasty* security."

"Can you send me whatever's on there?" Mike asked.

"Already packaged," Tony pressed a few buttons on his console, "and sent." Mike got an incoming message alert. "We kept it isolated. I'll leave cracking it open to you."

"Good idea. Was there anything else in that secret room?" Mike asked.

"Indeed there was. We're studying a cannon we found, meant for a fighter or a small ship. It's powerful, *advanced*. Really, nothing out there like it. The last couple of years there have been some new weapons floating around. Dealers don't even know who sells 'em. They make artillery and some energy weapons people call blasters. We found one of those in the room, too."

"I wasn't aware there were advanced weapons in the colonies," Mike said.

"You don't make purchases through the same channels as we do, do ya, mate?" Tony pointed out that since Mike usually made his own stuff it was reasonable that he would be out of the loop. "It's not that bad. This cannon looks like it's from a small production. These aren't made en masse."

The *Yellow Shark* had a reputation as the smartest ship in the colonies, at least within outlaw circles. On top of that, Tony was known for his honesty, and they were friends. If Tony said it, it was true.

"Okay then." Mike bit his lip, lost in thought. "Could you leave a few guys there? Brad isn't the type to do his own dirty work, so whatever he was up to I'm sure he has people working for him. Someone's bound to show up at some point."

"Consider it done."

"How much *money* did you guys find?" Mike asked, skeptical of Tony's obtuse amicability.

"Oh, Mike. Don't trouble yourself with the details." Tony smiled impishly.

Mike rolled his eyes. "All right, thanks for everything. Get back to me if there are any developments."

"Right-o." Tony gave Mike a casual salute. "Cheers, mate!"

Rebels

32

Honest Lies

WITH AN ICE PACK AGAINST THE BACK OF HIS HEAD, CALVIN lay on his couch watching cartoons and drinking beer. Water, beer and cartoons was his routine after a night of heavy drinking, and last night ended with getting bashed in the back of the head and robbed, so he thought a day-long dose of his routine was in order. Body aching, a slow, steady throb pounded at the inside of his skull and his stomach squirmed.

A loud pounding on his front door interrupted the tranquility of the apartment. With a groan, Calvin forced his body up to open the door. The hallway light assaulted his eyes. He squinted, hand over his face until his eyes adjusted.

In the hall was a man in a stylish charcoal coat with bulging eyes and a powerful brow. There were two large men at his sides. One was particularly massive and muscular. The other had a stone-cold stare, a crooked nose, and cauliflower ear; signs of a fighter.

Calvin's skin crawled. A shock ran from his tailbone to the top of his head and he froze in place. His heart rattled in panic, but the pain coursing through his body and queasy stomach disguised a lack of composure. If he failed at hiding his nerves, they could easily be mistaken for gangsters, so he had a plan B.

"Can I help you guys?" Calvin choked out.

"Mr. Perry, I'm Agent Jones, these are my bodyguards, Samson and Ken. We're from the UEG and we believe you may be able to help us. May we come in?" He was the meekest of the three, but somehow the most menacing.

"Hi. Yeah, come on in." Calvin stepped aside, heart racing. "Have a seat wherever." The three men entered and spread out. Calvin made his way back to the couch and fell into it. Ice pack back on his head, he lowered the volume on the cartoons. Samson and Ken explored the apartment before they joined them in the living room, each on different sides to cut off the exits. Samson had a good angle on the cartoons, so he watched contently, leaning casually against a bar-top kitchen counter.

"Are you okay?" Jones asked out of curiosity, not concern.

Calvin groaned. "I got mugged last night on my way back from the bar."

"Really?" Jones asked. "Do you have any proof?"

"That I was mugged? Are you serious?" Calvin looked back.

"Quite serious." The menacing agent's expression was unwavering.

"Uh, my head? My wallet's gone? I had to call off work and cancel all my cards today? What kind of a dick question is that?" Calvin declared, hoping that being genuine would be most convincing.

"I didn't see that you had filed a police report." Jones had already looked him up.

"Why? It wouldn't do me any good. My family has a history in law enforcement. I know it won't help find the guys who mugged me, not around here." Calvin shuffled in his seat. "Speaking of local authorities, what's the UEG doing on Ganymede?"

"Why didn't the muggers steal your mobile?" Jones ignored Calvin's question and noted his mobile on the small table next to him.

"Probably because it's a piece of shit." Calvin chuckled. Mobile computers were cheap tech, but he always lost smaller, more convenient devices.

"I see." Jones nodded. "I'll get to the point of our visit, then. We're investigating an incident that happened not far from here. Can you tell me about your evening?"

"Um, I went to High Borne last night to watch Smash International," he began.

"What is *Smash International?*" To Jones, the name sounded made-up.

"Seriously?" Calvin glanced around at the three men. Samson gave him a nod, but the other two had no clue. "It's a tournament for a fighting game called Smash. Invitation only, all the best players are there. It's wild, the bar was *packed*." Calvin became more enthusiastic as he spoke, but their serious faces gave him pause and anxiety crept back in.

"Please, move along with your night." Jones twirled his hand for Calvin to continue with the information he actually wanted to hear about. Now convinced it was real, it was clear nothing of value would come of the topic.

"Okay. So, I haven't seen my friend Tina in a while, she's a bartender there. I say hi and order my drink but the bar is slammed. This big guy comes up and orders a drink. We start talking about Steel Scorpion and beer. He invited me to his table. I hung out with him and his friend all night. James and Matt, *super* cool guys. Mad Scorpion-heads." Calvin smiled at the memory of them playing air guitar when a Steel Scorpion song played the night before. Matt broke a disposable utensil playing along to the drums.

"So you spent your entire night with two strangers you just met?" Jones asked.

"It is, you know… a bar. A social place where you drink and make friends." Calvin glanced around, uneasy. "Plus, I'm a bartender. I'm always spending my time with strangers. It's easy to make friends. Especially friends with good taste in beer and music."

Jones hummed and stared Calvin down, which made him uneasy.

"Relax, we're not going to hurt or arrest you. We simply need to know what happened."

"Sorry, it's just, you guys are a little intimidating. The last time I had a group of guys standing around my apartment like this, I owed someone money!" Calvin joked, but received no laughter. With a smile, Samson dropped and shook his head. Calvin's smile melted away and he stammered to course-correct. "Not that, like I don't participate in illicit activity. I-I uh…"

"I understand, it was quite humorous. Why did you spend so much time with them?" Jones clasped his hands together and listened.

"I don't know," Calvin said with a dogged sense they were about to pounce on him. "We don't get too many Earthers here. And, they were good company, fun, good tastes, good people. I don't need an excuse to hang out with good people."

"I see. So you spent your whole night with these men, and?" Jones pressed on.

"We got *wasted*. They were walking home so I offered to show them a shortcut that cuts from eighth to first. By that point though, it's all kinda fuzzy. We all leaned on each other for support. Then, I heard something behind me. I woke up alone in the alley this morning. My wallet was gone and I walked home with a *massive* headache. When I got here, I made my hangover breakfast and cocktail, made my calls, and I've been watching cartoons with ice on my head 'til you guys got here."

"Do you remember what you heard behind you?" Jones scooted forward with interest. He gave Ken a quick glance while he listened.

"Screeching tires. A door opened, like a van." Calvin tried to recall any detail.

"That's helpful. Did you see anything?" Jones asked.

Calvin shuffled through foggy memories of the night before. He caught a glance of two people, both wearing black ski masks and sweats. Leo's words shot into his brain like a bolt of lightning: *be honest.* "I kind of saw them, but they were wearing ski masks and sweats or something."

While they talked, Ken checked Calvin's head from a distance with the contact in his eye. Surprised at the damage which had been done, he fact-checked the other details Calvin had given them and it all checked out. He sent Jones a message confirming his story, which popped up discreetly in Jones's vision.

Jones sat back in his chair, elbow resting on the arm. He crossed his legs and studied Calvin, sickly and in pain but not a liar, only nervous and ill.

During the pause, Calvin took the mushy ice pack off his head. "Do you mind if I get another one?"

After a glance from Jones, Samson walked into the kitchen and came back with a bag of green beans. "I didn't see any more ice packs in there," he said, apologetic.

"Don't worry, you grabbed the right one." Calvin exchanged the green beans for the ice pack with a smile. "That one's all I got."

"So, why no hospital visit for your head?" Jones asked while Samson took the flimsy ice pack back into Calvin's freezer.

"I used to play Warball in high school. Quarterback. Got sacked a few times. I've had concussions, I can handle it." Calvin dismissed the injury even as he winced at the crisp cold bag on the back of his head.

"You're pretty short for a quarterback." Samson found a beam to lean against with his arms crossed.

"True, but I'm fast and I've got a *hell* of an arm. Or, I used to. I don't know *what* I can do now." Calvin was defensive of a time he was particularly proud of. Feeling the conversation out, he was more relaxed than when they first arrived, but there was still a trembling trepidation in his chest as Jones pensively stared him down. He was a wreck but within reason.

"Thank you Mr. Perry, I believe we have everything we need." Jones stood and tidied himself.

Calvin wanted to ask why they were there again, but he knew it had something to do with James and Matt. He did not want to test a fake surprise reaction when Jones explained why he was there.

"I'm glad I could help." Calvin followed them to the door. "And hey,

I'm assuming you guys are here on the same ship as James and Matt, so if you run into them, could you tell them to come by Hearthstein some time? I told them last night but we were pretty messed up, so they might not remember." Calvin switched the cold bag of green beans to his left hand and dried his right hand off on his shirt.

"Of course." Jones shook Calvin's hand. "Thank you for your cooperation."

"Yeah, any time. Good luck with your investigation," Calvin said.

"Good day." Jones dismissed himself.

"Hope your head feels better, man." Samson shook Calvin's hand as he passed.

"Thanks, take care, big guy." Calvin smiled, then reached out to Ken for a handshake, but he ignored Calvin and followed his team out.

Jones led the trio down the hall and into the elevator.

"That guy seems like he's on the level." Samson leaned back against the railing.

"He does. We made him nervous, but he was honest. If he had lied, I'd know. Wrong place, wrong time. But, that means someone took advantage of an opportunity." He sneered at the thought of losing pieces to an inferior opponent. "We have people watching us."

Calvin stayed home for the next two days until his head felt better. Chris was not at work when Calvin showed up. The following night, it was late after work when Calvin met with Chris and Leo in Ganymede's underground.

"What—the—hell, Leo? Do you know how bad my head hurts? Still?"

"Sorry, Cal. We couldn't tell you the plan in case that guy showed up at your house. Look, here's your wallet."

"My wh—damnit Leo! I canceled everything! You left me knocked out in an alley. I thought someone robbed me!" Calvin snatched his wallet.

"Well, that was kind of the plan." Chris scratched his head.

"Look, if any part of your story didn't line up, that guy would have tortured you until you gave up everything you knew, then he'd kill ya," Leo explained.

Calvin's eyes darted back and forth between Leo and Chris, his face melted at the realization of how close he came to a violent death. "Seriously?"

"That's the guy that killed Mad Mack, and he threatened to kill me, too," Leo said. "Still glad we've got some excitement around here?"

Although upset at how events had unfolded, Calvin understood the strategy. "What about James and Matt? What happened to them?"

Sam and Amber

33

Lost Friends

AFTER JAMES AND MATT HAD BEEN MISSING FOR ALMOST A WEEK, Sam and Amber faced their weekly lunch in the colony without their friends. On Amber's day off, they kept their appointment in the spirit of the duo who had proposed it.

Out of uniforms in casual attire, Sam and Amber picked a new place to eat from James and Matt's list. Each week they picked a new place from the highest rated pubs and restaurants in the city. This week's pick featured beer and gourmet sandwiches, but the experience felt empty without their friends.

"I'm really scared that we aren't going to find them," Sam admitted, a blank look on his face.

"I've… had that thought. But, it's natural to have it. Ultimately, we have to believe in Jones and our search teams. We have a good crew and we're working with the authorities. It'll be all right. If we were missing, they'd find us. We just have to be patient." Amber took Sam's wrist and squeezed it.

"I wish I could do something. I don't want to just sit here. They've got to be in the original colony, underground. That's the only thing that makes sense."

"Agent Jones already had all the entrances to it checked. They had some run-ins with local gangs, but that's it. Everything else has been closed," Amber said after a drink of her vodka with club soda.

"It can't all be closed. But, these people aren't going to trust us. We're outsiders. They're only going to trust their own, and that's an angle Jones can never take. As long as we're counting on *him* to find them, I don't know if it'll happen."

"That guy is a fuckin' psychopath. He'll cross boundaries we would never even think of. Don't underestimate him."

A pause gave them a moment to eat and Sam mulled over what solutions Jones would never think of. What approach would be in opposition to his?

"Maybe… if I can give an olive branch to someone who can get information about James and Matt, maybe I could actually get a lead on them."

"You'd probably have to deal with some rough people. After sparring with you, I'd say someone taught you to defend yourself, but you're not as formidable as you think. I recommend you avoid rough neighborhoods *and* any physical confrontation with Agent Jones." Amber leaned in with a raised eyebrow, knowing of Sam's brash actions when he first met Jones.

"Yeah, you made that clear, I know." Sam groaned. "But, I can't sit here and hope they come back safe. I have to try *something*."

"How do you plan on finding someone who can get you the info? Ooh! *Maybe* we could pretend to be *customers*?" Amber said sarcastically, then waved a hand in the air. "We're a couple from Earth fleeing a shady past, looking to get our chips removed."

Sam's attention was caught on the word *couple*. Pretend to be a couple. His previous relationship was over five years ago. He had barely been on a date since then. Surely, he would make it awkward and blow their cover.

Sam flashed a bashful smile. "We're both Alphas. Why would we leave Earth?"

"Honestly, if I hadn't found a sense of family in Earth Orbit Security, I probably would have left a long time ago," Amber said casually, then took a swig of iced tea.

"Why?"

"Eh." Amber rocked her head from side to side. "My parents didn't want me. I overheard them telling some friends one night, and a lot of things made sense after that. But, when I turned out to be an Alpha, they put on a show and pretended to love me because I was their meal ticket. So, I took advantage of the Alpha Development Program and relocated. Never looked back." Amber was not done, but what she said went against an assumption Sam had developed.

"Oh, I thought your parents died."

"That's horrible, why would you think that?" she asked.

"Because... my parents died when I was a kid. I was raised by my grandma. *She* died when I was a teenager."

"Oh shit, I'm so sorry." Amber put her hand over her mouth, wishing she could take back her candid reaction to his question.

Sam shook his head. "It's fine. We've never talked about our families, now I know why." He cringed. "I'm sorry about your parents, that's... really messed up."

"Yeah, well, whatever. Since then, if it doesn't feel like home wherever I am, I leave. If I'm just someone's tool or burden, I leave. Honestly, I want to buy a ship and recruit a crew and sail around the colonies, but I'm fine where I'm at right now." Amber shrugged off the pain of her past.

"Well, that's good. Because without you, I wouldn't have this ridiculous backstory about fleeing Earth," Sam said.

She smiled, smacking Sam in the shoulder, and took a moment to finish chewing and her food.

"If we *were* running away together, getting our chips removed would be *really* painful."

"Why?" Amber asked.

"Because the devices to get them removed are heavily regulated by the Ministry. Each one is accounted for and their designs are locked-up tight. So, removing them requires surgery or maybe hitting it with a zapper." Sam paused, then curled his hand into a fist and rested his chin in his palm.

"What are you thinking over there, Sherlock?" Amber inquired.

"Those devices make removing chips painless, and they probably don't have any out here. So, that would make it *really* valuable."

"Yeah, but if the designs are locked up, you can't get them without the Ministry knowing, right?" Amber looked to Sam, who gave her a sideways look with a grin. "Oh? Is that mischief I see?"

"I… may have a way to see the designs without anyone knowing," Sam said. Amber jabbed him in the ribs to press him further and Sam leaned in close to whisper. "That knife Jones gave me, the blood sample was classified. So, I asked my buddy, Koorosh, if he could help me out. He works in Ministry Security. He sent me a little something to crack through encrypted information, both Ministry and non-Ministry. So, I downloaded a copy of the *entire* Ministry system and used his hack. I know who Jones is looking for, but I can't tell him because it's classified. I can also look up the schematics for one of those devices and make it with the equipment available on the ship."

Amber's jaw dropped and she stared wide-eyed at Sam. "Wow, look at the cute little scientist breaking rules and going rogue. I didn't know you had it in you. Color me impressed."

"Technically, I'm an engineer. The Ministry uses *scientist* as a blanket term for the general public. But, thank you."

Amber rolled her eyes. "So you found out who that blood belongs to?"

"That's classified." Sam grinned and took a drink of his beer giving her a sidelong look.

"Oh, okay. I see how it is." Amber feigned offense, then returned to the main topic. "If you can make one of those things, then I could set up a meeting with you and the guy Jones is monitoring. He owns a parts shop here in the city. Jones has his devices tapped and multiple people monitoring him at all times. It's a legitimate shop, but it's also a front for smugglers and stolen goods. It's probably where our targets fenced the stuff they stole from your lab."

Amber's assessment was accurate.

"Oh." Sam leaned back in his seat, absently looking at Amber, mulling over an idea. "Can you get me around Jones's surveillance?"

"Are you kidding me? Nothing happens on my ship without me knowing about it. I can arrange for about a ten minute window so you can talk to him without anyone being the wiser, *especially* Agent Jones."

"If you can get me a meeting with him, I can make a de-chipping device and try trading it for some information. If we can establish a rapport, maybe we can even get them back!" Sam said.

"Let's not get ahead of ourselves, but if you're intent on doing this, let's give it a real shot at success. I'll set it up for tomorrow after Jones calls it a night. I'll be on shift, so I can make sure everything goes smoothly."

"Oh, man, thank you! I haven't been this excited to break the law since I was a teenager." Sam picked up the second half of his sandwich.

"Weren't you breaking the law getting that classified information from the Ministry?" Amber asked.

"Yeah, but I wasn't excited about it. Doing this, best-case scenario, we could get our friends back."

They enjoyed the rest of the day in a better mood than before, with a spark of hope brightening every step forward.

Amber worked her magic while Sam waited in the stairwell of an apartment complex. When he got word from her, he exited and hurried down a beige hallway to the door at the end and gave it three quick taps. Met with silence, he knocked again. This time there was a grunt and shuffling about from inside.

Sam tried to dry his sweaty palms in his pockets. Heart rattling in his chest, he bounced lightly in place, grinding his teeth.

"Who is it?" a voice called from the other side of the door, which had two peepholes, one at the normal height, one around chest level. Sam looked into the taller one, then leaned down to look into the lower one. Was the peephole from a former tenant? Did he have children? He leaned into the door so he could speak softly and still be heard.

"Uh, I'm a stranger. But, I've heard you're the person I need to talk to about selling something?"

"Come to my shop tomorrow."

"I can't do that. I have to talk to you right now."

"Why right now?"

"Because you're being monitored twenty-four-seven and for a few minutes right now, nobody is listening."

A tense pause followed. Sam checked his wrist for the time and clenched his teeth nervously. He had already lost two minutes.

"Who are you?" the voice asked.

"A friend."

There was another pause, then the latch on the inside clicked and the door opened. A short, round man in a bathrobe poked out from behind the door and ticked his head, signaling Sam inside.

Sam hurried in with a sigh of relief and a smile. Leo's apartment was neat and leisurely. On the coffee table in the living room was a bowl of nuts, next to it, a bowl for the shells. Sam took in the room with a nod and turned around. Leo was pointing a pistol at him.

"Woah!" Sam put his hands in the air. "That escalated quickly."

"Like I said, who the fuck are ya?" Leo demanded.

"My name is Sam." He spoke softly so as not to be heard through the walls. "I'm from the Ministry of Science and I don't have something to sell, I have something to trade. You can sell it for a lot of money, though."

"From the Ministry? Are you from that UEG ship?"

"Yes. That's how I was able to get around the surveillance. I have a friend who made the arrangements so we could speak privately, but I don't have a lot of time. When my alarm goes off, I have to go." Sam turned the back of his hand toward Leo.

"All right, *Earther*," Leo said with overt contempt. "What the hell do you want?"

"My friends, James and Matt, they went missing last week and our search crews haven't found anything yet. I know you're well connected, so I was hoping for some information. Even just knowing they're okay would mean the world to me."

"You fuckin' Earther scum are tapping my devices, following me wherever I go, and not even for anything *I* did, and you want me to help you? Go fuck yourself."

"Hold on, I said I have something to trade," Sam said.

"Yeah? I'm not a real big fan of you people right now, so it better be good."

Sam reached slowly into his jacket pocket and pulled from it a tube, but Leo could not make out the details. He pointed at the nearby table and Sam placed it on the corner closest to Leo then backed away.

Eyes on Sam, Leo shuffled over and picked up the item. His eyes narrowed, examining the white tube with a screen on the side and a plunger-like button at the top.

"What is it?" Leo asked after a moment, his gun no longer aimed at Sam.

"It's a de-chipper. You can use it for denizen and citizen chips. It'll make extracting them a painless procedure. These are tracked and regulated by the Ministry, but I made that one, so it's totally off the radar. They're practically impossible to get. Only a handful have ever been stolen and gone unrecovered."

"Are you for real?" Leo's posture relaxed and he examined the device anew, now with a proper perspective on what he was holding. "I didn't even know these existed. I thought surgery was the only way to remove them."

"Not on Earth. I don't know how you could contact me if you can find anything about my friends. Honestly, I'd like to get them back. I'll make a dozen of those if I have to. It'll take forever, but I'll do it."

"If this is legit, then I'll see what I can find out. If I can find anything, next Friday, go to the Hearthstein pub. My friends there will pass along anything I find out. Don't ask around, they'll come to you." Leo clicked the safety on his pistol and slipped it and the device in his bathrobe pockets. At last, Sam put his hands down with relief.

"Thanks. My alarm hasn't gone off yet, but I should probably get going."

"Yeah, no problem. Sorry about the gun, I thought you might be an asshole."

"Totally understandable. Thanks for not shooting me. This is a new shirt," Sam attempted to lighten the mood, relieved at the dissipated tension.

Leo chuckled, then waved Sam out. They shook hands as he passed and Leo closed the door behind him, the locks clicking shut.

The following week was an anxious one, and Amber switched her day off to Friday. Their pick for lunch had been decided for them, for the first time to a place not on their list. The Hearthstein pub had an excellent selection of beer on tap and the food was delectable. This pub was a local gem.

However, despite spending several hours there, nobody approached them. Sam became disheartened. They agreed to call it a day. On his way from the bathroom back to the bar, Sam bumped into his bartender.

"Oh hey, sorry about that," the bartender said.

"Yeah, same. I wasn't really paying attention."

"You and your girl gettin' another one?" he motioned to the bar.

"Nah, I think we're going to settle up after we finish this round," Sam said.

"Well, it's always nice to chat with Earthers about the homeland. You and your lady are great, come back any time. My name's Calvin." He held a hand out.

"Sam." He shook Sam's hand, but instead of flesh, there was paper in his palm.

"Nice to meet ya, Sam. You take care." Calvin returned to the bar and his duties.

When Sam returned, he opened the interface on the bartop to pay the tab and they were soon making their way through the light crowd of the plaza. Sam leaned in close to Amber and whispered about the note.

Amber's head pivoted in search of something, then she hooked her arm around Sam's bicep, dragging him into a clothing store. Customers used kiosks or personal devices to scroll through outfits, examining their mirrored holograms wearing the selected items. They hurried past them to the back of the shop where the private dressing rooms were located. As they entered one of the rooms, a lingerie menu appeared on the inner kiosk.

"Uh… what are we here for again?"

"The note." Amber grinned.

Sam pulled the note from his pocket and they huddle around it like excited school children. The note read: *Earther, thank you for the device. Your friends are well cared for. We are keeping them safe. They will be set free soon.*

"Safe?" Sam turned to Amber with a puzzled squint. "I expected more."

"Hmm." Amber looked Sam up and down. "Honestly, I thought even this much was a long shot. It says they're taking good care of them. At least we know they're okay. But, I agree. That thing you gave them was pretty valuable."

"All right, well. I guess we don't have to worry?"

"Yeah, looks like it." Amber pointed to the note. "Make sure you burn that when we get back."

Matt and James

34

Red Queen

A SPLASH OF WATER IN THE FACE JERKED JAMES AND MATT TO consciousness. They shook their heads like wet dogs and sprinkled water around them. Hands cuffed behind them, they were stuck in their seats.

By their count, it was October thirteenth, and it had been twelve days since they were abducted. Twelve days in an underground cell. Hardly anyone spoke to them and they had been well fed and well treated, but it did not make captivity any more pleasant. Now they awoke in an unfamiliar setting. An unexpected change in pace. It was safe to presume their last meal had been drugged.

They found themselves in a dark room with lights over their heads. A single figure silhouetted in front of them came into focus. It was a fit middle-aged woman. Her wavy reddish-brown hair was tied back, glistening with silver streaks. A long red-trimmed navy coat flowed behind her, boots clicking with each step she took toward them. She reached an arm out and motioned to the darkness.

From the shadows, a large man carried a stool with a low back and placed it behind her, then vanished into the shadows. Without looking or reaching back, she sat down, crossed one leg over the other, and rested her hands together atop her knee.

"Do you know who I am?" The woman looked down upon the two men. Her grayish-brown eyes glistened in the shadows.

The mysterious woman's expensive clothes concealed a layer of armor. A gun belt hung around her hips with a pistol, two small blades they could spot, and a long saber at her side, the type Russia used to give to distinguished officers. People at her whim meant she had power. The guy with the chair was likely not the only one lurking in the darkness.

"You're the Red Queen," Matt said. They had been ordered to familiarize themselves with the various pirate gangs, which turned out to be useful.

"Iskra Zekich, leader of The Red Storm." Her accent was hardly noticeable.

"So, you're the one that nabbed us?" James surmised.

"Of course not, we are only helping the ones who did," she said.

"Look, whateva' *this* is, we're professionals. You ain't gettin' nothin' out of us," Matt said, stone-faced.

"We want nothing from you." Iskra shook her head.

The men exchanged a confused glance, then James asked their mutual question. "So, what *do* ya want?"

"We think you would make excellent *pirates,*" she said with zest.

There was a brief silence, and then Matt and James broke out in laughter. It echoed in the dark room and settled. Iskra waited for them to finish.

"Seriously?" James asked.

"Yeah, I'm usually betta' at keepin' a straight face but that's funny, lady." Matt chuckled with a shake of his head.

"You aren't gonna try to find out how many people we've got? Why we're here? You're just gonna offa' us a job?" James asked in bewildered surprise.

"No. Red Storm is Russian-only. You would have to find another home," Iskra corrected him. "But, we can remove your chips and find you a home in the colonies."

"So, why recruit us for someone else?" James asked.

"Hold on," Matt said. "If you're on the level about this, why don't ya want any information from us?"

"We have what we need," she said casually.

"Why don't you need it? You think you know–"

"I know the name of the ship you seek, which *you* do not even know." Iskra grinned. "I know there is a force of eighty troopers on your ship. The man in charge is Agent Jones, and there is Captain Slater as well. Also a Ranger, those are illegal, no?" She waved her finger and clicked her tongue, tisk-tisk. "And, a man who is not like the others, he wears no armor and we have witnessed his strength. Genetically enhanced? Also illegal. He is flashy, foolish, full of ego. A Ministry scientist, who does not belong."

"How did you gatha' all this *supposed* information?" Matt asked even though everything she said was accurate.

"That is not your concern. Let us speak of your future." She moved the conversation along. They had used the chaos and search that followed their kidnapping to assess the *Rampart* forces, but it was off topic. "My friends on Ganymede say you are good people. So, we offer you asylum as pirates. Pirate ships, not bad."

"You ain't very good at interrogatin' are you?" James smirked.

"As I said, this is no interrogation."

"Why would we want to be pirates?" Matt asked with a hint of offense. "You guys steal from people and hole up in the colonies, hidin' behind civilians. With the UEG we fight for otha's, we got a purpose. We fight fo' the great'a good."

"You may have taken time to read about pirate clans, you know my name, but you are ignorant. You know nothing of our ways."

"Enlighten me." Matt challenged Iskra to defend her accusations. She sighed and examined the young men.

"Most of us were soldiers, like you. We wanted to fight for our country, for what we believe. We bled, held our dying comrades, witnessed the horrors of war, and when it was over we were kicked aside and forgotten. Injuries uncared for, promises of compensation un-kept. We lost our families, our friends, our legacies. Most pirates are the forgotten heroes of war, once hailed for their courage. Men and women who risked their lives for their people cast away when they were no longer needed. As you will be, like every soldier that came before you—in *all* of human history."

The room was still, without a sound, a moment frozen in time. The mood, solemn. In spite of their expectations, her words came from the heart.

"So, you're *serious* about us becomin' pirates." James tried to wrap his head around the bizarre situation. It was clear now why they had been well fed and never interrogated or abused.

"Yes," Iskra said, the recognition in their eyes clear now.

Matt and James shared a look, and with it knew their answer.

"My family has dedicated their lives to the service fa' generations. Both of us." James spoke first. "I'm sorry for whateva' you been through, but it ain't my experience. I joined 'cause I believe that fo' all the ugliness we see, we're doin' good things. If that ain't true, my life and the lives of those who came before me were in service to lies."

The room was silent again. After listening to James, Iskra nodded, then turned to Matt.

"Also, we took an oath. If our word means nothin', then neitha' do we. If by some twist 'a fate we become pirates, it'll be afta' we complete our service with the UEG. We neva' followed an unethical ord'a. Things ain't perfect, but I believe in *the people* to make the right choices."

Iskra's eyes fell in disappointment. Looking up again, she rose from her stool.

"There is a bet if you are brave enough to leave your corrupt leadership for a life of freedom." Her boots echoed with each step toward them. "People choose well, but leaders do not listen. I respect your answers. I hope you find happiness in your choices."

From behind, damp cloths were cupped over their mouths and noses.

They struggled, but the world faded into darkness. The last thing they saw before they fell out of consciousness was Iskra's silhouette. Her final words echoed in their minds.

"But, you are fools."

Natalie and Will

35

Next Level

"Happy Birthday!" Will surprised Natalie in the gunner room. The room was decorated with colored paper ornaments and a stapled-together HAPPY BIRTHDAY sign dangling from one side of the ceiling to the other.

Natalie jumped in surprise. Will stood in the middle of the room with a table behind him. Beneath the table were pillows, blankets, and small memory foam seats. The tantalizing aroma of meat, onions, and cilantro lofted in the air.

"Ssssshhhhhh!" She checked the short hall behind her with an ear-to-ear grin and hurried into the room. "Someone could have heard you!"

"They already know," Will said as if it should be no surprise. "It may feel weird to celebrate your birthday with them, but I haven't gone a year without celebrating it since we were five, so you're dealing with it."

She gave Will a loving smile, her cheeks flushed like pink roses. On the wall to her left two announcers sat behind a table, a big red mute icon hovered at waist-level. Above them was a large, half-destroyed title reading: Brawl. Watching pro gaming tournaments was one of their traditions.

Natalie took slow steps toward Will as she took in the room, but he held his hand out for her to stop. Excited and curious, Natalie stopped with a huff. Will twisted around and grabbed a small tablet from the table behind him.

"Today, the fourteenth of October, twenty-one eighty-four, Natalie Elizabeth Owens turns eighteen and there are many amazing things happening around the universe to celebrate this day!" Will announced.

Giddy at the reverence and extravagance of Will's efforts and tone, she could not keep still and rubbed her hands together with anticipation.

"In Korea, a young man selflessly saved a woman and her baby from a burning building. In Egypt, scientists increased the efficiency of air filtration systems for spacecraft by forty percent." His eyes skimmed the screen. "In ways that take too long to read!"

He coaxed a giggle from Natalie, who would have better understood the content of the news and looked forward to reading it later.

"In the Netherlands, scientists discovered... something. It's a lot of big words." Will shook his head. "I probably should have left that one off the list, but it sounded cool." Natalie giggled again, this time at his folly. "Last but not least, the news I know you're going to lose your mind over: In the USA, a new pro-gaming clan was jointly founded by Dax Guererro and Moxie Paige called The Free Radicals!" He boomed and motioned on the tablet to turn the headline into a hologram. Natalie's jaw dropped and her eyes all but jumped out of her head.

"Seriously?" she squealed, mouth covered with both hands.

"Dax, the Unstoppable Force, and Moxie the Queen of Carnage will lead what is sure to be the greatest clan in the American continents, if not the world!"

"Oh my god!" Natalie snatched the tablet from him. Holding the information in her hands made it real. Upon reading the news with her own eyes she jumped again and leaped onto Will, squeezing him. "Oh my god! I can't believe it!"

"And on the *first* day of Brawl, like they already know they're going to win." He let her down, but the excitement still overwhelmed her.

"Holy shit! I hope they win." She beamed.

"Of course they're going to win." Will eyed her as if she was crazy to consider their favorite up-and-comers could lose. "And, I think they're going extra hard since they weren't invited to Smash International."

"We've never seen them play Galaxy Fighter Three before," Natalie said. "But, they *did* get first and second at Arena, so we know they can work together."

"Exactly. I'm pretty sure they're going to murder everybody. But, let's not get ahead of ourselves." He stepped aside dramatically to reveal the table.

On neatly arranged plates were ingredients for tacos, chips, salsa, hot dogs, a small ice chest with beverages, and two caramel nut bars. There was also a small white box for warming up food. Handy, since they planned on being there for a while.

"Ian kind of helped me get the food together. Rick said I could grab a few beers and these are the last two caramel nut bars. I figured, my mom only had these at the house for Ash and since she can't be here with us, this might be a nice way to at least have her here in spirit." Will presented Natalie with the bars.

"Aw, how did I end up with such an awesome boyfriend?" Natalie wilted at the gesture and eased into a loving hug. She closed her eyes and listened to Will's heartbeat.

"We've known each other since we were little. It was destiny. But, getting stranded in space together helped."

"But, if we have free will, that means we can change destiny, right? Is *that* still destiny?" Natalie asked. She pulled away to look into Will's eyes.

"I never thought about that. I guess destiny doesn't mean anything if you don't go for it."

"Or if *you* don't go for it." Natalie leaned in for a kiss. The light peck spiraled into a passionate kiss and they eased apart with their foreheads together. Eyes closed, they held each other for a moment before separating, hands still clasped.

"It's going to start soon. Let's get comfy." Will pulled the pillows, blankets, and fluffy seats out from under the table and slid them to the middle of the room. Natalie grabbed a pillow and clubbed Will's bum. In retaliation, he threw a blanket at her face for her to unfurl.

"Oh!" Natalie bounced. "Did I tell you I almost blew us all up today?"

"What?" Will's voice rose sharply, peaking between panic and surprise.

Natalie laughed. "I'm exaggerating. Rick was showing me how to replace…" Natalie trailed off into silence. Will would not know what she was talking about if she went into detail. "Well, in a lot of these older ships there's these power regulators on four sides of a big ring above the reactor. In the middle is like a thing that you twist and pull up. I was holding a fat cable that runs around the power coil while Rick showed me stuff. I touched it to the ring, which he says if he hadn't cut the power to that node, it would have been like touching the wrong node when you jump a car but way worse and the ship could have blown up," she said in a delighted tone. "I guess it's an old design flaw."

"Why are you so happy about almost blowing up the ship?" Will was frozen in place, dumbfounded to find out he could have so easily died that day. He could have been pooping—and then boom! Dead.

Snickering, Natalie laid out a comfortable spot on the floor. "There was no real danger. How about you? Anything new?"

"I'm all right," Will said unconvincingly. "We don't really use the lower decks. After I cleaned the galley, gyms and recycling center stuff I don't have too many repeat jobs so I've been helping Farouk out in Hydroponics. He gave me a book to read about war by a Chinese guy. Did you know he grew up playing football too?"

"No, I didn't. Jeez, you have something in common with everyone."

"Don't we all?"

"I guess." Natalie's mind was not as focused on Will's insight so much as his hesitation and dishonest response. "Are you sure you're okay? Are you happy?" Natalie laid out a blanket on the pile of bedding and returned to Will.

"I'm happy I'm with *you*." A pillow in each hand, he wrapped his arms around her. "I do kind of miss cracking mobiles, and playing football, and my chickens. Sometimes, I wonder what happened to my chickens."

"Maybe we can play football here? Like, in the common room on deck two." Natalie said. "Farouk could join us, and Shin, right?"

"Yeah, he played too. That'd be cool." He smiled and gave her a peck on the lips. There was a chance he liked the idea, but it would not be enough to keep him happy. His response had the electrifying energy of a seashell.

"And for your job, maybe you can apprentice with the Captain and learn computer stuff from him? You think cracking mobiles is easy. Maybe you're good at that kind of stuff," Natalie suggested. This time, there was a spark in his eyes.

He contemplated the idea and made excuses in his head for why it would not happen before he finally conjured a response. "You think he would?"

"Totally!" Natalie beamed. "He gave *me* a shot, I'm sure he'll give you one too."

"But, he's always so awkward. I don't think he's comfortable around teenagers."

"He still let us on the ship, and he's been more relaxed since we started game nights. It doesn't hurt to try," Natalie said.

"Okay, I guess I'll give it a shot. Thank you." He pressed his lips to hers for a peck, then turned their attention to the table of food behind him. "So, are we starting with tacos or hot dogs?"

"Obviously tacos." Natalie gawked incredulously at Will.

Will fixed them plates and laid down to watch the fighting game tournament as if they were there. Once the pre-game show finished, every wall in the room became a screen and they were immersed in the crowd. It was three hours of pro-gaming action with intermittent making out and snacking. The final fight was everything they could have hoped for and their team had won the day.

"Free radicaaaaaaaaaals!" They cheered as bold letters appeared over two game characters: VICTORY. With jovial roars, Natalie and Will threw themselves into a hug, eyes still glued to the screen. They cheered alongside the booming mass of roaring attendees that undulated in celebration around them, some banging inflated tubes against each other, others whistling. The elated announcers prattled on about the match.

"Half volume!" Will cut the volume to a moderate, conversational level.

"Murder!" Natalie roared. "Straight – up – *murder!*" She pounded on Will's chest with her fist.

"Those two are a *monster* team." Blood still pumping, Will anxiously ran his fingers through his scruffy hair and let out a long huff. "Oh my god."

"It was like watching a dog play with a chew toy!" Natalie laughed. "Moxie and Dax with their own clan is going to be brutal."

"You mean Dax and Moxie," Will said.

"Moxie and Dax," she insisted.

"Dax and Moxie. You don't see people saying, 'Natalie and Will'."

"Uh, except *everybody*? It's Natalie and Will, Moxie and Dax. Sorry." Natalie put a finger over his lips with the faux apology. "That's just the way of the world."

"Okay, it *is* your birthday, so I guess *today*—today it can be Moxie and Dax. But Dax has a girlfriend and it isn't Moxie, so this is kind of pointless," Will pointed out.

"So? They're a good team." Natalie skipped past circumstances and more about what they were together.

"They are." Will nodded.

"And we are?"

"Natalie and Will." His head drooped in defeat.

She grinned back at him then reached over her head to get another drink of her beer. Will scoffed, his head plopped into the cushion.

"Moxie and Dax, Natalie and Will, super teams. Imagine playing with them." She leaned back on her elbow facing Will, who mirrored her body language. She took another drink then rattled her empty bottle and handed it to Will.

"I don't think we're on their level." Will placed the bottle on the table behind him.

"I don't know, our teamwork got us on a pirate ship in space, so I'd say we're pretty next level," Natalie reasoned.

"Okay, we've always been a good team. Getting here, though? That was luck."

"Luck, and you being brave enough to risk your life for me." Her big eyes fawned at Will.

"*I* didn't know I was risking my life," Will said. "I just wanted you to stay alive."

"And," Natalie looked away in pause, "I appreciate that. Thank you."

"Well," Will struggled to find the words, "You did exactly the same thing for me. I never expected a thank-you for any of it, but, thank you too."

"I know, um…" Natalie looked around, everywhere but at Will. "I know things worked out weird, but I'm glad you're here and I at least have *you*. I'd be so lonely if I didn't. This would have been so hard without you." Natalie took his hand and interlocked their fingers. Will's heart picked up its pace. They had been dating for weeks, but something was different.

"I'm glad too." Will could not break away from Natalie's eyes, not that he wanted to. "I thought that was going to be the last time I saw you."

"You know what I've been thinking about since we talked to One a few weeks ago?"

"What?" Will's voice was a faint whisper. Natalie's captivating doe eyes looked directly into his soul and pulled him deeper into their gaze like quicksand.

"At first I felt so worthless. I thought everyone else was going to live their lives and we were stuck in exile. Everyone was going to get a happily ever after except us. But, as I thought about everything he said, I realized that we're still living our lives, and we get to do whatever we want with them while we're here. We have *totally* clean slates and none of the things that used to hold us back matter anymore. Everybody's life is a story, and our stories are whatever we want them to be. None of the old rules apply. We can do whatever our hearts desire."

Will wanted to say something clever, but all he could muster was a soft breath. Still fixated on Natalie's eyes, long lashes fluttering at him, cheeks blushing, he noticed her mouth slightly ajar. He was consumed by the buzz of electricity between them. The rest of the world had disappeared and they had drifted closer to one another. Her last sentence echoed in his ears.

"What... does your heart desire?" he whispered. No sooner had the words left his lips than he realized it might have been beyond cheesy, but it felt right.

Natalie lunged at him and pressed her lips to his, squeezing his face to pull him closer. Will's heart skipped a beat, raced as hard as when they had run for their lives. A rumble swept through his body and he tingled from head to toe, arms coiled around her.

Natalie pulled away. They basked in their heavy breath on each other's lips before their eyes gradually peeled open. Natalie lunged and pushed him onto his back. His hands on her hips, Natalie's leg slid up his body and wrapped around him. She ran her fingers through his hair then pulled away and sat up on top of him.

Straddling him, she looked in his eyes, then his lips, then examined his face and ran her fingers down his cheek. She crossed her arms to grab the bottom of her shirt and pulled it over her head, then threw it against the wall. She reached behind her to unhook her bra and let the straps hang from her shoulders, then dove in for more.

Mike

36

The Wizard of Elysium

On the bridge of the *Ulfberht,* Mike left Nikolai in charge and entered his office through a side door, which closed behind him. He put two fingers to the back of his hand.

"Hey Al, knock-knock."

In front of the office door appeared a speck of light. It expanded into a bright ring of nebulous white light with the consistency of smoky plasma. Inside the ring was another place; a grassy green hill with a stone path and a starry sky. Mike stepped through the ring of light and was no longer on the *Ulfberht.*

A vibrant, colorful garden surrounded the path. Ahead, a small bridge passed over a peacefully trickling stream that cascaded down rocks. The garden was so beautiful and alive it was easy to forget he was standing on a large asteroid in space. Glittering stars covered the sky. A fluffy yellow nebula with tinges of red against a greenish cloud dominated the horizon ahead to Mike's right, towering higher than any skyscraper and more massive than any mountain.

The path led to and encircled a round exedra in the middle of a clearing atop a grassy hill. Sitting on the bench was an old man with unruly white hair. He drank from a teacup then set it down on the stone table in front of him, next to another teacup on its own saucer.

"Hello, Michael," he greeted. His large glasses, bright smile, and bulbous nose came together to make him look a bit goofy.

Mike swept his coat aside to sit on a small bench opposite him. "Hey Al, how's Elysium holding up?"

"Wundabah!" Albert took in the beauty of his garden. "I'm building a belvedere on ze south side. I zink I'll park somevhere with a good view of ze Milk Way to celebrate when it is finished." He held his hands out as if he could behold the view in front of him already.

"I'm sure it'll be as beautiful as everything else you've built here." Mike took in the majesty of the garden, his voice a mix of amazement and jealousy.

"I have no doubt. But, something troubles you, friend. Have you come with questions?" Albert asked.

"Yeeeeah," Mike groaned.

Mike spent the next half hour sharing his last three months with Albert. He started with the attack on the bunker and the kids. Then, he told him about One, the vision he had when he touched him, and their conversations since. Lastly, he shared what he learned from Bradley; that Lazarus was up to something in the colonies.

"Such peculiar events, especially ze alien. Why do you only now come to me?" Albert asked after Mike had wrapped up.

"Well, I had Brad to deal with and I can't come here while we're at warp. Also, I wanted some time with my thoughts and time to talk to One. But, nothing he says is helpful. I've just found myself at a loss of what to think. The only thing I'm sure about was that vision." Mike always found reasons not to bring One. He could have brought him then but chose not to.

"Why ze light?" Albert leaned in.

"That light." Mike's mind fixated on the fluffy white light that emanated from Natalie's house. "It was pure... love, man. I thought I hadn't felt it since before that night. But, I realized I have. It's not the same. I may not have her, but I have you, and Nikolai, and Maya, and this crew." Mike shuffled his body, searching for words and feelings he was not accustomed to expressing. "I realized that what I've been chasing all these years wasn't *just* my daughter, it was that love, that sense of family. And, in my search for that, I've built a new family around me. A family without which I'd be lost, and I appreciate the hell out of you all."

Albert smiled. "You've grown so much, old friend. I too am lucky to have you and ze friends we've made since our escape. I may have little desire to live in a world so cruel, but you remind me there is also good."

"There's a lot of good people out there." Mike pointed at the stars. "You've just gotta get out there and meet them, be a part of the world."

"Earth is that way." Al pointed. "And, a world where greed and corruption still reign, even after ze Union? There may not be hunger, but there is poverty, classism, and hatred. My inventions will be turned into weapons." He shook his head.

"Your inventions could also make the world a better place. A Hammer is a weapon if you need a weapon. Any tool is," Mike pointed out.

"Knowledge without wisdom is dangerous. It must be earned so you understand consequences." Albert was an animated character, which could make it difficult to tell if he was being serious. Even after all these years, it still made Mike nervous when Albert cavalierly discussed the horrible things that could go wrong with an experiment if he was ever wrong about anything.

"The world needs visionary idealists like you. You're at *least* a hundred years ahead of everyone else. You would *inspire* people."

"Inspiration is important, but I am not one to do it. I am old, that is a young man's game," Albert said.

"So, what? You live on an asteroid in space with an atmosphere, a garden, a waterfall. You make robots that build tunnels to make your home bigger, and you can travel anywhere you want in the *universe*. Your solution is to lock yourself away in this palace of self-indulgence, squander your talents, and hide away from the world?"

"That makes this the perfect place for One. My little asteroid is as far removed from the equation of our universe as anyone can be."

"Nice segue." Mike gave Albert a sidelong look.

"What?" Albert put his hands up. "You said One seeks not to interfere with events in ze universe. He goes where ze universe puts him. Ze universe is us, so we choose where he goes. Bring him here, he will be safe."

"I heard the kids talked to him. Maya won't tell me anything else, but I think they got him to talk," Mike said.

"Impressive," Albert said.

"Either they're impressive or I'm an idiot."

"Or both." Albert sipped on his tea.

"If they can get him to talk, I can get him to talk. If I can't get anything out of him before we head for Earth, I'll bring him here. Besides, it's not like there's anyone chasing us. He's safe on the *Ulfberht*," Mike said. "You two would *really* get along. He talks about the universe like it's alive."

"All things are alive, Michael. All things. If I do not understand this, I cannot do all the things I do."

"This table isn't alive." Mike knocked on the stone table.

"But, it is, like ze universe is alive. Let me explain in a way you understand easily." Albert straightened himself, fingers wiggling in front of him. "Ze universe is object-oriented program. All things are objects, and so all things have equal value in eyes of ze universe."

"You're right, it does make a lot of sense when you say it like that." Mike entertained the concept, but Albert was not finished.

"Be careful, Michael." Albert leaned in. "I believe he is trying to protect you."

"How do you figure?"

"You said he is anomaly, ze universe is trying to heal. Perhaps if something he says changes time, things can be worse. Think, what has changed since you found him?"

"Well, we picked up the kids. We were delayed in leaving for Freyja maybe a few hours at most. Nothing much, really," Mike recounted. Things had generally gone according to their original schedule with negligible differences.

"Ze kids," Albert said, wagging an index finger in the air. "If you attack later, ze kids die. If early, ze kids live, perhaps. But, you attack when ze kids are there, save them, and destroy enemy ship. You are almost killed by Dragon Claw at *Oasis*. Many things ze same, other things different. If Time has changed, there is no way to tell how. It is changing every moment in many places, and you would never know."

"I suppose, but I can't see how anything else could have changed."

"You are not looking at Time. You are looking at events in *your* timeline. *Your* struggle is not *ze* only struggle. *Your* story is not *ze* only story. The kids, their families are dead. What did these kids do in ze future? What happens now? What did their families do? What was their destiny?"

Albert paused his rant of questions, staring dead at Mike, who contemplated the butterfly effect of a single event. He had not taken into consideration the possible futures that had been changed, or how other lives may have been altered and how that could affect him. There was no way to tell how far the ripple of One's arrival would spread, even without him saying a word to anyone.

"Any changes." Albert regained Mike's attention after giving him a moment to process. "Any change at all can alter everything, ze whole world. From this vantage, we cannot see. If Time has changed, there is no way to tell how. It is changing as we speak. You must think bigger, higher." Albert motioned with his hands as if expanding an invisible plume of smoke in front of him, like the massive Nebula the sky.

"I hadn't considered all that." Mike leaned back, contemplative.

"Especially if you pursue Lazarus. He thinks on a grand scale. You must as well if you are to face ze challenges before you now," Albert warned.

Mike nodded and paused in reflection, then straightened his posture. "Thanks for the advice." He stood. "We're only a day away from Sol and I want to have at least one more chat with One before we head for Earth. We've got to stop by Leo's on Ganymede before we get along with our business."

"Why?" Albert pushed himself up, using the round stone table for support, cracking his back once he was on his feet.

"We took some damage during the Dragon Claw attack, need to replace a part."

"I could make *anyzing* you need right here." Albert thrust his hands around him, dumbfounded that Mike did not make the most of the resources available to him.

"Yeah, but we can't *always* do that. We've got to keep good relationships with the people in the world. You do that by giving them business sometimes and actually *interacting* with them." Mike took a stab at Albert's isolation, which was even greater than his own. "Oh, actually, could you make a bunch of gravity nets? After the attack on Endoria, those things are hard to come by, so we could make some good money on 'em."

"Okay, but I am not as isolated as you think. Goodbye, old friend." With a big toothy grin, Albert opened his arms for a hug, which Mike was happy to give. "And remember, time is changing all around us, we only have one piece of ze puzzle."

Sam

Oil and Water

High Archon Edison,

Thank you for clearance to vaguely discuss my objective with Captain Slater. He had invaluable strategic advice and I've finished modifying the tactical suit he gave me in case I encounter the enemy. This includes upgrading the gravity gear, which I found to be highly inadequate. The tech is out of date, we could do much better. I request the Ministry address gravity gear, and the standard issue equipment provided to Earth Orbit Security.

As for the energy weapon we confiscated from the Dragon Claw, my report is almost complete. I've run some experiments on its various components and refashioned it as a defensive weapon on my suit. Since I'm a terrible shot, I changed its form factor.

Two men from Jones's unit went missing shortly after my last report. I wish there was more I could do to help, but the crew is working around the clock to find them. Jones has ramped up security precautions. It has been over three months since we arrived, but there is still no sign of our targets. Samson

is worried we'll scare them off in the search for our teammates since they are
supposed to arrive soon.

Until next time,
- Sam

"Send message." Sam leaned back in his chair, but a red alert with a
downbeat tune popped up on his screen instead of a confirmation.

UNABLE TO SEND
PERMISSION DENIED

"You've got to be *kidding* me!" Sam pounded the table and shot up
from his chair. "*Rampart*, ping Agent Jones." A screen appeared over
his desk and placed Jones in the War Room. Sam had not been able to
call friends, but he damn well better be able to communicate with the
Ministry. Jones had overstepped his bounds and Sam needed to draw a
line. He gave himself clearance and sent the message, then stormed out
of his room with purpose and maintained a brisk pace.

The *Rampart's* War Room doors flew open and Sam burst in. Inside,
Ken and Samson stood around the center table with Jones at the far end.
A hologram of local city blocks was projected over the table. The meeting
came to an abrupt halt and they looked up at Sam with inquiry.

"The room, please," Sam ordered.

"We're in the middle of—" Jones was cut off.

"Samson, Ken, now," Sam commanded.

Samson and Ken made for the exit without hesitation.

"What the *hell* do you two think you're doing?" Jones's voice trembled
with rage.

"You're both our superiors. We're following the chain of command."
Samson put his hands up. Jones and Sam stared each other down while
the other two men left the room in a tense silence. Even after the doors
closed behind them, Sam and Jones's eyes remained locked.

"You've grown bold these last few months. What gives you the right to interrupt a strategy meeting with my team?" Jones demanded.

"I have every right that you do here, and I'm doing my job. What the hell gives you the right to prevent me from speaking with the Ministry?" Sam retorted.

"We restricted all non-essential use of comms. Seeing as it took you almost two weeks to notice, I'd say it isn't of particular importance," Jones said.

"The Ministry, like the UEG, shouldn't be classified as non-essential communications." Sam raised his voice.

"My mistake." Jones managed a disingenuous and sarcastic tone. "I'm sure you'll require some counseling and a warm blanket after this ordeal. Since you aren't useful to the mission, why don't you go do that?"

"I'm sure thousands of people on the *Oasis* would disagree about my useful-"

"Oh, who gives a damn about them? I asked one thing of you and you were useless. I still don't know who we're after because of *you*."

"Now who's the baby? You're still crying over that blood sample? It was classified, that's all I could get." Sam was keen to protect Ministry interests. It had become a point of contention between them. Sam spoke the truth, but after hearing it multiple times, it was a tired excuse to Jones.

"This again." Jones rolled his eyes. His body slouched as if physically burdened to hear it. "You've made no efforts to circumvent that lockout, though, have you? You're a little puppet, like the rest of the Ministry. You're smart but useless. You waste everyone's time and get *nothing* done."

"Are you *kidding* me?" Astonishment replaced Sam's anger. "Before the Ministry, science was like the wild west. There was no research coordination, no checks and balances, hardly any safety regulations. People created dangerous AIs, news stations would call random jackasses *specialists*." His fingers mimicked quotation marks. Jones took a deep, annoyed breath as Sam went on. "And we got stuff like the Reckoning and subsequent collapse of the late twenty-first century."

"Oh, yes, please remind me of the *nightmare* that was the late twenty-first century. The Ministry *loves* to remind everyone the world was bleak and hopeless before the glorious *Ministry of Science* graced Earth with its… bureaucracy…" Jones twirled his hand in the air, stepping away from the table.

"Vetoing dangerous and irresponsible laws not based in science is saving lives and keeping Earth prosperous." Sam tried to correct his perception. "We provide structure to a formerly unstructured system and help create responsible laws."

"Laws determined the lay of the land *before* the Union, and they do so *after* the Union. Laws are all we ever needed! Private Industry did fine before the Ministry."

"Uh, famines? Geo-catastrophes? Rampant corruption? War?" Sam listed the faults in Jones's logic. "*That's* doing fine?"

"War always has been and always will be. There may not be war now, but it will come again, mark my words," Jones said with conviction.

"That's a pessimistic attitude," Sam said. For the first time in human history, there were no nations, only one unified Earth. The world had known peace and progress like never before. Humans were finally a level one civilization and all that was left of war were the veterans of the last one. In another generation, they would be old, and a generation after that, gone. "We have abundant food, shelter, education, and people at their core are loving and kind. There's no need for war."

"People at their core are selfish and violent," Jones asserted.

"I guess I didn't account for trauma or sociopathy."

"You've had a very convenient life, haven't you, Chancellor?" Jones paced toward him. "You and the rest of your Ministry brethren are nothing more than obstacles in governance. You sit behind your desks in cozy chairs imposing your morality on the world while the rest of us do the work that is necessary to keep the world *safe* and prosperous."

"Imposing our morality? Your world view is more twisted than I thought," Sam said. In his eyes, if Jones considered scientifically responsible legislation as an imposition of morals, then his opinions were based on perception, not viable information. To Sam, he was a child who considers their parents oppressive because they won't let them touch a hot surface.

"Without people like me, this *peace* you've blissfully enjoyed would crumble to *pieces!*" Arm's reach away from Sam, Jones's eyes were a mix of bloodthirsty eagerness and disdain.

"The Ministry has propelled our species to new heights. Your inability to see past the tiny box you exist in isn't the Ministry's problem," Sam said.

"Excuse me?" Jones took another step forward, fists clenched at his sides. "Do you think me a fool, Chancellor?"

"I don't think that would be accurate," Sam said, ready for Jones to attack. "Even fools recognize their limitations. You mistake freedom with nihilism and practicality with a lack of ethics. You hide your insecurities behind authority and think your ideals are the only ones that matter, but that's because you can't wrap your brain around anything greater than yourself. You say you're keeping people safe, but you're just indulging your sick personal appetite for cruelty. Humans are a cooperative species, and people like you who are unable to think like that are broken, sub-par, and disposable," Sam said with a penetrating stare. Jones glowered at Sam, fists trembling. "For the layman," Sam continued, "trash."

Eyes bulging, teeth gritted with rage, Jones took a wild right swing at Sam, who did not react as Jones anticipated. Instead of retreating, Sam ducked under Jones's wild punch and slammed a fist into his jaw.

Jones's ears rang and his eyes watered. His body jolted from the blow. Sam slugged him in the mouth while he was stunned and shoved him into the wall. Jones looked back at him in surprise. He had underestimated Sam, and had not expected him to react as he did.

"I'm from Washington, raised by lumberjacks." Sam stared down Jones, cracked his neck, and clenched his fists. "I'm not going to take your childish shit."

Sam had some fight in him, but Jones has superior training. He killed for a living and was no stranger putting his life on the line. Sam, on the other hand, spent his time behind computer screens and in laboratories. He might have to take a few blows, but Sam was no match for him.

Jones charged into him. Sam swung and missed. Two quick punches to Sam's abdomen and a hook to his head sent him tumbling sideways, barely on his feet. Jones pressed his attack. He took another swing but Jones blocked and returned the strike.

With no more patience, Jones hit him with a flurry of precise blows, ending with a jab to his neck. Sam covered up to defend and swung again, but Jones snatched his arm and threw Sam over his shoulder, crashing into the ground with a thud. Jones quickly mounted him, a knee on his stomach, and drew his long razor-sharp dagger from its holster. Dagger in the air, Jones smiled at Sam, blood trickling from his nose, and took one last bloodthirsty look at his prey before he watched the life drain from his eyes.

With a grunt, he thrust the knife at Sam's throat, but his arm would not budge. A pressure on his arm pulled him off Sam and tossed him away like a rag doll. Jones crashed ribs-first into the table, onto some chairs and rolled to the floor. His knife tumbled away. In a fury, Jones thrust some chairs away and shot to his feet. To his surprise, standing by Sam was Samson. Captain Slater's shadow loomed in the doorway.

"Whatever this was, it's over!" Slater boomed. "Or both of you will conduct your business from the brig. Do I make myself clear?"

Sam nodded in agreement after Samson helped him up. Sam and Jones glared at each other.

"Agent," Slater said.

"Fine." Jones's annoyance was opaque. He took his eyes off Sam to give Captain Slater a hateful look. Then, he turned to Samson. "What do you think *you're* doing?"

"I told the Captain when we came aboard that I'm a joint asset. I'm on loan to the UEG from the Ministry. I was given special orders to ensure the Chancellor's safety." Samson motioned to Sam. "So, I went to the Captain's office when Sam dismissed us."

Jones's jaw fell slack, both bewildered and insulted, but before he could process the information Captain Slater took control of the conversation.

"Mr. DeLuca just got a call about the part. They're coming to pick it up late tonight. You two should get yourselves patched up."

Sam and Jones looked to Slater, then each other. Their adrenaline settled in recognition that it was time to work. Jones composed himself and cleared his throat, then picked up his knife.

"I have work to do." Jones sheathed his knife and marched by everyone. He gave Samson a begrudging look as he passed. With Jones gone, Slater stepped into the room and the doors slid shut behind him.

"You okay, sir?" Samson patted Sam on the shoulder.

"Yeah, I'm good. Thanks for saving my ass. Why didn't you tell me you had special orders?"

"Didn't seem important. Also, I didn't know you, so telling you could have put me in a compromising position. But, you're a good guy," Samson said.

"Thanks." Sam smiled, happy to find an unknown ally, and a powerful one.

"You're damn lucky my office is on the other side of that wall." Slater pointed to the wall they crashed into during the scuffle.

"I didn't expect it to turn into a fight, for some reason…" Sam trailed off.

"Be sure you're ready for next time. I get the feeling he'd be happy to stay in the brig if he gets to kill you," Slater warned grimly. Their fight was not finished.

"Well, if our targets are here, maybe there won't be a next time."

Ulfberht Crew

38

Ambush

With Elysium behind them, the *Ulfberht* crew continued their return trip to the Sol system and touched down on Ganymede the next day. It was three in the morning and the streets of the industrial district were dark and quiet. Most of the commotion at that hour happened in the bar district, which was open at all hours. Mike, Shin, and Farouk strolled casually to the Goblin's Burrow for their power regulator.

"You look like a cowboy when you throw baggy clothes and a poncho over your suit," Mike said, the Goblin's Burrow a few paces away.

"There are no cowboys in space." Shin shook his head at Mike, but old cowboy and samurai movies were his favorite, and it was on purpose.

"I know a guy that might disagree with that." Mike opened the door to the Goblin's Burrow for Shin behind him, who held it for Farouk.

"Leo!" Mike strolled into the room. There was no response or sign of his friend, who was usually at the front desk. "Leo?"

"Welcome to the Goblin's Burrow!" a strange voice called out.

Mike, Farouk, and Shin jolted into high alert. Agent Jones stepped out from behind one of the decorative engine parts in Leo's lobby, arms in the air showing off the shop with pride.

"Who are you? Where's Leo?" Mike demanded with a hand on his pistol, the burning sense of imminent danger pumping through his veins.

"No need to worry, Leo is safe at home. My name is Agent Jones and I've been following your bread crumbs without any idea of who is on the other side. I've identified Farouk Knight, the *former* heavyweight champion, and Shin Morikawa, the *traitor*." He gestured to each of them.

Shin's hand inched back for his pistol.

"That would be a poor choice." Agent Jones waved his hand. Ken stepped out from the second level doorway in full armor and dropped to the first floor with them. Armored UEG troopers swarmed into the room on both levels, weapons trained on the trio. Samson strolled in behind everyone else.

"We can take 'em," Farouk whispered.

"So?" Agent Jones gestured. "Are you going to be difficult about this? Bringing you in alive is the preferred option but not the only one."

Mike examined the room. They were surrounded, the enemy had their own Ranger with a new suit, and the big guy was sure to be genetically enhanced. Despite Farouk's enthusiasm, they were fish in a barrel. Mike put his hands in the air and glanced at Shin and Farouk to do the same. They followed his lead. Disgruntled by the decision, Farouk glared at Jones.

Samson approached the team with a black burlap sack. He took Shin and Mike's weapons. Farouk was unarmed and stared him down, arms open in a challenge.

"Hey, all this aside, it's an honor to meet you," Samson whispered.

"Are you mothafuckin' serious right now?"

"Hey, at least if you get any funny ideas, I'll get that one-on-one I've always wanted." Samson winked slyly.

"Oh yeah? I hope you get it too." Farouk nodded. His eyes burned a hole through Samson like a mad dog ready to pounce.

Samson smiled and returned to hand over the guns. Jones examined Shin's pistol, removing a bullet from its chamber, then slipped it back into the clip. He tossed it back into the bag and grabbed Mike's pistol. Three troopers entered from behind Mike's team.

One trooper had a pair of handcuffs for Mike. The second had a collar with four small silver boxes spread evenly around it. He placed it around Shin's neck and plugged it into his suit then handcuffed him as well.

The third trooper had a pair of special handcuffs for Farouk as thick as a beer can. Magnetic restrictors ran along the inside to keep his hands immobilized. He glanced at Jones and then pulled his hands apart in an attempt to break the cuffs. His arms dinged against the inner walls. The trooper in front of him jumped back in a startled panic.

"Not bad." Farouk nodded.

"Those are some quality arms if you actually managed to touch the casing," Jones said in wonder. Farouk smiled and relaxed.

"So, what is your name?" Jones examined Mike's pistol. He put a bullet back into the clip and approached Mike, eyeing him like the solution to a puzzle out of reach.

"You don't know who I am?" Mike asked.

"Should I?"

"Weren't you sent to track me down? Seems like a dick move not to tell you who you're after."

"Well, we didn't know your name. The Gerridae at the bunker you attacked caught a glimpse of Knight's ship and I surmised the traitor's identity from the description of a fight on the *Oasis Station*. You, however, I don't know who *you* are. I've been in suspense all these months. I see you're a respectable Earthling and I *could* scan your brand but I'd rather be civilized about this with a fellow Alpha. Still, I'll not ask my question again." Jones closed up Mike's gun and tossed it in the bag with Shin's. Samson pulled shut the bag's drawstring.

Albert's words rushed through Mike's mind. *Any changes at all can alter everything, ze whole world. From this vantage, we cannot see. If time has changed, there is no way to tell how. It is changing as we speak, and you vould never know.*

This is what he meant. When they attacked the Gerridae, they changed time a tiny bit, and this was the backlash. Mike cursed himself for not having greater vision and considering that someone might be after them for the bunker attack.

"My name is Michael Smith."

"Smith? If that's a fake name…"

"It's real." Mike rolled his eyes.

"Michael Smith," Jones said, two fingers on his hitch. It projected for him the results of the name search. "Your name sounds familiar." Jones shook his head, unable to shake the feeling. "Could you be more specific? There are almost four thousand Michael Smiths registered with the UEG, forty-two of which are Alphas."

"Michael Julian Smith. Born the fifth of November, twenty-one thirty-eight," he specified, careful to enunciate.

Jones returned to his search. Perplexed, he looked back and forth between his search results and Mike, then read aloud. "Software Developer. Alias: Axiom. Fought in World War Four. High Archon and *founding* member of the Ministry of Science?" Jones read aloud the single result that matched his name and birth date in astonishment.

"That alias is for a younger, more conceited person." The sound of his old alias brought with it a sting of shame. "I don't go by it anymore."

"I do rather like the dramatic flair of you space-faring vagabonds and your nicknames. I've been doing my homework on you all since I was tasked with this mission. What do you go by now?" Jones asked.

"Does it matter?"

"I've been waiting for you on Ganymede for three months from the single lead of that Gerridae's black box. I'm a bit curious," Jones admitted.

"Hmm." Mike shook his head. "I don't have an alias because I'm a pirate. I'm a software engineer."

"No, you're a criminal now, so you're a hacker."

"That's fair," Mike admitted.

"What's your new *hacker* name?" Jones mocked.

Mike could barely stand Agent Jones and his exasperating and useless line of questions. "Aries."

"So you've ascended to godhood? Good for you. Far less creative." Jones misinterpreted the name, but Mike did not care enough to correct him. "According to these results, you've been deceased for over a decade," Jones said with astonished intrigue. Usually, his targets were not such fascinating mysteries.

"I do often feel dead inside, I guess that explains it," Mike bantered, but his comment was passed over.

"You must know something very important for your blood sample to return no results when searched. I have a Ministry Chancellor on my ship and he was unable to procure any information for me."

"My results were probably classified. I wouldn't think a Chancellor would have clearance. I'm sure there are people who don't want anyone to know I'm alive."

"Well, if you don't cooperate, I will ensure they no longer have to lie." Jones paced away. The troopers behind Mike and his team nudged them outside.

Jones, Ken, and Samson followed them out of the building. Outside, over two dozen UEG troopers waited with a semi-circle of armored vehicles, all taking aim at them on their trek to a long armored truck in the center. Once inside, two troopers locked thick clamps around Farouk's knees which magnetically attached to those on his hands.

"All right, I get it." Farouk examined his restraints with annoyance.

"We aren't taking any chances. Since your cybernetics are so advanced, I had our Ministry official make the restraints *twice* as strong as the strongest restraints that exist for weaponized cybernetics. Apparently, he's good for *something*." Jones smirked, confident in his superior position. He took a seat across from them, Ken and Samson on either side, troopers at each end of the cabin.

"Whatever you say, man." Farouk shook his head, eyeing the troopers closing the doors from the outside.

The long vehicle lurched forward and everyone in the cabin swayed with the motion. The silence was overwhelming, with all six men on edge and biting their tongues. Riveted with anticipation, nobody expected their quarry to come so quietly.

"So, Michael Julian Smith," Jones broke the silence, still curious and intrigued. "Why are you so important that someone would conceal your death, or life?" Jones leaned back against the wall, arms crossed in contemplation.

"They didn't exactly hide my death, but had no choice but to support the evidence of it when I disappeared," Mike explained. There was no reason to lie, which both concerned and further fascinated Jones.

"Interesting, but who *are* you? What have you done?" Why was this outlaw so forthcoming with information? The real question he wanted to ask could not be asked bluntly. He needed to finesse the information out of him.

"Really? Every time you see the stars while traveling at warp, or marvel at the efficiency of essentials distribution on Earth, or use a Ministry console, you're interacting with my contributions to the world," Mike said with neither ego nor humility.

"That's right!" Jones perked up. His eyes bloomed and he uncrossed his limbs, a finger pointed at Mike. "I remember you! I watched a documentary not long ago. You're... what did they use to call you? The Tesla of software?"

"Yeah, a long time ago..." Mike trailed off.

"Fascinating." Jones was captivated. "How is it you ended up here?"

"I found out that life isn't as black and white as I thought. I've had to make some hard choices." Mike's words grew heavy with regret.

"I suppose I can't really fault my Ministry contact for falling short on this task. How did you come into the company of these two?" Jones swung his finger between Farouk and Shin. "You should play the lottery."

"The universe is a crazy place." Mike revealed nothing.

Jones grinned. Finally, Mike was not being forthright with information. Perhaps he cared more to hide some of these details than his personal ones, which meant he was not hiding, but he *was* hiding something.

"I'd be careful if I were you." Mike took the initiative in the conversation.

"Why do you say that?" Intrigued, Jones leaned forward, elbows on his knees.

"Whoever wants to keep my survival a secret is a powerful person. You knowing puts you at risk. You should watch your ass."

Eyes narrow, Jones leaned away, insulted. "Are you threatening—"

Everyone in the cabin was lifted from their seats and the vehicle jumped, landing with a bounce. It settled quickly. They fumbled in surprise and Jones rushed out of the rear double doors.

In such a hurry he almost tumbled out of the vehicle, the crackling sounds of gunfire welcomed Jones outside. Slugs dinged against the armor and the audio channel was abuzz with people calling out enemy positions. An explosion flipped the vehicle behind theirs in the convoy and knocked Jones to the ground.

Stunned, the world spun around him. Samson helped him to his feet. The sounds of the world were muffled and distant.

"Yarie?"

"Wha—?"

"You all right?" Samson asked again, his voice clear. Jones looked around to get his bearings. The troopers from his vehicle had piled out with him and were already firing at the attackers in the windows and rooftops, taking cover wherever they could.

"I'm fine." Jones pulled his arm away and leaned on the armored vehicle for support. He walked around the vehicle, past a trooper taking cover behind the door firing at attackers. Jones rubbed his ears to soothe an uncontrollable ring in his head and grabbed his rifle from the cabin then returned to Samson and Ken.

"Get the guys on the rooftops." Jones pointed at Ken, still in a daze, vision blurred. Then, he pointed at Samson. "Close the door, make sure they don't get out."

Samson hopped back into the armored vehicle and closed the doors. Ken ran for the nearest building. Jones headed to the front of the vehicle and fired at the windows that flickered with gunfire.

Inside the vehicle, Mike, Shin, and Farouk listened to the muffled, chaotic world outside. Samson leaned back casually across from them.

"You guys aren't going to try anything, are you?" Samson chuckled.

"Oh yeah, you bet." Farouk nodded. "Right, Shin?"

"Agreed. We're going to work together to break out of here," Shin said.

Samson glanced back and forth between them with a grin. "I like that you guys have a sense of humor even when you're in cuffs."

"We ain't playin' motha'fucka'. I can break these cuffs."

Samson clicked his tongue and shook his head. "You can't break those cuffs."

"I'm going to sneak attack yo' ass then break that collar powering down Shin's suit. After that, Shin's going to keep you busy while I break out of these cuffs, then I'm going to whoop your ass while they get out of here," Farouk relayed his plan to the others.

Samson scoffed, on the verge of laughter, then looked back and forth between Shin and Farouk. They glanced at one another in agreement. It became clear he was not joking. Their eyes promised impending action.

Samson unfolded his arms and held a finger in the air. "Don't!"

Farouk pulled the two sets of cuffs apart and charged into Samson. He deflected quickly, but Farouk was faster. He twisted Samson's arms and locked him up, then smashed him in the face with an elbow. Shin lunged from his seat and Farouk crushed the collar then ripped it off his neck. Samson pulled Farouk from behind and threw him against the back wall. Shin removed the collar and broke the cuffs in time to defend from Samson.

Samson tried to land a punch on Shin, but he was too fast. Shin dodged and tied up Samson's arms, landing quick punches when he could. He kept Samson busy while Farouk focused, took deep breaths, and pulled his arms apart with everything he had. The cuffs shattered and pieces fell to the floor, then he smashed his knee clamps.

"Help a brother out." Mike held his hands up for Farouk, who snapped his cuffs with two fingers.

Samson finally managed to grab a hold of Shin and pulled him into a powerful knee. He tried to clothesline him but Farouk grabbed Samson's arm and slammed him against the back of the compartment. They exchanged blows while Mike and Shin hurried out. They disappeared while Samson tried to fight his way out of a corner.

Samson locked up with Farouk and attempted some knee strikes or any effective blow, but Farouk dragged him against the wall and tossed him outside. Samson tumbled onto the street. He barely had time to get up before he was forced to defend against Farouk, who charged him into the overturned vehicle behind them. Farouk went on the offensive but Samson locked him up and tossed him into a building several meters away.

Every day for the last three months, Samson had trained intensely. He practiced every morning and every night, he watched all of Farouk's fights, and in the last two weeks, his training had become more intense, frustrated about his vanished teammates. This was the moment to which the mission and his whole life had been building. A one-on-one against the living legend, Farouk 'The Slapdaddy' Knight.

"You really want to fight the mothafuckin' Slapdaddy?" Farouk got to his feet.

"I'm not the best unless I beat the best." Samson cracked his knuckles, neck, and back, then took a boxing stance. "I've lived my whole *life* for this fight."

"All right." Farouk sauntered over to Samson, his fist far out in front of him. Samson held his fist out to meet Farouk's.

The two men bumped knuckles, then shuffled back.

The fight had begun.

Chaos

39

Battle Zone: Ganymede

THE ACCENTS OF KEN'S SUIT GLOWED A SOFT COBALT BLUE, FROM the soles of his shoes to the streaks on his head, holding him to the side of a steel building. He sprinted up the wall toward the muzzle flashes of attackers firing at the caravan below. Some fired at Ken when they saw him coming. He tossed grenades in the windows and pounced onto the roof.

The roof-perched attackers jumped at his sudden presence before turning to open fire, but he moved too swiftly. His blade jutted from his arm and cut through the rifle of the nearest attacker, then through his chest and he darted away. It was as if the bullets were rushing to catch him. Even when they did connect, they were ineffective.

Ripping through more enemies, a railgun shell zoomed past him from an adjacent rooftop. He jutted his left arm toward them and fired his composite-alloy nails. They ripped through their necks and chests then shot back toward Ken to re-arm themselves.

Ken continued his assault while the battle progressed elsewhere.

On the ground, Mike and Shin hurried from vehicle to vehicle, taking cover from the bullets that rained down around them, banging against the cars and paved floor like a hail storm.

"I wish I had my helmet." Shin tossed a dead soldier on the ground and searched the vehicle cabin for their weapons. Mike checked the dead soldier's rifle, but it was user-locked and would not fire.

"Found them." Shin pulled out the bag and handed Mike his pistol. Mike peeked around the back of the vehicle, watching troopers fall dead. On the far side of the street, Farouk flew through the air and smashed into a parked car. The roof caved in and shattered glass exploded around him. Farouk crawled off the car's hood dusting off pieces of broken glass and hustled away. Mike stayed low and hurried back.

"You see Farouk anywhere?" Shin asked.

"He's still fighting the big guy." A nearby explosion muffled the end of Mike's sentence.

"Pssst! Mike!" A hiss pierced the cackling storm of gunfire.

Mike and Shin searched for the source. Hidden behind some cars a safe distance away, Leo waved his hands for them to join him. A stranger kept Leo covered, firing at UEG troops. Shin covered them en route to Leo.

"Leo! You're all right!" Mike took cover with him, away from the wreckage-covered battlefield that was once a street. "That guy said you were at home."

"I've been giving these assholes the slip for weeks. Besides, this was all for me, I needed to be here for it," Leo said. "You haven't met Chris. Chris, this is Mike."

Chris ducked to take cover and shook Mike's hand. "Nice to meet you."

"Thanks for saving our asses. And Leo, I'm sorry for all the trouble. I didn't know we had a tail."

"It's not just us, we called the Red Storm. Let's get somewhere safe. I've got your package waiting back at your ship already. Wasn't Farouk with you?" Leo stayed low and followed Chris away from the battle.

"Leo, you're the best. Farouk will catch up." Mike looked back at the battle. "We broke radio contact with our ship, so backup should be here any second."

"If you've got backup, we could really use it right now. We need to retreat!" Leo hollered over his shoulder.

Not far away, Farouk was entangled in a fierce technical battle with Samson.

"You ain't bad." Farouk kept his head on a swivel and dodged a flurry of Samson's punches. Samson was a massive heap of muscle, but to Farouk's surprise, he moved quickly like a light heavyweight and was technically sound. Equally as fast and powerful, Farouk was not intimidated. Unlike Samson, Farouk was a former world champion who had conquered the best fighters of his generation and taught others to fight.

"Thanks." Samson gave Farouk a nod before a flurry of jabs, hooks, and crosses, trying to shuffle in close. Farouk was the best Samson had ever fought and winning this fight would define him forever.

Farouk retaliated with punishing blows to his body, circling him. Samson covered up and Farouk alternated between head and body shots. A thundering right hook from Farouk sent Samson stumbling sideways with fuzzy vision and a high pitched tone in ears. His bell rung, Samson applied pressure and pressed the attack with a series of fast, straight punches that caught Farouk off-guard.

Samson lunged forward and gripped his hands behind Farouk's head, punishing him with knee strikes. Quick to guard, Farouk smashed down Samson's knees before they could reach their apex then retaliated with an uppercut. Another exchange left Samson at an increasing disadvantage. He tried to take advantage of some openings but Farouk was ahead of him at every step.

Farouk was known for his striking with amazing boxing and two black belts. Farouk's ground game, however, was not a strength, but he did have extensive training. Samson believed it was unlikely Farouk could keep his grappling competitive without someone with whom to practice. If there was an avenue to victory for Samson, that was the surest one. He needed to change his strategy.

Bouncing and moving around Farouk, Samson shot in with a jab then dropped and tackled Farouk at the waist. Before he could make contact, Farouk's knee slammed into Samson's face and broke his orbital. It was the first time since before the gene therapy that he broke a bone. His left brow ballooned. The staggering blow was followed up with several dulling punches that slipped through Samson's guard like it did not exist.

If present, spectators would be cheering *Slap Attack! Slap Attack!* Samson was glad there was nobody watching.

In desperation, Samson threw a wild right cross. Farouk ducked underneath and shot forward, plowing his fist into Samson's already damaged face. Knocked off his feet, blood spurted from Samson's nose. He stumbled to get up, tipping to his side, blinking and shaking his head with the world spinning around him. Panic set in. Farouk put on pressure and Samson threw desperate punches to keep a distance between them.

Farouk bent at the waist and swiveled from side to side as he closed in on Samson, who could no longer keep track of his movement. Panting, Samson came to terms with the situation in which he had placed himself. Farouk's skill was as legendary as advertised. Matched up against a far superior fighter, and someone actually as strong as him, he was going to lose the fight.

He needed to figure out how to subdue Farouk and figured he could muster one or two good attempts depending on how the first one went. He did his best to dodge and defend against Farouk while he figured out his strategy.

Amidst Farouk's assault, Samson caught his arm and transitioned into a clinch from behind in an attempt to lock in a rear naked choke.

Pulling at Samson's arm, Farouk swung above him, holding his breath, but Samson kept his head down, chin to his chest. Moving to avoid the weak punches, his trembling clench squeezed tighter. Farouk struggled to pry Samson's arms off. Looking into the broken glass two floors up, there was a vehicle coming toward them from the street that ran perpendicular to theirs.

Farouk smashed an elbow into Samson's iliotibial band, giving him a dead leg. Samson's leg gave out underneath him and he lost his steel grip. Farouk took a deep breath and spun around with a quick elbow to Samson's head, breaking free of his grip. He gave Samson another uppercut and a hard punch to the gut, then grabbed his arm and flung him over his shoulder.

Samson rocketed through the air and crashed against the building wall. Farouk leaped away as Samson rose to his feet, sliding his back against the wall for support. His vision was blurred and one eye completely swollen shut, the world swirling from side to side. An overpowering ring in his ears and a pounding in his head made it difficult to focus. A blurry blob floating in the air came into focus.

Hovering over the street was a small red and yellow fighter with rows of thrusters on eight sides, built for space combat. After a moment, he recognized it to be a Razorback. It was in fact, Addie's Razorback: *Dragonfly*.

In the space of a breath, Samson contemplated why there was an old space fighter hovering in the middle of the street. *Don't they have zoning laws around here?* Then, *Dragonfly* opened fire, and everything made sense.

Samson was blasted into the building. Bright streaks of energy crashed into him. Powerful thuds slammed into Samson and the building until they stopped as abruptly as they had begun, leaving a cloud of smoke and rubble in their wake.

Farouk looked over his shoulder with pity at Samson's limp body on the ground covered in rubble, crimson blood pooling underneath him. Samson was an enemy, but also a fan, and a solid fighter. "Good fight."

Dragonfly rose higher, firing at the rooftops. Ken sprinted away and threw himself off the building to get out of the line of fire. The Ranger suit protected him from most weapons, but it offered little protection against weapons of that caliber.

Like a hummingbird, the *Dragonfly* floated through buildings, opening fire on what remained of Agent Jones's caravan. *Dragonfly* weaved from side to side, avoiding the modest enemy fire that remained.

Five fighters easily twice the size of *Dragonfly* swooped in, opening fire before they were in close. Their white and blue paint matched the *Rampart*. The *Dragonfly* made dodging them look easy, swooping around and between them, dispatching three with ease. The ships rained to the ground as balls of fire. The last two ships chased *Dragonfly* out of the city and into open space.

After the whirr of fighters and the cackling of gunfire had ceased, the road was a quiet battlefield, littered with UEG bodies and vehicles covered in bulletholes or flipped upside down.

"Ken!" Jones roared. Blood running down the side of his face, he waded through a sea of trooper corpses, rubble, and heaps of broken vehicles. "Samson!"

In the midst of an insane space fighter flying into the city and raining down hell, their attackers had disappeared. Only the whispers of crackling fires and pained groans filled the street. Jones glared into the open armored truck where his prisoners had been minutes earlier. He stumbled around the truck, through damaged cars and more dead soldiers. Then, he was rooted in place.

Samson's massive arm and other parts of him jutted from beneath a pile of rubble. On approach, it became clear that what remained of Samson's arms and legs barely clung to his tattered body and he was covered in burns. Parts of him had been vaporized. A massive pool of blood flowed from his body into the street.

"No…" Jones's voice was laced with rage. He approached Samson and kicked the rubble-covered corpse. "Stubborn… *idiot.*"

"Ken, checking in." His voice came in weakly over the audio channel, breaking Jones's baffled, wrathful haze.

"Thank you for not getting yourself killed," Jones replied and turned away from Samson's body.

"Almost did. I had to jump off a building," Ken grunted, lying on top of a smashed car not far away.

"How long 'til you're ready for battle again?" Jones demanded.

"Fifteen, twenty minutes if I see the ship's doctor."

"A medical team is en route," Jones said. "This isn't done."

Rebels

40

Freedom

THE WALLS OF MATT AND JAMES'S UNGUARDED UNDERGROUND cell rattled and dust sprinkled onto their heads from the ceiling. With a sigh, they shook their heads in dismay; unable to help with what was surely a confrontation which involved their people.

"Those shots were different." James stood from his seat.

"Yeah," Matt agreed. "Fast and heavy caliba'."

"Probably mounted, maybe an old tank or a ship or somethin'." James paced in frustration. "I guess the party is going to end without us." The walls shook again. The fighting was nearby, but it had died down.

"Hey guys," a familiar voice called from outside the cell. On the other side of the bars holding a six pack of beer was Calvin.

"You've got some balls." James approached the cell door, Matt stood to take an aggressive posture.

"Look, I got bashed on the head too. I didn't know what was going to happen. Also, you've eaten well, haven't you? Nobody has beaten you up or kept you up at night? I even made sure they brought you beer. You've been treated well, haven't you?" Calvin made a case for himself.

"Yeah, I'll give ya that. You're still a backstabba'," James said.

"You pretended to be our friend to get one ova' on us." Matt glared.

"Man, I didn't have to pretend. You guys are awesome and I loved hanging out with you. I'm sorry for how things went down, but we have to protect our friends. We offered you guys a way out of your lives working for the UEG, but you chose to keep doing what you're doing. So, I'm here to let you do that." Calvin looked back and forth between the two men, hoping they wouldn't continue to hate him.

"What are you sayin'?" Matt asked.

"I'm here to set you guys free," Calvin pulled a pair of keys from his pocket.

"What?" James shared a puzzled look with Matt. "You're breakin' us out—*and* you brought beer?"

"Well…" Calvin considered his options and realized things might go more smoothly if he rolled with it. "It kind of sucks that you're going back to your lives as soldiers or whatever on Earth and we'll probably never hang out again, but it's your choice. So, we should at least have a beer on the way out. I kind of owe you guys for all the trouble."

"The beer is a nice touch." James and Matt's angry stares softened, then melted away. With a smile, James stepped away from the door. Calvin happily unlocked the cell and handed his friends an open beer as they stepped out of the cell.

The three men raised their drinks together in the air. The celebratory clink of bottles dinging together was the happiest sound the dimly lit underground tunnel had heard in weeks. After taking a drink, James gave Calvin a warm pat on the back.

"You're a good guy, Cal," he said.

"You guys too. Are you sure you don't want to be pirates? I hear it's a lot of fun." Calvin tried one last time.

"Nah," Matt said. "We've got our own lives waitin' for us."

"Well, I hope your lives go good places. You guys can visit any time, I owe you a bunch of free drinks," Calvin promised.

James laughed. "Yeah? Well, if we can cash in on those free drinks, we'll take a vacation and come visit first chance we get."

"Oh yeah! I almost forgot." Calvin reached into his pocket and pulled out a speaker that fit in the palm of his hand. "You guys want to hear that secret track?"

"Hell yeah!"

"Crank that shit!"

Ulfberht Crew

41

The Fruits of Patience

THE *ULFBERHT'S* HANGAR RE-COMPRESSED WITH EVERYONE SAFELY aboard. Addie leapt from her beloved *Dragonfly* like a firecracker. First out of her vehicle she hooted and cheered, running to the *Slap Attack*. In the distance, a door into the long hangar opened and Nikolai marched across the spacious hangar with haste.

"Thanks for the backup," Mike said. Addie crashed into him with a big hug as they walked down the *Slap Attack's* ramp.

"Of course!" Addie jumped to hug everyone. "I'm so glad you guys are okay! What happened? That was like a military escort." She followed them to Iskra's shuttle, which had accompanied them to the *Ulfberht*.

"They tracked us after our attack on the bunker a few months ago," Mike explained succinctly, still shaken by what had happened and aware he would have to repeat himself. He had been caught by surprise. Bradley accused him of being arrogant and since he did not see this coming, was there a chance he had been right? He was so arrogant that he thought he could hit and run a Ministry-UEG bunker with no repercussions. He had not even taken measures to be made aware of such an event.

"Iskra! It's so good to see you!" Addie ran ahead of the group to give Iskra a hug.

"Oh, Addie, good to see you as well," Iskra said.

"Thanks for the escort," Michael said when their paths met. Iskra was dwarfed by six imposing Red Storm pirates, each almost two meters tall.

"Of course." Iskra hardened her stance, back straight and steely-eyed. "Leo called. You should thank *him*."

"I thanked him back on Ganymede," Mike said as Nikolai arrived.

Iskra's six-man escort stood at attention and saluted Nikolai. Iskra saluted as well, but more relaxed. Nikolai returned the salute then stood beside her.

"Addie, could you get us ready to head out?" Mike asked. Veins still coursing with adrenaline, she was play-boxing with Farouk a meter away.

"No problem. See you later, Iskra!"

Iskra gave Addie a wave as she ran off.

"Michael, what happened?" Nikolai asked.

"Apparently, the Gerridae we shot down when we hit the bunker caught a glimpse of us." He ticked his head toward the *Slap Attack*. "They've been waiting for us on Ganymede since then."

"That is not good," Nikolai said.

"You're telling *me*." Mike scoffed. "All I could think about back there was what Al said about the timeline changing. Gave me the creeps."

"You escaped. That is most important," Nikolai grumbled. "But, we should be vigilant. Surely, they will try to follow us. So close to rescuing your daughter, we can not afford confronting them again."

"And, so close to Nikolai's return to the Red Storm." Iskra crossed her arms and raised an eyebrow at Mike.

"Yes, and that. I know it's been a long stay but we'll have him back to you as soon as possible." Mike tried to answer for the numerous consecutive months Nikolai had stayed with them on the *Ulfberht*.

"He stays more and more, but now, four months?" Iskra tried to subdue her anger.

"Moya lyubov." Nikolai placed his hand gently on her back. Iskra huffed angrily. "I volunteered to help Michael, do not be angry with him. She is my goddaughter. I want us all reunited."

Iskra and Nikolai exchanged tense whispers in Russian, then paused. "The Red Storm misses its general," she said without spite.

"I understand. I know we've seen less of you the last couple years, but I'll be sure we visit more," Mike said. "Thank you again for your help."

"You're welcome." Iskra bowed. "I have a clan to lead. Poshli!" she roared. Her men saluted and returned to the shuttle, but Iskra stayed.

Mike, Shin and Farouk did not need to be asked to leave. Despite Nikolai's supportive attitude, he missed Iskra and his clan.

Once they were alone, Iskra's stone face softened and she smiled at Nikolai.

"Moya lyubov." *My love.* Nikolai held his arms out for her.

"Moya dusha." *My soul,* she responded softly. Iskra stood on her toes, reaching up to hold his face in her hands. Nikolai bent down low and they pressed their lips together affectionately. "Ya skuchala po tebe, moya lyubov." *I have missed you, my love.*

The couple shared a few minutes together while her guards waited in the shuttle. They shared a goodbye kiss, and with a dramatic sweep of her coat Iskra turned and marched to her ship. Nikolai left for the control room to open the bay door.

While they had their moment, Mike went to his quarters to wash up and decompress. The chirp of the ship's comms interrupted a welcomed moment of peace.

"Mike, come to the bridge, and bring your sidearm," Maya called. Mike grabbed his discarded pistol to meet Maya on the bridge.

"What's up?" Mike asked when he arrived.

"Michael, something troubles us," Nikolai said.

"I checked Shin's weapon already, give me your pistol." Maya got straight to the point without explaining anything.

"Why?" Mike held his pistol by the barrel and handed it to Maya. She checked the chamber then popped out the clip and extracted bullets into the palm of her hand.

"Shit," she said sharply. From the bullets, she pulled a small metal cylinder and showed it to Mike. "They've been *waiting* for you, Mike!"

"Nikolai, get the Red Storm back here," Mike ordered. "Addie, get us to warp, now!"

Nikolai was already on the nearest console sending the message. Addie jumped into her cockpit. Maya crushed the tracking device under the butt of Mike's pistol.

"Uh, Captain?" Addie worked quickly on her console. The warp meter was filling up, but not fast enough. The bridge's front screen displayed a three-dimensional map of the space around them, and three large ships appeared behind them with UEG signals.

For a brief moment, time stood still as the horror ramped up in Mike's chest. When the icons turned red, meaning the ships had fired on them, claws dug into his lungs. The *Ulfberht* jolted suddenly with Addie pulling the ship away to avoid enemy fire, but it interrupted their jump to warp.

"Michael, our signal is jammed. The message cannot send." Nikolai gripped the rail. The ship jolted from side to side with Addie dodging enemy attacks.

The situation grew more troublesome. Over a dozen enemy fighters emerged from the three large battleships and headed their way. There was a single course of action they could take if they sought to survive. On the nearest console, Mike held down the intercom and his voice boomed throughout the ship.

"All hands, battlestations!"

Chaos

42

Blindsided

"You should have digital security on defense!" Sam yelled on the chaotic bridge of the *Rampart*. "I told you what this guy can do!"

"Only once I told you his name, which I got from him *myself!*" Jones hollered.

"It's not *my* fault it was classified." Sam tried to conceal his deception.

"We will overwhelm our enemy on *all* fronts. Battle is not your domain, *Chancellor*. Know your place and let *us* do our jobs!"

"Fine, do what you want." Sam moved to the other side of the bridge by Amber, who coordinated their ships. Jones's eyes bore a hole through Sam for a moment before returning his attention to the battle.

The bridge's front screen was a hologram assembled with data from every ship in battle. An overlay displayed trajectories and weapons fire. Fighter squadrons and three friendly battleships had a green outline. Jones had used emergency measures to acquisition the two additional battleships. A red outline delineated the enemy Stinger – a powerful warship from World War Four. A shadow of Earth's past. It was half their size but moved more quickly and fluidly than anyone there had seen from a ship that size.

"Focus fire on their engines!" Captain Slater boomed. "They're too slippery to take random shots."

"Alpha and Beta squadrons, focus your fire on the enemy's thrusters." Amber relayed orders almost as quickly as the Captain dictated them.

The enemy ship kicked into a one hundred eighty degree spin and darted through the pursuing fighters. The fighters broke formation in disarray. Two ships were not so lucky and it smashed through them like bugs.

"What the hell are they doing?" Captain Slater wondered aloud, watching the Stinger stay a hair out of their effective weapons range and sweep beneath the three slow-moving battleships.

ON THE *ULFBERHT*, CALLING FOR BATTLE STATIONS SHUFFLED their ranks, Nikolai took the Captain's Chair and Mike was on digital security. Almost everyone except Rick and Addie rushed to the gunner room. Natalie and Will arrived first.

"Rick! Divert power to engines and weapons!" Another enemy fighter dropped off the battle screen, a credit to the gunner room. "Michael! How much time?" The swarm of fighters dove toward and away from them.

"I'm playing offense and defense, maybe a minute." Eyes fixed on screens of scrolling text, Mike typed commands and ran scripts as fast as he could.

"Addie, gather the fighters and crash us through them, then get us beneath the enemy battleships. Keep us out of weapons range." Nikolai sought to exploit the enemy ships' designs, which left their keel and poorly armored aft vulnerable.

"I turned off safeties and thrusters have full power. Go wild up there, Addie," Rick called in.

"Everybody hang on!" Addie maneuvered to corral as many fighters as possible then kicked the *Ulfberht* into a sharp one hundred eighty degree spin, boosting it in the other direction. Everyone on the ship grabbed onto something, fighting the inertia that swept through the ship. The fighters pursuing them scattered. Two bold pilots strayed too close and were smashed to bits against the *Ulfberht's* armored hull. It shot away, leaving the disorganized enemy fighters rushing to catch up.

"Hard turn to pass behind them, gun range!" Nikolai barked.

Addie followed without hesitation, sweeping the *Ulfberht* behind the enemies on the starboard flank. Fighters behind them dashed from side to side to avoid the *Ulfberht's* defensive fire. The battleships favored a heavily armored hull to maneuverability and were sluggish to turn. Addie easily swooped behind the enemy ships.

"All guns, fire on their engines!" Nikolai boomed.

Every defensive gun and side cannon facing the enemy cruiser focused fire on their rear thrusters. The *Ulfberht* took fire from enemy turrets, but their scramblers threw off most of the shots, causing a few to hit the pursuing fighters. They destroyed the main thrusters, crippling one ship's mobility. The other two cruisers continued their slow spins to follow the *Ulfberht*, while the third rolled awkwardly in place.

"Out of defensive range, keep us on this side," Nikolai ordered.

The *Ulfberht* pulled away from the battleships, leaving one unable to pursue. The guns turned their fire back to the enemy fighters, of which only half remained. Will and Natalie adjusted to intercept enemy fighters with the *Ulfberht's* every change of direction, giving Addie more breathing room as she pulled away from the enemy ships.

"I got it!" Mike pumped his fist and faced the bridge's front screen.

On the *Rampart*, Jones grew frustrated with the failure of the ship's fighters, with no regard for any lives lost.

"Captain, *Obelisk* is immobilized and we're down to *five* fighters," Amber called.

"Captain Slater, can't your people hit *anything?*" Jones earned a wrathful glare from Slater.

"That's the fastest, most mobile damn battleship ever made. We don't have the speed *or* maneuverability to keep up with it," Slater explained, aware that Jones had no clue what they were fighting or why it mattered. "Follow that ship!"

"Then send more fighters!" Jones said, further frustrating Slater, who had already seen losses to his crew on Ganymede.

"Have the fighters drive them toward us. Prepare Gamma squad and have all fighters from the *Obelisk* and *Titan* ready to launch."

"Captain?" Haynes called while Amber relayed Slater's orders. "The *Titan* is reporting that they've lost control of their ship."

"What? Tell them to shut down!" Slater watched the *Titan* lumber around to face them, already turning to follow the Stinger. It lurched forward and opened fire, thrusters at maximum. The *Rampart* shook violently, port side hammered by every forward-facing cannon on the *Titan*.

"Pull up! Hard to starboard!" Slater ordered. The sluggish *Rampart* crawled away but the *Titan* adjusted to compensate. The gap between the two ships evaporated.

"Brace for impact!" Haynes yelled, but everyone had already done so.

For a breath, the *Rampart* shook no more. The *Titan's* cannons stopped firing and it's engines stopped, but it was too late. With no friction to slow it down, it slammed into the *Rampart's* bilge, knocking people into the air and out of their seats. The crew picked themselves up off the floor, staggered but composed.

"Captain." Amber wiped away a trail of blood streaming from her head and applied pressure to the wound. "The *Titan* has cut power. They're on backup power, down to essential systems."

Slater smashed a hand against his chair in frustration, eyes on the *Ulfberht* dodging the four fighters still in combat. "Where's our third squad?"

"We can't launch them, sir. That hit took out our docking bay. Response teams are still assessing the damage. The *Titan* can't launch theirs either," Amber reported. "Both *Obelisk* squadrons are ready, though."

"Sons of bitches! How many people do they have on security?" Slater was losing his composure, fist stuck as a tightly clenched ball.

"Probably just the one guy." Sam arrived with a medkit and tended to a gash on Amber's head. Despite the dire situation, she smiled as Sam applied a healing balm and bandaged her injury.

"Enough of this!" Jones boomed, infuriated with Captain Slater's performance. "We don't need more fighters, we only need one." He approached the nearest console and pushed a bridge officer out of his way.

"What are you doing?" Slater asked.

"What you could *not*. I never fail to get my target, this will not be my first time!" He cleared his throat then opened a channel to one of the pilots. "Pilot, this is Agent Jones, do you copy?"

"Copy, sir."

"I need you to release control of your craft to me, I'm not losing any more lives to these criminals," Jones said.

"Uh, yes, sir." The pilot hesitated, but relinquished control.

Jones used the console to maneuver the pilot away and followed with a wider berth than the others. He watched the enemy's movements. They gradually moved away, zigging, zagging, and twisting in corkscrews. Like a flash, he saw his opportunity.

The commandeered fighter shot forward. While the other three fighters were trying not to get shot down, Jones rocketed in.

"Sir?"

Jones ignored the nervous pilot, focused on his target.

"Agent, what are you doing?" Slater asked, but was ignored.

"Sir, the Captain asked you a question," boomed the officer next to Jones, examining the controls in case he needed to intervene.

"I'm ejecting!" The shrieking pilot panicked in his cockpit. One of the Stinger's front thrusters came into view as the cockpit was jettisoned from the craft and avoided certain death by a hair.

The fighter crashed into the Stinger's thruster and burst into a raging plasma fire. The furthest depths of space were not as quiet as the *Rampart* bridge. The room was slack-jawed, frozen in horror. Jones would have let the pilot die, and did not hide it. None of them could believe what they had witnessed. Captain Slater barely restrained his rage.

"Have the rest of the fighters destroy the other thrusters, fire up the forward cannons and bring us into firing range." Jones moved back in front of the command platform as if he had not almost done something abhorrently immoral.

With a wrathful fire in her eyes, Amber stared at Agent Jones. After a moment she glanced between him and Captain Slater, who gave her a nod to carry out the order. The fighters were able to take out another thruster, then another.

"Move us in, pull the fighters back when we're in range," Slater ordered. The chaos on the bridge had died. Everyone quietly did their job while they imagined in which way they would like to kill Agent Jones.

The *Rampart* was the last ship that could move, and with the enemy's mobility progressively impaired they could finally get a fix on their target.

"We've got a shot, sir," the weapons officer called out.

"Fire!" Jones ordered.

The cannons on the front of the *Rampart* launched giant shells at the enemy ship. They ripped into its central starboard mass and spun the enemy Stinger.

"Second volley ready, sir," the weapons officer said.

"Fire," Jones ordered with a deep, satisfied growl. A second volley of railgun fire tore into its port side and left it a crippled heap floating alone in space. "Fire everything. Tear them apart!"

"No, stop! Hold your fire," Sam interrupted.

"How *dare* you." Jones turned slowly to eyeball Sam then strode toward him, teeth gritted.

"Watch it." Captain Slater stood up, taser pistol drawn and fixed on Jones.

Jones stopped and turned slowly to Captain Slater, then backed away. The other bridge officers were put on alert by the Captain's reaction. Two of them took flanking angles on Jones with their pistols out.

"Insolent trash." Jones's face glowed red.

"I can't let either of you kill each other. That's *my* job." Slater's deep voice rumbled over the quiet bridge. "Speak your peace, Doc."

"You better not have just destroyed what I'm here to retrieve, or you *will* find yourself on the business end of the threats you keep shooting at everyone else." Sam stepped toward Jones.

"Is that a threat?" Jones's fists clenched.

"If the package I'm here to retrieve is destroyed we could *both* find ourselves with a worm's eye view of a grave." Sam had never acknowledged that might be the truth until he said the words. He kept his cool, but in the back of his mind, he realized what was at stake, and what he had gotten mixed up in.

"Go on." Jones took note of a troubling thought Sam could not hide, and relaxed his posture.

"We need a landing party, and we need to retrieve what I'm here for before I allow you to destroy that ship," Sam said.

"Acceptable." Jones cringed with disgust. "Tell me what I need to grab and I will retrieve it. I will lead the landing party *myself*."

"No, I'm coming with you," Sam said.

"Excuse me?" Jones almost laughed. "You?"

"I can't tell you what I'm after, I have to get it myself." Sam stood his ground.

"You would be useless. You would serve only to put all our lives in jeopardy. I bet you've never even seen battle up close," Jones condescended.

"Maybe not, but I can handle myself. Do you think I've been sitting on my ass the last three months? I've been preparing for this, I've got something I can wear besides a Ministry coat."

Jones crossed his arms and gaped at Sam. "Is that why you've been requisitioning armor?"

"You won't need to protect me, I'll take care of myself down there." Sam's eyes were as determined and stone-cold as when he had challenged Jones on Earth and Ganymede. Jones straightened his coat, then his hair. He let out a long breath, but Captain Slater broke the silence before him.

"Going to be kind of hard to send a boarding party with our docking bay down," he holstered his weapon, but the other officers kept their pistols locked on Jones, weary of his unethical inclinations.

"Amber." Sam backed up. "What's the damage to the docking bay?"

Amber checked the damage reports. "It looks like the doorway has been crushed." She flipped the holo-screen for Sam. He examined the three-dimensional display of the hangar and its damage.

"Captain, would you be willing to depressurize the docking bay and remotely pilot a shuttle to crash into the bay door and push it open? We could even take shots at the clamps in the corners to loosen it up."

"I guess we've got to repair the whole damn thing anyway," Slater said. "If we put her on backup power the emergency latches will disable and we should be able to open it enough for a shuttle to get through."

"That's all we need," Sam said.

"Fine. I'll assemble my team and meet you in the hangar. Be quick about it."

On his way out the bridge, Jones's eyes met with a number of officers. Each one received the same cold, unapologetic look that told them he thought they were all scum. Likewise, he received the same murderous look from each of them. Once he was gone, the bridge crew put their pistols away and a deathly silence fell over the room.

"I guess I should get going." Sam's voice trembled. Captain Slater gave him a nod, and Sam left the platform for the nearby exit.

"Sam," Amber called. Sam turned, bridge doors open behind him. "Be careful down there. He'll take any opportunity to get what he wants."

"I'm not taking any chances," Slater said. "Haynes, Wells, go with 'em. Stay on the shuttle, make sure everything is on the level."

"Yes, sir!" they said together, Amber with enthusiasm, Haynes with determination. They eagerly ushered an astonished Sam off the bridge.

"Let's go." Haynes hooked an arm around Sam and dragged him off the bridge.

"Yeah, fuck this guy," Amber said. "We're not letting anything happen to you."

Chaos

43

Siege of K.R.A.Ken

THE *RAMPART'S* BOARDING CREW SQUEEZED OUT OF THE BUSTED shuttle bay and set forth to board the enemy Stinger. From the cockpit, Jones and Ken watched the enemy ship spin, dead in space.

"I see him." Ken turned and left the cockpit.

"Morikawa? He's out there?" Jones said.

"I'm off here." Ken marched with purpose through the upper deck of the shuttle for a ladder. "Good luck," he said to Matt and James before climbing down to the next level, which housed the troopers. Without Samson, the team was vulnerable to Farouk, but Ken had his own mission.

"Is he serious?" Matt asked, armored and ready for battle, clipping on an earpiece aside James. They had arrived in the wake of the battle in time to hitch a ride back.

"He is The Kraken. His ultimate mission is to slay every rogue Ranger. There are limits to the command I have over him." Jones turned back to the cockpit window. He was far closer to harm than was preferable.

Downstairs, Ken entered the airlock and closed the door behind him. The highlights of his suit lit up and he decompressed the airlock, sucking the air from the room. Ken remained rooted in place. Once the whirlwind around him subsided, the outer door opened. Ken disengaged his suit and floated out of the airlock, tapping on the console outside to close it behind him.

The shuttle left him floating in space or a moment before he engaged the small thrusters that popped out of armored compartments. Ken scanned Shin; he was making repairs to the ship, a magnetized tool bag nearby. Shin was armed with a large blade and a railgun but did not appear to have modified his suit. Even his scanners were out of date, as he did not appear to detect Ken heading for him. The railgun was the only cause for concern, and it was easy to dodge. The final assessment: Not a threat. Shin was, in fact, at a definitive disadvantage.

Several meters away from Shin, Ken landed on the bow of the *Ulfberht* with a thud. His suit tinged with a blue glow. Shin calmly put away the tool, zipped shut the bag, and closed the panel before he rose to his feet, facing Ken.

"So, *you're* the one hunting us," Shin broadcasted on a general short-range signal.

"Surrender peacefully, or die like the others." Ken's voice rumbled in Shin's helmet.

"At least show Kamila and Nigel the respect of using their names," Shin said. "Nigel said you two were best friends."

"Before he betrayed everything we believed in. Before he betrayed *me*." Ken took a stern and angry step forward, fists balled up at his sides.

"Nigel was sent to catch me when I ran. He let me go," Shin began, intending to share a heartfelt story, but Ken did not let him finish.

"I know, and it's because of you that I had to kill the best friend I've ever had." Ken's fists trembled at his sides.

"I don't make your choices." Shin's feet slid into a defensive posture.

"But you brainwashed him into deserting, and I couldn't let anyone else go after him. Because of you, I was forced into that position."

Scapegoat, a role Shin was familiar with. Ken could not cope with his actions, so he blamed Shin. Had Shin never spoken with him, Nigel would have never gone to do his own investigating and had a change of heart. Nigel acted according to his conscience once he knew the truth. When presented with the same option, Ken could not bring himself to question his beliefs. He had no one to blame but himself.

"You didn't like what he had to say? Did the truth hurt?" Shin taunted.

"The *truth* is that you're a traitor."

"So, if you had seen Alliance soldiers pillaging the colonies and killing civilians, you would have looked the other way?"

"The Federation was doing the same thing to *our* people in the colonies. It was war," Ken snapped. "And, we needed the resources to win. We finally achieved world peace and you weren't willing to make a few sacrifices for it."

"Your opinion is a valid one. But, if the foundation of a civilization is a lie, it will collapse. The UEG is built upon lies. Only when we confront the truth can we build a truly peaceful world. We won at the cost of our souls."

"Souls don't keep ships flying and people fed," Ken retorted with a growl. "You're an idealistic fool, and you got Nigel killed."

"I don't remember guiding your hand," Shin said.

A storm brewed within Ken, a pulsing bloodlust flowing through his body. Shin's best move was to remain as level headed as possible.

"This is your last chance to surrender," he said after a moment.

"I have only one more thing to say," Shin said, a hand in the air. Ken nodded for him to speak his mind. "I forgive you."

Ken took a stunted step back. "What?"

"You are consumed by rage and guilt. You may not be able to forgive yourself for what you've done and everything you're going to do, but it's difficult to challenge your beliefs. Especially if they have been a part of you all your life. So, blame me if you must. But, I forgive you for killing Nigel, and anyone else you pursue in your quest for revenge and justification."

A tear pooled into a bubble in the corner of Ken's eye and he trembled with fury. "You will regret not surrendering. I don't need your forgiveness."

"Then," Shin paused, "you have my pity."

In a flash, Ken fired composite nails at Shin. Two zoomed by his head. Three others slammed into his chest and abdomen, digging into his body. Shin's suit conformed around them, but he needed to pull them out and cover the holes while the suit repaired itself. His chest burned, blood pooled under his suit. He zig-zagged, narrowly avoiding subsequent shots, closing the distance between them.

Shin drew his blade and swung at Ken in one swift motion. Ken dodged and evaded the quick flurry of swipes. Most were aimed at the head. Shin was trying to put cracks in Ken's helmet screen, the greatest vulnerability in both suits.

A nail slammed into Shin's screen and bounced off. Cracks webbed out from the impact point. When Ken dodged, he had predicted the position of Shin's head and fired a blind shot. Alarms blared in Shin's helmet. A structural integrity icon flashed in the corner, already reduced to seventy percent.

Blade glowing red, Ken pressed the attack. Shin deflected and tied up his arms. Lunging under an attack, Shin jammed his thick blade in the projectile launcher on Ken's left arm and cranked it. The compartment splintered apart, spewing sparks and metal parts without a sound.

Shin spun for a backswing, but Ken blocked with his blade. To Ken's surprise, it did not cut through Shin's as it should have. His helmet's sensors labeled it as *Unknown Alloy*. Blade to blade, Ken pressed a needle deeper into Shin's chest. Crippling pain shooting through his chest, Shin was forced back, thrusters propelling him away.

Examining the broken compartment, Ken sliced through the wires tethering it to his arm. He pressed his attack again, pushing Shin through a cloud of debris along the central shaft of the ship. Pieces of the ship hung by a thread or were completely gone, filled with gaps and exposed cables.

In the storm of the assault, Shin let his guard down and Ken took the bait, diving in for a big right cross. Shin snatched his arm and slammed him into the hole. Ken went back-first into steel beams and a thicket of cables.

Shin grabbed a bundle of torn wire nearby and backed up. In a whirlwind, Ken was back on his feet. Shin deftly dodged another vicious attack, using the wires to tie him up, and flung him back into the hole.

Ken jumped to his feet, scanning the area for Shin. His instincts kicked in and he stepped to the side. A railgun bullet dinged off the hull and Ken's eyes were drawn upward. Shin had Ken in his sights, massive railgun pointed at him. He rained down shots, driving Ken back into the pit of steel and loose cords while he freed his arms of their bindings. Cords cut and untangled, a shot whizzed by his head. He launched away, zigzagging on his way to Shin, who struggled to line up a shot.

Thump!

Ken was abruptly halted mid-flight, stopped by a tug on his leg. Shin had tied up his foot before jettisoning away. That split second was all Shin needed to drill a shell into Ken's face. The hit rung his bell, structural integrity diving below fifty percent. Maneuvering to dodge, Ken cut himself free with a swift slice. How tactical display was damaged and flickering, missing information, but he retained most of his visibility.

Ken zoomed at Shin and closed the gap between them. Shin took shots before he got close, but Ken went untouched. He slashed at Shin. With only a railgun in his hands, Shin blocked. It was paper to Ken's glowing red blade, jutting out the other side. Ken sliced through the bulky, outdated weapon, then slashed it again.

Without his most viable weapon, the odds had moved in Ken's favor. Shin blocked his next strike and shot away.

Ken pursued him into the debris field toward the aft of the ship. Mangled chunks of metal and armor plating as thick as their bodies tumbled through space, careening in and out of their paths.

For a few seconds, Ken lost sight of Shin and he vanished. He paused, then spun and scanned the area, but Shin was gone. He could scan through the debris, yet Shin had disappeared. Surely, he was taking the opportunity to remove the needles.

"We're on our way back to the ship, we've lost contact with everyone else. Your time is short." Jones's voice popped into Ken's ear. They had retrieved their target faster than anticipated. There was no time for hide and seek.

"Hiding, again? You aren't brave enough to face the truth of your choices, why should I expect you to face the consequences?" Ken glided through the debris and mangled chunks of the *Ulfberht*.

"You are the one who can not face the reality of their choices. I accepted mine before I made them." Shin's voice buzzed in Ken's ears.

"Then you should accept your fate, like a man." Ken searched his environment. He kicked at large pieces of debris and carefully navigated the steel jungle.

"Accountability does not seem to be a priority for the UEG. A people is only as good as their government."

"The UEG has brought peace to Earth for the first time in history," Ken argued. He came upon a large slab of the ship's armor that spun so slowly it was hardly noticeable. Everything else had more energy to its spin. The slab was thick enough to disrupt his sensors, a perfect hiding spot. "Building a better world requires sacrifice."

Arm's length away, Ken kicked the slab. It spun slowly away then shot back, slamming into him. He shoved it away and prepared for an attack, but there was no sign of Shin.

"You can't build a better world without holding people responsible for their crimes," Shin said.

"If that's true, why aren't you turning yourself in for treason?" Ken searched the debris field again, blade ready.

"It would have been a crime against humanity not to have done what I did. That goes beyond laws."

"The words of a criminal. When is it *ever* right to betray your people?" Ken countered, spinning rapidly to check behind him. Before him, the wing had been torn asunder. He floated into the gash. Most of the mechanisms in the wings were for storing ammunition and firing the rail guns. It had been reduced to a scrap heap.

"A government and its people are not one and the same," Shin said.

Ken popped his head inside and scanned the area, still no sign of Shin. He eased out of the ship back into open space.

BEEP! BEEP! BEEP! BEEP! BEEP!

Ken's sensors picked up Shin behind him, only ten meters away and flying at him like a bullet. With a spin, Ken slashed at his attacker. Shin grabbed hold of his wrist and crashed into Ken blade-first. Helmet structural integrity: thirty-nine percent.

The two crashed into the rim of the jagged gash. Ken slashed, but Shin ducked underneath and smashed his knife into Ken's face again. Structural integrity: thirty percent. In the chaotic exchange of blows, Shin attacked his thrusters.

Pressed into the ship, Ken went into panic mode and fought back. It was unclear how Shin evaded his sensors, but he was here now, and there was no way Ken would let him out of his sight again.

Catching Shin's arm, Ken kept Shin's arm away from his face, blade less than arm's length away and getting closer. Ken punched, kicked, and slashed at Shin. He took a note from his opponent and retreated into open space in a spiral, with only one good thruster on his feet and two on his back disabled.

With Shin close behind, Ken's path took him past a floating steel punching bag. The deck-two gym was scattered around them. He snatched the chain dangling from the top and swung it behind him, slamming Shin into the side of the ship. He barely avoided Ken's follow up attack. A disc-shaped weight bounced off the wall next to his head. Again, Ken retreated down the length of the ship, Shin in hot pursuit.

With a spin, Ken tried a surprise attack with a furious hammer-fist. Shin blocked and the exchange locked them together, each holding the other back.

"Unfortunately for you, I still have tricks up my sleeve." From his projectile arm's lower compartment erupted a cord that stabbed into Shin's suit. "Zero-day exploit, courtesy of the UEG."

The interface in Shin's suit blinked, *REBOOTING*. Shin kicked at Ken's arm and sheathed his knife, then everything in his helmet turned off, shrouding him in darkness.

He shot his head to the side as the strength in his suit gave out and Ken's blade slammed into Shin's shoulder. A searing hot pain pounded through his arm. When he pulled the blade out, air from Shin's suit hissed into space.

Shin latched onto Ken's arm, wrapping his legs around his shoulder and upper arm. He hung on for dear life and pressed his shoulder into Ken's arm to keep the hole sealed while his suit rebooted. He kept his face tucked, arm up, making strikes ineffective. His suit, although powered down, was still resilient.

"Have it your way." Ken spiraled them into open space, then back toward the ship, accelerating all the way. Above Shin, the ship grew larger as they neared the stern. Ken punched at Shin's sides and tried prying his arms away. He retracted his blade and pushed Shin's helmet toward the ship so he could watch him die in the vacuum of space when they impacted, but he resisted.

Dangerously close to the ship, Ken let the momentum carry them the rest of the way. He smashed a knee into Shin from behind and pulled him close.

Shin used the attacks to change his position and minimize Ken's effectiveness. They became an entangled ball of yarn tumbling through space, the ship spinning around them less than a hundred meters away and closing. The interface in Shin's helmet lit up with a loading bar in the middle. It would not be online soon enough.

Overpowering Shin, Ken flung him over his shoulder. Shin crashed back-first into the ship with Ken ramming into him.

They impacted with such force that they altered the ship's spin. The force of the impact sucked the air from Shin's lungs and he gasped desperately for breath. Blade out again, Ken pulled back his arm and brought it down upon Shin. Wheezing for air, Shin barely avoided the strike, which dug into the ship next to his head.

ONLINE.

Shin kicked Ken away. His thrusters sparked to life and he darted away, skimming the surface of the ship with Ken on his flank. Shoulder burning, he pressed a hand over the gash while it repaired and pulled a cluster of smoke bombs from his belt. Tossing them in front of him, they bounced off the ship and released their thick black smoke.

Shin flew into the cloud and disappeared for a second, but Ken was prepared. Reaching out, a shock burst from his arm and rippled through the cloud, shorting out the artificial smokescreen. The cloud dissipated, its sensor-dampening effects disappeared. Tight on Shin's tail, Ken swung his blade, but Shin was gone.

Ken looked up and spun. Surely, Shin had used cover to come from behind, but there was nothing. Ken was alone. He scanned the area like before. Nothing. Shin had vanished.

"Where are you?" Ken roared. There was no debris, nothing to hide behind, nowhere to go, yet there was no sign of Shin. "Come out, you coward!"

No response.

He had been fighting a specter. His time limit was a bomb about to go off. So close to killing Shin and after taking so much damage, he could not let it end like this.

"Ken, we're headed back to the ship, hurry back or you'll miss the bus."

The shuttle was separating from the ship. Shin appeared to have access to secret cloaking technology, which was both troubling and infuriating. But, there was no more time. If Shin was too close when the ship exploded, he would die. If he survived, he would be flung into open space. Either way, Ken was forced to forfeit his search.

Thrusters aglow, Ken flew back to the shuttle looking over his shoulder at the empty battlefield behind him.

Natalie

44

All or Nothing

Natalie opened her eyes. After being tossed around the gunner room and then plunged into zero gravity darkness, she took in her surroundings. Emergency lights bathed the room in a soft red glow. Ian groaned, cursed, and made a fuss while Farouk and Maya tended to his leg. Everyone had rushed in and started shooting without putting on a vest and hooking into a harness. Injuries ensued.

"One, two, three!" Maya pulled on Ian's leg. He cried out, glowing red face contorted in pain, taking heavy breaths of relief.

"See? No big deal," Ian huffed.

"Come on, I'm taking you to the med bay," Farouk said.

"No, it's all right. I don't even need it. I can help with the repairs." Ian floated himself upright.

"Nikolai, do you copy?" Farouk radioed as they exited.

"I'm here."

"We're on our way to the med bay. Ian broke his mothafuckin' leg."

"Ye make it sound like I did it on purpose," Ian protested as they drifted down the hall, doors closing behind them.

"Will?" Natalie spun herself around. Nearby, Will floated against the

347

ceiling unconscious. "Will!" She pushed off the wall and hurried to his side, pulling him close. Maya floated to them and examined Will.

"He's unconscious but nothing serious. He'll be fine." Maya put Natalie's worries to rest. "I've got Natalie and Will in the G-R, Will is unconscious but Natalie is okay."

"I need help in engineering. If we can get to warp, we can get away," Rick prattled in their earpieces.

"Be right there," Maya said. "Anyone have any idea why they stopped firing? They had us dead to rights."

"They're either trying to take us alive or they're after One," Mike said. *"That means we're about to get boarded. I'm going to guard One. We need Addie ready to warp us out, so Nikolai is staying here to guard the bridge. Everyone gear up. Natalie, I need you and Will to lock yourselves in the gunner room."*

"What? Hey! I need to help with repairs," Natalie protested.

"If we get boarded, they'll shoot to kill. Will is out cold and neither of you are combat trained. They won't distinguish you from us. Stay in the G-R," Mike ordered.

"Natalie." Maya grabbed Natalie's shoulder as she opened her mouth to protest. "I know you want to help but when gravity kicks in, Will is going to fall to the ground and he could get hurt. His head is going to be killing him when he wakes up, too. He needs you here, okay? Just stay here, we'll take care of everything." Maya gave Natalie a quick kiss on her forehead, then headed for the door.

Natalie let out a disheartened sigh, looking down at Will's peaceful, unconscious face. "Okay…"

"Thank you." Maya floated away and closed the door. After a moment a red light appeared on the console next to the door followed by two beeps.

Holding Will close, Natalie gripped the floor to keep them stationary. At first, she intended to do as Mike and Maya had asked, but sitting alone with her thoughts she soon concluded that if they could not repair the ship, everyone would die. They would die alongside everyone else, and she could not stay in that room with Will.

There was no getting away from the danger. The urge to move built up inside her like a boiling pot of water. Within a few minutes, she could take it no longer and examined the room for options. There were no soft surfaces and nowhere to wedge Will safely if she were to leave him. Then, it came to her.

Pulling Will behind her, Natalie headed deeper into the room and opened the hatch into the maintenance shafts. She drifted inside then struggled to pull Will's limp body into the corridor, finally managing to squeeze him in. She nestled him inside, sitting him down, hooking his arms through the ladder. She tugged at him to ensure he was secure. Natalie tapped two fingers over her ear to turn off the earpiece and give them a moment of privacy. She pulled his chin up and pressed her lips to his.

"Stay safe," she whispered, then hurried into the maintenance shafts.

As she got closer to engineering, Natalie turned her earpiece back on. The channel was abuzz with activity.

"We need to replace half the fuses on the ship 'cause I turned off the damn safeties for the battle." Rick's normally tranquil tone was consumed with frustration and a trembling hint of desperation.

"What the fuck are these things?" asked Farouk.

"Just follow the instructions and replace the ones that are broken," Rick yelled. With everyone's lives depending on fixing the ship, Rick was under pressure. *"I'm puttin' up a map of the breached areas from the workin' sensors, there—"*

Rick was interrupted by the loud bang of a metal panel flying off the wall and Natalie diving out behind it. Ian sat on a table nearby, his good leg hooked under a bolted-down table to keep him stationary.

"What the hell?" Rick was as surprised as he was angry. "Natalie's here."

"Natalie!" Mike scolded. *"We told you to stay in the G-R!"*

"When I signed up with you guys you said I'm part of the crew. So,

I'm helping you guys make repairs. If we fail then we *all* die, right?" Natalie grabbed the side of a metal shelf to sweep herself around to Rick.

The radio fell silent for a moment. Despite her naiveté, these were desperate times and she would be helpful given her skill and speed. Ian and Rick exchanged uncomfortable looks, grunts, and shrugs.

"If anyone should be fixing the ship, it should be Natalie." Farouk broke the silence. *"I have no idea what the hell I'm doin'."*

"My daughter is headstrong, too. May as well give 'er what she needs to succeed," Ian suggested.

"Mike, we need Natalie to get main power back. I'm sendin' her out." Rick grabbed a duffel bag and filled it with tools, parts, and fuses the size of playing cards.

The channel fell silent following a hollow, far away thump. The ship creaked, and the sound resonated through the walls. Everyone's eyes moved to the ceiling, then the walls, and then to each other.

"We're being boarded," Maya said.

"God damnit. If we're sending her out, give her a stick." Mike submitted to their circumstances but still tried to keep Natalie as safe as possible.

"Ah'll get it." Ian floated to a weapons locker and grabbed a zapper.

"We're going to need a tactical advantage before we can protect One," Maya said. *"Mike, Farouk, meet me on deck six by the elevators."*

"Copy that."

"Comin'."

"Maintenance level two, I'm sending you the repair list." Rick floated the bulging duffel bag to Natalie, then an earpiece. "Ian, Let's lock up engineering."

"I've got this." Natalie kicked her feet against the wall, darting back to the maintenance shafts. Ian grabbed her arm as she passed.

"Aye lass. If y' find trouble, give 'em a good shock." Ian handed her a long, matte black zapper with a wink.

"Thanks." Natalie snatched it with a smile and pressed the button to test its wild blue sparks, then hurried into the tunnels.

"Let's play it safe, keep our audio open, do not engage until I give the

green light. Non-combatants stay out of the line of fire. Let's get out of here without any casualties," Maya called out.

"I already broke m'leg."

"Fine, just the one casualty, then."

Natalie's first two repairs were on the port side of maintenance level two, one toward the aft and the other toward the center of the ship. She opened the grated floors and yanked out the fuses, tossing the charred cards down the hall behind her. She replaced the cards and hurried off. The third problem was center-mass on the starboard side, forcing her to loop around the ship.

Adjacent a breached and sealed compartment, Natalie opened the floor and removed a fuse, but it was undamaged. She checked the others, they were all in one piece.

"What the?" Natalie put them back and examined the compartment. She traced the main power conduit with a finger until she came upon a T-shaped junction. The conduit in the breached compartment had been jerked out of place and took the T-junction with it, breaking the ends of the other two connecting points. To protect the meta-fiberglass inside, the conduits were segmented and clipped together. But under extreme pressure, they release to protect the conduit chain. Only the two conduit segments connecting to it had broken.

"I thought you'd be a challenge." Natalie shuffled through the bag, shoving aside spare fuses until she pulled out two power conduits and a handheld box with a round peg. She replaced the broken conduits and put the box's peg to the end of each one. A green indicator on the conduits lit up, confirming that power flowed down the chain. She connected the T-junction and tested it before connecting the other end, but this time there were no lights. The junction, which also doubled as a power regulator, was busted.

"Oh, no." Her hands trembled at the prospect of letting everyone down. She searched the bag already knowing she would not find what she needed. The world closing in around her, she pushed away the panic with an idea.

"I don't need a T-junction, I can use an L," she said. "The gun bays." Natalie grabbed a screwdriver and an adjustable wrench from the bag then spun around and hurried down the maintenance shafts to the nearest exit. The exit was in a supply closet on deck four directly across from the gun bays and escape pods. But, that meant passing through the hallway to get them.

The storage room was a mess of floating bottles, rags, toiletries, and a menagerie of frequently used items. Like a wall of vines, Natalie had to push her way through the floating mess to get to the door, still trying to be as quiet as possible. A thud against the wall made her flinch and recoil. There was a louder thump by the door and the erratic sounds of a struggle. Natalie hovered by the door and listened for a moment, zapper gripped tightly. She gathered her courage and with a deep breath opened the door to peek into the hall.

"Natalie?" Maya's voice called from the darkness, silhouetted against the soft red lights in the hall.

"Is it safe?"

"Yeah, what are you doing out here?"

"I need a part from a gun bay." She eased into the hall.

"Shit! They've got One!"

Following Mike's update, Natalie's heart skipped a beat. Shaken and anxious, Maya attempted to calm her down before leaving.

"Don't worry, we've got this. Just focus on what you've got to do, okay, Natalie?" Natalie gave her a stiff nod and a thumbs-up. "Okay, this deck is clear so you're safe, do your thing. *I'm on my way.*" Maya's voice echoed in Natalie's ears and her silhouette vanished down the central lateral hall.

Natalie hurried to the gun bay across from the maintenance closet, but it was closed, and the door was unresponsive. "Uh, Captain? I need to open a door and it won't open." She tried her best to look away from the dead bodies nearby.

"Which door?" Mike whispered.

Natalie checked the label above the console next to the door. "Room

W-S, Four-O, two." The consoles on her deck lit up. Natalie opened the door and hurried inside, closing it behind her. "Thanks."

Inside, the walls were lined with bullets the size of her arm. She opened the floor and removed the L-shaped junction that connected to it. She glanced through the window, then opened it and peeked down the hall. She was alone and back in the supply closet in seconds, door closed, chest heaving. Eyes squeezed shut, Natalie calmed herself and slowed her breathing, forcing the thoughts of dead bodies, and her family, out of her mind, then she flew back into the maintenance shafts.

A test after connecting it showed green lights. She clipped on the other end and hurried back to the supply closet. The fourth and final repair was in the starboard docking bay, which meant passing through the hall again, past the dead bodies.

The debris in the closet latched onto her duffel bag and hooked the zapper, She pulled away from the clawing darkness and pressed herself to the door. She tried to listen, but the team chatter was too loud, so she turned the volume to a minimum. Outside, there was silence. She hurried out, squirming away from one of the dead bodies. The other had floated away.

Floating into the docking bay, the top of a shuttle became visible through the windows. She stayed low and crept to the edge. Through the thick, monolithic windows of the starboard docking bay, Natalie saw a transport shuttle docked with the *Ulfberht*. She recognized the two-deck-tall XJB ship, complete with a small medical bay and a staging area for unloading troops.

On the level below was the airlock, guarded by a UEG trooper with his helmet off, feet flat on the ground. The fuses were located beneath the floor between her and him. If she could taze him, she could make the repairs. The only angle where she could approach undetected was from above.

Natalie nudged herself back against the convergence of steel and glass in the corner of the walkway. Before she crept over the railing, a trooper dropped from deck three with One over his shoulder. One looked at Natalie with a smile.

"Oh my god." She clasped a hand over her mouth to muffle her gasp at the sight of a large man carrying him into the airlock. Frozen, she held herself there for a moment, hands trembling, the prospect of failure on the horizon. Then, she remembered what Maya said to her. *Don't worry, we've got this. Just focus on what you've got to do.*

Natalie focused on the task at hand. She readied herself to launch toward the ceiling, then the ship shook violently around her following a thud. A metallic groan echoed through the ship. She groped for the wall slit and pulled herself to safety. Cradling the corner of the docking bay entrance, the ship creaked and moaned around her, echoing down the halls.

Natalie returned to the railing and took a deep, trembling breath, then propelled herself to the ceiling. Eyes on the guard, she went unnoticed, gliding along the ceiling, the stopped herself above the airlock, catching herself on a central beam. Eyes fixed on the guard, body pressed against the ceiling, she gritted her teeth and took deep, trembling breaths. Time froze, then she swooped like a hawk, arm out, zapper aimed at her target.

But, as she closed in, his head pivoted and he bounced away. Natalie reached out to brace herself so as not to crash into the airlock. She pivoted to the floor panel in the wake of the guard's unexpected exit.

"That was lucky," Natalie whispered to herself and raised the volume on her earpiece, un-muting herself. "Guys, they're docked at the starboard bay. I'm here fixing the last breaker."

"Natalie, get out of there," Maya ordered in a raspy hush.

Stuffing the zapper in the bag, Natalie opened the hatch and tossed the lid aside.

"This one is easy, I'm almost done." Natalie pulled out charred fuses and shoved new ones in, hands trembling.

"Natalie, get the hell out of there!" Rick shouted. Terrified or not, she had to finish. If she failed, the ship and everyone on it would die.

"Done!" Natalie pulled a lever and almost made her escape down deck five, but the dead bodies in the hall sent a chill up her spine. Leaving the duffel bag behind, she launched herself to the top level with a deep sense of accomplishment.

She did it.

She saved everyone.

Rampart Crew

Ghost Ship

THE *RAMPART'S* STRIKE TEAM WAITED IN THE STAGING AREA OF
their shuttle, rifles drawn, wearing black, gray, and cobalt suits of armor.
The troopers had their helmets fastened, visors down.

Matt and James had returned in the wake of battle and were ready
to go in their own custom outfits with their faces encased. Even Jones
wore a personal suit of black armor in lieu of his usual stylish garments.
Jones eyeballed Sam's modified suit. Sam had added bulky devices and
modified the armor to accommodate the various upgrades. He had also
copied Matt and James's helmets since the design offered more protection.

Jones's special unit was up front with fifteen troopers crammed into
the small staging area. A boom rippled through the shuttle then a click as
the shuttle docked with the enemy ship. Troopers lined up in the middle,
the two up front held riot shields. Sam opened the airlock and troopers
poured inside. Upon crossing the threshold the troopers floated off the
ground and bumped into one another.

"Hold!" Jones ordered.

The energetic charge came to a halt and the boarding party activated their gravity gear. The shield troopers in front looked through the airlock windows.

"It doesn't look like there's a welcoming party."

Jones rushed ahead to look for himself. Storage boxes floated throughout the room but there was nobody waiting for them.

Sam pressed a small round device against the console to power-up and gain access to the storage bay. Matt and James entered the airlock and stopped in their tracks. They looked at each other, then down at their suits and bounced in place.

"Heya, Sammy! You upgraded our gravity gear!" James said.

"You're the friggin' man, Sam," Matt added.

"My pleasure. Kept me busy while you guys were gone." Sam tapped the console then put the device away. The wide double doors pivoted out. A chirp in Sam's earpiece preempted James's voice, and a seperate vitals monitor appeared for each of them.

"Hey, Matt and I always run a private channel. We keep this one on auto so we can selectively talk in the main channel. Our helmets are soundproof, too. So, as long as you do that, we can keep some things between us."

Sam adjusted his settings while shield-bearing troopers led the group into the three-deck-tall storage bay, rifles hopelessly searching the room for an enemy. Jones followed close behind and scanned the room. He drew his pistol and fired. The pistol clicked but there was no shot.

"I'm all set up. Thanks, guys," Sam said privately to Matt and James.

"Gravity is off but weapon dampeners are still on. Wonderful." Jones put his pistol away and drew his dagger and a zapper. The troopers pulled out zappers or blades of their own. Jones prepared to give an order but noticed Sam tapping on his hand. "What are you doing?"

"Giving us a map of this ship with areas we think will be blocked off based on where we hit them." A digital map became available to everyone. Sam had also marked areas of interest. The Northwest and Southeast junctions were closed off.

"We're here because of Chancellor Bernard. He's after something on this ship, we're to help him retrieve it then return to the *Rampart*. Since it is Sam's mission, I'll let him brief us on what we need to do here." Jones stepped aside and gestured for Sam to speak. Sam stepped forward and nodded to the troopers.

"I've highlighted the living quarters and crew areas. I think one of the officers might have it in their quarters so I'm going there. I've uploaded a basic detection algorithm into your sensors. If you find what we're after your sensors should recognize it and I'll get an alert," Sam said.

"Is there any chance it could be on the bridge?" Jones asked.

Sam thought for a moment. "Maybe."

"Is there anything else we need to know?"

"No, it's all you." Sam stepped back and Jones stepped forward.

"This is a retrieval mission. It looks like they're on a skeleton crew, but engage the enemy with caution. My team will accompany the Chancellor to the officer's quarters on level two. Team B." Jones pointed to a trio of troopers. "Deck three. Team C, deck four. You four, team D, deck six. You two, bridge team. You guard the shuttle. You two with us." He pointed at the shielded troopers. "Let's move out."

The troopers assigned to levels five and six went straight into the hallway. Everyone else turned off their gravity gear and jumped up to levels three and four, splitting off toward their respective goals.

The groups kept in touch reporting their progress, but kept chatter to a minimum. The emergency lights gave the halls a soft red glow.

"Engineering is locked up tight," team C reported in.

"There's nothing down here," team D reported.

Jones and the two troopers hustled to keep up with the rest of the unit, who moved effortlessly through their eerie environment. They floated back to the floor with each step and zig-zagged through the halls, James and Matt took point, advancing in turns ahead of their high-value assets. Jones and the troopers covered their flank. Before they knew it, they had arrived at the officers' quarters, but several troopers from the other groups had turned from green to red in the team status monitor.

Sam used his device to access the room, which to his surprise was unsecured. James held up three fingers, then two, one, and a fist. He opened the door and Matt swooped in, pointing his zapper into the spacious common room. He and James entered first, followed by Jones and Sam, who scanned the rooms for his target.

"That one." Sam pointed at a door to their left with a red number one painted on it.

"All teams, check in." Matt kept an eye on the entrance to the community area.

Agent Jones stayed with Matt while James and Sam moved together. Sam opened the door and James rushed in, pointing his zapper into the room. Sam hurried after him and saw One with his own eyes for the first time.

One sat on his bed, not a wrinkle around him. Sam lowered James's zapper and stepped forward, hands up to show he meant no harm.

"My name is Samuel Bernard. We're here to retrieve you. Would you please come with us?" Sam was amazed to see how young he looked, and how human.

"As you wish." One got off the bed and followed Sam outside.

"We need to get movin'," Matt said. "Only team C checked in, one casualty."

"Team C, status up… date." Jones's eyes locked onto One as he walked by, unaffected by the lack of gravity. An unsettling churn in his stomach urged Jones to kill him. With Sam's eyes burning a hole through him, Jones buried the strange urge. To move his mind along, he sought to settle his curiosity. "How is it he can walk?"

"That's classified."

Jones glared at him, then focused on his mission. "Team C isn't reporting in."

"That's everyone." The rattle of alarm was clear in James's voice. "There's nobody here. They weren't even watchin' this guy."

"Keep your eyes open," Jones said, disgruntled. Losing the entire strike team was an unexpected complication. They were yet to even see an enemy crewmember. In some unseen way, eyes were on them. Surely, a trap lay ahead.

"All right fellas, let's get out of the spooky ghost ship," James said in the private channel. "Let's move out."

"I don't like this," Matt whispered.

"Ken, we're on our way back, hurry or you'll miss the bus," Jones said.

James and Matt hustled down the hall, the team close behind them. At the elevators, they stopped and checked around the chamfered corners. All clear. They signaled for the troopers to watch their backs and took a right around the elevators. Instead of a staircase, there was a steel wall. A pressure panel had swung into place.

"That wasn't there when we came in." James moved to the lift across from the stairs and tried to access it, but it was unpowered. "That's a dead end."

"Stay sharp," Matt said. "Check our immediate area, search for alternate routes."

"Stay near me." Sam guided One by the elevators. Matt and James tried the officer laundry room, but it was restricted.

"Sam, open up this door for us," James called him over.

"Wait here," he told One, who nodded. Sam tried to unlock the door, but it required special permissions. He used the scripts Koorosh had given him, but they got him nowhere. "The security here is out of my depth and this area is restricted. It looks like I can only access unsecured common areas."

"Then why could we open the officer's quarters?" James asked.

"They weren't restricted. They should have been, though. Right?"

"Yeah," James said. *"It feels like we're bein' watched."* James moved down the hall to the temperature control room.

"But, they shouldn't have security cameras or sensors on backup powa'."

"Still can't shake it." James tried the door, also restricted.

"I can't wait to get out of here. This place is kind of out of my nightmares,"

"I hear ya, Sammy." Matt checked the docking bay control room. Restricted.

"Thanks, we got it from here." James signaled Sam away and he hurried back to One. "Map says there's a staircase in the laundry room."

"Copy that." James took point and opened the door then he and Matt disappeared into the laundry room. The eleven seconds it took them to return were like the moment before the fall on a rollercoaster.

"Looks like the starboard staircase is the only option," James said upon return.

"We can't all go down that stairwell safely," Jones pointed out.

"Not as a group." James peeked over the staircase, wide enough for two people. He jumped onto the wall and his gravity gear held him to it. He knelt down and peeked beneath the floor, but saw no one. With a signal, Matt hustled down the stairs and guided Sam down, James followed. They checked the next level below, but the pressure panel at the next level was closed.

The pressure panel next to the stairwell on deck three was sealed from damage in the next section, as well as the one in front of it, which led to the bridge. Matt and James led the group around the elevators. Jones kept the troopers between him and their flank. With each corner they turned, Matt and James moved ahead, followed by Sam and One, then Jones and the troopers, who were always one junction behind.

Turning the corner into the port hall, their path was again cut-off. The pressure panel past the offices and the airlock ahead was closed, as was the port side pressure panel to the bridge on their right.

"Sam, can you open and close these things?" Matt asked.

"I'd have to remove the wall panel next to it. I'm pretty sure I won't be able to hack it digitally, but I can hack the hardware."

"Okay, let's do this quick. We'll cova' you while you crack it open. You three wait here, watch our flank," James said.

"There's nobody behind us," one of the troopers said.

"We ain't takin' no chances. Watch our flank," James commanded.

"Yes, sir."

"Let's go." James hustled away with Matt behind him. He peeked around the corner of the offices, his back to the wall. "Clear."

Matt crossed the hall and checked the airlock. James signaled to Sam.

"Stay close to me." Sam guided One down the hall and stopped in front of the pressure panel. It was then he realized he had nothing with which to pry open the wall panel. "James, can I borrow a knife?" James handed Sam a knife and the panel popped off with ease.

While Sam examined the wiring, the creak of a pressure panel moving caught their attention. Jones peeked around the corner of the stairs, it was the panel from above.

"The one above us is opening." Jones kept his eyes on the stairs, ready for anyone who dared attack. "One of you, with me," he called a trooper over.

All four of the short hall's office doors opened unexpectedly. James and Matt were put on alert and eased into the hall, zappers ready. They ignored the sound of the opening pressure panel on the floor above. "We've got movement."

With all the commotion splitting their attention, no one noticed the pressure panel rising between the two groups. A thud echoed from behind and their attention was brought to the chunk of the floor that had risen to divide the two groups.

"That's not good," Sam said.

"Chancellor, can you open *both* of these?" Jones approached the panel.

"Finishing this one first. Matt, can you open up that panel over there?" Sam pointed to the wall and Matt hurried to it with his knife.

Another icon turned red in the team-view. Jones and the other trooper whipped around. The body of the trooper who had been watching their flank pumped blood into the air, gravity gear pulling him down. Blood spewed from his neck like a lava lamp. Still, there were no enemies in sight. Jones and the other trooper took a defensive posture.

"I'm not picking up a cloak," the trooper said.

"Careful, they might be able to circumvent our scanners," Sam warned.

"What a delightful thought," Jones groaned. "Stay close, trooper."

"How's that door comin' along?" James asked.

"I didn't download the electronic schematics, but I think I've got it figured out."

Matt and James backed up, closer to Sam, weary of his comment about their sensors. Then, a voice came from nearby.

"I'd gladly open the door for you if you leave him with us."

"That's a negative," James said. "Why don't ya come out and talk face to face?" Like a switch flipped, their screens turned black, leaving them all in darkness. "Shit, helmets off!"

The team unclipped and tossed away their helmets then readied their melee weapons. At the end of the short hall was a man with intense eyes and scruffy brown hair.

"Uh, James?" Matt said. "The friggin' champ is behind you, bro."

James turned to look behind him but stopped when he spotted the giant stranger behind Matt. "Bro, you've got some big Russian guy behind *you*."

The two looked over their shoulders to see who had flanked them. Behind Matt was a massive Russian holding himself in place on the far side of the airlock, closest to Sam and One.

"Oh shit, Farouk Knight!" James squealed at the sight of Farouk gripping the inlet on the far wall.

With a grin, Farouk nodded. "'Sup."

Chaos

46

A Killer Escape

JONES AND THE TROOPER STOOD SHOULDER TO SHOULDER, BACKS to the pressure panel's carpet surface. Examining the map, Jones spotted a maintenance shaft behind the stairs they could take to the next level. There was no need to engage if they could destroy the ship from afar. When their screens turned black they discarded their helmets, but still, there was nobody in the room with them.

"If someone is cloaked in here…" Jones pulled a small sphere from a pouch and tossed it in front of him. A white mist sprayed from it and filled the compartment. Visibility diminished but there was no sign of cloaked enemies. Then, it struck Jones that they had not looked up.

Lightning fast, Jones spun and swung above them, a trail of light followed the zapper's vibrant sparks. The unseen enemy kicked it out of his hands and smashed a small foot into his neck. Jones rocketed to the ground then was kicked in the ribs and floated across the room.

The trooper lunged with his zapper, shield between them. A knife through his hand, he howled and released his weapon. Jamming a zapper into his neck, the attacker scurried over his shield then slit his throat with the blade.

Jones scrambled for his zapper. The maintenance shaft from the map was in front of him, and blowing up the ship would be safer and more efficient than coming to blows in enemy territory. The attacker pounced before he could go for it. He deflected and retreated, but in the dim light got a look at the muscular brown woman approximately his height, hair in a ponytail. He bumped into the port reservoir and grabbed the wall inlet.

"Aren't you The Raven?"

"You recognize me? I'm surprised you haven't pissed yourself," Maya said.

"It must be easy to assassinate people when one looks like you do. But, I find sleeping with my prey distasteful."

"The weak always make insulting excuses for the hard work and talent of others. Or, maybe you just can't get laid because you're an insufferable dick."

"Weak? You'll not find me as easy to kill as my inferiors." Jones readied himself.

"And still, you can't take the lead."

The pressure panel rang like a gong and Jones was distracted. Maya threw herself forward and charged at him along the wall. He deflected a zapper attack but she flowed with the movement and zapped his hand.

His hand spasmed at the shock and he let go of his zapper. Maya swatted it away. He retreated to retrieve it but was tackled into the ceiling. She wrapped her legs around him and they wrestled for control.

Maya's adaptability and tenacity overwhelmed Jones. She was an ever-shifting body of water that peppered him with powerful elbow strikes and slashes of her knife. Jones got in a few strikes, but could not free himself.

A slash from Maya skimmed his face from jaw to brow. She slammed her blade at him, but he grabbed her wrist before she cut into his neck. Holding back the knife, Jones pulled on her ponytail to pry her away. She kicked his elbow to get her arm loose but was slammed into a wall.

While she tried to pull free, he kicked off of her to send them in opposite directions. The shield was nearby, but she was too fast. He barely brought it between them to block the blade meant for his eye. A crack sprouted from the blow.

Jones kicked off the ceiling and threw the shield across the room with her on it. He rushed to the maintenance shaft and yanked off the hatch. The hairs on the back of his neck on end, he spun around, using it as a shield. Maya's knife dinged against the hatch and she hammered it down with her zapper.

With a grunt, Jones pushed the hatch away with Maya on it. She flew across the room and he dove into the shaft. Upside down, he unlatched the hatch on the deck below and tossed it away. Squirming through the opening, he pulled a grenade from a pouch. Before he was out, a hot iron burned his lower left leg.

Maya stabbed into his Achilles tendon and like letting go of a stretched rubber band, his calf whipped into his leg and balled up behind his knee. With a scream, he threw the grenade into the shaft behind him. Maya rushed back up to level three and dove out. An explosion consumed the shaft behind her.

"The agent got away. He's on deck four," Maya called in, catching her breath.

On the other side of the pressure panel on deck three, the encounter had progressed differently.

With Matt and James both dwarfed in might by the enemies flanking them, even without gravity gear, they tried a more tactful approach in order to give Sam time to open the panel. Their circumstances for such a tactic were more favorable.

"Hey, how about you guys just let us go? You don't want to fight fans, do ya?" James asked Farouk.

"Fans trying to kidnap a guest, yeah. Why not?" Farouk said to James's dismay.

"I can't let you guys take him back to the Ministry," Mike said.

"What's wrong with the Ministry? That's the best place for him." Sam stripped the ends of a wire. For Mike, it echoed of lessons past.

"*You* must be from the Ministry. You realize they wouldn't have sent you unless you were expendable, right?" Mike floated to the hallway junction.

"That was my bunker you attacked. You think he's safer on a pirate ship?"

"Aren't you the one that put him in danger by attacking us?" Farouk asked.

"That was Agent Jones." Sam gestured toward Jones in the other compartment. "I stopped the attack."

"That doesn't change the fact that you know he's going to be a lab experiment for the rest of his life if you take him back to the Ministry," Mike said.

"We can learn about his species, try to establish a dialogue, protect him from pirates." Sam looked over his shoulder to see who he was talking to.

"Real great job you guys did there, huh?" Farouk cracked.

"Establishing a dialogue with his people is impossible," Mike said. "You seem well-intentioned. But, having good intentions doesn't mean you're doing the right thing."

"Aren't you M.J. Smith? How did you end up a pirate? How did you fall so far?" Sam continued to work.

"You don't look favorably upon pirates. But, how about a former High Archon? A former General? A former Ranger? We're not riff-raff. We've seen behind the curtain. Shin was cast out as a traitor for doing the moral thing. The Ministry tried to kill me when I learned too much about something I shouldn't. Most pirates are former soldiers betrayed by the system they faithfully served. It's been the same throughout history. And, I picked that bunker because *I'm* the one who built it."

Matt and James shared a concerned look. They had heard these words before, but this time they resonated. Regardless of their doubts, their priority was surviving and getting Sam out alive. They could sort out the rest later.

"Doing good deeds in the past doesn't justify or excuse you from doing bad deeds now," Sam said.

"We do good deeds, but not for the glory of the UEG," Nikolai bellowed. "For someone so intelligent, your world view is limited."

"Like slaughtering the security team at my bunker? Yeah, super noble."

"They made their choice. It is a soldier's life." Nikolai's words echoed what Fuller had said to him about the loss. "We kept the rest safe."

"There are people out there playing a bigger game than you're aware of, but you're caught in the middle of it," Mike said. "One will be taken away from you. You will be discredited and you will disappear because you know too much without already being on the inside."

"You're telling me to turn my back on the Ministry? You're asking them to turn their backs on the UEG, the means by which our species has finally found peace?"

"Found peace? Look at us. Why is our species not united? A peace founded on lies is unsustainable. Earth is healthy, peaceful, technologically advanced, there's barely any disease left. But, we're branded like they used to do to farm animals, and your potential is limited based on arbitrary guidelines. Earth isn't a utopia, it's a gilded cage, and there are people willing to assassinate in order to keep it that way. What do you think that agent's job is? You'll realize that one day, like I did. But, by then you'll probably be discredited and silenced."

"You're deluded to see Earth as the villain, blaming the UEG and the Ministry for all your problems. You're just upset you can't do everything you want, the way you want to do it." Sam was appalled at the image of Mike that formed in his mind. After what he learned from Leo, he could not leave Earth when he could stay to change things for the better. "Earth has issues, but those don't get fixed by running away."

"Do the right thing and leave One with us. We'll get him somewhere safe. All you've got to do is say you didn't find him here. Go back home and be happy. This is your chance to get out alive."

There was a moment of pause, then Sam touched the other end of the wire to the pressure panel's control mechanism and it began its slow pivot back into the ground.

"I *am* doing the right thing," Sam asserted.

"Then, I guess that's our cue," Mike said.

Farouk pushed off toward James. He swung at Farouk with his zapper but it dinged against his hand and was easily ripped from his grasp. Farouk snapped the zapper in twain and tossed away the two halves.

"Aw hell." James drilled a stiff right jab into Farouk's face and his fist crumbled to rubble. James collapsed to his knees with a wail, cradling his trembling hand. Farouk tossed him into Matt, who had wearily kept Nikolai at a distance with his Zapper. James thudded into him and they tumbled to the ground. Farouk headed for One.

"Come on brotha'." One walked toward him.

"No, come back!" Sam squawked. One returned and Sam hurried between him and Farouk.

"Come on, for real?" Farouk advanced and reached out to grab Sam.

Trembling, but ready for an encounter with Farouk, Sam stepped forward and threw a big right cross into Farouk's chest. Because he was out of range and even if he made contact it would only hurt Sam, Farouk did not react. As Sam's punch reached its apex a fat rod shot out of the compartment on his arm and slammed into Farouk with the voltage of a lightning bolt.

Farouk rocketed away and slammed into the pressure panel between the two groups. The bellowing clang echoed down the hall and the room froze.

"Let's go!" Sam rushed away with One.

"One, stop!" Nikolai was quick to get his wits about him and One stopped at his command. Sam's loose grip slipped from One's arm.

"Let's go!" Sam insisted, and One followed.

"Come back!" Nikolai leaped across the hall and grabbed Sam, then tossed him into the short hall of offices like a rag doll. In the corner of his eye, James lunged at him with a left hook. Nikolai deflected and threw

James across the hall. He snatched Matt's zapper mid-swing and threw him into the pressure panel alongside Farouk.

Sam recovered quickly after being hurled into the wall and hurried back to One, but Mike tackled him and his gravity gear pulled them to the floor.

"Farouk, you okay?" Mike asked, wrestling Sam's arms out of his way.

"I can… barely move, but I'm good." Farouk clung to the wall inlet, an arm over his throbbing torso.

"If you get out of here it won't be with him." Mike rained fists down upon Sam with furious passion. Sam put his arms up to protect himself.

"James! Pick him up and get him back to the shuttle. Avoid contact and protect him at all costs. We need to get him back to the Ministry! That's an order!" Sam's world shook around him, the piercing sting of bony fists clipping him from every angle.

"What about you?"

"I got him. Go!" Matt torpedoed into Mike.

"Michael!" Nikolai moved for Mike, but paused. James threw One over his shoulder and ran the other way. Mike had trained, it was time to trust him. Nikolai lunged at James, but he dodged and booted Nikolai in the chest. He flew back to the office hall and James ran off with One.

Sam's superior mobility made it easy to avoid Nikolai and chase after James. Nikolai grabbed Matt and slammed a knee into him, then hurled him down the short hall. Before he had finished dispatching Matt, Mike was on his feet and in pursuit of One

"Come on!" Mike followed James down the hall gripping the inlets to stay grounded and move faster, Nikolai close behind. James opened the compact hallway to the galley service entrance that connected the port and starboard halls, Sam behind him.

"Cover me." Mike opened a screen to lock the opposite door of the hall. Nikolai hung back and grappled with Matt, each trying to land a blow. Nikolai landed a giant boot to his chest, then they raced away.

With the weight of a feather on his shoulder, James zoomed down the hall unimpeded. Whatever the Ministry did to this guy was amazing.

The value of his return was clear. At the far end of the hall, he swiped over the console and almost rushed face-first into a closed door. He tried the console again: RESTRICTED. Mike flew into the narrow hall behind them.

"Here." Sam opened a nearby door, the only one in the hall. They hurried inside and were surrounded by stoves, ovens, and racks of bottled ingredients magnetically held in place. They found the galley. Straight ahead, a long opening into the lounge past a waist-level countertop.

They slid over the countertop and regained their footing on the other side, but the backtracking and obstacle had slowed them down enough. Nikolai burst into the lounge. James tried to hurry off, but a kick to the back of his knee dropped him. He flung One into the air. Mike grabbed him and kicked James to the floor.

He turned to exit but was intercepted by Matt. He flung One away to fight Matt but Sam tackled him over the counter into the galley, leaving Nikolai to tussle with James and Matt. James was knocked away and took advantage to snatch One and run away while Matt kept Nikolai tied up. Nikolai did not have the leverage to incapacitate or rid himself of Matt.

"The agent got away. He's on deck four."

Sam and Mike exchanged blows in the galley. Sam was tempted to use the weapon that incapacitated Farouk, but it would surely kill him. He was no killer. He could escape without sinking to their depths.

The ship rocked to the side, its spin altered. Haunting, metallic groans echoed through the ship and it spun around Mike, who bumped into a console and accidentally opened the freezer door. Stuck to the floor, Sam clashed clumsily with Mike and in his attempt to take advantage of the situation was charged into the freezer.

Sam stumbled to get his bearings and stood up in time for Mike's elbow to smash into his temple and knock him out in the cold, unpowered freezer.

"Nikolai? What was that?" Mike closed and locked the freezer door behind him.

"I don't know, but I'm still fighting the small one!"

"I've got the agent." Mike hurried down the galley's stairway to the door on deck four. He reached the hall behind the galley as Jones hobbled by, an eye swollen, bleeding from various shallow knife wounds. Mike opened the door and tackled him into the side of the narrow hall.

Jones's defense was instinctual, slashing at Mike. He dodged and pressed his attack. Unaware of the locked door ahead, he easily defended and retreated toward the door. There, he swiped his hand over the console and charged face-first into it. Mike gripped his hair and slammed his face into the door again. Jones grabbed his wrist and twisted, swiping Mike's hand over the console.

The door swooshed open and Jones hurried out, shoving Mike away. "I need backup!"

"You're not getting out of here." Mike tackled and wrapped him up, pounding him in the face, trying to make his other eye swell so he could not see.

With his suit numbing the pain in his leg, Jones struck back and slammed Mike into the inlet, splitting him open. Forehead pouring blood, Mike tried to regain the advantage, but Jones was an avalanche. His impending death was palpable, clawing to pull him into oblivion with every grazing blow, and he refused to die on a dirty pirate ship in space. He flung Mike back into the narrow hall, closed the door, and hurried to the shuttle.

Barely passing the lounge entrance, a giant crashed into him and flung him inside. Matt lay unconscious on a broken arcade machine nearby surrounded by a cloud of broken glass. Nikolai stood poised between him and his exit. Mike would arrive soon, and there was no telling where Maya was. Luckily, Jones's call for backup was answered and the former shuttle guard tackled Nikolai from behind, giving Jones the opening he needed to slip away.

Fingers hooked under the inlets to keep him grounded, Mike raced down the hall. He sped past Nikolai and the brawling trooper.

Ahead of Jones, the door to the docking bay was still open. Jones was too close for Mike to stop and close it, but he was close enough to catch if he pressed on. Jones bounced down the hall on one leg with Mike gaining quickly. At the threshold, he turned off his gravity gear and kicked at the doorway toward the airlock.

Mike leaped after Jones with more momentum.

Only a few meters away, Jones pushed off the railing to move faster, but as he crossed over the edge of the second level he was tackled from below and they spun in place. It was a petite shadow with a ponytail.

Arm high, he slashed down her jugular and dug his knife between her ribs and into her heart. With a kick he sent her crashing into Mike and gave himself the momentum he needed to reach the airlock. Blood poured from her chest and neck. Death would come quickly, but it did not matter. The rest of the crew would soon join her.

Jones pulled himself into the airlock, slamming on the console to shut the door behind him.

Chaos

47

Saved

HEART POUNDING, EVERY BEAT RUSHING THROUGH HIS BODY, Mike could almost feel his knife digging into the agent's throat. Another agent had once caught up to him and escaped, this one would not get away. He would have to change direction when he hit the airlock, and that would be enough to catch him.

A shadow crashed into Jones from below. They twisted together and spun in place, then Jones kicked the silhouette into a collision course with Mike, launching himself toward the airlock.

The red lights illuminated the silhouette flying at him. A boulder lodged in his throat and his heart dropped like an anchor. It was Natalie, trying to clutch her injuries. Streams of blood poured from her chest and neck, spewing into the air, pooling in red bubbles.

Natalie and Mike crashed into each other. Her bloody hand gripped his collar. Terror-struck, she looked into his eyes. He applied pressure to her wounds but could not stem the flow of blood. Natalie opened her mouth to talk but gargled her own blood. Mike held her close, tears pooling in his eyes.

"I'm sorry... I'm so sorry," Mike trembled, holding her, pressing his arm to her wounds, but the blood flowed unfettered. Her convulsions for breath diminished and her labored breathing slowed, then stopped. The panicked look in her eyes softened, turned distant, then faded away.

Tears streamed down Mike's cheeks, eyes transfixed on Natalie's lifeless body in his arms.

"Way to go Natalie!" Rick yelled in the audio channel. *"We've got power!"*

Gravity kicked back in first. There was a light pull before a sudden drop to the ground. Mike pulled Natalie closer and the weight of her in his arms dropped him to his knees. The boxes in the room fell in a thunder of bangs and thuds, blood rained down around them.

A hand landed on his shoulder. Vision blurred, he turned to see Maya standing over him, looking down at Natalie with a hand over her mouth.

"Oh, no…" She knelt down next to him and caressed Natalie's head. "It's okay, stay here. Nikolai and I will give 'em hell."

A metallic boom echoed around them, the shuttle detaching. Massive lights flooded through the loading bay windows, turning to head for the *Rampart*, leaving them in darkness again.

It was exactly like before.

The lights flickered back to life, but Mike was unmoving.

"Nevermind, we need to get to the bridge," Maya said.

"She just needs a couple minutes and we can go to warp." Rick referred to the *Ulfberht*, paying no attention to the audio channel. *"That S.O.S. went out, hell of a lot of good that'll do us now. You guys all right up there? What's goin' on?"*

Mike's voice cracked, and he could not form words.

"Rick." Maya cleared her throat. "We lost Natalie."

IN THE SHUTTLE, HAYNES FOLLOWED JAMES INTO A PRIVATE ROOM in the medical bay where he set down One and left, closing the door behind him. "Where's everyone else?"

"Sam told me to get him back here, avoid contact, and keep him alive at all costs," James said.

"Is he what Sam was after?"

"Yeah, he's an experiment or somethin'. Can you watch him for me while I go back for Matt and Sam?"

"No, I'm here to make sure everything is on the level. What happened to the rest of the strike team?" Commander Haynes inquired.

"The other teams dropped off one by one, then our team got split up. They're in our goddamn tech!" James threw a hard left punch at a nearby console. Its flexible surface rippled, then settled back into place. He examined his numb, limp right hand. "We couldn't see 'em. They were all around us, and we couldn't see 'em."

"How many of them are there?"

"It's just a few of 'em," James paced back and forth in the medical bay, chest heaving with each breath. The medics left to give them privacy.

"You okay?"

"No! I'm not fuckin' okay! They, we… we've never lost the whole damn strike team before." James put a hand over his ear. "Matt, Sammy! What's goin' on?"

Neither one responded. Their private channel was silent, but the channel's private team view still showed their vitals as green, so they were alive.

"Matt! Sam! Copy!"

No response.

"They're still alive but not responding. I need to go back for 'em." James marched to the staging area.

"No, Sam gave you orders to guard him. Look, Coleman, look at me!" Haynes said. James snarled and paced, running his fingers through his hair. The towering warrior stopped and faced Haynes. "You and Akers are talented, smart, and tough as hell. I have faith in both of you. You made it back, give him a chance to do the same. But, I need you to tell me what happened. Come on, let's take care of that hand, then I can send you back out there. How the hell did you even shatter your hand?"

While Haynes tended to James in the shuttle's medical bay, Amber kept an eye on the airlock. When Jones tumbled in, she grumbled at his safe return.

"Medic!" she called. Two medics hurried in to assist Jones. "Where are Sam and Matt?"

"They're still back there." Jones cradled his injuries on the floor.

After ripping his boot off, a medic snaked metal prongs into the cut in his heel to retrieve his calf muscle. The other opened the wound farther so they could reattach it.

"And you left them there?"

"I barely made it out alive," Jones growled.

"I'm not asking about *you*."

"They're still alive, check the team view. Ken, back to the shuttle, now."

Amber had monitored the team view. They were still alive, but it did nothing to assure her of their safety. She stepped into the airlock and looked through a window. There were only floating boxes, nobody had followed Jones to the shuttle.

The medics reattached the tendon and injected his leg with a sedative to deactivate the muscles, then mended the wound and wrapped his foot in a brace to keep it still. Once they left, Amber turned sideways so as not to turn her back on Jones. She kept an eye out for their team in the airlock while Jones crawled to rest against a wall.

He watched Amber, who only passively monitored him, keeping her attention on the airlock for their team's return, keeping it closed in case enemies lurked nearby. Sam and Matt still had not returned and had likely been neutralized. If they were unconscious or stranded somewhere on the ship, there was no way to reach them.

With their numbers so depleted, if the enemy counter-attacked, it would be a massacre despite the bottleneck of the airlock. They could not afford to stay, but would not leave until the team was back, or until the team view confirmed their deaths.

Jones discreetly accessed his admin tools, careful to make sure Amber did not notice. First one then the other, Matt and Sam's names turned red in the team view.

Amber jumped, her chest tight.

"We need to go," Jones said. "Lieutenant, inside. Pilot, disembark. Get us back to the *Rampart*, double time."

Amber stared at Sam and Matt's red icons glowing in her eye and meandered into the staging area in a daze. A cloud of dread enveloped and dragged her to the floor against a corner opposite Jones. As a commanding officer, she could not return to the ship distraught and attempted to compose herself.

The door to the airlock closed and the ship disembarked. A boom echoed through the ship as the shuttle detached. Jones pulled his hitch from a pouch and unfurled it, slapping it onto his wrist.

"Captain, prime weapons and prepare to fire as soon as we're clear."

The shuttle pulled away and Jones set the walls of the staging area to be transparent so he could see the ship's destruction with his own eyes.

"Stop! Go back!" James rushed by the staging area to the cockpit, a strip of gauze dangling from his half-wrapped hand. "What the hell? Matt and Sam are still back there!"

The shuttle pulled away from the spinning ship, lights aglow. Their power was back, but it would do them no good.

"Take us back! They're still alive!" James burst into the staging area.

"They're dead, Coleman," Jones said. "Check the team view. There's nothing we can do."

James rushed Jones and lifted him off the ground, slamming an elbow into his face. "We have a private channel, asshole! They're still alive!" James roared in his face.

Amber jumped to her feet.

"Your desperation is getting the better of you, Coleman!" Jones attacked James's arm but the brawny mass was rooted around his neck.

The medic troopers jumped on James to pry him off.

"Take us back!" James roared, spit spraying on Jones's face. The troopers pulled him away but James shot forward again and slammed Jones into the wall.

"Oh shit…" Matt's voice buzzed in James's ear.

"Matt! Jones is going to fire on the ship! You and Sam get to an escape pod!"

"What? I don't…" Matt struggled to get his wits about him. *"I don't know where Sam is. I don't see his waypoint."*

"Get out of there! Now!"

Matt rolled off the broken arcade machine and stumbled to his feet. He hurried to the hall, exterior walls lined with escape pods.

"Shuttle's clear." Captain Slater's update rang in Jones's ear.

"Fire!" Jones boomed.

Giant metal slugs zoomed past the shuttle and slammed into the *Ulfberht*, tipping it into a corkscrew spin. Car-sized shell after shell drilled into the ship.

A guttural roar erupted from James and he head-butted Jones, then pummeled him with elbows.

"Stop firing! Stop! Stop!" His heart clenched, every synapse screamed for him to stop what was happening, to save his friends. Helpless and desperate, he pummeled Jones. Without him, Sam was their only superior, and he was on the ship.

The troopers pulled him off and fell to the floor in a pile. Jones collapsed into a bloody heap, face swollen, painted red and purple.

Ken entered and examined the room in an attempt to figure out what he had missed. An icon turned red, but James was in too much of a rage and did not want to see who it was. He fought against the troopers to get back at Jones.

"Rampart, hold your fire!" Amber yelled. Before the *Rampart* could comply, a burst of light appeared behind them and from it appeared a massive red and gray ship. Several shots slammed into it before the *Rampart* stopped firing.

All around them, flashes of light preceded Red Storm ships bursting into the vicinity, surrounding the UEG forces without end in sight.

The powder keg around them exploded, the full contingent opening fire on the UEG ships. The *Rampart* veered toward the shuttle, pummeled by enemy cannons.

Once the shuttle was in range, the stars disappeared into shimmering streaks of oscillating light. The connection to Matt and Sam terminated.

"No!" Jones roared, bloody pulp of a face fixed on where the *Ulfberht* had been. "Nooooooo!"

"Matty..." James collapsed and the troopers untangled themselves. James sobbed on the floor, fearing his best friend dead.

Jones dragged himself onto his good foot, using the rail to get up. He hopped past James and the troopers, hobbling to the medical bay, drawing his blade.

Commander Haynes stood at the door to One's room and drew his taser pistol as soon as Jones limped in leaning on the rails, a wildfire of murderous intent burning in his eyes.

"Is that where he is?" Jones asked.

"Stay back or I *will* open fire," Haynes warned, charged with caring for One the moment James ran off. Jones was only a couple hops away.

"Out of my way! Retrieving that thing cost me my target!"

"We are under orders to protect this asset and return it to the Ministry, stand down or be shot."

A hand gripped Jones and slammed him to the floor face-first, arms yanked behind his back.

"Agent Oliver Jones, you're under arrest for the suspected murder of Ministry Chancellor Samuel Bernard and UEG Specialist Matthew Akers." Amber made sure the cuffs were uncomfortably tight.

Instead of spouting insults, Jones laughed.

"Put me in the brig, but when you file," he coughed, "the report or *whatever* it is you do, you'll be told to let me free."

"How do you figure?" Amber said with a mix of doubt and concern.

"You stood in the way of my mission." He hacked, spitting blood on the floor. "I don't officially exist. I'll be back in my quarters by lunch."

"We could kill you now and say you died on that ship," Amber threatened.

"You always had more guts than Commander Haynes, but I doubt you have the stomach for it." Over his shoulder, Jones looked Amber in the eye.

She was tough, but she had a solid moral compass. Jones banked on her inability to commit murder.

Amber pulled him up and tossed him into the trooper behind her. "Lock him up!"

ON THE *ULFBERHT*, THE CREW HAD RETREATED TO THE BRIDGE, the safest place on the ship. But, tucked away behind the gunner room wall, Will remained safe. With a pained groan, his eyes slowly fluttered open in the depths of the *Ulfberht*. His head pounded and his body ached. "Where...?" Will examined the dark, unfamiliar corridor. He had been in the gunner room with half the crew and now he was alone in some strange compartment.

Groggily, Will untangled himself and climbed through the opening in the wall before him. He tumbled into the gunner room. The lights were on, but there was nobody there. He looked back at the hatch in the wall.

"I didn't even know that was there," he grumbled to himself, holding a bump on the back of his head. Natalie's cherry flavored lip-gloss was fresh on his lips. "Natalie?"

Part

4

A New Reality

Jones

48

The Devil's Right Hand

On a shipyard orbiting Earth, Agent Jones burst from an office in a furious march. He had been released from the brig several hours late and without food. Upon release, he had to take a call, which went poorly.

"Mission status?" In civilian attire, Ken pulled alongside and accompanied Jones down a walkway overlooking one of the shipyard's busy streets.

"They're not happy about losing Samson, or one of the battleships. But, I'm not benched, they still want me to find Smith and bring him in, dead or alive. I'll have to rethink my approach. They won't give me reinforcements."

"Samson wasn't your fault. He shouldn't have tried—"

"My command, my fault." Jones sneered. Ken hated being interrupted but kept his outrage restrained to a quiet snarl.

"In any case, I still have to get Morikawa. He disappeared on me. He's got some kind of stealth—"

"Do whatever you want, just give me some damn space." Jones's powerful stride rushed him away. Ken stopped with a scoff and left in another direction.

Agent Jones got something to eat and found himself a table high above a promenade atop the massive shipyard overlooking Earth and its moon, Luna. He was as isolated as he could be from the busy crowd below and as close as possible to the window. Looking upon Earth, watching its various systems at work helped him think.

Jones sat alone for a while after his meal until two men entered the promenade. One man looked around the empty balcony and nodded in approval. To Jones's displeasure, he headed directly for him. He left a large, muscular man in a suit and matching fedora standing stoically in the archway with his hands together in front of him.

"Special Agent Oliver Jones? Do you mind if I join you?" asked the light-skinned man with red eyes in a fine black suit, hair combed back.

"Is that how you were taught to introduce yourself?" Jones asked.

"My name is Lazarus." He grinned, entertained by Jones, who gestured for him to sit. "The name doesn't bother you at all?"

"I'm accustomed to dealing with codenames. Until recently I knew a man whose codename was Samson, yet he had no hair. I don't ask needless questions. How do you know *my* name?" Jones clasped his hands together.

"There's little I *don't* know, Agent Jones. You may not have a codename but your reputation as The Bloodhound precedes you. You live in Montana, close to the bunker that was attacked a few months ago." Lazarus drew a tablet from his coat and placed it in front of Jones. There was a picture of Farouk on the screen. "To which you were called in order to follow one Farouk Knight, flying a third generation Armadillo. You recently caught up with him and his crew only to lose them. Shall I continue?"

Jones flipped through the tablet. There were pictures of Farouk, reports from the bunker's personnel, and videos that would play silently as he pulled them off the screen. He kept them projected to one side while skimming the heap of information.

"Only if you have a point." Jones navigated out of the *Bunker* archive to reveal an archive bearing his name. There were archives for the various members of Mike's crew that Jones had reported and one for each of the assets he had acquired for the mission. Amidst the folders was a name that he did not recognize: Nikolai Markov.

"Oh, I do. As you can see I've done my research. And you, despite your reputation, got a valuable genetically enhanced asset killed, lost a battleship to pirates, and all but *destroyed* two others. Not to mention the attempted murder of a Ministry Chancellor and losing your targets. I believe this is the first time you've blundered an operation so badly. Congratulations on a stunning record thus far, but I really can't fault you for letting this one get away." Despite his words, Lazarus did not come off condescending. There was empathy in his voice.

"Attempted?" Jones could not move on before addressing that word.

"Haven't you heard? Dr. Bernard arrived unconscious in a life pod eight hours after the *Rampart's* arrival." Jones clenched a trembling fist and restrained his anger, but Lazarus continued before he could respond. "I wouldn't worry about him. He's got his own problems to deal with. Let's focus on you."

With a groan, Jones set the tablet down and slid it away. "What did you mean about letting them get away?"

"You didn't know who Farouk Knight was flying with. Axiom is a slippery son of a bitch, he's managed to evade even *me* all these years." Lazarus pointed at himself. "And, with that crew? I'm truly amazed you even got as close as you did."

"He goes by *Aries* now," Jones corrected him.

"Does he?" Lazarus's brow furrowed with intrigue and he shook his head. "Cute. Well, *Aries* has formed quite a team. I'm sure you didn't expect the Red Storm, the largest pirate clan there is, to come to his rescue. But I do have a theory about this." Lazarus waved a finger in the air. "You mentioned in your logs a large Russian?"

"My logs. Yes, I did." For Jones, that confirmed this man worked for somebody well connected and important. He had spoken with the only people who should have access to his logs and they were not happy with him. Not to mention, they would not have sent someone to meet with him so soon.

"Nikolai Markov is the former Russian Spaceforce General and founder of the Red Storm. We've come to be informed that he takes weeks or months away from his clan, leaving his wife Iskra Zekich in charge. We don't know where he goes, only that he is absent and unaccounted for anywhere else. It has been a mystery that I believe you solved."

"What luck," Jones deadpanned.

"Since the Red Storm showed up to rescue that ship, I think we can safely assume that was him." Lazarus rolled his eyes. "Somehow, he and Michael became friends after the war, so it isn't far fetched."

"I should have listened to that Ministry moron." Jones shook his head. "He told me to put all my digital security on the defensive."

"Good advice. There is no one better when it comes to that sort of thing." Lazarus gently rocked his head from side to side. "I believe your operation fell apart when you put the *Rampart* on emergency power. It restricts power to the essentials, which does not include signal jammers, which is why they got a signal out when their power came back."

"I do appreciate that informative lesson and all of... this." Jones waved at Lazarus and his tablet. "But, information is never free. Why are you here? What do you want from me?"

"Want? Nothing." Lazarus sliced his hand sideways through the air with a foreboding grin. "Nothing more than to see Michael and his crew blown to pieces."

"*That* is a request I would be overjoyed to accommodate." Jones sat up straight. The stranger caught him in a bad moment when he arrived, but there was a growing kinship between them as the conversation went on.

"Do you have a plan to find him again?" Lazarus asked.

"If the founder of the Red Storm is indeed on that ship, then the Red Storm will probably guard them until their repairs are complete. So I *should* just have to wait for them to show up at a shipyard somewhere. That is, if they don't have their *own* shipyard like the Dragon Claw."

"To our knowledge they do not," Lazarus said.

"Then the only shipyard large enough for a ship like theirs to go unnoticed is the *Olympus* shipyard at Avalon. I would start my search there. Either way, I'm stuck here for at least a month while they repair the *Rampart*. They won't give me another ship." Jones growled bitterly, eyes on a storm forming over the Atlantic ocean.

"The *Olympus* shipyard, you say?" Lazarus asked, eyes drifting away. "Repairs for both ships should take about a month," he mumbled, calculating something in his mind. His eyes squinted as he pondered something, then shook his head. "Never mind that. You said you need a ship. Is that all you need to kill Michael?"

"I would prefer stealth to firepower, so perhaps a stasis cocoon?" Jones grabbed the nearly empty beverage he had ignored since before Lazarus arrived and took a drink.

"If I get you a personal ship and anything else you need will you, literally," Jones emphasized with an affirmative gesture of his hands, "bring me back Michael's head? I'll make sure you can get out of here in *hours*."

"You *really* want his head." Jones nodded with a grin. His kinship with Lazarus was no illusion. They were birds of a feather.

"Well, the last idiot I sent said they killed him." The frustration in Lazarus's voice burned like wildfire. "A shot to the back of his head was too easy a death for him."

Lazarus cleared his throat and regained his composure.

"I prefer working covertly, and alone. The only person you can rely on is yourself. He won't even see me coming. But you know, I think you and I could become good friends." Jones gestured warmly at Lazarus with a smile.

"As do I. When you've killed Michael, give me a call and I'll have a spot ready for you in the big leagues." Lazarus pulled a clear business card and a small coin-sized item from his pocket with a wink and slid them across the table. His grin was like a news anchor smiling through lies and half-truths.

"I thought the UEG *was* the big leagues." Jones placed his mobile on the table and grabbed the small silver item, examining it pensively.

"Not to me," Lazarus said. "I don't request a new ship, I demand one. That power could be yours as well." He eyed the silver item with a raised eyebrow. Jones twirled the coin-sized item in his fingers, then placed it on his mobile.

His mobile blinked black and white, and then brought up an unfamiliar screen. Lazarus took back his disc so Jones could read the screen in detail.

"Lazarus, was it?" Jones scrolled down.

"That's right." The ominous man smiled. Jones put his mobile down and turned his body to face the man he knew as Lazarus.

"I was having such a…" Jones sighed, "an exasperating day. But, it has been an *absolute* pleasure making your acquaintance."

Ulfberht Crew

49

Moving Forward

Red Storm pirates raided the powerless UEG ship. The crew fought at every junction, but one by one they fell. They overtook the *Titan* within an hour. Most troopers were killed in the assault. Survivors were sent to Earth crammed into life pods.

Sam awoke alone on the *Ulfberht's* cold freezer floor. The door creaked open and a ray of light streamed into the room like a scar. Red Storm pirates surrounded the exit with their weapons fixed on the opening, dampeners temporarily turned off.

Hands up, Sam stepped out of the freezer staring down a dozen rifles. A pair of Russians searched him for weapons. Mike stood alongside Nikolai in the center of the group with a grim, tired expression, devoid of the victorious bravado Sam expected. Surely, the team had got away with One and had no choice but to leave him behind. The pirates cleared him of weapons and cuffed his hands behind him.

"Your crew left you and your friend behind then fired on the ship with you on it." Mike brought Sam up to speed so he understood his circumstances.

"Who else got left behind?"

"The smaller guy that was with you."

"Where is he?"

The look on Mike's face told him everything. He averted his eyes to the steel floor. "He was in one of the compartments that got hit when your people fired on us. His body was floating outside."

Stunned, Sam's eyes welled with tears and he stared blankly back at Mike. "No, he…" The words got caught in his throat.

"You've never lost someone before?" Mike asked.

"My parents when I was a kid." Sam shook his head and rocked in place. "My grandma."

Nikolai put a comforting hand on his shoulder. "You have our condolences. There is no greater pain."

Mike took a deep breath, burying his own mournful emotions. "You really didn't belong on that mission."

"I guess not." Sam's remorse simmered to a wrenching squeeze on his heart.

"Look, you've got a choice to make and you're pretty screwed either way," Mike said flatly. "We don't take prisoners. You can stay and we'll get you a new identity so you can move to the colonies or you can go home, get arrested, tried for treason, and killed in your sleep."

Taken aback, Sam looked to the crowd in confusion. "That's extreme."

"It is the most likely scenario," Nikolai said.

"How do you figure?"

"You had a chance to talk to me. The things I know they don't want getting around, and you don't have much motive to stay loyal after being fired on by your own people. They're going to silence you if you go back."

"I think that's a bit much. We haven't talked about anything, and when I file my report I can just leave this part out."

"They're going to assume you left out *everything* they want to know. If you want to live in denial, we'll throw you in a life pod and shoot you at the shipyard your people went to. Despite doing this, you seem like a good guy, so I wanted to give you a chance."

Sam considered what he was saying, but could not bring himself to believe it.

"I believe in the Ministry. Can you please send my friend's body back with me?"

"You lose objectivity when you believe in things." Mike looked over Sam's shoulder at the pirates behind him. A prick in his neck turned his world to darkness and Sam collapsed into the arms of his captors. The last survivor released, Sam was sent home with Matt next to him in a body bag.

The Red Storm got the *Titan* running, then towed the *Ulfberht* to the Avalon system. With his return, Nikolai assumed command of the Red Storm. The crew took residence in his capital ship, the *Gorynych*.

Before going to Avalon they stopped at Alpha Centauri A. A crowd of Russians joined the *Ulfberht* crew in paying their respects to Natalie. The young hitchhiker had saved the life of their leader. Through the bay's large windows the domineering sun shined upon the funeral service as Nikolai praised Natalie's bravery. Mike followed, admitting he was skeptical about bringing teenagers onto his ship, but he had never been so wrong.

Will requested to watch alone and Nikolai made the arrangements. From an unlit observation room on the second level, Will watched the men from the *Ulfberht* carry Natalie's coffin into an airlock. They lined up in front of the window and at Nikolai's command, the room stood at attention. Boots stomped in unison and shook the room. Mike released the airlock and Natalie's coffin sailed into the star. Nikolai sang in Russian, soon joined by the rest of the room.

Eaten away inside by a growing void, Will could not hold back his tears. Though he could not understand the song, it resonated within him as he watched the coffin shrink into the distance until it was gone. Not even two weeks had passed since they celebrated her birthday, and he found himself at her funeral. He sat in the darkness long after the service ended. She was all he had left. What was there to go back to?

The trip to Avalon was a somber one. Natalie's death weighed on the crew. Will was hit especially hard and spent most of his time alone. He was hardly seen and barely ate or talked. Attentive and caring, Addie made sure he had whatever he needed, but the crew tried not to bother him. Shin communicated with supportive gestures, but not a single word. He could offer none that would help.

The loss reminded Ian of his daughter. He watched old home videos and called her. Once repaired, Farouk spent most of his time with his steel punching bag and drinking with the Russians. Combat helped him deal with his emotions. With no such outlet, Rick's drinking got so out of hand that even the Russians grew concerned.

Come the fifth of November, Mike was so consumed with guilt that he had forgotten his birthday. Had Nikolai and Maya not shown up with drinks and a small ice cream cake, the day would have gone overlooked.

Friends and drinks helped him talk through his feelings about Natalie and Hope. For years, the fear of failing his daughter had plagued him, and now they had manifested with the first teenager he brought aboard. Was it an omen of what was to come if he ever rescued her?

After a month-long journey, the arrival at the *Olympus* shipyard in the Avalon system for repairs did nothing to comfort Mike. The ship could be fixed, but the loss was permanent, and he had a newfound sense of doubt.

A network of segments extended from the shipyard's large, dome-like central body. Ships stuck to it like flies in a spider's web, and now the *Ulfberht* was one of them. The crew stayed on the *Gorynych* surrounded by a loyal pirates to protect them.

The day after their arrival, the *Ulfberht* crew ate lunch together in the officer's lounge overlooking the *Gorynych* mess hall, with the exception of Maya and Will. With the news in the background, they caught up on current events. Their casual conversation came to a halt when breaking news took over the screen.

There had been another attack.

"What's that? The fifth Dragon Claw attack in six months?" Ian took a drink of his beer. In Russian, Nikolai bellowed a command to raise the volume. The tagline under the reporter read: *Pirates obliterate major Freyjan port.*

"Five months," Nikolai grumbled. "One each month."

"Do they still not know it's the Dragon Claw? Or are they saying pirates anyway?" Farouk asked, ever suspicious of the media.

"*Pirates have left this busy port in shambles. Once the center of interstellar commerce in the region, they have done untold damage to the local economy. This surge of brazen pirate attacks has caused outrage and demand for action, making the people of Earth uneasy about leaving home.*"

"If I didn't know Tony was on his way, I'd call to check up on him," Mike said.

"*That's true, Jill. The attacks took a heavy toll on the upcoming launch of the* Felicity *cruise ship, which saw a wave of cancellations. But, up and coming pro-gamer Dax Guererro bought tickets for his entire family. Many others followed suit and the remaining tickets have already been purchased by others who didn't have a chance to get them before since the colossal ship's maiden voyage has been booked for a year.*"

"I bet those guys from the *Oasis* got away, or they'd know it's the Dragon Claw." Addie watched the devastated Freyjan port.

"Wiley sods," Ian said.

"Unless they know and aren't telling anyone." Shin mirrored Farouk's sentiment. Farouk pointed in support.

"*Donald Brown, owner of Arc Industries and Babylon Mining, has joined in the outcry for action, citing his concerns for the safety of the* Felicity's *passengers, as well as his employees.*"

"Safety my ass. You're just worried about your money," Farouk yelled.

"*Somethin' needs to be done about the rampant lawlessness in the colonies. They are so infested with crime it's oozing into space. Who knows how the people of the colonies became so immoral, but when it threatens our lives, our children's lives, the lives of loving mothers and fathers working to put food on the table, it is despicable that our government does nothing!*"

"Pirates been around more than twenty years, now all of a sudden he's worried. That two-faced asshole is up to something." Farouk pounded the table, denting it.

The video cut from Brown back to the newscaster.

"After the increasingly devastating attacks, Regents have enacted emergency aid policies and increased the budget for the EOD, which is currently looking for an alternative contractor to XJB as their contract expires this year. With pressure mounting, some are pushing for a summit next month to discuss the growing pirate threat."

"His partner died a little white ago. I bet you he tries to get that contract," Farouk said.

Addie's head turned to check the door, which opened slowly. Then, Will's head popped in, followed by the rest of him.

"Hey Will!" Addie said. The table's attention turned to him and they paid him various greetings, inviting him to join them.

"No thanks. Captain, can we talk?" he asked.

"Sure. Nikolai, you mind if we use your office or something?"

"Why use office when you have the room." Nikolai's scooted his chair back and rose to his feet, grabbing his empty plate and drink. The rest of the table followed suit. Farouk handed his off to Ian and headed for the couch while everyone else left.

"Hey Rick, we're clearin' out, let's go." With a kick, he awoke Rick, laid out on the couch with an almost full plate on the coffee table and a flask in his hand. Grunting, he wobbled upright and tried to get to his feet, crashing to the floor with a thud. "Come on, man, I got you." Farouk tried to help, but Rick pulled away.

"I d'nee jer help," Rick mumbled. He leaned on the couch to get on his feet and stumbled to the door, leaning on whatever he could. He tried to take a drink from his flask, but it was empty. Farouk followed him out, ready to catch him if he fell.

"Is he going to be okay?" Will asked.

"I don't know." Mike leaned back in his seat with a heavy sigh. "How are you doing? You look better."

"Yeah, I'm doing better. It's kind of sucked not having anything to do because I just sit around all day."

"It's good to keep busy, keep your mind off things. Do you want me to find something for you?" Mike offered.

"Actually, that's what I wanted to talk to you about. Like a couple days before everything happened, Natalie and I were talking. She convinced me to ask you if I could be your apprentice like she was for Rick. I used to crack mobiles and mod games back home. So, I was wondering if you could teach me?"

Mike stared at Will for a moment. Whether it was out of compassion or guilt, his answer was, "I'd love to. I've never taken on an apprentice before, but I'll do my best. I feel like I've failed you both, and I'm sorry for that. I've been mad at myself since the attack, but if I can send you into the world with a great career and knowledge, then I can at least ensure you live a prosperous life."

"Natalie got to live her dream. Working on the ship with Rick, she was happy." Will wiped away a tear and for a few breaths, the loudest thing in the room was the memory of Natalie.

"I'll get you started with some reading material. Are you sure being on this ship won't be too hard?"

"Natalie was all I had left, and she *loved* the ship so much. It's all I have left of her. So, I'd like to stay if that's okay. I don't want to leave yet."

Leaving would mean letting go, and he could never do that.

Rampart Crew

50

Be True to Thyself

THE *RAMPART* AND THE *OBELISK* LIMPED INTO THE *SAGAN SHIPYARD* on the fifth lunar lagrangian point. The crew hustled to empty the ship. Personal effects, tools, weapons, vehicles, supplies, bodies, it was all gone within two hours. A heavy security detail transferred Jones to the shipyard's brig, where *Rampart* troopers remained on guard.

Once the ship had been cleared out, Captain Slater relieved his officers and took the long shift. Orders would await them when they awoke. The gracious Captain had promised his officers seven hours, but Amber and Haynes were awoken after five and a half. Their orders when they awoke: *Report to the Med Bay immediately.*

When Amber arrived in the station's white-walled medical bay, she was directed to a private room with fogged windows. Inside, Slater and Haynes stood by the bed with their backs to the door. With a turn, they pulled apart to reveal the patient. Lying in the bed, alive and awake, was Sam.

With a gasp, she ran and wrapped her arms around him. "You're alive!" She pulled away to regain her composure.

"Didn't think I was going to be, but yeah."

"Is Matt okay? What happened?" she asked.

Sam's grim expression answered her question.

"I didn't want to say who arrived for security reasons." Slater turned to Sam. "I kept your arrival under wraps since you showed up so much later than everyone else. I woke you up because we need to know how you survived without so much as a scratch and what happened on that ship."

"We docked at an empty docking bay and split up into teams. Our team got to the target without any trouble, but the rest of the teams died one by one. Our way back was blocked by a pressure panel. I had to open up the wall to get at the power. Another pressure panel separated us from Jones and the troopers with him. While I was getting the panel open..." Sam cleared his throat. "*M.J. Smith* started talking to us and we realized they were in our tech. They'd been watching us the whole time and we couldn't see them."

"M.J. Smith? Isn't he dead?" Slater asked.

"Turns out, he's very alive."

"How the hell did he get in our tech?" Slater leaned in with alarm.

"I don't know, that's not my field of expertise. They probably got into our system through one of our helmets but that's all I can figure."

"How did you guys get left behind?" Haynes moved things along.

"I got the door open and we made a run for it. For some reason, the target kept going back and forth doing whatever anyone told him to do, so I told James to pick him up and go. They caught up to us in the galley. Smith knocked me out and locked me in the freezer. When they let me out, they told me the *Rampart* fired on us and they found Matt floating outside."

Hands on her face, Amber paced away in a circle, balling them into fists. Haynes buried his eyes in one hand and turned around. Captain Slater let out a muffled groan.

"I can't believe we fired on our own people... I'm glad you're okay. I uh, I'm sorry. I know there ain't a damn thing I can say to make up for it. I'm going to have to live with that," Slater said.

"What happened? Couldn't you guys see the team feed?"

"Your status turned red," Amber said. "I thought you can't alter team member status, even if you're team lead."

"If anyone has a way to do that, it would be that asshole," Haynes said.

"Where's James? Did he make it back?"

"He made it back. Left me guarding your guy when he took off. Last I saw him, he was at a bar," Haynes said. "Poor thing."

"What about the guy you were guarding?" Sam asked.

"I arranged for quarters, he's got twenty-four-hour security. Haven't contacted the Ministry, though. I know it was a sensitive issue so we wanted to make sure we got it into the right hands."

Sam sighed. "Thank you so much. If it isn't too much trouble, could you make the call for me? They aren't letting me out of here and it's a dead zone for my implant."

"No problem. I'll get you some clothes, too," she said.

"That tracker you put on Jones is still goin', so I'll check up on him," Slater said. "Haynes, post some security outside."

"Yes, sir. Glad you're all right, Sam." Haynes strode out of the room with purpose.

"Thanks. And, I appreciate that, Captain."

Sam gave Amber the details and she was off. She tried to get a hold of James, but he was a ghost. Amber addressed other tasks first but was soon on the line with the Ministry trying to get a hold of High Archon Adison. For over an hour she was transferred and put on hold a half dozen times before his thin face appeared on the screen.

"Commander Wells? How can I help you?"

"High Archon Adison, it's a pleasure. I'm calling on behalf of Chancellor Samuel Bernard."

"Is he all right?"

"He's fine. Gave us a bit of a scare, though. They've got him in sickbay until regulations allow him to leave."

"What happened?"

"Sam and another teammate got left behind during the infiltration and we thought they were dead. They returned in a life pod about eight hours after the survivors from the ship we lost. I've forwarded his report to you, I'm sure he details the events there."

"Thank you, Lieutenant. I'll read this right away. Please tell the Chancellor that I'll send a ship for him soon. It'll be good to have him home."

"Will do, sir."

Amber asked station personnel to be informed when a Ministry ship arrived and went about her duties. A couple of hours later her hitch beeped with the alert she was waiting for, so she took Sam a change of clothes.

"Time to go home." She strode into the room holding a pile of his clothes.

"Ship's here already?" Sam sat up.

"Back to a glamorous life on Earth." She handed him the folded stack.

"I'm going to miss my time here. This has been more adventure than I think I've ever had in my whole life."

"Maybe you should visit once in a while?" Amber strolled away and turned around. "Don't worry, I won't peek."

Sam hopped out of bed and disrobed. It was quiet for a moment, but then Sam gathered up some courage. "So, how would I visit? Just hang out on the ship?"

Amber erupted with a delighted chuckle. "Oh yeah, that'd be great. Just linger around the ship on your vacation."

"I don't think I've ever actually taken a vacation."

"Neither have I."

"Maybe we should? Both? Like, at the same time?" Sam strung his belt through the loops on his pants.

"Are you asking me out?"

"I think so? It's been a long time since I've done that, too. But, we both travel a lot for our jobs, so I was thinking we could coordinate a few days of vacation time."

"What took you so long to ask?"

"I was going to do it the day James and Matt disappeared."

"Hah!" Amber burst. "That's some bad timing. Things were hectic after that."

"Yeah, but, what do you think?" Sam buttoned his shirt.

"Sure." Amber nodded. "It's worth a try."

Shirt tucked in, Sam threw on his Ministry coat and turned around. "Dressed."

With a slow pivot on her heel, Amber turned around and gave him a thumbs-up. "Looking sharp, Chancellor."

"Thank you." Sam sat on the bed to slip on his shoes.

"I read your report, by the way. You got lucky." Maya leaned back against a table.

"You read my report?"

"I read all the reports. That's part of my job."

"Ah, well, there's actually something I left out." Sam looped his shoelaces together with a tug.

"Oh? Tell me more," Amber approached with intrigue.

"M.J. Smith offered us the chance to be pirates." Sam chuckled, slipping on his other shoe.

"Oh my god, really? Wow. That's some balls right there. Why would he think you would leave? You're a Chancellor, life is good."

"As a Ministry founder, he respectfully disagreed. He said I was expendable and they were going to throw me under the bus. I told him to fuck off." Sam hopped off the table, shoes tied.

"Good, because I wouldn't stick around here if it was like that."

"Really? Would you take off like you did on your parents?"

Their conversation was interrupted when the door slid open and James burst into the room, his right hand still encased in a silver regenerative cast.

"Matty?" Leaning on the doorway for support, James's tired eyes searched the room for Matt. Only Sam and Amber looked back at him. "Sammy," he said. Eyes welling with tears, he stumbled into the room. "Is Matty with you?"

Sam shook his head, looking up at James, whose face melted. "I'm sorry."

James collapsed to his knees and covered his face with a croak. Sam and Amber hurried over and knelt to hug James.

"I'm sorry," he said.

"You don't need to be sorry." Amber rubbed his back.

"I heard there was anotha' surviva' and I ran ova' here." He took a stuttered breath. "I'm glad you're okay, Sammy. I just…" James shook his head. "Matty's gone. He was my brother. It's like someone cut out a piece of my goddamn heart and every time it beats, I feel it missing. I feel like I'm dyin'."

"They sent me back with his body, so his family will get closure."

"That's good." James nodded with a sniffle. "Yeah, that—that's good 'a those guys."

"Yeah, they're not what we thought." Sam wiped away a tear.

"I tried to get a hold of you earlier to tell you," Amber said.

"I turned off my hitch." James rolled out of his hunch and wrapped his arms around Sam and Amber. "I'm sorry. I'm pretty trashed."

"It's fine, we understand," Sam said. James pulled out of the hug and wiped his face on his sleeves and hands.

"You guys want to grab a drink?" he asked.

"Hell yes, I could use one," Sam said. "My ship will wait for me."

"I'm on duty, but I'm supposed to be seeing off our Ministry VIP, so I go where he goes," Amber followed up.

"Let's go then." James led the group out of the private room. On their way through the medical bay lobby, the double doors on the far side opened and a half dozen troopers in two rows entered with their taser pistols at the ready. In the middle of them was High Archon Adison. Important as he may be, the escort was excessive.

Sam smiled and waved. "I didn't expect him to come himself. Let me make sure I can still grab that drink."

"Chancellor Samuel Bernard." Adison raised a hand in the air, then sliced it down. "You're under arrest for suspected treason."

Before Sam could process what Adison was saying, troopers swarmed him. His hands were behind his back and a glove was slipped over his left hand, blocking his implant, followed by handcuffs.

"What? Treason? What the hell are you talking about?"

"You were alone on the enemy ship for eight hours and returned unharmed, no signs of interrogation. It was your facility that was attacked. And, somehow, the enemy crew had an unexplainable drop on the assault team. Until the extent of your crimes has been determined, you are under arrest."

"Hey!" James pushed by one of the troopers, but two others aimed their taser pistols at him. Amber pulled him back.

"James! Stop! Hold on, this is bullshit! All the survivors of the *Titan* were returned alive, why aren't they being detained?"

"Because they weren't on that ship. I'd mind my business if I were you," he said.

"Adison, what the hell?" Sam struggled, but a signal from Adison cued a trooper to smash him in the stomach and the others dragged him away.

"Commander, please have all his belongings taken to my ship." Adison eyed Amber, then followed the troopers out.

Instead of doing as ordered, Amber stormed all the way to Slater's office. At the sight of her furious posture, strangers moved out of her way.Groups parting before her, she stopped at the door to his temporary office and tapped the console.

"Lieutenant Commander Wells." The console confirmed her voice, turned green, and she exploded into the room. "Sir! The Ministry arrested Sam for treason! With our own troopers! What the hell?"

"I ain't happy about it either, but he outranks me."

"But, treason? He didn't—he *wouldn't* do that." The device Sam made for Leo popped into her mind, but that was their secret. "He believes in the Ministry like I believe in the UEG. He risked his life out there for it and now he's being arrested for suspected treason? It's *wrong*, sir."

"I know, but if you think you're havin' a bad day now, wait 'til you see what I've got for you." Slater motioned for her to take a seat and typed on the tabletop. Over the table appeared a box with an audio waveform. "I came to check on Jones earlier. Turns out he's M.I.A. I went digging through the backlog of his bug and found this."

Amber sat down and listened to Jones and Lazarus's conversation.

When it finished, Slater sent a copy to her hitch. He stood in front of the floor to ceiling windows to look upon Earth. He already had time to process everything, Amber needed a moment.

"You said Jones is gone?"

"A couple hours after this conversation, the device died."

"So, he gets to do what he did and gets off just like that? He even got a promotion, and Sam gets thrown in jail for treason? This isn't... right."

"Wells, something I always admired about you was your morals. You do the right thing and you don't let anyone get in your way. It's the trait I admire most, so I understand if this doesn't sit well with you. But, there's no legal way you can help. Sam's fate is what it is. If you try to do anything, you'll be throwing away your career with Earth Orbit Security and there won't be a damn thing I can do about it."

"Sir, are we really going to let this happen? Isn't there someone we can talk to or something we can do?"

"Not if you like the life you've got," he said.

Amber sat for a moment with her fists on her knees. The sense of family she got from Earth Orbit Security had vanished. It had kept her there for eleven years, and in an instant, it was gone. She was an expendable cog. They all were.

"You going to be okay?"

"I don't know. May I be excused?"

"You're excused."

Amber shot out of her seat but before she left, she paused. "Thank you for the advice, sir. You've been an extraordinary role model and a fountain of wisdom."

"Thank you, Lieutenant. You've been an exemplary officer."

Amber marched out in a daze. Leaving the office lost in thought, her journey came in flashes without any conscious direction. She found herself by the brig. As a Lieutenant Commander, she had clearance to see Sam. Before she could go in, James's voice caught her attention. He was arguing with two troopers who would not let him in. Amber hurried to him, arriving as things got physical.

"James!" Amber rushed between them, hands on his chest, pushing him away. "Let's go, come on. I'm sorry guys."

The troopers' aggressive stance softened. They waved them off with a nod and returned to their posts.

"Come on." Amber pulled at James's arm and dragged him back to his room despite constant protests that he wanted to see Sam. "Oh my god, shut up for a minute. Which way is your room?"

"Woah, how did we get here so fast?" James pointed down the hall. "That way."

Once they arrived, James opened the door and Amber shoved him inside. Amber checked down the halls. All clear, she closed the door and locked it.

"What the hell were you doing out there?"

"I wanted to see Sam. After they took him and you left, I followed them to the brig. I checked my hitch. Missed a *bunch* 'a messages. One of 'em was from the UEG." James wobbled then sat on the bed, elbows on his knees.

"What did it say?"

"I've been assigned to a new team. Already. They said to take some weeks leave, then report in. We haven't even been back a day." James shook his head. "It's like the Red Queen said."

"The Red Queen? What are you talking about?"

"The lady from the Red Storm. She said the UEG is going to shit on us, that they don't care."

"Were they the ones that abducted you?" She sat next to James.

"No, the rebels called them. They gave us a chance to bail. If we would have bailed, Matty would be alive. Maybe Sam wouldn't be under arrest right now. Maybe that dickhead Jones would be dead."

"Look, James, Agent Jones is M.I.A. Not only will he not be punished, he got a job for it."

"What?" James shook his head. "No. No, that—that ain't right." He balled his fists and restrained his rage. "So, we can just kill our own people on purpose now?"

"Do you want to help Sam?" Amber asked. James gave her an agreeable nod. "The Captain said there's no legal way we can help Sam without throwing away our careers. But, there isn't going to be a fair investigation, Sam's getting thrown under the bus, so I say we help him."

"How?"

"You're going to need to sober up a little, because we're going to bust him out and make a break for it."

Ulfberht Crew

51

In the Path of Destruction

"It breaks my heart to see her like this, Mike."

A slur of words approached Mike from behind. He stood in the middle of a long interior walkway that crossed over the *Ulfberht*. The ship was dwarfed by the monolithic columns and cross-sections of the massive shipyard, which regularly took in ships larger than the *Ulfberht*. Mike turned around to see a pear-shaped Latin man with a goatee and curly black hair, his dark blue mechanic's uniform smudged in grease.

"I know the feeling." Mike cleared his throat.

"Hey man, I can never remember how to spell her name. Can you take care of this for me?" He handed Mike a small tablet with paperwork.

"Seriously, Javier?" Mike shook his head, taking the tablet. "You were Rick's number-one guy for like four years? You can't spell her name?" Mike typed in the name for him.

"I know there's an H in there somewhere. It's like German or something, I don't know. Why would you give her a crazy name like that?" Javier's joke was threaded with honesty.

"It's the name of these old Viking swords. Some of the best swords ever made." Mike handed back the tablet.

"She *is* one of the best." Javier nodded in agreement, stepping up to lean on the oversized windows, looking down at the battered *Ulfberht*. "We'll have her fixed up in no time. After we upgrade her warp systems, you'll be able to fly back to Earth in less than two weeks. Maybe then, you guys can visit more."

"We promise to visit more." He nodded, smiling at Javier's subdued affection. "I uh, heard you guys dropped a big job for us?" Mike asked sheepishly.

"Yeah, I was walking by right here when you guys pulled in." Javier pointed down the hall. "I almost dropped my lunch. We don't give a fuck about no other job if *you* guys need us."

Mike smiled and patted Javier on the shoulder. "Thanks, Javi."

"Bah." Javier smacked Mike in the gut then gave him a firm hug and a strong pat on the back. "We've made a lot of money here, and people offer us jobs all the time, but this baby's our home." He ticked his head at the *Ulfberht*. "If you ever need your crew back, we're there."

"You've got it, Javi." Not particularly emotional, the loyalty of Mike's old crew moved him. He had barely kept in touch, and yet they were willing to come back at the drop of a dime. One could not wish for better people.

"So..." Javier fidgeted, eyes on the floor. "I think Rick might need someone to talk to him."

"What's up with Rick?" Mike's brow furrowed with concern.

Javier shrugged, holding his hands in the air for a moment. "I don't know man, he came in a couple nights ago with a bunch of booze and was like 'here, take this shit off my hands.' Since then he looks all sick, and he's being kind of crazy and pissed off all the time. It's weird, man. I tried to bring him a beer and he smacked it out of my hand and said he had work to do. I don't think he's slept. He's been making mistakes, too. We've been cleaning up after him, but don't tell him that part." Javier waved his hand in the air, not wanting to step on Rick's ego while he was down.

Mike recoiled in astonishment. "Do you know where I can find him?"

"He's on the *Ulfberht* somewhere. Go down there and ask around, you'll find him. He hasn't really left."

Mike headed straight to the *Ulfberht*.

"Hey, you know where I can find Rick?" he asked a passerby in the noisy machine shop on his way.

"What's up, Captain!" said the skinny, pale-skinned guy covered in tattoos.

"Oh! Uh… Shayne!" Mike had not noticed with whom he was speaking, having asked the first person he encountered.

"Yeah! Good to see ya. Which Rick you lookin' for?"

"Walker."

"Oh yeah, he's down the hall in the control room." Shayne's long arm pointed down one of the hallways.

"Thanks, Shayne." Mike walked off with a polite wave goodbye.

"No problem, Captain." Shayne waved and went back on his way.

Mike spotted a pair of double doors amidst a high volume of foot traffic. Easy to find, as Mike approached the door Rick charged out of the room, body tilted to one side because of a heavy duffel bag over his shoulder.

"Rick!" Mike jumped. "Where are you going? You got a minute?"

"No, I don't, Mike! Since you gotta do everything yourself around here!" Rick yelled behind him, voice echoing down the hall. He had bags under his eyes and his skin was pale and drooping, his hair scraggly and wild. Rick marched away with Mike on his tail, looking behind him at the control room, confused.

"Rick, you don't look too hot. You feelin' all right?"

"I feel fine," Rick huffed, worn down and annoyed. "Why do people keep askin' me that?"

"Because you look like shit, Rick. Now stop for a minute and talk to me." Rick stopped with an angry sigh. He motioned for Mike to get on with whatever he wanted. "Let's go to Javi's office and talk in private." Mike did not wait for Rick to acknowledge the stern suggestion and walked off. Rick followed him begrudgingly into Javier's office. "Room, close the blinds," Mike ordered, closing the door behind Rick. The insides of the windows turned black in stripes, mimicking horizontal blinds.

"What do you want, Mike? I've got a lot of work to do," Rick grunted.

"Not looking like that you don't. Are you sure you're not sick or something? What the hell's wrong, man?" Mike leaned back onto the desk.

"Nothing's wrong," Rick raised his voice, a fire in his heart stoked by the question. Rick set the heavy duffel bag on the floor. It slammed down with a heavy thud and clank of metal. "I'm fine!"

"Rick, why don't you have a hover-ball in there?" Mike pointed at the heavy duffel bag, which would be reduced to almost no weight at all with a quantum-locking ball keeping it buoyant.

"I… I don't know. I guess I forgot to grab one," Rick said, groaning and cracking his back.

"Rick, if you're forgetting simple stuff like that I'm not letting you work on my ship." Mike pointed at the duffel bag.

"I'm fine, Mike! Everyone forgets things." Rick sat down, rubbing his eyes.

"When was the last time you slept?"

"I slept last night."

"For how long?"

Rick paused, looking up, thinking back to his evening. "I fell asleep in engineering for a couple hours. I woke up and got back to work, then took another nap for like an hour this morning, maybe around six."

"When was the last time you had a full night's sleep?"

Rick shrugged, looking away. "What does it matter? We've got to get our ship back on her feet. We gotta get her flyin' again."

"You're going to make a mistake like this. You haven't slept. I can tell you haven't showered. Have you been eating at least?" Mike grilled Rick, glad that Javier had updated him on the situation.

"Of course I eat! I had a…" His eyes darted around, thinking back to his last meal. "Javier brought me a burrito earlier. Woke me up from my nap."

"So, the last time you ate was around seven in the morning when Javier brought you a burrito?" Mike confirmed, amazed that Rick nod0ded with satisfaction at his answer. "That was ten hours ago."

"Was it?" Rick shook his head in disbelief, searching for his mobile to check the time. "Where's my mobile?"

"Rick, when was the last time you had a drink?"

"I gave the crew all my booze, it was just slowing me down." Rick looked away, waving it off like it was no big deal.

"Oh man." Mike's shoulders dropped. "Rick you're not sleeping, not eating, and having alcohol withdrawals? No wonder you look like hell took a shit on you."

"I look fine." Rick waved him off.

"How do you feel?" Mike asked.

"I *feel* like getting back to work, but I've got some dick stopping me from doing that," Rick yelled, staring angrily at Mike. As soon as he finished speaking, his eyes softened, flooded with regret. "I… I'm sorry, Mike. I didn't mean that."

"I know, but you're cut."

"This is bullshit, Mike." Rick stood up and paced back and forth in frustration.

"You know it's not. Now, why don't you tell me what the hell is wrong?" Mike was not going to change his mind but still needed to get to the bottom of Rick's issues.

"I just… I just need to get her flying again, Mike. I just need to get her back out there. I need to fix her. She needs us." Rick's eyes began to water and his voice cracked. He choked on his words and leaned against the wall, trembling hands together in front of him. He wiped tears from his eyes, looking to the ground.

It became evident what was eating at Rick, but Mike was at a loss of words. If only he had brought Maya with him. She always knew what to say.

Mike cleared his cracking throat. "Rick, we all miss Natalie." Rick huffed, still looking away. "Do you think we don't?"

"Nah, I… I'm sure you do," Rick admitted, still looking away, trying to stay angry instead of giving in to his sadness.

"Then, what?" Mike pushed Rick to face his problems.

"I don't know," Rick said, wiping tears from his face. "I just… You know I never wanted kids." Rick shook his head. "Not in this shitty world. They could put a stamp on *my* kid, and tell them what they can and can't do? A world that'll hate them for being who they are? And, I figured with my luck, my kid would be a little shit that hates me."

He tried to dismiss the thought of having children. After months of working alongside Natalie, who loved machines and ships even more than he, Rick had grown closest to her. She was everything he dreamed was never possible.

"Natalie was perfect," he croaked, sniffling and wiping his nose with the underside of his shirt. "That girl was everything I ever wanted in a kid. And I thought…" Rick took a moment to compose himself. "Life had kind of worked out funny. I never had a kid, and she lost her family, but we found each other. I didn't want a kid around at first, but that girl *knew* her machines. I thought…" Rick began to break down, covering his face and turning away from Mike as if that would conceal him.

"Rick." Mike put his arm around Rick's back, pulling him in for a hug, a tear running down his cheek.

"We were supposed to keep her safe," Rick said through stuttered breaths.

"I know, Rick. But, she was an adult, and we should be proud of her. She fixed up our ship like a pro."

"She died getting the ship working again and saved us. I can't stop until she's flying again, Mike. For Natalie, let me keep working," Rick tried to reason.

"Sorry, I can't do that. Natalie wouldn't want you doing a half-assed job for *any* reason. She'd bring you a beer, tell you to take a nap and let her pick up your slack. That's *our* crew out there." Mike pointed outside. "They're not some random crew hired to fix our ship. This is *their* ship too, they're going to take care of her."

"I guess you're right." Rick sniffled.

"I know I am. Now get yourself together and let's go get you a whiskey and something to eat." Mike patted Rick on the shoulder.

"Shouldn't I, uh, keep *not* drinking?" Rick wiped his face clean of tears, rubbing his wet hands on his jeans.

"Maybe we should ease you out of it. You've still got a ship to fix," Mike jested. Rick smiled and nodded, then cleared his throat. The back of Mike's hand buzzed.

"Thanks, Mike. I'll try not to turn into a little crybaby on you again." Rick patted Mike on the shoulder extra hard.

"If you need to cry, I'm here." Mike tapped on the back of his hand. "Tony just docked. Let's go meet him and grab you some food."

"Yeah, I'm feeling hungry now that you got me thinkin' about it." Rick followed Mike to the door. When they stepped out of the office, Javier and a group of their mechanics had gathered outside, all pretending to not have been trying to listen. Amongst them was Addie with an innocent smile.

"Oh, hey Mike," Javier greeted, scratching behind his ear.

"Addie? What are you doing here?"

"Hanging out with the guys." She motioned to them, wiping away a tear.

"You guys need something?" Mike asked.

"Nah, I was just going to uh… have a meeting, but we were waiting for my office to be available," Javier said.

"Enjoy. We're going to grab food and meet Tony." Mike walked off with Rick following him to the food court.

"Ooh! I'll join you! I love me a British accent." Addie hurried after them. Holding two fingers to her wristband, she attempted a British accent. "Will, we're going to grab a bite to eat. Please, meet us in the food court."

Mike made Rick chug the first beer he could get his hands on then poured him some water and a whiskey to sip on for lunch. The group found a seat far away from any crowds at a table overlooking the food court. With Addie perched on the back of the booth, she and Will ate alongside Rick. Halfway through a chicken wing, he pointed at Ian and Nikolai hustling toward them, Maya close behind, unrushed.

"Michael, we have serious problem," Nikolai said in a hush upon arrival. He looked over his shoulders and sat at the table. Ian grabbed a seat from another table and placed it outside of the booth to join them.

"What is it now?" Mike asked, more annoyed than surprised.

"Well…" Nikolai twisted his hand in the air as if weighing out options in his mind. "We could let people die. It is not *our* problem."

Mike looked back and forth between Nikolai and the others. Rick was still stuffing his face. Addie's eyes were judging him. "What is it?" he asked.

"Five Dragon Claw attacks in five months. That is very precise. Dragon Claw is not usually so organized. I look at the attacks. All attacks are *exactly* twenty-seven days apart." Nikolai presented them with a tablet full of information he had jotted down and linked together for Mike to peruse. "Then, look at targets." He pointed to the right side of the screen with pictures, dates, and thin lines connecting them to a timeline in the middle. "Endorian shipyard, Atlantean moon factories. Those factories produce many materials for ships and machinery in the colonies. *Oasis*, Ternarian port, Freyjan port: all very busy, important to bounty hunters, smugglers, and private industry."

"Okay." Mike nodded. "I agree it doesn't make sense that they're attacking places that benefit them too if that's what you're getting at."

"Aye, that's part of it," Ian chimed in. "But someone's got to be payin' 'em a lot of money for it, which is a troublin' notion on its own."

"Even *more* troubling," Nikolai pulled Mike's attention back to him, "these targets hurt pirates and colonies, not UEG. Very carefully chosen. And, the last target like these I can think of is right here." Nikolai tapped the tablet with his index finger for emphasis. "At Avalon, *this* shipyard, the most successful shipyard in all the colonies. Look how busy it is now that rival Endorian shipyard is destroyed."

"You think they're going to attack *Olympus*? When?" Mike shot up with concern.

"Hey, you all caught up?" Maya arrived, leaning on the booth wall.

"Yeah."

"Cool. Scoot over." She bumped Will with her hip and he scooted in. Maya sat next to him and picked at his steak fries.

"Twenty-seven days apart. So, the next attack should be ninth of December," Nikolai said.

"That's not good at all." Mike looked over the information on the tablet. "So you think someone is, what? Targeting critical infrastructure in the colonies?"

"That's what it looks like," Ian said. "You going to eat all those wings?" He pointed to Rick's plate, wings dwindling. Rick glanced between Ian and his wings, then pulled his plate closer.

"Wing?" he offered Will.

"Sure, thanks."

"We've got to tell command right away." Mike went to leave the table but Nikolai stopped him.

"No." He guided Mike back into his seat. "If we alert the authorities, they will tell everyone and the Dragon Claw can attack early, or postpone. We must be careful about who we tell until the eve of the attack. Then, we can strike at the Dragon Claw when they reveal themselves." Nikolai punched his palm. His eyes shot up, spotting someone in the distance.

Mike spun around to see Tony headed their way with a large entourage of men and women. They stuck close together, on guard, checking their environment. Tony had a more serious face than they had ever seen on him. He was on high alert instead of strolling down the promenade with a gleeful pep in his step.

"Rick and I were waiting for him here, then you guys showed up." Mike raised an arm to wave at Tony and call him over. He stood from the table. Nikolai stood with him. The others continued to eat.

"Mike, good to see ya, mate." Tony shook his hand and then greeted everyone else.

"Good to see you too. I'm sorry to hear about the attack on Freyja. I hope any friends you got there are all right."

"Thanks, we're all quite upset about that, but I'm a bit more concerned with what arrived at the house we were watching for you." Tony leaned in to ensure Mike could hear him.

"What happened?" Mike leaned in too.

"Some bounty hunters showed up with their bounty." Tony signaled over his shoulder to his crew.

"Who was their bounty?"

Tony smiled and took a step to the side, waving a hand in his wake to reveal a chubby, balding man in slacks and a corduroy jacket. He fidgeted, looking at the crowd of pirates around him, who had been hiding him from view. "I'd like to introduce you to Adam Ward."

"Oh shit, Adam?" Mike said.

"Did you say Adam fucking Ward?" Maya hissed. She stood up and the circle of pirates opened for her.

"Maya! Mike!" Adam threw his hands up. "Why didn't you guys tell me this is who you're bringing me to? I've been scared out of my mind for weeks!"

"You've been well treated, haven't you?" Tony said.

"Yeah, but I didn't know who you're working for."

"Well, we rescued you from those thugs, didn't we?"

"Okay, stop your weird bickering," Maya halted them. "Adam, what the hell?"

"I don't know. They found me somehow. Kept bragging about how they're the best bounty hunters in the colonies, yadda-yadda. They put a bag over my head and took me somewhere. Then I hear shots and these guys are pulling the bag off my head."

"I made your ID and faceblock implant, there's no way they used tech to find you," Mike said defensively.

"I think they did it the old-fashioned way. But, boy am I glad to see you two."

"So are we. You're the guy Lazarus was looking for," Mike said.

"Lazarus?" A wave of panic rushed through him, destroying his relief.

"Hold on, so you three already know each other?" Tony said. "I was under the impression his disappearance has been a mystery for twenty years, how the bloody hell do you know Adam Ward?"

"I'm the reason he disappeared," Maya said. "I was supposed to kill him. I talked to him and realized I'd been lied to and was about to make a mistake. So, we fled to the colonies together. That's when I met Mike."

"So you're the one that's been making all these high-tech weapons?" Tony surmised as Adam was the son of a famed weapons designer from the war.

"Yeah." Adam nodded with a toothy grin, pleased with himself.

"That wasn't smart. That's how they were able to track you down. So I ask again: what the hell, Adam?" Maya pressed.

"What? I'm sorry. In retrospect that probably wasn't a great idea, but a man's got to make a living."

"Michael," Nikolai grumbled. "If Dragon Claw has been attacking critical infrastructure and Lazarus is hunting a weapons designer hiding in the colonies," he said gravely, looking at Adam.

"He's going to make a power play for the colonies," Mike concluded quietly.

"Who's the Russian guy?" Adam asked.

"This is Nikolai Markov, former General of the Russian Space Force and founder of the Red Storm," Mike introduced Nikolai. Adam's eyes lit up and his posture straightened.

"The Russian Superman?" Adam reached out to shake his hand. "It's a pleasure to meet you."

"You as well."

"What was that about a power play for the colonies?" Tony said with focus.

"Let me fill you in. Nikolai was doing the numbers on the Dragon Claw attacks and it looks like they're exactly twenty-seven days apart. Not only that, it looks like they're going to hit the *Olympus* shipyard next," Mike explained succinctly.

Tony's crew glanced at each other, hearing the news for the first time. A murmur of concerned whispers rippled through them.

"You're sure about this?" Tony asked.

"Positive." Nikolai grabbed the tablet from the table behind Mike and handed it to Tony, who wasted no time in looking through Nikolai's notes.

"Well," Tony said after a moment, handing the tablet back to Nikolai. "That's an interesting development. Have you alerted station command yet?"

"No, I just found out myself, but I don't think we want to warn them, yet." Mike crossed his arms, biting his thumbnail in contemplation.

"Why not?" Tony said, his body personifying how perplexed he was to hear that as if there was no other logical course of action.

"Well, we should call Iskra." Mike glanced at Nikolai, who nodded. "Then, maybe find somewhere discreet to talk." He glanced around at their public surroundings to leave, but his hand buzzed with an important alert. Upon checking it, he shook his head with an uneasy look.

"What is it?" Maya asked.

"It's a message from the Captain of the shipyard. She wants to see me immediately."

"Woah, freaky."

"You two are coming with me." Mike motioned to Maya and Nikolai. "Tony, keep Adam safe and out of view."

"Aye-aye mate."

Rampart Crew

52

Early Birds Feast on Victory

IT WAS NOT LONG AFTER SAM WAS THROWN IN A CELL THAT ADISON paid him a visit. He stood on the other side of the hall beyond arm's reach. Sam shot up from his seat and gripped the bars.

"What the hell is going on? Why am I under arrest?"

"M.J. Smith, huh?" Adison raised an eyebrow. "What did you think of him?"

"Not what I expected."

"What did you expect?"

"Not a pirate."

"He's supposed to be dead. I'm sure you couldn't help but satisfy your curiosity. Did he tell you why he's out there?" Adison asked.

"He asked for the package back, I told him to eat shit. Then, they pulled me out of that freezer at gunpoint and told me Matt died. That was the extent of our conversation. Is that treason?" Sam growled.

"What did he say?"

"He said he'd let us go if we left the package with him."

"Why did he want it?"

421

"I don't know," Sam said in exasperation. "We didn't share a chat over drinks. I was their prisoner."

"And yet, you returned *eight* hours after the rest of the survivors who were sent back after a siege. No, Samuel. I believe you had plenty of time to chat, and that man is dangerous. Now, we know he's alive. Unfortunately, I can't allow someone we can't trust become an Archon, or handle such a sensitive subject. I'll be taking it back to Earth with *me*. You'll be picked up later by a security team," Adison said.

"Come on, Adison. You can't do this to me. I've lived *my life* for the Ministry. I don't have a family, the Ministry *is* my life. I dedicated everything to it."

"I'm sorry, but I don't believe you. You're a threat to the Ministry. I hope what remains of your life is pleasant." Adison marched out the exit.

"This is bullshit!" Sam roared. "Adison!" Adison vanished from the block of cells and Sam was left alone to contemplate his choices.

Traversing the station with his escort, an alert buzzed on Adison's hand. One had been cleared for transfer. "Finally." The new course took them past James, who tried to maintain a low profile despite his size.

"I got eyes on him. He's goin' to pick him up," James said, an earpiece in place so he could communicate with Amber.

"Copy that." Amber crossed the plaza where she had found James. The security office double doors slid open for her and she approached the front desk with a no-nonsense attitude. "I'm here to transfer a prisoner." She accessed her hitch and turned in a fake transfer order, which her rank enabled her to make freely.

"My screen says this guy's getting transferred later," the guard said.

"Yeah, this Ministry asshole changed his mind and sent me to grab him myself. If he asks me to get him a coffee I'm breakin' his friggin' nose."

The man behind the front desk let loose a hearty chuckle. "Yeah, those bigwigs think you'll wipe their ass for 'em with a smile, too." The guard cleared the transfer. "He'll be out in a minute."

While Adison escorted One from his room, two troopers escorted

Sam to Amber. Sam gave Amber a baffled look. The Troopers stayed at his side.

"Troopers?" Amber asked.

"We were ordered by the High Archon to stay with him until he departs, sir."

"This way, then," she said. "We're taking the service areas to avoid crowds."

"Amber, what's going on? Where are we going?"

"Chancellor, I ask that you remain silent while we transfer you," she said coldly. Following the kick to his pride, Sam looked to the floor and did not speak again.

"He's moving again, package in tow." James's voice buzzed in her ear.

Amber touched two fingers to her hitch. "That's approved, please proceed."

While Amber escorted Sam and the troopers to the Ministry shuttle, James followed One, Adison, and his escort of four troopers into discrete halls far from the bustling plazas. One of the troopers briefly caught a glimpse of him, but the next time he looked back there was no one.

The escort continued through the winding halls of the infrequently traveled area full of small businesses and vacant offices. With no sign of trouble and no reason for concern, they strolled through the empty halls without a sense of danger or urgency.

From behind, the two rear troopers were pricked in the neck. For all of James's mass and power, he had a delicate touch, even with a broken hand. The world spun around the two troopers and after a groggy attempt to warn the others they collapsed.

The caravan spun around. James zoomed by Adison and One, smashing into one a trooper like a truck. The other went for his weapon, but an elbow to his face toppled him to the ground, unconscious. James injected them like he had the others and pocketed one of the tear-shaped injectors.

Adison stared, wide-eyed and trembling. "Did the UEG send you to take him?"

"Nope." James's brawny arm loomed over Adison to inject him. He put both his arms up to push it away, but may as well have tried to stop a steamroller. Seconds later he was on the ground, unconscious.

"How's it goin'?" James greeted.

"Hello, James," One said.

"Uh, want to help me move these guys?" James hurried to the door of a vacant business space and slid his knife between the door and the frame.

"I can not interfere, only observe."

"All right, whateva'." The door opened and James put away his knife. Two at a time, he dragged the unconscious bodies into the room. "Come on."

James hurried down the hall with One close behind, still in Earth Orbit Security's navy and gray armor.

"Hey, how come you do whateva' people say?" The question had lingered in James's mind since their attack on the *Ulfberht*.

"I go where the universe tells me to go."

"What if the universe tells you to help 'em drag some bodies into a room?"

"That is interference because it is in assistance of a life form's objectives."

"Okay, I get it. You talk like you're an alien." James reached a corner and looked both ways. The bustle of the plaza between them and their destination echoed down the hall.

"Are colonials not aliens to Earth?"

"Hey, I neva' thought about that." James paused in contemplation, then focused again on his environment. James turned the corner into the next hall. "Stay close."

One followed James, who cut through the crowd. People moved out of his way without a glance in his direction.

"I'm in the plaza," James called in, eyes scanning the crowd for a path to the maintenance halls.

"Copy that, I'm escorting the prisoner to the Ministry ship. I should be available in five minutes. I'll see to it then."

"So, I've got two minutes," James said. His pace picked up, now in a rush to the rendezvous. By a service entrance was a short Latin man with wide-set eyes and shaggy black hair. James gave him a nod and the man opened the door. With a cash card in his palm, James clasped hands with the man as they passed and brought it into a close embrace with a pat on the back. "Hey, you take care of ya'self."

"You too," the man said. He and One exchanged a nod as he passed. The man made sure the door was locked then strolled away.

In the service tunnels, littered with empty boxes and trash, Amber led the group through the rock and steel-walled hall with Sam behind her. The two troopers brought up the rear. After passing a series of nooks and recycling chutes, the troopers did not check corners as they passed. It was easy for James to wait silently and sneak up behind them.

BEEP—BEEP—BEEP—BEEP!

The station's alarms blared and red lights flashed in the hall. Startled, the group paused, and James was quick to inject them with the sedative.

"Whoa!" Sam's jaw dropped. "What are you guys doing?"

"We're busting you out, dummy!" Amber boomed, barely audible over the alarms echoing through the hall. She unlocked his handcuffs and tossed them, and her hitch, on the ground.

"Looks like they found that High Archon, let's move!" James signaled behind him and One appeared from the shadows.

"How did you guys know to get him?" Sam yelled. Amber shook her head with a confused expression. "How did you guys know to get him!"

"I'll explain later!"

The group ran down the hall, James far ahead of the rest of the group. He cleared their path and led the way again, following signs to the dock which housed the Ministry ship. Once there, he motioned everyone against the wall and approached the service door slowly, then peeked through the narrow window.

"Two guards at the door," he said.

"Do they know who they're looking for?" Amber asked.

"They probably know about me," he said. "They'll taze me before I get to them."

"I'll take care of it. Give me a sleeper."

James handed her one of the injectors. She palmed it and opened the door without pause. She marched into the hallway and approached the troopers with stalwart authority.

"Troopers! Why do you look so relaxed? Do you not hear the alarms? Look alive!" she boomed.

"Yes, sir." The two panicked troopers took a more assertive stance.

"Both of you are staring at this wall like that's where danger is going to come from. You, watch that side of the hall, you watch his one."

"Yes, sir."

The two men turned away from each other and before they knew what happened, they were asleep. James erupted from the service hall with Sam and One close behind. Amber opened the dock's double doors and they hurried inside.

Awaiting them in the round dock was no basic, run-of-the-mill shuttle. Instead, Adison had arrived in style with one of the Ministry's cutting-edge warp-capable relief shuttles, decked out with full amenities and a top-of-the-line medical bay.

"Sam." She stopped him. "We need to lock this. Can you put a Ministry lockout on it? Maybe they haven't revoked your credentials yet."

"It's worth a shot." Sam accessed the panel and closed the doors. "Did you grab the suit I made?"

"I had it delivered here along with the rest of your stuff, and I kind of had our stuff sent here too."

Sam chuckled at her foresi while he worked, but the interface locked him out. His credentials had been revoked.

"Okay, you lock it with yours, I need to grab something."

Sam sprinted into the ship, the alarms still blaring in the hall, only a quiet murmur in the bay. Sam opened crates and tossed them aside until he found the one with his suit and pulled from it the small device he had used to open doors on the *Ulfberht*.

"Sam!" Amber called from outside. Sam hurried back with the device. From afar, Adison's scowling face glared through the glass with a squad of troopers. He rushed to the console, pressed the thin metal device against it, and worked the interface as he normally would.

The double doors slid apart, but stopped, not enough room for anyone to pass through. The doors closed again and Sam pulled the device away.

"We've got a few minutes." Sam rushed to the shuttle.

"But, if your credentials are revoked, how are we going to start the ship?" Amber closed the door behind her and followed Sam to the cockpit awaiting an answer. "I was kind of counting on you being able to use this ship."

"The ship we were on was too custom for this to be super effective, but my buddy said it works on standard *and* Ministry systems." Sam placed the device on the console and typed as he talked. After a moment, the console lit up and the ship was operational. "We got lucky he brought this ship and not a regular shuttle, though."

"It wasn't luck, I saw this thing. It looked pretty snazzy," Amber said.

"In that case, great job." Sam worked the console, which lacked a yoke, unlike most ships. It was purely console-controlled since it was not meant for combat. "No Haynes?"

"I don't think his husband would appreciate him running away from Earth."

"Right, married. It's too bad I didn't get to say goodbye. Let's get going."

The ship rose slowly and spun in place. They passed through the dock's open ceiling and before them was Earth. The blue ball of life that nurtured them and most of humanity throughout history was peppered with swirling clouds and wrapped in a thin, delicate blue atmosphere like a soap bubble ready to pop.

"This might be the last time we see her," Sam said.

"It really is so beautiful from up here." Amber took in the view one last time.

"Goodbye, home," James said.

"Your departure is unauthorized. Set the ship back down and prepare to be boarded by security." The cockpit blurted, but Sam cut the transmission.

"Where are we going?" Sam asked.

"Avalon," Amber said.

Sam set the destination while James and Amber took in the view of Earth. Outside, fighters closed in on their position. However, once Sam took them to warp, they disappeared alongside Earth, the station, and the stars.

The group reconvened in an office adjacent to the medical bay. There, Amber shared with them the recording of Jones and Lazarus.

"Is that why you brought him?" Sam asked about One.

"I had a feeling in my gut and I followed it. It felt like the right thing to do."

"Thanks for that. Smith was right, he would end up as an experiment at the Ministry. I didn't want to think about it that way, but that's how it is."

"It can be tough to realize the truth about stuff you believe in, Sammy," James said. "I wish I could say somethin' to Matt's family."

"I'm sorry. I know busting me out cost you that. Thank you guys so much," Sam said. "I don't think I'll ever be able to pay you guys back."

"I couldn't watch that happen to someone." Amber's head dropped in shame at a memory long passed, then examined her uniform. "But, I can't wear this uniform anymore. I feel disgusting. I'm going to change."

"You know what?" James looked down at his own uniform. "Me too."

Ulfberht Crew

53

Common Enemies

Not knowing what to expect, Mike was uneasy on their trek to the Captain's office. He checked his environment, looking for something out of place, but there was nothing. Soon they were deep in the halls surrounded by offices and the only people there were station personnel, which only worsened his alarm. They had caused no trouble in the few days they had been on *Olympus*, so the station's Captain should have no reason to summon them.

"Once, before the war," Nikolai said, commanding Mike's attention. "A commanding officer called me into his office. Someone had taken his Vodka, a recent gift from his family, and I believed he suspected me. In reality, he wanted my help in finding the thief because he placed so much trust in me."

"I'm guessing you took the vodka?"

"Yes, as a gesture to our soldiers. They had done a good job, but I did not have time to replace it."

"So, what did you do?" Mike asked curiously.

"I told him I would begin a thorough search for his vodka. I found the unopened bottle in the case his family had sent. He thought he had misremembered, so he bought me one of my own for all the trouble."

Mike laughed, his tension relieved. "I guess there is a way out of every situation."

"That is correct." Nikolai grinned. "So, relax."

"Your stories help."

"Hell, maybe the station needs a hacker," Maya said.

"With how much we're spending to repair the ship, I would love a gig."

"We're making good money selling gravity nets right now. Silver linings to being stuck at a shipyard," Maya pointed out.

"I thought Nikolai was the positive one."

"Positivity usually wins the day."

Ahead, two imposing guards stood on either side of a large door with a round frame for its handle and a large bulletproof window, fogged over. They wore the station's sapphire and yellow uniforms, underpinned by armor. The guards brought back the ominous cloud which had enveloped Mike after the urgent summons.

"Identification." The guard motioned to the screens next to him, with a matching pair on the opposite wall.

They each stood in front of a screen with a tap. Nikolai was the only one without fake identification. Maya was Moira Gonzales, which she could pronounce with a Spanish accent if she needed to. Mike was Hugh Schwartz. With a snort, he held in a laugh at his name, which he had forgotten. When he turned around, Maya shook her head at him.

"All clear. Please leave your weapons with us." One guard opened a locked hatch next to him and pulled out a shallow, rectangular bin.

"We aren't carrying any weapons," Maya said.

The hall fell silent, and after a moment of the guards examining the trio, he nudged the bin at them. "Miss, please don't waste our time."

"You're literally just standing here, but you did call me *miss*." Maya smiled and reached behind her.

From her waistline she pulled a knife, hidden by her coat, and deposited it in the bin. Nikolai did the same. The guards looked at Mike. With a sigh, Mike held his hands in the air. They would not simply let him through if he claimed to not have weapons.

"Weapons check," the guard said. A strip on the walls around them flashed, then two holographic red spheres appeared on Maya's arm and lower leg.

"Goddamnit, Mike." She pulled a blade from her forearm and a taser pistol from her ankle, depositing them in the bin.

"Really, lady?"

"Lady? What happened to *miss*?"

"You lied to me."

"Your whole life is a lie."

With a smirk, the guard took a step back, put the bin in the compartment and closed the hatch. "All clear."

The other guard grabbed the rod encircled on the door and turned it ninety degrees, then pulled the door open for them. Mike was the first one in.

The spacious office had a lounge-like seating area on the right and a cabinet with coffee, a fridge, and snacks on the left. Centered on the far side of the room was a massive wooden desk stained a dark walnut, a console surface fitted on top of it. The walls of the room displayed the shipyard as seen from the top of the central dome. The section behind the desk, however, displayed the *Ulfberht* from above. The Captain was standing in front of it, arms folded, looking upon the battered ship. She turned around and placed a hand on her luxurious high-back office chair, eyeing the new arrivals.

The small woman was of mixed Asian descent. She had big eyes, flawless skin, and silver highlights ran through her midnight black hair, tied back in a bun, the only sign of aging. As she turned her head to look at each of them, light glistened off a scar on her chin. She could have got it fixed but kept it.

"I'm Captain Kathryn Kim. It's nice to meet you," she said.

"My name is Hugh, this is Moira and Nikolai."

"Hugh Schwartz? Are you a fan of comedy movies, Mr. M.J. Smith?"

"I'm sorry, have we met?"

"I have been informed of a threat to your life. That threat puts a dangerous individual somewhere on my station. I don't like that one bit. But, I also don't know if I can trust the source of the information. We've got to be careful with Earthers." Her big eyes bore a hole through him, figuring out who she was dealing with.

"As I've recently been reminded." Mike played into her cautious inclinations.

"And, of course, I know who Mr. Markov is. We've had a small army of Red Storm ships orbiting *Olympus* since you all arrived, making everyone nervous."

"Apologies. That is not our intention," Nikolai said.

"As long as you aren't planning on blowing us to hell, I guess I don't have to worry. There hasn't been an increase in crime and somehow you people seem to have *all* the gravity nets, so if anything I'm grateful for your presence."

Nikolai gave her a stern nod and the Captain turned to Maya.

"Who are you?"

"Moira Gonzales," she said with a fluent Spanish accent.

"You're not Latin."

"I'm mixed."

"I can see that, but everything else is bullshit. I need to know who you are or you can wait outside."

She and Maya stared each other down for a moment, then, Maya made the prudent move and told the truth.

"I go by Raven."

"I know you. You're a mercenary."

"Not so much these days," Maya said casually.

"What a fine bunch we have here. All options considered, I kind of trust you the most, even though you're supposed to be dead and the first thing you did was lie to me." She looked at Mike. "Not being armed helps, though."

"Thank you. I'm still not really sure what's going on, though."

"Have a seat." She sat and motioned to the chairs in front of them. "I have a recording of the threat and the pictures of the people who brought it to me. Which would you like to see first?"

"Let's see the people," Mike said.

Captain Kim worked the interface on her desk and brought up three pictures. From left to right was Sam, James, and Amber. The trio recoiled in their seats and shared looks of confusion and concern.

"It doesn't look like you have a good history with these people."

"They're the reason my ship looks like it does."

"So, it was a good idea not to trust them."

"Well…" Mike rocked his head. "The one on the left here, he's misguided, or was, if he's here. I don't know. This guy was protecting him. Her, I don't recognize."

"Me neither," Maya added. With a glance from the Captain, Nikolai shook his head. The blonde was a mystery.

"About a month ago these people became wanted by the UEG, so I put them under arrest. But, I don't trust the UEG. You seem to be shooting straight with me, so allow me to share the recording with you." Captain Kim removed the pictures and brought up the recording. "This is what left me… troubled. And, the reason I called you here right away." Captain Kim played the audio file.

"Special Agent Oliver Jones? Do you mind if I join you?"

That voice.

"Is that how you were taught to introduce yourself?"

"That's the agent that attacked us," Maya said.

"My name is Lazarus."

The threat was real. They did not need to hear the rest, but they listened without saying a word. The waveform of the audio fluctuated with the speech until it stopped and the recording ended with a polite goodbye between two terrible people. The room was left in a stunned silence. Captain Kim gave them a moment to process before she spoke.

"A lot of things about this conversation disturb me."

"None of us travels alone anymore. I will increase Red Storm security right away," Nikolai said.

"We're with you there," Mike said. "Well, I guess first of all, I'd venture the threat to my life is real, and thank you for informing me."

"You're welcome. And the people who brought me this?"

"Undecided. The guy in that recording, Lazarus, he's bad news. I have no idea how they got this, but I'd like to know. That's the only thing still bothering me."

"What bothers *me* is that mustache-twirling asshole pausing at the mention of my shipyard!" she boomed, then pressed an icon on her desk. "Bring in the little guy!"

"I love your fire. You seeing anyone?" Maya asked.

"Barkin' up the wrong tree, but thank you."

"I like both trees, thought I'd throw it out there."

A moment later, Sam was escorted in wearing handcuffs. He stared wide-eyed at Mike, their encounter a clear surprise. Mike and his crewmates stood from their chairs and Captain Kim shot to her feet. The guards aimed their taser pistols at the group.

"Everyone better be fuckin' chill," the Captain said. Nobody caused a scene, but the room was tense. "Go ahead," she dismissed the guards. "Explain yourself, Earther."

"I, uh… did?" Sam replied.

"Where the hell did you get this recording?" Mike asked. "His eyes are genetically modified, there's no way you could have eavesdropped without him seeing it."

"When I boarded the *Rampart*, Captain Slater asked me to bug Jones. Within a day or two, I implanted him with a subdermal. It's been recording everything from then until the day of that recording."

"And you, here, why?" Mike said.

"Everything you said, happened. Beat for beat. It defied mathematical probability. My friends busted me out and we booked it here looking for you. We brought One with us," Sam said.

"One what?" Captain Kim asked.

"One is a person," Mike said. "But, why are you here?"

"The agent that wants to kill you fired on me and my teammate, killing one of my best friends. Adison arrested me for treason, and I came to terms with the reality that One was going to be poked at in a lab for the rest of his life and I didn't mean as much to the Ministry as the Ministry meant to me. Jones thought you were coming here, so this is where we went. He's probably here somewhere, too. I wanted to make things right."

Sam was like him, long ago. He believed in the Ministry. If anyone knew how difficult it was to go against the Ministry and his own beliefs, it was Mike. For Sam to turn his back on everything and show up to help meant he had crossed over like they hoped he would when they first encountered him. Now, Sam understood the truth.

"Seeing as you all have some sort of understanding of who the people in that recording were, I want to be brought up to speed or everyone here is under arrest," Captain Kim commanded.

"Lazarus works for someone. I never figured out who, but he's their errand boy. That person works within and above legal boundaries," Mike said.

"I'm listening." Captain Kim leaned in with interest.

"Nikolai, do you have that tablet from earlier?"

"Michael, no!" Nikolai said in a scolding tone.

"Captain, we think it is prudent to keep this information to ourselves and quietly prepare for it, but it seems it's in everyone's best interest to be honest, given the circumstances," Mike said.

Nikolai glanced between them, then pulled the tablet out from a pocket inside his coat and handed it to Captain Kim. She looked over the information and set it down, her hands trembling. Everything lined up. There was no plan, but their information was in line with her alarm at Lazarus's mention of her shipyard.

"How long have you had this information?"

"We only just figured it out before you called us here," Mike said.

"You'd better not be lying to me."

"That is the tablet these two brought to me not five minutes before I received your summons. Nikolai advised we keep it to ourselves, citing the risk of the Dragon Claw getting wind of our awareness. But, given your gracious nature here, today, I thought sharing and honesty was the prudent move." If ever there was a time to start things off on the right foot, it was that moment.

"How do you know it's the Dragon Claw?" she asked.

"Because we intercepted a group of them before their attack on *Oasis*. They send small groups into the target, place beacons, and leave. They have a few minutes to get off the station before the fleet drops out of warp and fires upon their pre-designated targets. That's how they're in and out before anyone can react."

"We could put a ban on Dragon Claw," Captain Kim growled.

"*Oasis* had an open bounty on them and they still slipped in," Mike pointed out. A bedeviled scowl from Captain Kim made the hairs on his neck stand on end. But, beneath her wrath was the acknowledgment that he was right.

"So, former General and Leader of the Red Storm. I've seen my share of scraps during the war and since, but to deny your expertise would be stupid. You figured out what's coming. So, how do *you* think we should handle this?"

"We should keep this a secret. If the Dragon Claw know we expect them, they could change the date."

"And what about this jack-in-the-box bullshit? Do you have any ideas on how to deal with that?"

"Actually, that's on me," Mike said. "We took one of their beacons on *Oasis*. I can make a program to piggy-back off their signal and cut their weapons lock. That might buy us a minute, but it's enough time to counter-attack."

"They can fight us or fire on the station, but not both," Maya chimed in.

"You took one of the beacons?" Sam asked.

"Yes, why?"

"We arrived after the attack. We stayed for a few hours assisting in rescue and repairs. They didn't know why G-sector was untouched, but it was a godsend."

The weight in Mike's heart lifted. He could not stay and help, but he had helped in the end. Then, Sam's ship did what they could not.

"Thank you for helping." Mike looked Sam in the eye and gave him a stiff nod.

"I don't think I can get the Avalon defense fleet to do minuteman drills without telling them any of this." Captain Kim brought the conversation back around. "And, once it's out, it'll spread like wildfire. Unless the Red Storm is volunteering to take point, we wouldn't have a fleet to fight with."

Nikolai was quick to respond. "The Red Storm, alongside some friends. We should be discreet and careful, but we can ask for assistance from ships we trust."

Captain Kim nodded and leaned back in her chair, arms crossed. Eyes on her desk, after a moment she sat up. "Due to all the attacks this year, we can run *random* drills on the station and make upgrades to our defenses. When the real thing comes, we can call it a drill. That should lessen the panic. If your fleet can engage them, *Olympus* will support you once our blast shields are up."

"Is there anything I can do to help?" Sam asked. No longer being addressed, he was out of place, and it was discomforting.

"You're the reason their ship looks like that." Captain Kim jabbed a thumb behind her at the video feed of the *Ulfberht*. "The only reason I haven't turned you over to the UEG is because I hate the UEG, and you've brought us good information. You're going back to the brig." She reached to call in the guards.

"Hold on a sec," Maya stopped her. "You said you helped out at *Oasis Station*. If someone there can vouch for his aid, then I see no reason why we can't trust him a little."

Captain Kim eyed Maya, then turned to Sam. "Is there anyone I can talk to on *Oasis* who can vouch for you and your friends?"

"I worked with Chief Engineer Brian O'Neil. Amber helped with their communications and logistics. James was evacuating people who were trapped, but I don't know who they worked with."

"I can work with that. You'll stay in the brig with your friends while I sort it out. But, if I like what they have to say, you're free to go. You can rent a room if you need a place to stay, and your help will be welcome."

"That works for me. Thank you, Captain. And, you." Sam motioned to Maya. She gave him a nod, but not a name.

"I was wondering, how did you get here?" she asked.

"A warp-capable Ministry shuttle."

"Really?"

"Yeah, why?"

"Can I borrow it?"

"For what?"

"The attacks are too extreme and out of character for the Dragon Claw. While you guys mount a defense here, I want to go to the Dragon's Den and talk to Plunder himself, maybe get to the bottom of what's going on."

"Well, it isn't a standard ship. I've spent the last few weeks teaching Amber how to use it. One of us would have to go with you."

"Let's talk more about that later, then."

"If that's all, then I'd like everyone to get the hell out of my office." Captain Kim stood up and motioned to the doors.

"I have one last thing," Mike said. "You said you brought One. Where is he?"

With One waiting on Sam's ship, security allowed Mike to board. Instead of taking him back to the *Gorynych*, Mike called Al and give him new coordinates. It took a few minutes to open a portal to a new location, but it was safer than moving him through the shipyard. One smiled at the trapdoor in space and passed through with delight.

"I should have brought you here when I first picked you up and you told me what you were," Mike told One as they crossed a stone bridge over a trickling stream.

"Why did you not?"

"I don't know. Ego, pride, desperation? I thought I could get more out of you than cryptic answers about the nature of the universe."

"I wish I could give you the answers you seek."

"Yeah, I know." Mike led One into a garden courtyard where Al was checking on his flowers under a starry night sky, his hair as wild and frazzled as ever. He stopped to greet his guests.

"Al, this is One. One, this is Albert," Mike introduced them, even though he did not need to.

"You can go anywhere you want in your universe." One nodded with a look of respect. "You are far ahead of your time."

"Thank you." Albert's posture straightened as he grabbed his overcoat. "It is a pleasure to meet you, at last."

"I knew we would meet, given enough time."

"Okay, I can see you two are going to get along great." Mike stepped away. "We've got a lot of work to do back on *Olympus*. See you later."

"Michael," Albert stopped him, "what have you learned of Lazarus?"

"Well, cracking the information on Lazarus's card was interrupted when we got attacked and lost power. So, we're stalled on that, but we've got a lot going on."

"Bring it here. Create a proxy and run your programs while you handle your affairs on *Olympus*," Al offered graciously.

"Thanks, Al! That would help a lot. I'll call you." Mike hurried to the portal.

"See you soon."

Mike

A Glimmer of Hope

Over the next few weeks, the Red Storm and the crew maintained intense security precautions, but there was no sign of Agent Jones. The *Ulfberht* was coming together when Mike took Will on a stroll through the command level. He ran his fingers along the pristine new paint job.

"It looks brand new," Will commented.

"Yeah, I forgot what she used to look like." The bridge doors opened in front of Mike and he guided Will to a hatch on the floor near Addie's cockpit.

Feet hanging over the edge, Mike slid into the extra-large maintenance shaft with Will close behind. They crawled to a fork in the short shaft. Mike lay on his back and Will rolled over, lying down next to him. Heads next to each other, Mike pointed at the overhead console.

"So, this whole maintenance shaft is restricted access, you can only access it from the Bridge and beneath us is a thick panel of armor. But, all the accesses here are genetically and passcode-protected. So uh… close your eyes real quick."

With a begrudging grunt, Will squeezed his eyes shut and covered his face. Mike input the access code and eight beeps echoed down the chamber.

"Okay, you can open your eyes." Mike opened the panel above them and the lights inside lit up. "This is super simple, but you wanted to see this, so here we are." Mike pulled out a drive the size of a brick. "We plug these in here like this. This is the power, and the rest of these are system connections." Mike plugged them in and clicked a button on the side, turning on his custom drive. "Then you click it on."

The box lit up, followed by several beeps. Mike slid it into the compartment and closed the hatch.

"Okay, let's back up out of here." They shuffled out of the corridor and closed the hatch, then started everything up. Screens projected over the consoles.

Happy to be using his personalized interface again, Mike ran maintenance and update scripts. He paused, puzzled to see some unexpected notifications. His eyes scanned over the information, which was not organized but a jumble of words, letters, numbers, and symbols.

"What's that?" Will asked.

"It's a... hold on a sec." He sifted through everything and pieced the message together until the information became clear.

Before Mike was a message to Donovan Fletcher, the man who had taken over after Bradley Summers. With the little useful information he got from Bradley, Mike had updated the parameters of the malicious software he had planted in the Ministry's systems. Message decoded, Mike's eyes lit up and his whole body was ready to explode with excitement. He gripped the arms of his chair to read it again.

Archon Donovan Fletcher,

Subject 319's transfer has been moved up in response to a possible security threat. The new residence is almost ready for launch, but not fully functional. Be prepared to relocate Subject 319 on December 20.

There was no name to the memo, merely a destination and text. The geolocation on the message receipt placed it in Ukraine.

Mike thrust his fists in the air, eyes wide and jovial.

"Yes!" he yelled. Fixated on the screen, Mike lowered his hands to touch the console and smiled. "Hope. Daddy's coming to get you."

Pirates

55

New Friends

CAPTAIN KIM'S INQUIRIES PROVED FRUITFUL, WITH HIGH PRAISE showered upon the Earthers she suspected to be infiltrators. The crew of the *Oasis* even passed along messages and updates on the station's ongoing recovery. After being released, Sam, Amber and James made accommodations on the station.

Maya wasted no time in again asking to borrow their shuttle. After several hours of convincing, Amber agreed to go with her. She could help more by getting to the bottom of the attacks than helping the station to prepare for battle. They departed within a day.

James was not allowed to work security, so he got a job bartending. Sam, meanwhile, assisted Adam Ward and the engineers in upgrading the station's cannons. Chief O'Neil and the Captain's Chief Engineer had worked together in the past, and his comments made it clear that Sam was not only trustworthy but a tremendous asset. Although tossed into the depths of a storming new world, they stayed afloat and found a place for themselves. Sam and James understood that it would take time before they earned Captain Kim's trust, so they paid little mind to her heavy monitoring of their activities. Mike, however, protected himself against her digitally.

The *Olympus* crew checked and upgraded every possible defense. The drills had to wait a week and a half while the station's marketing team raised awareness. The first drill yielded poor results. Accustomed to safety, instead of funneling into the nearest business, people lingered in the quads and went about their business. Some people even lodged formal complaints. If that was how people reacted on the day of the attack, people were sure to die. To improve results, Captain Kim imposed fines.

While some people found themselves fiscally motivated to comply with the second drill, the station made a pretty penny from the fines. By the third drill, Captain Kim had achieved the level of cooperation she sought, and a fourth drill normalized the activity.

Mike and his crew reached out to trustworthy contacts to recruit ships for the battle. Tony's ship, the *Yellow Shark*, was their first ally. Farouk recruited the *Milagro*, where the friends he ran into on *Oasis* served. They hoped to get back at the Dragon Claw, as the attack on Endoria had cost them a security contract. Ian called his daughter on the *Phoenix*, and their moral obligation signed them up. Addie's old racing crew, the Starblazers, signed on as well. As many of the volunteers as they could possibly manage were outfitted with energy weapons designed by Adam Ward. Mike took advantage to upgrade the *Ulfberht's* warp system as well.

Captain Kim spoke with a few trustworthy Captains in the Avalon Defense Fleet, and they agreed to join, vowing to participate in drills and show up to defend the station if called upon.

For Mike and Sam, the month of preparations was laced with paranoia at the thought that Jones could be on the station stalking them. The extra security took the edge off, but almost every night, they would awaken in the middle of the night. With more in common than they realized, their shared state of alarm brought them together. Mike advised Sam to keep a taser pistol behind the head of his mattress. They shared a unique bond in their history with the Ministry. It was not long before Sam joined the crew for lunch, and James after that.

All the crews involved, in fact, developed a camaraderie. With maintenance crews at work on their ships, they found themselves with a surplus of downtime, and none of the assisting ships had met each other. Several members of the fun and adventurous *Milagro* were taken with the bold and dramatic crew of the *Phoenix*, which was over sixty-percent female. The intelligent, diverse, and sexually fluid crew of the *Yellow Shark* enjoyed the company of both. All crews found themselves in drinking contests with the Russians, to mixed results.

After making so many new friends, there was no way anyone was going into battle without throwing a party. The covert battle group came together to rent out an arcade bar with a stage and dance floor called Game Dorado two days before the anticipated day of the battle.

The gold-trimmed venue was a smoky throbbing of music, dancing, and laughter alongside a whimsical cacophony of video game sound effects. Trills and dings, buzzing and bangs. Colorful lights and sweet aromas danced in the air alongside the party goers. No matter where one of the hundreds of attendees found themselves in the venue, vigorously uplifting energy pumped through them.

Farouk's appearance was a cause for celebration. To the attendees with prosthetics, he was a hero. To everyone else, he was a legend. Always appreciative of fans, he took pictures all night and signed every autograph. A woman from the *Phoenix* asked for his signature on her right butt-cheek and ran off to get it tattooed. To protect the ink, her pants were pulled down half-way on one side.

After Jorge, leader of the Starblazers, won a dance battle against a *Yellow Shark* crew member and was crowned dance battle champion, Ian's daughter, Miranda, was coaxed on stage to sing. With a thicket of natural orange hair under a black tricorn hat with a long, cerulean feather from a Freyjan bird, the nineteen-year-old beauty trotted to the stage with a cackle. "Someone record this for my dad!"

"I got you!" Addie called out from the menagerie of shadows speckled in blue, purple, and pink light.

"He's not here because he hates big parties, but he's always asking me if I still sing. My mum was a singer. She used to sing all the time when I was young. When she died, I told him I wanted to go to the stars to be closer to her, so he moved us to the colonies without a second thought." Miranda wiped a tear from her eye. "Shit, my makeup." She giggled and composed herself. "Anyway, I have the best dad in the galaxy. If you disagree, I'll fight you over it!" She shook a fist at the laughing audience. "This one's for you, Dad! And, everyone here, of course. You're all amazing."

After a pause for laughter and cheers, she cleared her throat, took a deep breath, then the small woman let loose a powerful voice that ripped through the club and captivated all who heard it. If ten was the scale, she was eleven or twelve. Her siren's song stopped people in their tracks and drew them to her. When her melody ceased, the building erupted in whistles and raucous applause.

"Atta girl!" cheered Captain Joan Jemison of the *Phoenix*, a tall woman with jet black skin and powerful tree trunks for legs. On her feet, she applauded. Her crew, then the rest of the room followed her example and the cheering grew even louder.

Of the Captains, Jemison was the one that showed up most ready to party, in order to show people how it's done. Her bright heels matched a short red dress and sparkling golden phoenix earrings. Tony disappeared after finding some good company for the evening. Captain Arturo Gomez of the *Milagro* showed up, but remained stationary at his table, drinking tequila with lime and reminiscing with a captive crowd about life in space when he was their age.

Despite the threat Jones presented, Mike showed up to the party with Shin at his side for protection. But, they did not stay long. He had a drink, shook a few hands, and made a quiet exit. Sam, however, caught him on the way out.

"Hey, Smith. Got a sec?"

"Sure. Come on this way, though." Mike got out of sight and behind some tall bushes with his back against a wall. "What's up?"

"Well, since all this is going to be over, James and I were talking about what to do next. We were thinking that since Amber and your friend have our shuttle, uh, we were wondering if we can fly with you guys? We're fitting in here all right, but don't want to stay. We realized we're actually fitting in with this group. And, we want to make up for our part in you… losing a crewmate."

"You guys lost one, too." Mike tried to shrug it off, blaming Jones, not Sam.

"Killed by our own, who we are both now living in fear of."

"Well, you'll have me in your corner, but we vote over this kind of stuff. I'll bring it up tomorrow. We've got somewhere to be, though. We're leaving after the battle. Won't be staying to celebrate or mourn, so you'll have to move in within a few hours if you're voted in."

"Thank you. It would mean a lot. We don't have much so we can work with that timeframe. Thanks M.J."

"Hold on, if you want to crew up, please, never call me that again. Nobody has called me that in ages. It's weird. Call me, Mike."

"You've got it."

Ulfberht Crew

56

Battle of Olympus

THE DAY AFTER THE PARTY WAS ONE OF RECOVERY AND LAST-minute connections. The night before battle, *Olympus* and the battle group went on a forty-eight-hour alert. After orbiting the shipyard for a month, the twenty-two Red Storm ships withdrew, waiting at warp nearby. Station security was told to anticipate a drill in the next day or two, but the truth was kept from them. Only those going into battle knew what was to come. A battlegroup channel was created, with the Avalon Defense ships in a separate channel, ready to merge in.

Addie's old crew, the Starblazers docked with the *Ulfberht* so they would not have to stay confined to their cockpits for two days. They mostly played board games with Addie, Will, or whoever was on shift on the bridge, which was a quick sprint away from the docking bay. Mike and Nikolai were vigilant but did their best to stay fresh before the battle.

For the first half of the forty-eight-hour alert, there was no activity. Life on *Olympus* was business as usual. With Sam and James voted in, Will trained them on the turrets. An alert was set to inform the battlegroup as soon as one of the beacons was activated, so after Mike fell asleep on the bridge following a twelve-hour shift, he tried to take a nap, leaving Nikolai ready for the prime hours of the anticipated attack.

Mike found it difficult to sleep. He rolled around in bed, fully dressed and uncomfortable. The lights were off, but he was not tired. His mind was astir with technical challenges and points of vulnerability. The Dragon Claw, for all their rough-and-tumble reputation, had great technical skill. Was there a chance they had changed the signal of their—

BEEP! BEEP! BEEP!

Mike's eyes burst open and he flailed out of bed. His implant was going crazy and the ship speakers boomed around him. The first Dragon Claw beacon had been activated.

He jumped out of bed and sprinted downstairs to the bridge. As he arrived, a herd of young Starblazers sprinted by on their way to the docking bay. Right behind them, Will broke off and bounded up the stairs to the bay's control room. Mike hurried to a bridge console and turned off the alarm, then began to work. Nikolai jumped into the Captain's chair and addressed the battlegroup.

"The first beacon has come online. Battlegroup is on alert status."

"*Finally,*" Captain Gomez said eagerly. "*Milagro, checking in. We're ready.*"

"*Phoenix here. We've got our dragon-slaying gear on,*" said Captain Jemison.

"*Oi, the Yellow Shark is here and hungry for blood!*"

"*Really, Tony?*"

"*I was just following your lead.*"

"I am in command of the battlegroup, so follow *my* lead," Nikolai boomed.

"*Aye, sir,*" Tony said humbly.

"*The Red Storm is ready,*" Iskra reported in.

"*I'm on my way to my office. Dispatching security to the locations your app is sending me. Let me know when to run the drill,*" Captain Kim whispered, still in public.

"*Make sure they're discreet,*" Mike said.

"I've got it handled." Captain Kim made the calls as locations popped up one by one. Once in her office, she made preparations to sound the alarms.

"Starblazers here, my team's ready to go." Since the group had a dozen members, they operated independently and communicated through Jorge, who prayed and traced the sign of the cross in the air over himself before he grabbed the yoke.

"Jesus, how many of these goddamn beacons are they going to place?" Captain Kim dispatched her pre-recorded order to follow the Dragon Claw as they appeared. There were over twenty beacons and counting, popping up in close succession.

With most of the Red Storm's ships tied up in other systems, the defense fleet consisted of twenty-four Red Storm ships, the *Ulfberht*, *Milagro*, *Phoenix*, *Yellow Shark*, and an attack group of a dozen Starblazer fighters. Captain Kim had managed to get six ships from the Avalon Defense Fleet to sign on with her. That made for a total of thirty-four including the ADF ships and twenty-eight without. Already on alert, they set course for Avalon, where they would wait at warp until called upon.

"Gunner room?" Nikolai asked as Will rushed onto the bridge, straight into a seat next to Mike.

"We're all good here. Strapped in this time," Farouk answered.

"I think that was the last beacon. They haven't activated another one," Captain Kim updated the chat.

"Shit." Mike typed feverishly, face glued to the screen.

"What's the total?" Captain Jemison asked, taking her seat on the *Phoenix* bridge.

"I count thirty-five becaons in the last ten minutes."

"We're outnumbered," Mike muttered, still at work.

"Captain Kim, as soon as the last Dragon Claw departs the station, run the drill," Nikolai ordered.

"You got it."

"Michael, status?" Nikolai lit up the front of the bridge with a hologram of the station and surrounding area, with defending ships marked as allies.

"He's in," Will spoke for him.

"I've received confirmation the last group is off the station. Running the drill."

"He's looking for something in the beacon data," Will said hastily. "Negative Z?" He paused. "Oh! He's turning the ships around. When they come out of warp they'll be facing the wrong way."

"Be advised, ships will be facing away when they come out of warp. We are outnumbered, but we have surprise and position to our advantage," Nikolai said boldly, assuaging anyone's fear of being outnumbered.

"I'm glad I'm on this side of the fight," Captain Jemison said.

"Michael, we need coordinates," Nikolai pressed.

Mike continued to work without responding.

"He's working on it," Will said.

"I think you are taking your job here today too literally," Nikolai eyed Will.

"Got it," Mike burst. He ran the coordinates through a script and coordinated the battle group's destinations. Large ships went to warp and relocated to their assigned location. The Starblazers stuck close to the *Ulfberht* to piggyback off its warp bubble.

"Target weapons so they can not fire on the station even if they get around us," Nikolai ordered. "Target thrusters on the first ship you see."

The quiet anticipation and vulnerability rattling through the bones of everyone in the fleet was shattered seconds after they arrived at their locations with massive flashes of light blooming before them, each quickly blocked out by a warship, patchworked together from pieces of other crafts. Once the storm of light had finished, there were not thirty-five ships, but forty-five. Some beacons had several ships targeting it, which meant that some ships were outnumbered by a cluster of Dragon Claw battleships.

"All ships, open fire!" Nikolai bellowed.

The moment the Dragon Claw ships dropped out of warp and saw a canvas of stars instead of a shipyard, they scattered. Some ships only took light damage from the defense fleet's opening volley. A few ships were handicapped but pushed on.

The cluster in front of the *Ulfberht* was a group of five. The *Ulfberht's* massive central forward cannon disabled the ship that spawned before them, but the other four broke off in separate directions.

"George, go left!" Addie called the move, leaving Nikolai to focus on the larger battle at hand.

"It's pronounced, Jorge!" Jorge and the Starblazers zoomed after one of the ships.

"We've got the other ones." Addie leaned into the Yoke and charged them forward, rocketing toward the enemy. They moved to evade and she followed, closing the gap. Once she was breathing down the back of their necks she fired the forward cannon and obliterated its aft thrusters. Newly-installed blaster cannons on the wings fired a volley of shots before Addie pulled out of her dive, shredding several thrusters and turrets.

"Olympus blast shields are up," Captain Kim said.

"Done. Their weapons lock on the beacons are down, and they're not getting it back," Mike said.

"Good, now attack. Addie, bring us around, we need to fully disable that ship."

"Aye."

"This one's bricked," Jorge said, the Starblazers breaking away to swarm another Dragon Claw ship.

Addie lined up her shot and crippled her target. "Scrapped."

"They have disabled six Red Storm ships," Iskra updated Nikolai.

"Starblazers, the *Yellow Shark* has enemies closing, assist them," Addie ordered.

"On the double," Jorge said. The squad of fighters zoomed away.

"We took down one but having some trouble over here," Captain Jemison said, boxed in and narrowly evading three Dragon Claw ships circling and firing on her ship. Facing four to one odds, they managed to take out one and narrowly avoided destruction at the hands of the other three.

"We're already on our way," Captain Gomez answered from the *Milagro*. An old battleship armed to the teeth, they had obliterated their own targets. The *Milagro* blasted its way in, splitting a Dragon Claw ship in half. The *Phoenix* took advantage and went on the offensive, cutting off a retreating Dragon Claw ship to pinch them with the *Milagro*. Together, they cleaned up the last two ships.

"That's a third of them down," Tony pointed out.

"But, our advantage is gone," Captain Gomez shot back.

"Michael, status?"

"They've got some good security. Still working on it."

"Nikolai. Uh, Captain. Captain Nikolai, we're getting reports of disabled ships but not a lot of casualties," Will reported.

On the Bridge's front screen, the Dragon Claw ships broke off and helped each other out, then proceeded as a group toward the station after being forced out of range to evade the ambush.

"They do not want a fight. Red Storm group one, disengage and warp to these coordinates," Nikolai sent the coordinates for the three ships to intercept the closest attacking group of five. They exploded into their path firing their cannons with no weapons lock. The Dragon Claw leaned into them and fired, then broke off. They passed close by and fired their side cannons, ripping through the port of a Red Storm ship. The two groups circled each other in a dogfight.

The outnumbered Red Storm ships tore into the enemy, but went down one by one. They took down three Dragon Claw ships until the last of the group defended its comrades, fighting the fourth ship to a standstill. The fifth Dragon Claw ship dove at the *Olympus* shipyard's main body and opened fire. The *Olympus'* upgraded cannons fired massive bursts of energy that roasted the ship, forcing it to break away. The shots smashed into the blast shields protecting the massive windows but dealt no significant damage. The booming collisions reverberated through the large dome. Many then realized it was not a drill.

"Phoenix, Milagro, Yellow Shark, Starblazers, intercept the second

group with us," Nikolai ordered. "Remaining forces, do not let anyone attack the station."

From all angles, the *Ulfberht's* group charged into a cluster of ten Dragon Claw ships that had amassed nearby and were gunning for the *Olympus*.

The *Ulfberht* was the last of its group to arrive, intercepting the forward-most ships which had slipped by the *Phoenix*, *Milagro*, and *Yellow Shark*. The Dragon Claw ships unleashed a torrent of shots upon the *Olympus* with three Starblazers in pursuit, trying to disable enemy thrusters, zipping around to dodge turret fire.

A flash of sparks on one Starblazer ship caught Addie's eye, then it exploded into a ball of light and plasma. Addie screamed and clicked both thumbs down on the yoke, unleashing cannon fire upon the Dragon Claw ships.

"George! Jorge, who was that?" She screeched.

"It was Ben, It's okay, he eject—" A shell smashed into Jorge's cockpit and his audio cut out. Addie screamed again and barrelled into the Dragon Claw ships. Stingers were built reinforced for head-on collisions so it could dive-bomb enemies in a pinch and not splinter itself apart. The Dragon Claw ships were forced to scatter or be cut in half.

"Oh, my god, Jorge. No me digas... *Wh-what's this fuckin' icon?"*

"It's a switch for the battlegroup chat, you're in charge now. Look at it to turn your voice on and off," Captain Jemison updated the mourning pilot.

"You got this, Jessi," Addie huffed, watery eyes glued to the half dome in front of her, hunting down the Dragon Claw enemies, not letting them get a shot in.

"F-f-f-fuuuuck," Jessica said through sobs. *"All right then, kill* **all** *these motherfuckers!"* she roared.

The *Milagro* broke off its battle to support the *Ulfberht* and a Starblazer against five enemy ships. thirty seconds later they went to warp and reappeared in front of the ships making a pass at the *Olympus*. The *Milagro* charged into the cluster, firing cannons and turrets in every direction. Enemies fired back, and two of them turned into the *Milagro* to absorb the brunt of its devastation. The *Milagro* itself was battered by enemy fire and left crippled and floating away with limited thrusters.

Three Dragon Claw ships survived the altercation but found themselves in the *Olympus* weapons range, pelted by defensive fire. Forced to turn away, they circled back around and took aim at the crippled *Milagro*.

The *Phoenix* swooped in and bore down on one of the enemy ships, chasing it as it circled away from the cannon fire. The *Ulfberht* circled around to protect the *Milagro* from the other two ships. The main thrusters of one Dragon Claw ship splintered and bloomed into a plasma fire, and the other broke off to regroup. Instead of pushing the attack, they disengaged and went to warp, alongside most of the Dragon Claw ships.

"Done. Right on time, it looks like," Mike said.

"All ships, go to warp!" Nikolai commanded.

"Phoenix, give us a ride!" Jessi, the new Starblazer captain, said.

"You got it."

The front screen displayed various Dragon Claw trajectories. The defense fleet's courses adjusted to match.

"Put us between them. *Phoenix, Yellow Shark,* Starblazers, stay at warp with the ADF units. ADF team, sending coordinates, on my command drop from warp and open fire." Nikolai sent them coordinates flanking the Dragon Claw ships.

The defense fleet reappeared between the Dragon Claw destination and the *Olympus.* When the Dragon Claw dropped out of warp in formation, a wall of enemy ships awaited them. Face-to-face with an enemy that would not quit, both sides gritted their teeth and braced for the coming assault.

"Fire at will! ADF team, now!"

The two fleets erupted in a booming storm of weapons fire, with the defense fleet protecting the *Olympus* from enemy fire. A few stray shots slipped between the ships and smashed into the station's armor, ships in repair, and bursting open corridors. Most of the shots crashed into the defense fleet, crashing into their armor, knocking people off their feet or out of their chairs. Breached compartments sucked an unlucky few into space. Bright bursts of energy and metal slugs slammed into Dragon Claw ships, but they trudged through it, firing every cannon which had not already been disabled.

From their southeast flank, the Avalon Defense Fleet team burst out of warp with the *Phoenix* and *Yellow Shark*, unleashing hell from behind. The Dragon Claw's right flank melted. Husks of Dragon Claw ships were left tumbling through space as the storm of weapons fire drifted through their ranks. They closed in around the Dragon Claw, now attempting to retreat. They swerved to avoid enemy fire, pelted until flashes of light consumed them and the Dragon Claw disappeared.

"Hold fire!" Nikolai commanded.

A deathly calm fell over the fleet as they waited for whatever came next. Mike and Nikolai monitored the enemy fleet's movements. They repositioned by their stranded comrades littered around *Olympus* space.

Dragon Claw ships dropped out of warp and fired tow cables, pulling their friends in close, then extended their warp fields around them both to tow them home. One by one, the fleet zipped away, headed back to Sol, leaving not one ship behind.

"The enemy retreats! Victory is ours!" Nikolai roared, then relaxed into his seat with a sigh of relief.

The crews of the defense fleet burst into jubilant celebration. Jumping out of their seats, hugging each other, hooting, cheering, clapping, the fleet was bursting at the seams with joy made all the more potent by the adrenaline still pumping through them.

"Well done everyone!" Tony shouted.

While the fleet celebrated, Nikolai looked over the casualty reports. In the end, fifteen Red Storm ships had been heavily damaged or disabled, five of which were the result of the final head-to-head charge. The *Milagro* had taken heavy damage but also had the highest Dragon Claw kill count, crippling at least seven ships. Two Starblazer ships had been destroyed and they lost their leader.

Addie cried in her cockpit while everyone else celebrated. Will knelt down next to the cockpit and wrapped an arm around her. She leaned into his chest and returned the hug, sobbing into his shirt.

Despite the damage it took, the *Milagro* reported only seven deaths and a few dozen injuries. The *Phoenix* and *Yellow Shark* reported injuries and only two or three deaths. The Red Storm had also seen a minimum of casualties.

The Dragon Claw had been more focused on getting to the *Olympus* than engaging the defense fleet in battle. Until the final showdown when it became clear they would continue to stand in their way, the Dragon Claw engaged in combat only as much as they had to. For a clan known to love a good fight, it was strange that they prioritized firing on the *Olympus*.

"Looks like we're in decent shape." Mike pulled Nikolai's attention away from the statistics. "We've got some repairs to make, but nothing major. Main systems are intact. We should avoid a fight for the time being.

With the alarms on *Olympus* turned off and the blast shields folding back over the cannon bays, Captain Kim addressed the battlegroup.

"Thank you, everyone. We all here at the Olympus owe you a debt of gratitude."

"It was our pleasure, Captain. I about shit my pants when I saw how many ships they had," Captain Gomez said. *"Thank you, Nikolai, for leading us through that."*

"Aye-aye!" Tony burst.

"My condolences for any losses out there," Captain Jemison said.

"Yes, today was a success and we saved many people, but we did lose some, and they should be honored and remembered for their heroism," Nikolai said.

"Captain Kim, the Red Storm has many damaged ships, is there room for us in the shipyard?" Iskra asked.

"I'm already making arrangements for everyone in the fleet who needs repairs. Please send me the ships and damage so I can figure out where to put you. But, rest assured, we'll pitch in on the fleet's repairs."

"We will return for repairs at another date. We must go," Nikolai said.

"You sure you can't stay for a little while?"

"Sorry, Captain, we've got to be somewhere in a hurry," Mike said.

"Thank you again, Nikolai, Mike, for saving my station. If you ever need anything, you know where to find me."

"We're glad we could help, Captain. Let's grab a celebratory drink the next time we're out here."

"Looking forward to it. Happy trails, gentlemen."

Addie pulled out of her hug and wiped her tears. After a deep breath, she set a course for Earth.

"Thank, Will. I'll be okay." Addie sniffled, drying her hands on her jeans.

"I'm here if you need me." Will left her side and found his seat again. Addie's loss brought back thoughts of Natalie, who would have loved to be in that battle. It was something she would have never thought she could experience, and it was thrilling.

"Good job today," Mike said.

"Thanks," Will said absently. "Do you think she was watching?"

For the first time, Mike pulled himself away from his screen and turned to Will. "I, uh… don't believe in an afterlife. But, One has made me question the nature of the universe. So, the best answer I can give you is, I don't know? Whatever we believe, it has to be something we choose for ourselves. Whatever you think it is, is what it is, because we can't prove anything."

Mike returned to his work and Will returned to contemplating the nature of life and death. If what we believe is what dictates how we behave, then why can it not go the other way? If we can prove nothing, then what does it matter what happens after we die?

We should live the best lives and do the most good we can while we are here. We should live happily and full of love, as Natalie did. What we do while we are here is all that matters, because it is all we can experience. If there was an afterlife, he would tell her all about the battle, if not, oh well. People don't worry about the weather on another planet when they're getting dressed because it doesn't affect them.

Lazarus

57

The Righteous

Donald Brown sat on the empty rooftop terrace of his favorite chic restaurant surrounded by treetops as he did most mornings when a smooth, familiar voice approached from behind.

"Good afternoon, Mr. Brown." Lazarus approached with a smile in another dark suit, this time carrying a large box under his left arm. He was more chipper than before.

"Lazarus, call me Donald. It's good to see you. You seem to be in good spirits." Brown stood to greet him at the same white table where they had met before. They shook hands and Lazarus pulled up an empty seat next to Brown, placing the box on the table.

"Today is a big day. I'm expecting some good news in the next couple hours," Lazarus shared.

"What's that you got there?" Brown sipped his black coffee.

"A gift. To commemorate your new contracts with the UEG *and* your sole ownership of Arc Industries. It really is a shame that poor old business partner of yours met such a sudden and unfortunate demise." Lazarus slid the box to Brown. "My condolences."

"No tears shed here." Brown eyed the box from a distance. "It isn't a bomb or a human head, is it?" He chuckled.

"Please, Donald. Would I hand deliver a bomb? It's a gift, open it." Lazarus leaned back and crossed his legs, hands together in his lap.

Glancing between Lazarus and the box, Brown put down his cup and pulled the box closer to open it. Inside were two bottles and a cigar. Brown recognized his favorite cigar, examining and sniffing it then putting it back in its place. Pulling out the bottle of whiskey, he was taken aback.

"Is this really a hundred-fifty-four-year-old bottle of whiskey?" Brown asked, his eyes blooming, jaw slack.

"Twenty-thirty, the same year your great-grandfather was born."

"Where the hell did you find this?" Brown slipped the whiskey back into the box and pulled out the wine, which was also over one hundred years old.

"Don't worry about that, just enjoy them." Lazarus smiled.

"Thank you, I… this is amazing. Thank you for the gifts." Brown put the bottle away and closed the box with care, then moved it aside.

"And still, those gifts fail to express our gratitude for making such bold moves to position yourself as you have," Lazarus said.

"Well, I would be a fool not to embrace the future. It's inevitable. All you gotta do is put yourself in the right place to ride into it prosperously."

"I love your work in the public eye, as well. You have such passion, such vigor. Has anyone ever told you that you have a gift for public speaking?" He spoke candidly, pleased with Brown's performance thus far.

"My great-grandfather's gift is a talent we've passed on from one generation to the next," Brown said smoothly. "People want to hear what they want to hear. They want to be assured they're right, and they want someone to blame for their woes. Be it the devil, pirates, terrorists, rebels, criminals, it all works just as well."

"I'm truly in awe of people who sway the masses. I can get an individual or a small group to work with me, but large groups are far more difficult to control without leverage. And, I'm not particularly fond of crowds, as it were."

"Oh, crowds are no trouble at all. See, you've got to think of a crowd as one person. Any one person might have ten thoughts about whatever you said, but they're only going to react to one. A crowd will react to all of them. There's so many people they all react differently. You've got to convince the crowd to listen to that one voice in the sea of noise that agrees with you. Start with something they all agree with. It's what makes talking to people in churches so damn easy."

"I've seen videos of your great-grandfather speaking. He was quite a sight to behold." Lazarus nodded.

"He was the *best*. You know how he started Babylon Mining?" Brown asked.

"I'd *love* to hear the story." Lazarus sat up straight.

"For years, he talked about a war on religion. How atheists and other non-Christians were undermining Christian values. He said that in *the heavens*, God had blessed man with an abundance of resources; resources with which we were to build a paradise here on Earth." Brown spoke with zest as if he was delivering the message himself. "And, if people wanted to help realize God's vision of paradise for his loyal believers, the church needed the people's help to create a company that would allocate those resources the way God intended, bringing the common man to the stars, ever closer to God himself. Oh my lord, did those people eat that shit up."

Lazarus chuckled at the story. "And now, who remembers any of that?"

"We're just another company with *Christian* values." Brown imitated quotations with one hand. "He promised those people all kinds of stuff but he didn't give them a damn thing. Only ten years later, nobody remembered those promises. People don't have that kind of vision. They don't think two years ahead or behind them. They just want to know how God can help them right *now*." Brown stabbed the table with his index finger.

The story delighted Lazarus. It was a pleasure to meet others who understood the true nature of people, as he understood it. Then a buzz circled the back of his hand. "Donald, I do believe we've made an excellent choice with you." He drew a circle on the back of his hand and a screen appeared over it. As he read the incoming message, his smile faded and his face turned stone cold. Eyes closed, he took a deep breath. Opening them, Lazarus dialed a contact. Their face appeared over his hand after the first ring.

"Yes, sir?"

"Withhold payment. Payment requires success. Go ahead with the contingency as well," Lazarus ordered.

"Sir, during the attack all the assets for the contingency were extracted. We destroyed the two prime assets before they could be taken."

"Well then, I guess our relationship with them is concluded. Goodbye." Lazarus ended the call and turned his attention back to Brown.

"It can be difficult to find people who can get the job done these days, isn't it? Care to join me for a drink?" Brown gestured toward the box Lazarus had brought him.

"Quite difficult. All the more reason you are deserving of these gifts." Lazarus stood and straightening his suit. "I appreciate the offer, but it appears I have quite a bit to attend to."

"I hope your problems work themselves out," Brown said with a tip of his cup.

"Thank you, I'm sure they will. I'll be in touch." Lazarus gave Brown a nod and left him alone on the patio to drink his coffee in peace.

Ulfberht Crew

58

Plan of Attack

AFTER LEAVING AVALON, THE CREW MET IN THE LOUNGE FOR drinks, as much to relax as to console Addie. After about an hour of socializing, Will entered the room holding a zapper with both hands and Mike brought things around to business.

"So, this has been nice, but for you two to be officially welcome here on the ship, there's one thing left to do."

Sam groaned and Farouk put his drink down with a grin.

"All right, let's get it over with."

"Thank you, Will." Farouk took the zapper from him. Will hopped onto a couch with the crew, where Addie prepared to record.

"As part of the agreement for you to join us, Farouk gets to taze you, and we're all here as witnesses."

Mike circled around to join the crew while Sam and Farouk stood before them, facing one another. Farouk twirled and shook the zapper, mostly to release pent-up anticipation. Sam finished his drink and set his glass down. With another groan, Sam shook his body, as if shaking out all his fear.

"I was down for five days, you'll be down for five minutes," Farouk said.

"I know, it's fine. It's fair. Let's get it done." Sam stood with his arms at his sides, chest out, squeezing his eyes shut. "I'm ready when y-nnnngggg!"

Farouk did not let Sam finish and jammed the zapper into his ribs. He shook and twisted, face contorting, and dropped to the floor. He shook on the ground for a moment, then Farouk reached the zapper out. "Here, grab on."

After taking a moment to recover, Sam reached out and grabbed the zapper. Farouk pulled and lifted Sam off the ground. He got halfway up before Farouk activated the zapper again. Sam yelped and shook in place, then dropped back to the floor.

The room laughed at the gag, then Farouk reached out with an arm to help him up. "All right, we're even now."

After some hesitation, Sam grabbed his wrist and Farouk pulled him up. His body was not ready to stand on its own and he collapsed to his knees.

"You okay?" Farouk patted his shoulder and hooked under his arm under Sam's. Sam nodded, then braced himself to stand with Farouk's assistance.

"All right, welcome to the crew!" Addie shouted.

The crew cheered and applauded. Ian and James whistled. Shin's clap was the slowest in the room, more polite than out of excitement or celebration. Once Sam was firmly on his feet, they hugged, patting each other on the back. Farouk helped Sam get back to his single-seater couch where he flopped into the cushions. Farouk found his seat and placed the zapper next to the sofa cushions behind him.

James loomed over the couch and gave Sam a hug, roughing up his hair and patting him on the chest. "You took that like a champ, Sammy. Way to go."

"Ouch." Sam groaned, covering up to protect himself.

"That's done, so let's have our first crew meeting since, I don't know, it's been a couple months now." Mike took his place in front of the group again. He pulled up a screen and read through his itinerary. "The topics I want to cover in this meeting are: What are we doing, where are our friends, security, Lazarus, and what's next. What do you guys want to hear first?"

"I'll take where our friends are at for four hundred," James tipped his beer bottle at Mike.

"The last message I got from Maya, she and your friend are almost to Sol. Next."

"Security." Shin said.

"I think an agent good enough to track us down and get away from Maya and also almost kill us all is dangerous and might be on the ship. Our sensors aren't picking him up, but working for Lazarus, he could have cutting edge tech. So, I want to do some sweeps of the ship. Everywhere he could be hiding, we're looking, from stem to stern."

"Oh, I'm so ready." James pounded a fist into his other hand.

"Whuh…" Sam tried to speak, then groaned and rolled over, still shaken.

"What are we doing?" James asked for him. Sam nodded.

"We are on our way to Earth to rescue my daughter, Hope. I haven't seen her since she was three and the Ministry is holding her somewhere in Ukraine."

Sam winced and shook his head, mumbling.

"From the Ministry a' Science?" James asked. "Are you serious? Can I help? Do you have a team lined up already? Really, the Ministry?" He followed up, disoriented. A desire to help someone rescue their daughter clashed with the thought the Ministry could do such a thing.

"Sort of. We won't turn down a volunteer, but I'll circle back around to that and you can let me know if you still want to be a part of it."

"You got it." James nodded.

"I want to know about Lazarus," Farouk said.

"I've been scrubbing Lazarus's card. It had a lot of thorns, but I got into his network. It's an isolated and limited. I don't know how much I'll be able to get from it, but I'm still picking it apart. Whatever I find, I'll send to Maya," Mike said.

"I don't know who Lazarus is, but his name would make an awesome gamer tag," Will said. "What's next?"

"Next is our trip to Earth. With the new warp system, we'll make it in about nine days. That's all the time we have left to make preparations to rescue Hope," Mike's voice rose in excitement and a smile crept onto his face. After over a decade, he was less than two weeks from seeing her again. "A memo I intercepted puts her somewhere in Ukraine and they're getting ready to move her. I've got to figure out where in Ukraine and work with Nikolai on an extraction plan."

"Can I ask a question?" James raised his hand.

"I'm sure you and Sam are going to have some questions here, so ask away."

"Why is the Ministry holding ya daughter captive?"

"She's telepathic."

"Woah, seriously? That's wild."

"I haven't heard of her, but I probably didn't have the clearance." Sam sat up, feeling better, but still queasy. "If I didn't have the clearance and she's in Ukraine, then she's being held at the underground Chernobyl bunker."

"That was one of my top choices, are you sure?" Mike asked eagerly.

"I've been to all the locations in Ukraine, that's the only one where I had restricted access."

"That's helpful," Mike gushed. "Now, I just have to look up the coordinates for it and we've got our target."

"I can get it from the Ministry system for you."

"How do you have access to the Ministry System?"

"I made a copy of it. We brought it with us."

"You what?" Mike exclaimed. "Why would you make a copy?"

"Your DNA was restricted access, so I made a copy and got a hack from a friend in digital security," Sam explained. "I didn't want to get in trouble."

"May I have access to both of those things?"

"It's all yours." Sam pulled up a screen over his hand and linked Mike to his copy of the Ministry system and the hack.

"God damn, Mike. You sure made a lucky pick with these two," Rick grunted.

"Betting on good people always works out," Mike said, unaware of the bitterness fueling Rick's comment. He looked over what Sam had sent him and remotely accessed Sam's Ministry system clone. "Oh man, you've saved me days of work."

"Glad I could help, but that base is massive, and heavily defended. How the hell do you plan on getting in? Are you going to storm in like my base? Because, as a result of your attack they've upgraded security across the Ministry."

"Yeah, you come in through the tunnels, you're fightin' your way out of a hole," James added. "You hit it from the front, you'll be taking on the most heavily defended part of the base."

"Knowing that, you still want to join us?"

"Hell yeah," James said with an assertive nod that flowed through his torso. "I'm goin' full pirate."

"If you're in, then you're in. Anything we discuss is confidential and restricted to this crew. But, you need to know it in order to discuss the battle plan."

"Deal," James said.

"Yeah, okay," Sam followed.

"Am I still allowed to be here?" Will raised his hand.

"Yeah, you're fine. So, we can talk more about this later, but we have the ability to portal through space."

There was a pause while James, Sam, and Will contemplated the news. He watched their faces, their minds working through the revelation of something that does not technically exist being at their fingertips.

"Like a portal-portal? Like you jump through it and poof you're somewhere else?" Will inquired.

"Yes, exactly," Mike said plainly. The three looked at each other in disbelief.

"That's a *huge* tactical advantage," James said.

"Do you know how much you could advance our species?" Will shot to his feet, hands on his head.

"I agree, but that's obviously not your invention. How do you have that?" Sam asked, then a revelation glossed over his eyes. "Oh my god, is Schulze still alive?"

"Yes, I do know how much that technology could advance our species, but it isn't my invention to distribute." Mike pointed at Will and Sam respectively. "Got it in one."

With no idea who they were talking about, Will sat down and pulled out his mobile to do a search on Mike and Schulze.

"You think the old man's going to be happy you're telling people?" Farouk asked.

"They're going to find out eventually, particularly when we jump through a portal into the base I'm looking at. Given the odds, I already asked Al."

"All right, let's get on with it." Farouk twirled a hand in the air.

"Let's indeed. This thing has the *exact* coordinates of the station." Mike pulled up a hologram and enlarged it for everyone to see, letting the ship take over the projection. There were trees, lakes, and at the center an archaic nuclear power plant covered by a massive dome. "This is Chernobyl."

Zoomed in on the power plant, Mike swiped his hand up and the hologram scrolled down. The ground on the outer edges of the hologram disappeared. Beneath the surface, not far from Chernobyl was a long t-shaped box. From it ran an elevator shaft that reached one kilometer down and fed into the center of a tall, cylindrical building, segmented into six sections reminiscent of a spine. Each level was several stories tall.

"And, this is the Ministry bunker hidden underneath it." Mike reached out and stopped the hologram's scrolling. "I've been here once and it was in the early days. What can you tell us, Sam?"

"Well, I've only been to the top three levels." Sam shuffled in his seat. "Those are clear of psychic prisoners. The fourth level is the habitat level, but I didn't have the clearance to go lower when I was there. I don't know anything about level five, but there was a rumor that on level six they're holding genetically enhanced prisoners from World War Three that became killers because of problems with early gene modification." Sam did not hold back his amusement at the rumor.

"That could be misinformation," Farouk pointed out.

"That's true. She could be at either one," Sam admitted. "But, I'd put my money on level five since it was a mystery. If it turns out to be the wrong one, six is only one level down from there."

"One level down is a small building worth of hauling ass." Mike shook his head. "I'm going to see if I can work on it from here to get confirmation on what level she's on. But, that'll have to wait."

"Does this thing have layouts for the levels?" James asked.

"It should." Mike expanded the top level to reveal a floor plan. He scrolled down a level, then another, then another to the habitat level, but the next two floors were empty shapes. "Looks like no, but that might change."

"If it does not change." Nikolai stepped forward and scrolled back up to level four, then three. Reaching into the hologram, he pointed at a room behind the elevators. "This looks like storage room on every level. If layout is the same, then we can enter through this room on the level we pick."

"So, we portal in there. Once we're inside, I get control of their security. We'll have to get a hold of an enemy security guard to get into their tech like we did with you." Mike motioned to James.

Shin stepped forward and examined the map, his nose a hair away from the hologram. He circled the outside while the others talked.

"Most of the security is probably in the basement and the dock, but if this level has its own security, they could slow you down enough for the others to pinch you," James said.

"They're going to have to take the stairs because I'll be in control of the elevators. That should buy us some time," Mike joked. "The one thing I'm afraid of, though, is Lazarus. If he is there to guard and escort her, he keeps a golem with him."

"Shit, Mike. That ain't nothin' I can't handle." Farouk shrugged off the threat.

"It might actually be a test for you. Lazarus has access to all the deep undercover tech. His golem is going to be made for battle. Your tech wasn't made to be revolutionary, it was just made by a genius. You and Shin work together if we run into the golem. I'm not taking risks on this. I intend to get everyone back alive, my daughter included."

"All right, I'm cool with that. Let's get the job done."

"These maintenance tunnels." Shin leaned away from the hologram and pointed at shafts that ran through the base like the ones on the *Ulfberht*. "They're probably on every level. I could follow one to their security room and cripple their defenses before we begin. That would also draw attention away from the rest of you."

"That's good idea," Nikolai said.

"So, you kick security's ass, we grab ya daughter, we portal out, bing-bang-boom." James clapped his hands together. "Easy peasy."

"Actually, we can't portal out. We won't be able to send Al a message, so we'll have to get to the hangar and steal a ship," Mike corrected him.

"Damn, I thought it was going to be easy."

"I wish it were. But, we've got a rough skeleton to work with. I'll try to get us more and we'll go from there. Is there anything else anyone wants to talk about?"

"I've got a question. I was still queasy when it came to mind," Sam said.

"What's up?"

"You mentioned intercepting a Ministry memo? How?"

"When I hit your bunker, I loaded up the latest system restore files and implanted some custom software, then put them back. I crashed the system so you would all restore from backups. When you guys did that, you propagated my software through the Ministry's computers."

"Holy shit," Sam leaned back in disbelief.

"Speaking of that night, how come you guys put One in a cell?" Farouk asked.

"The honest answer is because I wasn't there."

Will's attention was piqued by Farouk's question. He did not know Sam was from the bunker until that moment. "I have a question." The room looked to Will, who paused. "I...I saw the video of One's ship crashing and you guys were on top of it already. How were you there so fast?"

Sam looked back with a contorted, confused expression, glancing between Mike and Will. "What video?"

"Natalie recorded One's ship as it crashed. We have it in the shared drive. I'll link it to you." Mike accessed his implant to share the video with Sam.

"Thanks. Well, his ship came from an anomaly we had been monitoring for weeks. We ran some experiments and beamed some signals into it but our results didn't make sense. Later on, we realized that we were receiving the signals we had sent in reverse. It was like a time-mirror. Because of that, we could calculate when it would terminate. We sent ships to get some up-close readings for us as it did, then a ship shot out with a hole in it. Our ships followed as best they could to keep it cloaked. The security crew relayed the situation and I was called back to my base."

"That's fascinating. I want to hear more about it, but does anyone else have any questions or concerns?" Mike asked.

The crew responded with a series of various *nos* and head-shakes.

"Okay then, this meeting is adjourned. Let's grab some lunch and after that, we'll figure out how we're going to go about our sweeps of the ship."

Ulfberht Crew

59

Life Goes On

Passing by the *Ulfberht's* gunner room, Ian noticed a green light on the room's console, indicating it was unlocked and likely had someone inside. The internal sensors did not detect anyone onboard that was not from the crew and they had searched the ship from stem to stern, but they played it safe anyway. Most of the crew carried with them a taser pistol which had been synced to the ship.

"Aye," Ian called to Farouk, who stopped and took a few paces back.

"It's probably Will." Farouk drew his pistol, holding it in front of him. It was common knowledge Will and Natalie used to spend most of their leisure time there. "Mike's being paranoid thinkin' that agent could'a snuck on the ship."

"Will ain't been 'ere in a while. I wonder what he's doin'." Ian scooted closer to the console, holding a six-pack of beer in one hand.

"If you're goin' to open the door, I hope he ain't cryin'." Farouk shook his head, uncomfortable imagining the awkwardness that would follow if that were the case.

"Wan'nit just the one time? And, right after she died more'n a month ago?"

"Yeah, but it was weird." Farouk shuddered. "I ain't equipped to deal with that."

"Well, only one way t'find out," Ian tapped the console and the door opened.

Inside, Will sat in the middle of the room eating a bowl of rice and lab-grown chicken. Projected on one wall was a fight between a flashy jester and a bulky, spike-riddled monster. Surrounded by angry spear-wielding imps, the cartooney stone ring around them fell apart as they crashed into it.

"Hey, guys." Will glanced over just long enough to see who had walked in.

"What'cha watchin' there, lad?" Ian passed behind Will, watching the fight unfold. The two men sat on the floor on either side of him.

"I'm watching pros play a fighting game called Smash."

"Man, I used to love shooting games when I was a kid." Farouk thought back to his youth.

"It shows when you're on the guns." Will scooped up another bite.

"Thanks." Farouk's posture straightened, a proud grin spread across his face. "Who we rootin' for over here?"

"The jester. He's become my all-time favorite player. I haven't been watching, though, so I'm catching up before the big fight."

"Why's he your favorite?" Ian asked, happy to see Will doing so well.

"Two big reasons. His debut was in an elimination rumble. He was first seed out of fifty players and won," Will said. Farouk and Ian both gawked at each other in amazement.

"Holy shit. He won as the dark horse?" Farouk said.

"Yep. And, the second reason is: he's going all Highlander on bitches. No two people in a league can have the same name. If you want someone's name you have to take it from them. This guy wants the name, Jester, so he's been stomping out everyone with jester in their name. It's down to him and the guy named Jester. They fight for the name on Saturday. People call him, The Unstoppable Force."

"So, this game is so hot, people use it to fight over their names?"

Farouk asked. The jester pummeled the large spiky beast into the air, followed by a lightning strike that sent him flying away.

"Well, it's the most popular game right now. But, to take someone's name you have to play a series of different games. This guy can play anything. He's been talking shit all year to get this fight."

"When I was comin' up, I used to talk a lot of shit. You get the matches you want, and you get in your opponent's head before the fight." Farouk recalled his early days as a fighter with a smile.

"That's Dax and Moxie all day long. They're a lot of fun to watch. Natalie and I followed them. Made things feel normal, like we were still part of the world, but on vacation or something." Will's eyes fell, then returned to the match. "Do you guys have anything like that?"

"Like what?" Ian grunted.

"Something that makes you feel connected to the world. You guys are both from Earth. Do you ever miss it?" Will took another bite.

"I moved to the colonies for my daughter, Miranda. *She's* my world."

"We *are* connected to the world. What do you think the world is? Earth? People talkin' online?" Farouk shook his head. "Nah man, the world is all of us."

"Aye, I agree with the big oaf for once." Ian scratched at his scruffy orange beard. "When ah think back t' Earth, it isn't Earth I miss, it's people. Years from now you'll miss people you ain't met yet. This here's the only thing that'll 'mind ye of Earth. There's a lot of new stuff for ye in the colonies."

"Still, I kind of miss my old life."

"I feel you brotha', I feel you." Farouk wrapped an arm around Will and squeezed.

"It feels like I'm watching it for the two of us. Our favorite up-and-comers started a clan together, and my guy's been trying to earn his name all year. Now he's got his match coming up, but Natalie won't be here to watch it with me."

"So, uh… watchin' this stuff doesn't bring ye down?" Ian asked.

Will shook his head. "No. Somehow, it kind of helps."

Ian cracked open three beers and handed out one to each of them. "Aye, cheers to that, lad." Ian held his drink in the air. Farouk and Will clashed their bottles together with his. Fat red and yellow letters appeared over the goofy, dancing jester: *VICTORY!*

Maya

60

Blood Money

It was a month-long journey for the Ministry vessel to travel from Avalon to Sol, headed straight for the heart of the Dragon Claw. As they neared they got good news about the Dragon Claw attack. A digital package from Mike soon followed, giving Maya the ability to track Lazarus. Limited in capacity, the script could ping Lazarus every time he accessed the network, but it could not track his movement. Knowing Mike, Maya was sure that feature could come with time. Until then, unless he accessed his network, it was useless.

It was the fourteenth of December when Maya and Amber arrived at the Dragon's Den. They expected the *Ulfberht* to arrive in a few days. If Maya's theory about Lazarus's plans was correct, he could make his move at any moment. In her eyes, she was already out of time.

"Remember, Plunder knows me as Raven. While we're here, that's my name. In fact, most of the time that's my name. If anyone ever asks you my name, it's Raven," Maya reminded Amber, who worked to establish a connection with the Dragon's Den.

"Raven, got it. Do all pirates have a nickname? Should I come up with one?" Amber wondered how much she should reinvent herself now that she was on the run.

"Well…" Maya bobbed her head from side to side, making faces as she considered the question. "It helps me a lot since I meet people for different purposes and from different places. A nickname or an alias is a form of identity, and it helps me identify who I am to someone. How do you identify? How far away do you want to keep people? Or, how close? Why are you doing it?" The console beeped and paused her. She sat up straight, head in the game.

"Your security code and ship don't match. Identify yourself." A grim man appeared on a screen in front of them.

"My name is Raven, I borrowed the ship. I'm a friend of Plunder's. I'd like an audience." Maya kept a serious face.

"One moment." The screen switched to a blank background with 'hold' at the center.

Maya's demeanor switched back to relaxed and friendly. "Anyway, there are a lot of things to consider. But, if you're trying to hide from the UEG, you should *probably* take a new name, at least on paper. But, the farther you are from the UEG, the less you have to worry about that."

The screen switched back on and Maya faced it again, adopting a commanding stature.

"You've been cleared. Docking coordinates are being sent to you."

"Thank you."

The call ended and Amber took them out of warp. In a flash, the front screen was consumed by an expansive starbase. Parts of the Dragon's Den stretched beyond what was visible on-screen. The interconnected masses of the base were patchworked chunks of starships stitched together, jutting out in different directions. A handful of Dragon Claw ships orbited the station, but the base looked otherwise deserted.

Amber set them down at the designated coordinates on a platform with an open dome roof that awaited them. The dock recompressed and the women exited the ship into a well-lit gray room with red and yellow demarcations.

A tall man with a goatee waited for them in front of the bay's double doors. He wore a crude black leather jacket covered in patches decorated with skulls and the logos of metal bands. He had several visible piercings and a misshapen nose that had been broken several times and poorly mended. He had a mean face but a welcoming smile.

"Welcome to the Dragon's Den." His deep voice echoed off the nearby walls. The women greeted their host and with a swivel of his head, he led them out the double doors and down the hall.

After a couple turns and a jump through a zero-gravity vertical hallway, they arrived at the trolley pods. The large room was broken into two smaller sections, each of which hosted a pod the size of a van. There was enough room for eight people to sit inside, but the three of them had a pod to themselves.

The bay door opened and the pod was launched along a magnetic rail on the ceiling. Amber watched the base pass around them in wonder, laying eyes upon it for the first time. They flew from the outer edge of the base to the mass at the center, which was built around one or more asteroids. The base was abundant in sparks and construction machinery, seemingly undergoing heavy renovations.

The pod slid smoothly into a receiving room like the one from which they had launched. While the outer section of the Dragon's Den was newer and less refined, the main section of the station could easily pass for a commercial station, albeit not a wealthy one.

The silent giant led them to a banquet room with an ornate throne on a platform against the far wall with smaller chairs on either side. A second level balcony and columns wrapped around the room. A red stripe was painted in lieu of a rug from the doorway across the room and up the steps to the throne.

Upon entering the room they spotted several guards on their level as well as on the level above, each of them carrying rifles and ready for trouble. The only person in the room not standing was the man slouching on the throne.

"Raven," greeted the man with dirty black hair, face cloaked in shadow from the light above him. He wore a dark brown overcoat, black jeans, steel-toed boots, and leather gloves.

"Plunder," Maya greeted with a bow.

"I've told you before, call me Paul," he said, a weary rattle in his voice. "Why are you here?"

"If we're getting right to it, I know the Dragon Claw has been behind these attacks the last six months and you're working with a guy named Lazarus." Maya's accusation got his attention, and he sat upright. "And, I'm here to see what you can tell me about him. I can sort-of track him, but you're the best lead I've got otherwise."

Plunder shuffled in his seat with intrigue. He glanced at his guards and back at Maya, fidgeting in his seat.

"Did you say you can track him?"

"So, you're going to gloss over your attacks throughout the colonies?" Maya said. Plunder looked to the ground, then around at the guards.

"Everyone out." His booming command bounced off the walls.

Without question, the guards on both levels walked out. The doors clicked in echoes around them, and then they were alone with the leader of the Dragon Claw. There was a brief, tense silence, but Maya had an excellent poker face. Amber fidgeted, but a stern glance from Maya helped her find her nerve.

"Lazarus showed up here in June to hire us to pull off these attacks." Plunder got right to the point, nothing to hide. "He offered a shit load of money, but I turned him down. He said he wasn't going to take no for an answer. I told him to fuck off." Plunder repositioned himself with a grunt.

"So, what happened?" Maya pressed.

"Agatha was on a trip to Atlantis, where you introduced us. When her shuttle returned, Agatha and her escorts were all dead. There was blood everywhere. I could see the... pain on her face when she died..." Plunder leaned forward, elbows resting on his knees, face in his hands. "Written on the walls in her blood was a message: Nobody is untouchable." He brooded for a moment before continuing. "So, I called the collective where Agatha and I keep our kids to tell her daughter that her mother was dead. But, she wasn't there. None of our kids were."

Maya and Amber's eyes widened and the women looked at each other in alarm. The rest of the story was clear, but they dared not say a thing.

"I had barely hung up the call before I get a request to dock from Lazarus." Plunder clasped a trembling fist in front of him. "Smug son of a bitch comes in here and tells me they've got every secret Dragon Claw collective under watch, and they took the kids from me and Agatha's collective somewhere. If we tried to take our kids back, they'd die. If we tried to rescue them, kids in other collectives would die. We had to find them." Plunder's head swayed from side to side. "Nobody in the clan was willing to let any of our kids die. Lazarus still paid for every successful attack, so we performed them as instructed until we could get our kids. We thought it would be one or two, but... it took time." Even with his face covered in shadow, Plunder's regret shined through.

"I'm sorry for accusing you of working with him," Maya said. Such an accusation had surely been hurtful.

"It wasn't an unreasonable assumption," he grumbled.

"Did you rescue the kids?" Maya asked with deep concern. Plunder looked back up at her and sighed, then shook his head.

"We tried." His voice came out as little more than a trembling whisper. "We found where they had me and Agatha's kids. We moved on every collective, every single one at the same time as that last attack on Avalon. After that, he didn't need us. It was our last chance. We got most of 'em, but they killed mine before we could get 'em." Plunder's voice cracked, but he managed to keep going. "They killed my boy... and her little girl. We got the other kids out, but I failed my family." Plunder smeared his hands over his face, rubbing his eyes, sniffling. "I'm going to kill that son of a bitch." He nodded. "So, you said you can track him?"

"So to speak," Maya said. "We can get a location when he connects to his network but we can't track him in real time. Did he give you a card to reach him?"

"No." Plunder shook his head with a sniffle. "He'd contact us."

"Well, you can still help us make up for all the damage that's been done. I believe Lazarus is planning to incite a military incursion into the colonies. The Dragon Claw attacks crippled pirates and colonists and lined him up to start a war. He hasn't made his move yet, but I need to figure out what it is so we can stop him. Will you help us?"

Plunder's head drifted off as if in thought, then he turned back to Maya with a stern nod. "During the war, they leave us to starve, suffer, and kill each other to survive. They kick us to the gutter and twenty years later they decide they want the colonies, huh?" His voice was calm but trembled with a deep-seated rage. "Damn right I'll help."

He stood from his throne and sauntered down the stairs. As he walked into the light, his face came into view. He had one blue eye and one red eye with a prominent web of scars that ran down his cheek and the side of his neck. His face was pale and drooping with bags under his eyes. "If there's an incursion into the colonies, we'll be the first ones they come after."

Maya walked toward him, stopping an arm's length away. "Ternarians suffered the worst during the war. You lost your eye, I lost my brother, we were all lied to, and it's all because of people like him; heartless people who think that everyone is expendable as long as they get what they want. Let's find him, and *end* him." Maya's vicious eyes swirled with a bloodthirsty shadow. A fire in Plunder's eye fixed on something far away, then wavered.

"What is it?"

"I uh… I sent a ship to follow him. Our ship with the best long range sensors," he admitted.

"How did you follow him? What happened?" Maya leaned in.

"Put a bug on his ship. But, we haven't heard back. Their last known position was in the asteroid belt." In his mourning, Plunder had forgotten about the ship until then.

"Seems like as good a place to start as any," Maya said.

"How about we go with some of our ships, just in case. Your little shuttle can't handle trouble if you find it," Plunder teased, clearing his throat and fixing himself up to look more presentable. "But, I'm skinning the son of a bitch alive when we find him."

Maya

61

Chasing Shadows

Heading to the bridge of Plunder's capital ship, the *Minokawa*, Maya's train of thought was broken by Amber calling her name from behind.

"Ma—" Amber almost called her the wrong name. "Raven, I have a question I've been wanting to ask." Amber's jog turned into a stroll alongside Maya. "I've heard of food collectives. Out here, what is a collective?"

"Oh!" Maya snapped her fingers. Amber was new to life outside of Earth, and this was the first knowledge gap she had encountered. "Pirates don't carry their kids with them on their ships, neither do merchants or smugglers or the like. So, if they don't have any family to leave them with, they leave them in a collective. Collectives are full of kids whose parents are gone for months at a time. Some are public. Others, like the Dragon Claw collectives, are strongly guarded secrets."

"Thanks. I got the gist of the conversation but I wasn't clear on that." Amber looked to the ground, imagining how the Dragon Claw must have felt with all of the clan's children held hostage. That would drive any decent parent to insanity.

The bridge doors opened for them, bringing Amber's attention back to the world around her. Plunder glanced over his shoulder to see who had entered.

"You know, you'd think there'd be more asteroids in the asteroid belt." Plunder stood a few steps away from his seat, arms crossed, face stern.

"It's a planet worth of asteroids scattered around the entire orbit, they're more sprinkled than clustered," Maya explained.

"Yeah, that's what Lore said." Plunder watched the bridge's front screen like something was about to pop out of it. A menagerie of stars dominated the screen, but there was nothing of interest.

"Who is Lore?" Maya asked.

"My Digital Security Chief. Lore!" Plunder called out.

"Hey there," called a voice nearby. Maya searched for it and found a middle-aged Latin man with long hair, a goatee, and a leathery battle-worn face. He gave her a wave and turned back to his console.

"We're pulling up on an asteroid with a trajectory that lines up with our coordinates and timestamp," Plunder said. The ship's lights brought into view a lumpy, lifeless brown asteroid, spinning alone in the abyss.

"Do you think there's anyone home?" Amber stepped toward the screen.

"Sure as hell hope so. Lore," Plunder called.

"Yeah, I got ya, boss. There's definitely a base down there, under the rock. It's hard to tell what's inside."

Plunder stepped to his chair and tapped an icon on the arm.

"Boarding party A, suit up. You're going to clear the path for me and a team. Lore, I want you with me. Raven, you coming?"

"Mind if we *both* come?" Maya gestured to Amber, sure that she would not like to be left alone, surrounded by pirates.

"The more the merrier." Plunder left the bridge, Lore only a few steps behind him.

Maya and Amber borrowed space suits to join Plunder and a half dozen well-armed men and women on the unassuming asteroid. There was a shallow cave with a large metal wall, thick and sturdy. Lore disabled the security system and the group descended into the hidden base. They passed through the airlock into a vast steel-walled room complete with artificial gravity.

The inside lit up as the group removed their helmets. Some people set them down while others carried it with them while they explored the large room. It was a laboratory or workshop. There were connected rooms with metal desks covered in wires, parts, and lab equipment. Drawn to the chemicals, Amber looked through the well-labeled vials and bottles until Maya's voice carried from deeper in the hideout.

"We've got some bodies over here."

Amber carefully set the vials down and joined Maya. She arrived alongside another pirate. Plunder was flipping one of the two bodies over.

"These guys seem familiar," Amber said, a strange feeling pulling at her gut.

"They aren't dressed like Ministry. Colonials?" Maya speculated.

"I wouldn't recognize them if they were from the colonies." Amber shook her head. "Does someone have a device with a secure connection? I haven't got one yet."

"I got you." Lore pulled a tablet from his backpack and handed it to her, slinging the pack back over his shoulder. Amber got to work searching on the tablet while the others investigated further.

"Look at these entry wounds." Plunder turned one body's head to emphasize the wound. "These guys were executed."

"They became loose ends." Maya shook her head, feeling sorry for the poor scientists. Had circumstances and timing been different, could she have saved them?

"The wounds are recent too." Plunder let the head go limp and it rolled back into place. "Someone was here *recently*. My guess is someone will be by to clean this up soon. They probably intend on using this place again."

"That's not a bad thought. We should do our work and get out of here as quick as we can. Maybe put your ship on alert." Maya said.

"I notice a lot of the machinery here is for precision work. Blondie here was checking out chemicals in the other room, too." Lore gestured to the dead bodies. "Counting the two stiffs, that's a bad combination of things to be in one place."

"I got it. Missing persons from Earth early this year." Amber tapped on the tablet to bring up holograms of the banners for the missing scientists. "It was a big deal for a while, then people kind of forgot about it. Their faces were all over the place, though."

Maya stood up with her hands on her hips, eyeing the corpses. Nothing they were finding was good. "Let's figure out what they were making here. Plunder, have your ships keep an eye out."

Plunder's order came in the simple form of a look to one of his crew. With a nod, the crewman stepped away and contacted the ship.

Maya, Amber, and Lore examined what was left in the base. It took them almost an hour to come to a conclusion. Plunder paced around the group, listening keenly until they agreed.

"You guys sayin' these guys made a bomb?" He stepped into the group, hoping he heard them incorrectly.

"No, *bombs*, multiple," Maya corrected him.

"How many you think they made?" Plunder asked. His crew's body language echoed his concern. They had also been listening, pacing and shuffling about, now moving in closer.

"Two, Four, maybe more? Can't really tell. It depends on the yield." Lore tossed aside some scraps.

"They made multiple bombs, we need to figure out possible targets. We can discuss the details on the ship, though. Let's see where those other locations take us," Maya said.

After clearing his throat, Plunder looked around at his crew and boomed, "Let's move out."

Ulfberht Crew

62

One Way Trip

DECEMBER EIGHTEENTH AT FIFTEEN MINUTES TO MIDNIGHT, Eastern European Earth time, Mike, Nikolai, Shin, Farouk, and James stood around the table of the *Ulfberht's* dimly-lit war room. A hologram of the secret Ministry base they planned to attack hovered in the middle of the group. Each of them was armored up, double-checking their equipment.

Adam Ward had gifted them with custom blasters for their mission with non-lethal attachments, at Mike's request. With no desire to carry such a large weapon, Farouk asked for something smaller. Adam made him a powered down version resembling a bulky pistol.

While Nikolai stuffed explosives into a small pack, Mike flipped up a console on the table and held a finger down on the console. "Hey, Al, we're in the *Ulfberht's* War Room, could you set the entry coordinates here instead of the usual place?" He let his finger off and continued checking his equipment. After a moment the console beeped and Mike played a message from Al.

"It will take a minute to adjust."

"In the meantime," Mike said, "let's run through it one more time before we go."

"We enter base through portal into storage room." Nikolai zoomed in on the entry room.

"We toss a holo-projector through the portal to hide us from any cameras and I disable the base's security system," Mike said.

"I take access tunnels to level's power station and destroy it, forcing them to backup power." Nikolai slung the bag of explosives over his shoulder.

"I take the access tunnels to the security room, crippling it at the source." Shin clipped his new railgun onto his back.

"Farouk and I stay with the Captain," James added.

"You snatch a guard and I patch us into their system to keep us two steps ahead," Mike said.

"Then we scoop up Hope and put a hurtin' on anyone that gets in our way." Farouk nodded confidently, punching his palm in anticipation of the fight to come.

"The only hitch is the single shaft of elevators we have to take to the hangar where I steal us a ride home," Mike finished.

"That's what grenades and explosives are for. Easy peasy." James shoved his pistol into a holster, clipping it shut.

"Fingers crossed. The last bunker we hit went smoothly, let's hope this one goes the same." While Mike made sure his tablet was ready, the desk beeped. "I've got a message from Will." The message was titled, GLHF, so Mike played it for the room.

"Hey Captain, I wanted to wish you luck on your rescue mission. I'll see you guys when you get back." The hologram of a cartoon thumbs-up sprang to life before them then faded away after a few seconds, and the message ended.

"Aw, Will's a good kid." Mike smiled and took a deep breath, swelling with confidence. "Everyone ready to go?"

"We are ready, comrade," Nikolai nodded.

"Let loose the mothafuckin' dogs of war already." Anxious to begin their assault, Farouk bounced in place with a grin.

"Oh yeah, I'm ready." James affectionately rubbed the upgraded arm piece Sam had added to his suit.

"You use that thing on me, I'm kickin' your ass." Farouk raised a threatening fist in the air, rousing a chuckle from James.

"I can't thank you guys enough for this, for putting your lives on the line to help me rescue my daughter, not just this time but all the times before this. For the years you've dedicated to this ship, this crew, and to me. And, I should say something rousing, but I'm a computer guy. I don't do speeches. Let's do what we usually do: keep a level head on our shoulders and kick a lot of ass. Everyone good with that?" Mike held out a thumbs-up and the team jokingly cheered and applauded his speech.

An alert popped up on his console, a message from Al. *"Ze portal is ready. Good luck, mein friend."*

"That took more than a minute, old man," Farouk grumbled.

"I'm with you there." Mike tapped a button on the console, then shut down the hologram. They strapped on helmets and readied their rifles, facing the door.

Between them and the door appeared a speck of light that expanded into a bright, nebulous ring. As it expanded, Mike tossed a holo-emitter through the ring. Through it was a dark storage closet with tall shelves stacked with office supplies and boxes. Taken aback, James curiously examined the ring of smoke curling in on itself. It had begun forming as a circle, but when it reached the floor the smoke squished against it as if it was physical.

"Okay, let's do this." Mike took a deep breath, staring into the storage room, then readied his rifle. "Shin."

Shin leaped through the portal, cloaked, then scouted the room. "All clear."

One by one, the team stepped through the portal, staying low. An astonished James was last, watching the portal shrink to a point and disappear like a hologram, leaving them in darkness.

"Trippy."

"Give me a sec to lock things down." Mike sat down and gestured with his thumbs and index fingers to form a square, then pulled them apart. A holographic screen appeared in front of him and he got to work. It was a quiet few minutes. There was nothing anyone could do but wait, crouched and huddled together in a dark storage closet.

"Does the *Ministry* even have tech like that?" James could not contain his amazement at what he had experienced.

"Nah, only us." Farouk answered for the others.

"Okay, we're good." Mike closed his screen. "I got us schematics, too. Looks like this level is a little different than the others."

The group stood up and spread out, stretching their legs. Mike had turned off the motion sensors, so the lights remained off. Any curious passerby who saw the lights on might be drawn to it, and it was best to minimize risk.

"There's a massive habitat in the middle of it." Mike studied the map while the others stretched. "I think we picked the right spot. Let's get going. The hatch should be over there." Mike picked up the holo-emitter and pointed to the far side of the room. They moved to the maintenance hatch. Shin pulled it off the wall and examined the tunnel. "It will be tight for Nikolai."

"Usually, she does not mind." Nikolai chuckled and sauntered to the open hatch.

"Good luck." Shin rushed into the tunnels on all fours, speeding to his destination. Nikolai examined the hatch then readied himself to enter, turning to Mike.

"See you soon, comrade."

"Be careful out there," Mike said. Nikolai hurried into the tunnels and Mike closed the hatch behind him.

Palms sweating in his gloves, bones shaking, the butterflies in Mike's gut spun into a blizzard of tiny daggers that made his stomach churn. This bunker was massive compared to the one they had attacked that summer, and this mission was the culmination of ten years of his life.

Nothing before this moment had ever been as important. Finally, he would set his little girl free.

Mike sat in place and began to work while James and Farouk watched the entrance. After a few minutes, Shin checked in that he was in position. A minute later, Nikolai. They waited for Mike, who cleared his throat when he was done.

"Ready." Mike took a long, deep breath to calm his nerves. "Security system is going down in five, four, three, two, one." He pressed the button and the screen changed, spitting out several lines of code and finally a confirmation that the security systems had been shut down. "Off."

James crept to the door and peeked through the tall, rectangular window. The elevators were a round batch of four in the center of a spacious walkway. They waited for an update from their team for what seemed like an eternity. Three minutes after Mike turned off the security, the building shook and the power went out. The level went dark, light from the hall no longer streaming into the room. A moment later, blue emergency lights lit up.

On the other side of the elevators, well-armored personnel rushed by. "More coming your way, Shin. Heavy armah."

"Thank you."

"Let's go. We need to nab a security guard," Mike said. He rushed to the door behind James, Farouk nearby.

"Hey'a Farouk, you don't have any military experience, do ya?" James asked.

"Nah, but I'm pretty much bulletproof."

"That's what I thought. I'll take point, you watch the rear. If someone comes up behind us, be bulletproof."

"Sounds good to me."

James nudged the door open and raised his rifle, scanning the perimeter. They were alone in the dim blue hall. He ticked his head for Mike and Farouk to follow. With the security system down, there were no alarms. It was an eerie silence, but helpful, making it easier to hear the rushing boots of security. In that section, the rooms had no windows, only chrome handrails and directions to different rooms at the junctions.

Creeping quietly down the hall, the pitter-patter of a single pair of boots echoed behind them. They hurried around the corner and listened to them grow closer. Rushed, heavy, combat boots were accompanied by the jingle of armor and metal attachments.

When the steps rushed around the corner, James jammed a sleeper into his neck and dragged him to the floor. The guard struggled but soon fell into a deep slumber. James unclipped his helmet and tossed it to his teammates. Farouk snatched it out of the air and handed it to Mike. He sat against the wall and opened his holographic interface, plucking an icon from the side. As he pulled the icon away, it transformed into a holographic cord and he touched it to the helmet.

James dragged the body near them, anticipating another lengthy and dangerous wait while Mike worked, but in less than thirty seconds, Mike closed his interface.

"Done. We're invisible, but we can see them. Let's keep moving."

"It'll be nice being on the otha' side 'a this."

Moving through the halls was easy once they knew where security was. To minimize their suspicion of his digital malfeasance, he kept their functions operational. He sent fake orders, moving troops out of their path as much as possible.

"*I have a problem,*" Shin groaned into the channel.

"Copy that, Shin. What is it?" Mike asked.

"*I've encountered a golem.*"

"Shit." Mike's pace slowed to a full stop.

"*So, Lazarus is here,*" Nikolai said.

"Shin, get somewhere safe. Don't engage the golem without Farouk." Mike stepped his pace back up, running down the hall. "Rendezvous with us."

"*Copy,*" Shin said in relief, eager to put some distance between him and the mindless cyborg.

Sprinting down the halls at breakneck speeds, their path clear of security, they paused only to deal with a small group of scientists they crashed into. James's sleepers knocked them out and they were off again.

They reached a long, empty hallway with a single door on one wall. A large porthole in the thick, titanium door was the only window in the hall. Below the porthole was a steel plaque with a black background and silver lettering.

Subject 319

Mike searched for a console with which to open the door, but there was none. There was no doorknob, lever or anything. He peeked into the colossal room, trying to see inside. It was a messy lounge with clothes strewn about. There was a couch, a television, and stairs to a second level. On the far side was a shelf filled to the brim with board games.

"I'll get the two we've got coming." James jogged down the hall to deal with the incoming security guards.

THWACK!

Mike jumped, his attention shooting back to the porthole. With a gasp, his mouth dropped and his eyes grew three sizes.

On the other side of the glass was a fourteen-year-old girl with thin lips and sparkling blue eyes. Wavy, blonde hair cascaded over her shoulders like a waterfall. Mike put his hand to the glass and leaned in. A spitting image of her mother, she smiled at him, and tears welled up in his eyes.

"Dad!" she yelled, overjoyed to see her dad's face with her own eyes. But, it was inaudible through the thick door. Mike cringed with a pang of sadness. Her head tilted, then understanding washed over her face and she reached a hand out to touch the glass, closing her eyes. Mike touched his hand to the glass, overwhelmed by the moment. Then, her head lifted, she looked him in the eyes and spoke again. *Dad?*

This time, her voice echoed in his mind. He took a deep, stuttered breath. "Hope. I'm here, baby. I'll get you out of here."

Her smile was a ray of sunshine beaming into his heart. Mike went to open his interface, but she stopped him.

It won't work! It's analog now. The switch is in the control room.

"Shit." He could not hack an analog system and the control room was two floors up on the other side of the level. Preparations had been made to specifically counter his skillset. Someone knew he was coming.

"Michael," Lazarus said over the intercom like they were old friends. *"I was beginning to think you wouldn't show."*

Mike's stomach dropped like an anchor and a chill of terror crawled up his spine.

"I have to say, you caught me off guard. How did you get in here? Wait, don't answer that. I can't hear you anyway." His voice boomed in the empty hallway alongside the clicking of James's footsteps upon his return.

"Guys we've got security coming from all around us," James said.

"Someone ran your DNA through the ministry a few months ago, and I haven't heard from Bradley in quite a while now. But, when Agent Jones confirmed you're alive, I thought it might be safe to move your little girl before you come charging in, but I took precautions just in case," Lazarus blared in the background, in love with the sound of his voice.

"Damnit," Mike grumbled. "Farouk, can you punch through this thing?"

"I could try, but I don't think so." Farouk shook his head, stepping forward to look through the porthole. "This thing is more than a meter thick." He rapped his knuckles against the door.

"I'm a fan of trying." Mike threw his hands up in the air, then leaned into the porthole again. "Hope, sweetie, stand back, and to the side."

Hope nodded and hurried away from the door. Farouk took a step back and balled up his right fist. Like a statue brought to life, his back foot planted, Farouk shot forward and plowed a big right fist into the door.

Light cracks crept into the porthole glass and the metal dented, but the door was largely unaffected. Hope's return to the porthole was met with a look of disappointment on Mike's face.

"Sorry, brotha'."

"I'm coming back for you!" Mike put his hand to the glass. Hope put her hand over his, smiling with watery eyes.

I know you will.

Mike ran off while he still had the courage to leave her there. Fired up, anger boiling under the surface, Mike pushed the pace as he ran with no destination. The control room was two floors up on the other side of the level.

"Michael," Nikolai called. *"I have an idea. Come to secondary control room."* A pin appeared on their maps, which Mike and his team followed. Small groups of security were easily dispatched. As much as Mike wanted to head for the main control room as per his daughter's directions, if he was to raid it he needed to do so with Nikolai's mind and experience at his side.

Nikolai's pin led them not to the secondary control room, but to the nearby restroom where Nikolai and Shin waited. Shin's helmet was cracked and his suit was repairing itself, but several parts were broken or crushed and one of the thrusters had come off. His brief encounter with the golem had gone poorly. Security rushed by, their stampeding footsteps a dull murmur. The restrooms had the added benefit of muffling Lazarus's obnoxious and ceaseless pontificating.

The plan involved them splitting into two teams to attack the secondary control room. Outside the control room, Mike opened his interface and prepared to open the doors for them. He grabbed the holographic button and closed everything else, readying his rifle.

"On go. Three, two, one." Mike pressed the button, opening both doors. "Go."

Shin darted into the room, killing the nearest guards. The others drew their weapons, but not before the rest of the team charged into the room, guns blazing. Some of the staff tried to grab pistols hidden under the desks or call for help, but it was all over in a few seconds.

"We have few minutes before they come for us," Nikolai said.

"This will only take two seconds, I already did most of it outside." Mike's interface was already open and he had got to work on his task.

"When you finish, take Shin and Farouk with you to control room, James and I will retrieve Hope." Nikolai motioned for James to move out.

Ulfberht Crew

63

Cornered

"ASSAULT TEAM, CHECKING IN, READY TO BREACH AUXILIARY control room." A squad of armored security with railguns had split into two groups and gathered on either side of the room. The security force spoke Russian, relying on translators to facilitate their communication with Lazarus.

"Breach when ready," Lazarus responded. *"And, fire at will."*

The squad leader began the assault. The doors shot open and canisters rolled into the room, emitting black smoke from both ends. The teams rushed into the auxiliary control room, scanning it for targets. Only the dead bodies of their own personnel greeted them. The doors closed automatically.

"They're not here." The squad leader searched the room. "Check our perimeter." Some of his troops hustled to the doors, tapping on the console, but there was no response. They tapped the consoles several more times, but the doors did not open.

"Control, this is Assault Team leader. We're locked in here, could you unlock the doors for us?" He paused, waiting for a response. "Control."

The channel remained silent, but the connection was open. "Control, are you reading me?"

Both sets of doors to the main control room burst open and Mike, Shin, and Farouk rushed in from both sides. Security and staff drew weapons to defend themselves but they were too slow. Within seconds, the room's occupants were on the floor and they searched the bodies for Lazarus. They opened closed eyelids but found no red irises.

"He's not here. Watch your ass, Nikolai." Mike paced in frustration, then recalled their objective. "Find the switch."

"We are in position," Nikolai whispered. *"But, there is a team here extracting her. James is circling around. I do not see Lazarus or his golem."*

"Golem came out of nowhere for me. Keep your eyes open," Shin said.

"If they're already there, we don't need to be here to flip the switch. We're on our way, Nikolai," Mike said.

"No, wait,"

"What? Why?" Mike stopped, head shaking.

"Because there is no cover in this hallway. Stay by the switch. I will tell you when to press it."

Shin and Farouk guarded the room's entrances while Mike waited by the switch.

A trio of scientists dragged Hope out of the habitat, protected by a small squad of guards. She kicked and flailed as they struggled for every meter they moved her. She threw elbows, fists, kicks, and even bit at the scientists. Vicious and unrelenting, the scientists urged her to stop.

"Stop it! Why are you behaving like this? Young lady, I'm going to sedate you!" A female scientist shouted, her frustration bleeding through in her tone. After Hope kicked her in the face, she had no patience left and pulled out a tear-shaped sleeper.

"In position," James checked in as the scientist tried to grab her leg to inject her.

"Switch to non-lethal and attack!" Nikolai ordered.

From either side of the hallway, Nikolai and James opened fire.

The scientists ducked, dodging shots whizzing over their head while they worked to restrain Hope. The guards formed a semi-circle around them, firing back in both directions. The ministry woman with the sleeper finally got control of her leg and looked back at her with contempt.

"Get *away* from me!" Hope boomed, looking her dead in the eye.

The woman shot to her feet and backed up. She dropped the sleeper and ran away murmuring, "get away get away get away."

Hope and the other two ministry personnel froze in surprise and watched her run. One confused guard watched her run away and James shot him in the neck. The guard collapsed to the floor, shaking from the shock of the non-lethal round.

They snapped out of their daze and the woman scrambled for the sleeper as Hope flailed, elbowing the man in the face. He stumbled back with blood gushing from his nose. James kept him from pursuing Hope with some steady rifle fire. Hope tackled the other scientist to the ground and held her wrist back with both hands.

"Stop *resisting!*" The woman pushed Hope away with her free arm. Hope bit her and flailed her legs, getting in a lucky gut shot. With the woman's grip loosened, she took the sleeper from her and jammed it into her shoulder.

"Never!" Hope squeezed down the button and scrambled to her feet. The scientist reached an arm out but fell unconscious. Hope sprinted away along the wall.

"James, push them into the room!" Nikolai ordered. Once Hope cleared his line of fire, James switched to lethal fire and a storm of crackling light erupted from his blaster. The guards hurried into the habitat for cover, dragging their sleeping comrades.

"Michael, close the door!" Nikolai ordered. Mike hit the switch and hurried out of the control room to meet them.

Inside the habitat, an alarm sounded and the door began its slow journey to closure. They fired at the entry until the giant door slid shut, sealing them in.

Hope crossed the hall and turned the corner. The skinny girl crashed into James and bounced off his massive, unmoving frame, then scurried behind him.

"Hey! It's okay, I'm with your dad," James said.

"I know! Oh my god, did you see that?" she asked. "She did what I said! I've only done that with small animals. I didn't even do it on purpose!" the skinny teenager rambled, staring off into space as if listening to something.

"What are you talkin' about?" James looked at her, perplexed. Gunfire from the far side of the hall caught his attention. On his mini-map, Nikolai moved away, but there was no security near him. "Look, we gotta get you outta here." James grabbed her upper arm to usher her away, but she did not move.

"They figured out you're in their helmets so they're taking them off. You can't see where they are anymore. There's more coming from that way." Hope pointed in the direction James had wanted to go. "We need to go this way." She ran off the other way without waiting for James.

"I guess what they said about you is true." James caught up to run next to her.

"Yep."

"Hey'a Mike, ya girl here says they figured out they're hacked and took off their helmets. You might have incomin'."

"Thanks for the heads up. Take care of my little girl."

"Will do, boss man." James followed Hope around a corner. "Nikolai, we're headed fa' the South hall."

"Good. I'm taking the back way to you," Nikolai updated him.

"Let's take the maintenance shafts to the elevators and wait for them to rendezvous with us there," Mike said.

"I'll draw security away from that area," Shin said.

"Copy that."

"Why does Shin get to have all the fun?" Farouk joked.

Hope stopped in the middle of a junction and James alongside her. She took deep, heaving breaths and spun in a circle. With a wince, she clasped her head with both hands. "They're so loud. Coming from everywhere." Her head swiveled from side to side. "Over here." She ran into a nearby storage room. James closed the door behind them. He found her nearby, removing a hatch to get into the maintenance shafts.

"We takin' the shafts to the elevators too?" James whispered.

"No. I'm not the only science experiment here. We need to go down a level." Hope crawled into the tunnel on all fours. "Come on."

"Woah, the bottom level is off-limits." James leaned into the tunnel, still trying to whisper. "We can't go down there."

"It's the only way we're getting out alive with that Golem here." Hope crawled down the tunnel without looking back.

"Shit." James glanced between the door and the shaft, then crawled in feet-first to close it behind them. "Nikolai, change of plan. We're going down a level." James slid himself back down the shaft, hoping for a junction to turn himself around.

"Copy. See you there." Nikolai did not question it. *"Michael, please disable security for the entire facility."*

"You got it. Be careful down there."

Ulfberht Crew

64

Unleashed

Hope led James through the maintenance shafts into a rectangular room with entrances on the short ends. It was empty aside from a thick door in the middle of a long wall. They were surrounded by metal panels and hatches leading to various access tunnels, compartments, and machinery.

"This must be the hub of all the electrical systems passin' between each section. Probably makes it easier to service." James spun in a circle, examining the secluded room that only construction crews and engineers had ever laid eyes upon. Hope walked to the middle of the room and stood in front of a windowless steel door with a simple plaque.

Maintenance Access
Level 6
Subject 57b

"Fifty-seven?" James wondered. "Yours was three-nineteen. Are you guys numbered sequentially?"

"Yeah." Hope leaned back against the wall by the console, hunched over with her arms crossed.

"Wouldn't that make this guy really old?"

Hope turned to James with a smirk. "Yep. You're not going to tell me not to hunch?"

"It ain't good for ya spine, but you can do what you want. So, how many—"

Clank!

James nestled his rifle into his shoulder and aimed it at the other entrance, jumping at the clamor.

"It's okay," Hope said.

The door burst open and Nikolai barged in.

"Comrades!" He threw his hands out towards them. Then, his eyes fell upon Hope and he removed his helmet. A whirlwind of affection flooded from Nikolai and he opened his arms. "Oh, malenkiy angel. I have not seen you since you were a little baby."

Hope did not know who he was, but a deep love for her spilled from him alongside vivid memories of her as a baby. She ran at him and jumped into a hug, nestling her face into his chest.

That feeling. It was love. Real, genuine love, up close. It was no wonder it shined so brightly.

"Are you my uncle?"

"I am your godfather, but you can call me Uncle Nikolai if you'd like."

"What's a godfather?" she asked.

Nikolai released his warm embrace and placed his hands on her shoulders. "If your father dies, it is my responsibility to take care of you."

"Oh, so you're like my second dad. Cool!" A brilliant smile spread across her face and she hugged him again. She had been well treated, but after she gleaned from one of the scientists that she was kidnapped, her attitude toward her captors changed, and she had been increasingly solitary since. Imprisoned her whole life, she knew the concepts of family, but never first hand until that moment. "I have *two* dads!"

While Nikolai was warmed by her words, James had to hold back a tear, heart squeezed by grief's clawed hand. Matt flashed in his mind. James's birthday had been three days prior, but he told not one. It was his first without Matt to celebrate with him.

"I like this feeling," she said. A few seconds later she let go of Nikolai and looked over her shoulder at James. Then, she walked across the room, wrapped her arms around him and whispered, "I'm sorry about Matt."

"Don't worry about it. It's not your fault." James patted her back and shuffled until she let go.

"Okay, what now? Where are we going?" Nikolai asked to get them on task, counting on Hope having a reason for guiding them there. This was home and her abilities could warn them of danger.

"I heard the code for these places from one of the maintenance people." Hope hurried to the door in the middle of the room. "Those people think *so* loud." She entered the passcode and the door clicked open. She bounced with excitement and hurried inside. Nikolai and James followed her into the depths of level six.

The doorway led to stairs and a similar room one level down. From there, Hope guided them through the maintenance shafts into a vacant laboratory. After closing up the wall panel, she led them through the halls. She warned them of an incoming scientist, whom they suppressed, dragging his unconscious body out of sight.

It was not long before they entered a room two floors high, designed around a tall, liquid-filled cylinder with a youthful, muscular man inside. A face mask and a helmet with a cloudy transparent tube encasing a bundle of wires were strapped to him. At the foot of the chamber was a rectangular space with a meter-and-a-half-tall barrier that terminated in a semi-circle.

The single scientist in the room sat at a desk with her back to them. She checked to see who entered, scrambling to her feet at the sight of armed strangers.

"Don't move." James aimed his rifle at her. The woman glanced between them and a nearby alarm button. "Don't do it," James warned, but the woman darted for it.

She slammed her hand down on the button and looked around, confused when nothing happened, unaware the base's security systems had been shut down. The trio crossed the room toward her. Trembling, the woman put her hands up.

"If you listened, I would have let you sit first." James jammed the sleeper into her neck and she crashed to the floor, unconscious.

Hope found a console and began typing. Not a minute later, she hurried to the edge of the barrier next to Nikolai and James and pulled two towels from a cabinet. A soft alert sounded and then the water drained from the tube, rushing into the irrigated barrier below. When the water level passed under the man's waist, the helmet and face mask unbuckled automatically and he sank into the rushing water.

"You guys should take off your helmets. He'll like you more."

Nikolai and James looked at each other. With a shrug, they removed their helmets and laid them on a table nearby.

The giant naked man washed into the barrier's terminus with a grunt, water draining away around him. He squirmed, lurching out of his slumber, rolling onto his hands and knees. Reaching up to lean against the wall, he pulled himself to his feet. As he rose, so too did Nikolai and James's chins, their heads tilting back to look up at the behemoth.

The herculean juggernaut stretched and cracked his back, rubbed his eyes, and moved his jaw around as if to stretch it. With a yawn, he examined the people before him. He looked upon James and Nikolai with neither aggression nor concern, but his eyes lit up at the sight of Hope.

"Hope! You've grown so much!"

"Uncle Slayer! It's so good to see you!" She threw the towels at him.

"It's good to see you, too." Slayer rubbed the towels all over himself and tossed them over the edge of the barrier. "All right, bring it in!" He leaned over the edge of the barrier and twirled his hands in the air. She jumped into a big bear hug, his muscular arms enveloping her. "How old are you now? You were eleven the last time, right?"

"Yep! I'm fourteen now." Hope's posture was better, and she smiled.

Her entire demeanor improved in his presence. "I'm sorry for waking you up. This is my godfather, Nikolai, and this is James."

"Great to meet you guys. I don't remember my name, people call me Slayer. I guess it's a nickname I got before my early memories got... scrambled."

"You mind if I ask how old you are?" James asked, eager to settle his curiosity.

"I don't remember what year it is. I was born in twenty-twenty. I see the Boston accent hasn't changed one bit." He smiled, pointing at James.

"Holy shit, yeah." James nodded, amazed at the relic towering before him. "Nikolai, he's a hundred and sixty-four years old."

"Yes, James, I know math." Nikolai looked over at James, then back to Slayer. "So, you are *Uncle* Slayer? You slay uncles, huh?"

Slayer chuckled with a nod, smiling at happy memories. "Yeah. They woke me up one time and said that they needed to do some maintenance for a few months but someone was living in my habitat. I wasn't too happy about having a roommate until they walked her in here. She was four, and so damn cute. They told me her family's dead, so I told her she could call me uncle. They wake me up once in a while and we get to visit. I see you take your duties as godfather seriously. That's goddamn righteous. Good man."

"Her father is not dead. We are here with him to retrieve her," Nikolai clarified.

"Oh, what? Your dad's not dead?"

"No! He's been looking for me for years. I found out he was alive a few months ago!" Hope bounced with excitement, a smile stretching from one ear to the other.

"What about your mom?"

"The UEG are the ones responsible for her death," Nikolai said.

"Sons of bitches!" Slayer leaned on the barrier shaking his head. He balled up a fist but relaxed quickly. "That's messed up. But, I'm glad she's got a family that's willing to break her out like this. This little girl deserves it. Shit, you guys even brought her here to say goodbye."

"I'm not here to say goodbye."

"Oh, Hope." Slayer shook his head. "I can't go with you. That's not my world up there. There's nothing for me. You go ahead. I'll be fine."

"No, I mean, only if you want. But, we need your help to get out of here. I know you like… hate the world, and think it sucks, but I've never seen it. I've never hugged my dad. I've lived here my whole life, learning about what's going on out there, watching movies, thinking I'm here for my own safety when I'm actually a prisoner. You can come back if you want. I just want to be free."

Slayer sighed, looking down at the floor, shaking his head. If he did not help, he would deprive her of a life. He would condemn her to live as a lab rat, living underground, treated as property. This was her chance to escape and forge her own future.

"I'm going to need some pants."

With an oversized smile, Hope ran off to find a change of clothes, leaving the three men alone. There was a brief, awkward silence. James looked around the room, and his brand caught Slayer's attention.

"Mind if I ask about those tats on your necks?"

"Our brands?" asked James. "They represent genetic potential."

"Wow," Slayer said wide-eyed. "That's some good ole' *Nineteen Eighty-Four, Brave New World* shit right there, huh?"

"What happened in nineteen eighty-four?" Nikolai asked.

"Uh…" Slayer glanced between the two curious faces looking back at him. "Never mind, don't worry about it."

Hope returned with a change of clothes, which was always ready in a room nearby. Wearing jeans with combat boots and a Pink Floyd shirt stretched to its limit, Slayer accompanied them to the elevators. A single one of the four elevators was the size of a small room and could hold more than a dozen people. Most notably, Slayer could stand in it without slouching.

When the elevator doors swooshed open, a dim blue light shined on Mike and Farouk waiting on the other side. Mike hastily removed his helmet, his eyes met Hope's and they rushed toward each other.

They crashed together and squeezed as hard as they could, holding on as if letting go would mean certain death. Mike could not find words for everything rushing through his mind. Should he simply say 'hello'? Should he apologize and explain why he has not been there her whole life? Should he tell her how good it is to see her again? To hear her voice and hold her close like when she was a baby?

"They told me you were dead," she whimpered.

"I'm sorry. I'm sorry I haven't been here."

"It's okay. I understand. Uncle Slayer said it would take an army to get in here, but you came for me."

Mike reluctantly pulled out of the hug and faced the leviathan standing nearby.

"Slayer. Nice to meet you," he introduced himself, shaking Mike's hand.

"Mike. You're a friend?"

"Oh, yeah. I've known Hope since she was four. They've been doing all kinds of renovations to these bottom two levels so they've been waking me up a lot the last few years. I'm here to help you get her out."

"Thank you. We appreciate the assist. What exactly do you bring to the table?"

"Let's take this thing up to the top. When we get there, you guys stay here while I take care of the guards." Slayer waved his hand around as if pointing at guards. The ordeal was little more than a formality to him.

A quick patter of feet grew louder, ending with Shin's arrival.

"All right. It's a pleasure making your acquaintance. This is Farouk and Shin." Mike introduced them with a nod over each shoulder.

"Pleasure to meet you guys. How about we get this party movin'?" Slayer said.

"Couldn't agree more. Let's go." Mike moved aside so the others could enter.

Even with everyone aboard, the ride was so smooth there was no sense of acceleration or deceleration. They arrived at the hangar level with a soft ding.

"I'm going to give them a chance to run away," Slayer said.

"They are Russian." Nikolai grunted, head shaking. "They will not surrender."

"Well, that sucks for them."

The double doors slid open and Slayer stepped out into the well-lit lobby. Over two dozen security lined both levels of the room guarding the elevators, rifles trained on Slayer. Mike closed the doors behind him. The lobby's acoustics made it easy for them to listen in on the conversation, especially with security yelling at Slayer.

"Don't move! Identify yourself!" A guard on the second level yelled in Russian, his voice booming from his helmet's speaker. Unlike the security forces, however, Slayer did not have a translator of any kind. So to him, it was just incomprehensible shouting.

"Let's all calm down," Slayer put his hands in the air, looking around both levels of guards, armed to the teeth and locked on him. "I'm the experiment from level six. I want to give you guys a chance to put down your weapons and lock yourselves in that room right there." Slayer pointed at a nearby room. Some of the men chuckled. The commanding officer's body language and a shake of his head communicated his disbelief.

"We don't know anything about the contents of this facility. Return to where you came from immediately," the commander ordered. Again, Slayer did not understand. He looked around at them, gauging their response to be uncooperative.

"They say go back to where you came from," Nikolai shouted through the doors.

"Kind of figured it was something like that," Slayer said, disappointed. "Sorry guys. That's not going to happen. I'm going to demolish everybody that stands between me and the docking bay, so this is your chance to uh... not die."

"You may be big, but you are unarmed. We are in armor, we have guns, and there are more of us. Go back now, this facility is on lockdown," the security officer commanded, this time with a gesture of his rifle.

"They told me to go fuck myself, right?" Slayer asked over his shoulder.

"More or less," Nikolai's muffled voice answered. Slayer sighed, trying to think of how he could reach them and convince them to stand down.

"Proverte lift," the commanding officer said. Slayer caught the word lift and noticed one of them in his peripheral moving toward the elevator.

"Hey, don't do that." Slayer moved toward him, and the other soldiers took a stern stance. The room shuffled in place as the man heading for the lift stopped, looking to his commanding officer.

"Don't move! You move again and we will open fire!" the Russian officer yelled at Slayer, who did not need a translator to understand his aggressive body language and the officer jamming the rifle in his direction. *"Idti."*

The guard moved cautiously toward the elevator again, eyes on Slayer, who shuffled toward him. The security detail fired several shots at Slayer. The metal slugs slammed into him, crunched into mangled cubes, and fell to the ground like raindrops. After the gunfire stopped, the dinging of the bullets on the floor echoed in the cavernous room. Slayer looked back at them with annoyance and the befuddled guards glanced between him and their commander.

"Pirsing broni," the commander shouted. The guards tapped on their rifles and each one rang out with a click, which Slayer took to mean an upgrade in firepower, probably armor-piercing bullets judging by the sound of *pirsing*.

Slayer did not intend to let them assail him with explosive, armor-piercing, or any other special bullets, as he had dealt with it more than he wanted. The sensation of being attacked by a swarm of hornets was always fresh in his mind.

They had made their intentions clear. In one big motion, Slayer dashed at the nearby guard and flung him upstairs. He crashed into the commander with such overwhelming force that they slammed into the ceiling.

The room erupted in a hail of gunfire. Slayer dashed through the storm, bashing security through the air or flinging them at those on the second level. He leaped upstairs and thumped an open hand into an enemy's chest, sending him through a window.

Guards shuffled away in a panic, firing as Slayer charged through them, un-phased by their attacks. The bullets bounced off him like tiny beanbags. The guards with railguns were no more effective. He swatted projectiles away or caught the slugs in mid-air, throwing them back with impeccable aim. The final clattering of gunfire stopped when the last soldier fell to the first level with a thud.

Slayer hopped downstairs to rejoin the team. He knocked, the elevator doors opened, and he strolled away to give them space. Exiting the lift, they looked upon the bodies strewn about the room, some dangling lifelessly over the railing of the level above. The room itself had been destroyed and the ground was covered in rubble and glass.

Nikolai nodded approvingly.

With a hop, Slayer was on the second level and turned around to address them. "I'm pretty sure one of those guys called this in, so I'm going to clear the path ahead. See you guys in a bit." He sped down the cement hall, leaving them to find the stairs.

"Jesus," James whispered once he was gone, looking in bewilderment at the sea of broken bodies. "What the hell is this guy made of?"

"He's one of the earlier genetic experiments when things started getting interesting. We're as good as we are now because of all the stuff they did to these guys," Hope explained, having learned from their time together.

"There's more than one?" James asked with a panicked laugh.

"Only one other." Hope reached the top of the stairs in the middle of the group with Mike, Farouk, and Nikolai pulling up the rear.

"But, extreme genetic enhancement leads to a half-life. Overly-modified people don't live as long," James contested.

"Don't believe everything you hear," Farouk said.

"Humans can't speak telepathically either, but…" Mike motioned to Hope.

"Did you know some people can see *the future*? They'd *love* to find one of those." Hope took deep breaths to keep pace as they ran down the hall to catch up to Slayer.

"No shit?" James said, beside himself in amazement.

"Someone thought it was possible to push the human genome beyond its limits, and Slayer is the result. Let's stay focused." Mike brought an end to the topic. They had been reunited, now they needed to escape.

"Hope, can you sense the golem like you can sense security?" Mike asked, eyes vigilant and looking for danger.

"He doesn't, uh, have thoughts." Hope squirmed. "So, no."

By the time they reached the double doors leading into the hangar, Hope was out of breath and leaning on a wall for support, her legs ready to buckle, throat and lungs ablaze. Being a prisoner had limited her exercise.

"You need me to carry you?" Mike asked with compassionate concern. She had anticipated escape but did not realize she needed to prepare for it. She did not care if the fire in her lungs spread to her whole body, she was getting out of there.

"No thanks." She took deep breaths. "We're almost there, and you guys might need to fight, or shoot, or whatever." She stood up straight, ready to go again. A beam of pride twinkled in Mike's heart.

From the hangar ahead came the crackle of gunfire and yelling. With one of the doors ripped off its hinges, Shin glanced through the open space to scout ahead.

Hope hung onto her dad's arm as they followed Nikolai into the middle of an expansive seven-story tall hangar. Hallways cut deep into the thick, cement monolith. Large tracks ran along the walls and columns at every level. Shuttles, fighter craft, and workshops littered platforms which connected to the tracks on either side of the hangar.

Slack-jawed at the grandeur of the space, Hope noticed white specks falling down a chasm between the two sides of the hangar half the size of a football field. She approached the edge, mesmerized, even as Mike called for her to come back. She reached out and watched the snow fall onto her hand. Her smile grew until it could grow no more, and she reached out with both arms, grabbing at the snow until a hand fell onto her shoulder, startling her out of her trance.

"Come on, sweetie. We've got to stay together."

"It's snow." She smiled, looking at the sky, the chill biting at her bones dull and distant.

Mike watched the innocent girl experience a tiny slice of life for the first time.

"Is that how the sky looks?" she asked, expecting stars.

Mike leaned over to look up at a flat white sky instead of clouds or stars. "No, that's a hologram to hide the hangar. Come on, we've got to go." He ushered her along and she hurried back to the group. Everyone stayed low and Shin peeked around the corner of a pillar at the end of the walkway.

"There's our new friend," he said. Before anyone peeked, Slayer soared by, leaping across the room. Security fired in vain as he thrashed through them.

On the ground level two floors down, a pair of guards snuck into two fighters. Cockpits shut, the small crafts lifted off their platforms and faced Slayer, but he had already taken notice. He leaped into the air before they opened fire, giant slugs bouncing off the platform in his wake. He crashed into a fighter fist-first like a meteor, smashing it to the ground. Grabbing hold with both hands he swung it into the cement wall, smashing it to pieces.

Slayer darted away again, dodging a volley of fire from the other ship. He jumped again, soaring high above the fighter. Before he came down, the fighter shot up to meet him. The craft slammed into Slayer's face, but he grabbed hold of it. His fingers crunched into the hull of the craft, weighing it down in the front. The pilot pulled up, higher and higher, passing through the hologram and into the night. He flew erratically, but Slayer held on tight, body flailing.

"Fuck, it's cold!" Slayer punched the underside of the craft with his free arm and pulled himself to the wing. He chopped at it to break it off. The ship spun and stopped gaining altitude. There was a loud click then a swoosh. The top of the fighter flew off and the pilot shot into the sky, parachute opening above him.

Slayer climbed into the cockpit, looking over the edge at the shadows of the abandoned city of Prypiat below. The fighter rattled around him, the wing shaking apart.

"This is going to suuuuuuuuck," Slayer roared with laughter, sailing into the darkness below.

Ulfberht Crew

65

Gauntlet

"Aaaaand... he's gone." James peered up into the white holographic sky into which Slayer had disappeared.

"During the war, me and small platoon fought off battalion of Americans for *two* weeks waiting for reinforcements. This will be cakewalk," Nikolai boasted.

"While we've got some cover, I'm going to find us a ride." Mike dropped the holo-projector in front of him and sat on the floor with his back against a pillar, opening his interface.

Hope sat next to Mike, watching him work in wide-eyed fascination. His thoughts were different than most. There was no fluid string of words, images, or emotions. Instead, various threads branched apart and zipped ahead on their own. Fast and abstract with bursts of images, memories, and scripts connected thoughts, then the various threads converged at one point in the end.

"Okay, here's what we've got to work with. The platform system is offline and the ships are on an independent network. To control ships in the network, I need access to it first. So, once I get into one of those ships, I can get into all of them."

"That sounds like good news," James said.

"Yeah, but we're in the middle of the hangar. These two ships Slayer wrecked were the two nearest space-worthy ships. There's one at the end of this side here." Mike pointed down the hall. "But, there are about a half dozen on that side." He pointed the other way, across the center section of the hangar's t-shape.

"This one's closah," James said.

"But, only one. More ships is better," Nikolai said.

"Why is more ships better? We only need one."

"We have options. We can use as weapons, camouflage, misdirection, backup."

"What if it's a trap?" Farouk asked.

"Since the golem disappeared, I'm inclined to agree with Farouk," Shin said.

"Which one is the trap then?" Mike asked.

"Both," Nikolai grumbled. "If we go to one ship, they destroy single ship and we are cornered. If we go to multiple ships, they are waiting for us."

"I don't need a space-worthy ship to gain control. Those *should* be the only ones they're watching." Mike turned back to his interface and searched for what he needed, then stretched an arm out toward the closer end of the hangar with a single ship. "Right over here, there's a ship I can use that isn't space-worthy but is plugged into the system. It's close, one level down. Stairs are around the corner."

"Let's go, then to the other ships." Nikolai slid his back against a pillar, rising to his feet. Mike closed his interface and picked up the small, black holo-emitter, shoving it back in its pouch while the rest of the group checked their surroundings for danger.

"Looks like we're clea'," James said.

Led by Shin, the group hustled to the stairs. In the enclosed stairwell, Hope clutched Nikolai's arm and watched Mike disappear with James. The group waited for them to sneak onto the small, unpainted shuttle missing numerous panels. Likely a proof of concept, connecting it to the flight network meant they were preparing it for an uncrewed test flight.

Once inside, Mike powered it up and got into its systems. "This will take a few minutes."

In the enclosed stairwell, Farouk stayed on the center platform aside Nikolai and Hope. Shin guarded the bottom of the stairs. Snow fell, but the air was still, not a sound disturbed the tranquility.

The team maintained radio silence while Mike worked. Shin peeked across the way at something that had caught his attention. Hope and Farouk watched him until he tucked himself behind the wall. Farouk's eyes returned to the upper stairwell, where an imposing shadow loomed in the hall.

POW! POW! POW!

Shots burned into the golem's skin with a sizzle. Unfazed, it charged down the stairs and crashed into Farouk, slamming him into the cement wall behind him, a web of cracks rippling out from the impact.

Nikolai rushed downstairs with Hope, ducking under Shin, who ran up the wall to give them a path. His railgun zipped with a quick charge then blasted five slugs into the golem, nailing it down with each consecutive shot. Farouk slammed it into the cement wall, shattering it, burying the golem beneath a pile of rubble and dust.

Shin recalled the slugs to his railgun and Farouk retreated, rubble tumbling to the floor behind him. They backed down the stairs and Shin kept his railgun fixed on the golem. Exiting the stairwell, hollow thuds of stone echoed behind them.

"The golem has found us. He is in the stairwell," Nikolai warned.

"What?" Mike went to jump out of his seat but James already had a hand on his shoulder, keeping him in place.

"You gotta trust ya team. If you don't do this, nobody gets outta here."

With an angry groan, Mike returned to his work. The situation outside was a monkey on his back, but James was right, he was most useful where he was.

The group ran across the platform. Through the shuttle's openings, flashes passed in and out of Mike's vision, but he focused on his work.

"It is coming. We require transportation as soon as possible," Nikolai huffed.

"Working on it," Mike said through gritted teeth.

Dust billowed into the hall and the golem stomped out of the stairwell. In powerful, unrushed steps, it marched onto the platform, lifeless eyes fixed on Hope. Skin hung from gashes that revealed armor. The steel behind a gash on its face glistened red with blood. The golem's fine suit was stained and in tatters, with jagged chunks dangling from its blocky frame.

They backed into the hall until the elevator dinged behind them. The doors opened and a squad of guards raised their weapons.

Shin leaped into the elevator before they could take aim, smashing his hand against the console next to the doors. Amid a storm of gunfire, he thrashed the thicket of security with kicks and elbows, using his railgun like a club. The doors closed and the elevator began its ascent.

"Nikolai, I'll hold him, you get her out of here. Go as soon as I engage." Farouk handed his heavy pistol to Nikolai and took a fighting stance, bending at the knees, hands open.

"Hope, I'm going to carry you so we move faster, okay?"

With a nod, she reached her arms into the air. Nikolai knelt and scooped her up, draping her over his shoulder, hanging onto her legs.

The golem crossed into the hall and Farouk inched to meet it, watching its steady gait bring it to within a few paces.

"God, I hope you've got my back." Farouk shot forward with a jab.

Nikolai sprang into the stairwell, pausing to contemplate whether to go up or down. A fall from the second floor would not be lethal, making it the safer bet. He took the stairs down, Hope bouncing on his shoulder, and sprinted down the hall toward the other side of the hangar.

Upstairs, Farouk exchanged blows with the golem. His combos fell short against an enemy that did not feel pain, or could not respond to it. He snatched Farouk's punches out of the air and responded in kind with its own, then tossed him away. The golem marched for the stairs, but Farouk was in his face before it made progress, pushing it away and landing whatever blows he could.

Giant hand palming Farouk's face like a basketball, the golem charged him into the wall by the stairs. His head made a crater in the cement. Farouk tried to fight out of it, but the golem regained its grip and smashed him again, then five more times in rapid succession and tossed him away.

The golem entered the stairwell and scanned the room. Recent footprints went downstairs. It followed. There, Nikolai had made it a good distance down the hall.

"Oh, shit. Watch out, Nikolai, he's comin'," Farouk said, short of breath.

"I am on the second floor!" Nikolai checked behind him. The golem was already on his level and looking at him. It pivoted its body toward him and broke into a terrifying sprint. The cybernetic monstrosity was a truck that moved like a race car. "I require assistance!" Nikolai fired Farouk's pistol behind him at the golem. It burned holes in its skin but did little to deter it.

The golem barrelled toward Nikolai. Behind it, Shin swung in from above and fired his railgun. The golem's bounding feet kicked one slug away but the other caught it in the crook of its knee. The golem dropped, face slamming into the pavement. With so much momentum, it tumbled across the ground. Nikolai continued his mad dash to escape.

"Finally! Done." Mike burst. He closed his interface and ran outside with James. Sparks flew and metal dinged against the floor. Bullets rained down on them from high above. They rushed back into the half-finished shuttle and Mike opened his interface, finding the nearest fighter. "I am not in the mood for this shit."

Two floors up and one platform space over from Mike's position, a space fighter lifted into the air. A holographic yoke appeared in front of Mike and he gripped it with both hands. Around him appeared a hologram of the fighter's environment. There were spots missing, most likely due to being in the middle of repairs or upgrades.

The top two floors were lined with dozens of armed security. A few examined the rising fighter and brought it to the attention of others, but it was too late. Mike unleashed a fury of railgun fire, pulverizing the assailants and the building around them. He continued firing at the floor so it would collapse onto the guards on the next level.

Security in the opposite halls fired on the fighter from behind. Mike held down the trigger and zipped the craft around, blasting everything along the way. After burying the other groups, Mike brought the ship to their platform.

"You sure you don't want to drop the rest of the buildin' on 'em to make sure they're dead?" James joked.

"I was thinking about it, but we're in a hurry." Mike fired up the unfinished shuttle to see what it was capable of. "Looks like she can fly. Hey team, we're on our way. Sit-rep?" Mike lifted the small shuttle off the ground.

"Level two, crossing the central corridor. I am running with Hope. Farouk and Shin are fighting the golem."

For all of Farouk's grace and power, the golem's reaction time was impossible to contend with. Blocking and counter-attacking was more effective, but if Farouk did not attack, the golem would break away and go after Nikolai. When the golem tried to throw him off, Farouk latched on, tying it up as much as possible. The golem's heavy punches crashed into him, slamming Farouk into the wall, denting the armor beneath his skin.

Shin would get knocked away but was always quick to return. With Farouk in the line of fire, the most he could do was attack from behind, darting in and out too quickly for the golem to catch. When the golem managed to shove a boot into Farouk's chest and sent him flying, Shin fired another slug into its knees.

"Shin, focus on the head and neck. If we rip its fuckin' head off, we win. Fuck mobility!" Farouk charged in again.

Beads of sweat rolled down Farouk's forehead. If they did not kill the golem, there was no way they could take off without it stopping them. It was so intense, maintaining a relentless pace was Farouk's only course of action. There was no bell, no rounds, and no stopping because this abomination would not tire.

The golem rushed into Farouk and threw him at Shin. He dodged and Farouk tumbled away, but the golem was unrelenting. A boot narrowly missed Shin, who dropped his gun and drew his knife, lunging for the golem's eyes.

It caught his arm in the air before he could land the blow and slammed Shin in the ribs with several powerful uppercuts. A final hit slammed into his helmet, bringing its structural integrity down to fifty percent. He tossed Shin away and turned to pursue Nikolai, ignoring the friendly fighter hovering outside the hall, unaware it was under Mike's control.

The hangar echoed with the rapid booming of the fighter's railguns. Each boom interrupted the last, launching rugby ball-sized slugs into the golem, setting off a cascade of crumbling cement. The ceiling, walls, and floor around the golem were obliterated and crashed down on top of it.

The booming stopped and the fighter rose in altitude, stopping at the top level. It swept across the top floors, firing at security. Churning booms of railgun fire and rumbling echoed throughout the hangar, walls shaking with each strike.

"Nikolai, hold position. We're coming to you. Shin, Farouk, you okay?" Mike called in.

"We're good." Farouk helped Shin to his feet. Holding his ribs, Shin picked up his weapon and recalled the slugs. They whirred out from under the rubble and down the hall, sliding into the weapon with a clack. Mike's raggedy shuttle hummed by and they followed it to Nikolai, each finding their own way around the hole in the floor and mountain of rubble.

Across the hangar's central corridor, Mike landed the shuttle on a platform with a machine shop. Nikolai backtracked down the hall with Hope to meet them.

When Mike stepped out of the shuttle, Hope was already running to him. She leaped into his arms and squeezed. Behind him, James was using Mike's tablet to fly the fighter and clear out security, joysticks and buttons projecting over it. He walked idly out of the shuttle, taking slow, careful steps, focused on the tablet.

"Well done, comrade."

"Thanks. I'm glad you guys were able to hold out," Mike said.

Farouk arrived sweaty and winded. Shin cradled his ribs with a stiff walk and his helmet covered in cracks.

"You guys all right?"

"Nah, Mike. That golem's tough as shit. I don't think that took him down."

"That ship's railguns aren't much higher caliber than mine, and mine barely dented him. We should get moving."

In the distance, an explosion brought their eyes to the sky.

"Ah, shit. They've got RPGs." James handed the tablet back to Mike.

"Damnit." Mike put away his tablet and opened his interface, taking cover behind a cement pillar.

"Nearest ships are two kilometers away. Shin, we need you to take care of the last of their security and get rid of their RPGs," Mike said. "Farouk, James, if we run into the golem again, keep 'em occupied."

"Copy." Shin sprinted up the wall to the upper levels.

"Nikolai, you're with me. We're getting a ship. Shin, when you're done, swap with James. You and Farouk—" With a loud crash, the shuttle tumbled across the platform. They jumped and shuffled into a semi-circle facing the platform.

The golem had stayed silent and off their radar by traveling on the first floor. Crouched only a few meters away in the shuttle's place, it turned to scan them.

Fists clenched, its clothes clung to it by threads, draping like the branches of a willow tree. The skin on its face was shredded, its armor glistened in swaths across its body and jagged plates of dislodged armor jutted from it. A piece jutting out from under its neck was especially jarring. Wires sprouted from an empty eye socket. The golem stood upright, examining its target.

Hope scooted behind Mike and clenched him tight. The group mirrored the golem's overall stillness, but slowly shifted into taking proper hold of their weapons or preparing to move.

"Looks like it's increased our threat level." Mike backed away, one hand on his blaster, the other holding Hope.

"We got this Mike, you and Nikolai get her safe." Farouk kept his eyes fixed on the golem, which had bounced its sight between everyone in the group.

"It's not moving. Should we make a break for it?" Mike said.

"It's figuring out a strategy, god damn right ya should!" James did not wait for Mike to go. He raised his blaster and fired at the golem. The crackling shots dissipated, burning black streaks into the platform. The golem jumped out of the way and Mike sprinted down the hall holding Hope's hand, Nikolai behind them.

The golem leaped after them, but Farouk slammed into it, gripping its wrists, slamming a knee into its ribs. James rushed to corral it. The golem twisted to shake off Farouk, then plowed a boot into him, sending him crashing into the shuttle.

James circled around and held the trigger down on his blaster. The golem jumped out of the sparks and flames. He tilted up to follow the golem through the air and shuffled back as it descended. It landed with a boom, shaking the platform. Lunging at him with a massive swing, James stumbled back, doing his best to dodge the blow, but it crashed into him nonetheless.

With the blaster in front of him, it took the brunt of the attack and cracked in two. The golem's swing drilled through it and crashed into James. The force of the blow sent him rolling away. Beneath his sundered armor, his body was bruised from the impact. He gasped to catch his breath, rolling to pick himself up.

Farouk leaped in with an elbow from above, slamming the golem down. He followed up with powerful strikes to the back of its head and neck. Only a few centimeters thick, the panel of armor jutting from its neck popped off, flipping away.

The golem swept Farouk and held him down, pounding its fist into his arms, which covered his face to defend from the hailstorm of punches. An unsustainable strategy, Farouk wrapped his legs around its shoulder and grabbed onto the arm holding him down. With a twist, he yanked back on the arm in an attempt to break it.

The golem lifted him off the ground. Anticipating a slam, Farouk uncurled himself and pressed the attack. Jab, cross, hook, bobbing and weaving to avoid counters.

It weathered the storm and found an opening, bull-rushing Farouk, lifting then slamming him into the ground, denting the platform's steel surface. Farouk gasped for breath. Looming over him, the golem raised a leg to stomp on Farouk's head but a hail of railgun fire from above knocked it off balance. The golem stumbled, raising an arm to protect itself while Farouk put some distance between them.

Shin landed on the platform between Farouk and the golem. The railgun whirred and unleashed a storm of thick slugs, trying to anticipate the golem's position as it dodged. He pushed the golem back until he was out of shots. When Shin raised his railgun in the air to recall his ammunition, the golem charged. The platform shook beneath Shin's feet with each thunderous step. Shin held his ground, staring it down, the clacks of his rifle reloading above him.

The last slug clacked into his rifle with the golem a few meters away. Shin took aim and fired. The whir of his railgun charging prompted the golem to pivot. The shot zoomed past its head. The next shot was swatted away, the golem's arm cranked back, fist balled up tightly.

Shin cloaked, vanishing from the golem's view. It followed through on its attack but Shin had leaped away. Charging in from behind Shin, Farouk crashed into the golem, slamming it onto its back.

He fell on top of it and transitioned into a mount, wrapping his legs around it. He pummeled the mindless monster, letting loose a guttural roar. The golem put its arms up to block but Farouk slipped around them. A powerful open-handed strike to his abdomen sent him tumbling back, and the golem was back on its feet.

"It's missing a panel of armor on its neck. If I can get in there and slice up its connection to the brain, I think we can get him." Shin put away the railgun, trading it for his knife.

"Let's do it. I'll keep the pressure on," Farouk said.

"I'll stay on its flank." James caught up to the fight, which had meandered toward the edge of the platform. Farouk had kept the golem engaged. Shin shot in from behind while James circled to look for safe openings. The golem blocked and dodged, focused on Farouk and Shin, unable to mount a counter-offensive.

With Shin's foot behind its heel, a powerful blow from Farouk tipped the golem back. James darted in with a punch, the rod in his arm shooting out, slamming into the golem's spine. It shivered in place, rocked by the jolt. James retreated and cranked his arm back to reload and recharge the weapon.

Shin leaped in to jam the knife into its neck, but the golem was quick to recover and snatched his arm out of the air, smashing a fist into his helmet. The force was distributed throughout the helmet but structural integrity plummeted to twelve percent.

Farouk charged in to help but was met with a boot to his chest and he tumbled back. James rushed in, but the golem swung Shin into him like a weapon and knocked him away.

Shin jammed his blade into the golem's arm, using it as leverage to shoot himself forward. He kicked at the golem's good eye to blind it, but the golem snatched his foot out of the air and slammed him to the ground like a ragdoll. Shin's helmet shattered and he lay unconscious on the floor.

Before the golem landed the finishing blow, Farouk tackled it from behind. The golem rolled with the momentum, flinging Farouk away.

With the golem's back to him, James lunged in again and jammed the high voltage rod into the golem's spine. The golem twitched and shivered, then twisted, swinging at James, who was already retreating. Its fist swept within a centimeter of his face. James made a tactical retreat, putting significant distance between them.

Determined and unwavering, adrenaline pumping, Farouk followed up James's attack and charged the golem. The relentless pace was wearing down on him. But, years ago when Mike and Shin saved him, he swore to help rescue Mike's daughter, and he would be damned if he was going to fall short at the finish line.

"Come on, mothafucka'. I ain't done with you."

In the midst of Farouk's assault, the platform shuddered, then ascended to the higher levels. Caught off guard, Farouk lost his balance and the golem capitalized, clotheslining him into the platform.

James charged in with another jolt from behind and dashed away in time to avoid a retaliatory strike. Farouk propped himself up and kicked the golem's leg, dropping it to one knee. James rushed in from behind again, but the golem pivoted with a right hook.

James had seen a sniper bullet blow a torso apart. To see his own arm exploding in chunks of flesh and bone with pieces of it flying away was more than he could take. The pain in his shoulder from the bone being ripped out of the socket spread throughout his chest and body, but it was dull in the face of losing an arm.

He stared, falling to his knees. The audio channel buzzed in his ear, his heart pounded in his head, and he could not get enough air into his lungs. The edges of his vision blurred, then the shock consumed him and a curtain fell over his world.

Ulfberht Crew

66

Escape

MIKE, NIKOLAI, AND HOPE REACHED THE NEAREST PLATFORM with ships. Despite panting for breath, Hope refused help. Shin had already cleaned up the last of the security, but they still took precautions before moving into an open space. The coast was clear.

They crossed the platform, vigilant of their surroundings. Halfway to the nearest shuttle, the platform jolted. Hope grabbed Mike's arm to catch her balance. They paused, then the platform rose along its rails to the higher levels.

"I thought you said platform system is down?" Nikolai said.

Mike opened his interface and checked again. "It is. They must have switched over its controls like they did for Hope's room."

"Poshli!" Nikolai picked up Hope and they sprinted to the shuttle.

"Farouk, Shin, James, we've reached the ships but the platform is moving on us. We're going to get airborne." Mike opened the bus-shaped shuttle. The side door lowered, it's interior turning into a staircase. They rushed into the single-cabin shuttle and Mike sat at the helm, powering it up.

"Our platform is moving too," Farouk said through heavy breaths. "James and Shin are down."

Mike and Nikolai locked eyes, a bolt of alarm shooting between them. Nikolai put two fingers to his wristband and checked on their teammates' vitals. Shin was unconscious but stable. James was unconscious, his body in shock, but his suit cut off blood flow to his arm to keep him alive.

Mike focused on his interface, accessing the shuttle and fighters on the platform. The vertical movement stopped and jolted forward, taking them back the way they had come. The console lit up and the shuttle hummed to life. The movement beneath them slowed, followed by a thud. A metallic boom echoed throughout the hangar. If both platforms had moved toward each other, they had been brought to the golem's doorstep.

Blaster ready, Nikolai rushed to the door as it opened. Mike closed his interface and grabbed his blaster. Turning to Hope, he grabbed her arms and looked her in the eyes.

"I need to get you out of here, so I'm sending you back to my ship. We'll find our own way back, but I need to get you to safety, okay?"

"But..." Hope shook her head, shaken by the uncertainty in her father's mind.

"Please, trust me. The shuttle will take off as soon as it's ready. I'll see you soon, Hope. I love you." Mike kissed her on the forehead and squeezed her. Eyes clamped shut, she clutched onto him without a desire to ever let go.

They pulled apart, Hope looking fondly into her father's eyes. They were resolved to die for her if necessary, as long as she was free. She wiped a tear from her eye and sniffled. "Come back safe."

"I will." Mike smiled, then ran outside after Nikolai, closing the door behind him.

Outside, the platform had risen to the highest level of the hangar. In the distance, the golem pushed Farouk back toward the far edge of the other platform. Blaster tucked into his shoulder, Nikolai took aim, holding his fire until Farouk was out of the way.

Farouk tussled with the golem, panting for breath, arms protecting his body more than throwing punches. Beads of sweat rolled down his forehead, dripping from his brow. He floated on his toes trying to circle around, but the golem did not let him pass. It pushed him back until he could retreat no further, teetering at the edge of the platform.

When the golem charged in, Farouk grabbed hold and clinched, blasting a knee into its gut. He twisted to throw the golem off the edge, but it dipped low and stopped short. With a thud, the golem's boot slammed into the platform and it pummeled Farouk's abdomen with a flurry of blows. When Farouk defended, the golem charged and thrust him off the platform. He reached for the ledge, the world slowing around him as he realized it was out of reach.

Once Farouk was airborne, Mike and Nikolai had opened fire. An avalanche of energy blasts encroached on the golem. Sparks and light erupted above Farouk as he fell into the depths of the hangar.

The golem raised an arm, fist over its ear like a boxer, protecting its eye. It sprinted out of the way, circling to close the distance. Mike and Nikolai attempted to lead their fire, but the golem was too quick, adapting faster than they could, changing direction and avoiding most of their shots.

Behind them, the whirring of the shuttle had grown louder than their blaster fire. The golem no longer circled, instead running directly at them, zig-zagging to avoid their fire. It crashed through them like a bus. Mike dove out of the way, rolling back onto his feet. The golem swatted at Nikolai. It missed but smashed his blaster in twain.

It raced for Hope's shuttle, which was hovering several meters in the air and ascending.

Mike pursued, blaster fixed on the golem, a finger held down on the trigger. The golem zig-zagged, and leaped into the air, slamming a fist into the shuttle's door. The shuttle jerked with the blow then swayed as it descended with the golem latched on. Mike and Nikolai unleashed a relentless stream of energy blasts upon the golem as it fell.

After the shuttle slammed into the platform, the golem ripped the door from its hinges and marched inside. Hope's panicked screams echoed in the cabin. A moment later, the golem emerged from the shuttle with Hope over its shoulder. It took a few steps out then crouched and sprang into the air. It soared over the edge of the hangar into the outside world. With a yelp from Hope, they vanished behind the curtain of the hologram.

The world ground to a halt. Mike's heart stopped beating and the dread of failure bored into him, trying to drag him into premature despair, but he would not relent.

"Farouk! Are you okay? What's your status?"

"I'm good," he grunted. *"On my way back up to you guys."*

"Nikolai. What do we do?"

"We can only delay it until Farouk can return!" Nikolai raced back the way they came, headed for Shin.

"Farouk, hurry back. We'll try to hold him here." Mike put his thumbs and forefingers together in a square and opened his interface. He hurried toward the other shuttle on the platform, working to seize control of it and three available fighter craft as fast as possible.

Engineered for quick deployment, the fighter crafts were the first to lift off. Mike navigated them above the hologram to get his first glance at the situation outside.

A dropship with two fighter craft on either side of it had landed less than a kilometer away from the edge of the hangar. In front of the ships, two squads of security accompanied two Ministry scientists and a familiar red-eyed demon, Lazarus.

In the snow near the hangar was a crater. From it was a straight line in the snow carved by the golem, which strode toward the group.

Security took a defensive stance and fired past the golem. Mike traced their fire to Nikolai hiding behind a thick steel door in the ground. He had grabbed Shin's railgun and taken the stairs to the surface, firing past the golem at security.

Mike set his fighters on an attack vector and they zoomed past the group, obliterating one of the enemy fighters. They zoomed away and circled back around for another pass. The other enemy fighter lifted off the ground and teetered away, but they had already returned. The enemy ship rocked from side to side at low altitude, trying to land a shot on the fighters and avoid a crossfire at the same time, but was overwhelmed. It spun and splintered into pieces, raining flaming debris into the snow.

Flickering yellow lights from the burning wreckage danced atop the pristine white snow. The force of each explosion sent security crashing to the ground. They scrambled to their feet and opened fire on Mike's fighters as they circled around, but he focused on the dropship.

The railguns on Mike's fighters unloaded a volley as they made another pass, but the shells bounced away as if they collided with an invisible bubble around the ship. Shells tumbled into the unsuspecting guards, knocking them into the snow.

"No way. I can't believe the Ministry already has forcefields," Mike growled. His shuttle whirred to life, ready to go.

He looked to his blaster, considering his options. "You shoot concentrated fields of energy. Let's see what you do to that forcefield." He guided the shuttle out of the hangar and landed it on the left flank of the battle. Rushing outside, he jumped over the stairs before they had opened, taking cover behind them. Bullets dinged against the steel. The fighters made another pass but did not fire.

The golem had met with the group and handed Hope off to the scientists with Lazarus. Kicking and flailing, Hope resisted, but they stuck her with a sleeper and her struggling ceased. She fell limp, and he took her over his shoulder.

Mike raised his blaster and fired at the dropship. The shots slammed into the forcefield and dissipated, leaving a crackling ripple in their wake. Consecutive shots turned it into a wild cacophony of thrashing lights. Seeing the forcefield could be disrupted filled Mike with the hope that his plan was viable.

Making the half kilometer trek back to the dropship, Lazarus jumped at the sight of a fluctuating forcefield. He spun, pointing a finger at Mike.

"Lenny, kill him!" he roared.

Mike was setting the fighters to pass and fire on a timer when Lazarus's order ripped through the bitter cold. He looked up from his interface, the golem already charging at him. A pitiful distance to the golem, it would be upon him in seconds.

"Shit!" Mike took aim with his blaster held his finger down on the trigger, unloading on the dropship. Like a storming sea, the forcefield rippled and thrashed, some of the shots slipped through and scorched the inside of the dropship. Before the fighters could fire, Mike was forced to leap out of the way or be torn asunder by the golem. His ships opened fire, the forcefield stabilized and the shots bounced off, not one making contact.

He fired at the golem, but it charged into him. Snatching the blaster, it swatted him in the chest. Mike tumbled into the snow, gasping for breath, vision spinning, his body pulsed in pain and he squirmed helplessly on the floor, the world fading away. The golem crushed the blaster in its hand and dropped it into the snow.

When the golem bolted after Mike, a rush of panic swept over Nikolai. The railgun barely put a dent in the golem, but it was all he had. For the golem to break off its pursuit, he needed it to follow an order that superseded its most recent command.

He took aim at the guard behind Lazarus, then targeted the knees and fired. Leg broken, the guard collapsed. The following shots slammed into the back of Lazarus's leg. Without armor, the shell ripped through his calf and he collapsed with a scream.

The golem spun around. Lazarus had been injured. Security guards helped him up but were under attack. The golem traced the shots back to Nikolai, reloading a railgun, staring it down challengingly. It charged at him, leaving Mike in the snow.

"The golem is coming," he said, railgun high above him. With Farouk crouched behind the steel door, Nikolai stared down the golem as it charged, the repeating clack of reloading shells above him almost as fast as its footsteps. With the golem within spitting distance, Nikolai dove back down the stairs.

The golem leaped at the door, ripping it from its hinges in pursuit of its prey. From behind a cloud of snow and steel, Farouk buried Shin's knife into its exposed neck. Pouncing onto the golem as it collapsed into the snow, he continued stabbing the opening in its neck, cracking the spine and splitting wires. With the golem weakly tugging on his arms he yanked at the head and twisted, roaring as he ripped its head from its shoulders, spine dangling from the base. The golem's body twitched and went limp, collapsing to the red and blue-speckled snow.

Pulling himself off the ground, Farouk dropped the golem's head into the snow. Panting, he turned around to get a bearing on their status. Nikolai was making his way to Mike, lying unconscious in the snow by the shuttle. Zooming away, the lights from Lazarus's dropship faded into the sparkling night sky.

Ulfberht Crew

67

Looming Threats

THE DAY MIKE AND HIS TEAM ATTACKED THE BUNKER, MAYA'S leads took her to Canada. A public push for a UEG summit to discuss the growing pirate problem was held in Vancouver. When Maya arrived, instead of the placid atmosphere she expected, alarms blared and security personnel swept through the building to usher people outside in an orderly manner. The murmuring crowd calmly oozed out of every exit, annoyed by the blaring alarms and general inconvenience.

She watched alongside other spectators from the junction of a pedestrian bridge across the street. Wearing aviator glasses with a hijab to remain inconspicuous, she eyed an evacuee crossing the pedestrian bridge toward her, a screen projected in front of him. Maya's tech helped her eavesdrop on his conversation.

"Yeah, seriously. A goddamn bomb threat."

"It's probably a prank," said the person on the other end of the call.

"Well, they're wasting everybody's time," the man grunted.

A bomb threat? With such few people who would know about the attack, there was a good chance Lazarus had called it in himself to raise tension, and the real target lay elsewhere. With the throbbing of sirens closing in, Maya vanished into the crowd.

On the *Ulfberht*, Mike's eyes fluttered open, bringing the blurry medical bay ceiling into focus. Groggily, he lifted his head from the pillow to look around the room. Shin and James were lying in beds next to him, still unconscious.

Body aching, head pounding, he struggled to sit up and rested on his elbows, rolling his legs off the side of the bed. His armor was gone, but he was still wearing the protective underclothing. There was a patch on his arm to aid his healing.

"Take it easy there," Sam's voice called from behind. Between Mike's groans and the new whisper-quiet doors, his entry had gone unnoticed. "You've got a concussion."

"How long have I been out?" Mike cradled his throbbing head.

"Almost five hours, I think. It's nineteen-hundred Pacific," Sam brought over a transparent tablet and checked on Mike's physical condition. "You should rest up here for a while. The crew has everything under control."

"Everything? What's going on?" Mike asked.

"Amber and Maya came back. The few leads they had were dead ends. Maya and Nikolai figured there must be another target."

"What do they think?" Mike took the tablet from Sam and turned it so he could read the blurry words, handing it back when the pounding in his head overpowered his will to read.

"They think the best prospects are the Joust gaming tournament in Los Angeles or the *Felicity* cruise ship. They couldn't decide on which one, so we split into teams," Sam explained. "Amber and Maya went to the gaming event. Nikolai is on the *ISS-Four* making his way to the *Felicity*. Farouk flew him over, he's still out there in his ship."

Mike slid off the bed, leaning on it to hold himself steady. "Hold on, you shouldn't be moving around," Sam warned.

"I need to get to the bridge." Mike's knees shook beneath him. Sam hurried to his side, helping him stand.

"You should stay here."

"I can't. I've got to try and help," Mike put his arm around Sam's shoulders. "If you want to take care of me, help me to the bridge."

"All right." Sam rolled his eyes, hoisting Mike up. With Sam's help, Mike hobbled out of the medical bay. The lift doors opened and Sam leaned Mike against the wall. He sat on the railing and laid his head back.

"Where's the guy we set free?" Mike asked.

"Nikolai took him to Schulze." The door closed and Sam tapped on the console to take them up one level to deck three.

"How are they doing?" Mike nudged his chin toward the medical bay.

"They'll be all right. James barely made it." Sam said. "Oh, and I took the shuttle you guys flew back off the grid."

"Thanks," Mike said. The lift doors opened and Sam scooped his arm under Mike, wrapping it around his back to help him out.

Mike had failed to rescue his daughter and Sam could not think of anything comforting to say. Everyone made it back alive, but it would be of little consolation. The short walk to the bridge was a quiet one. When the bridge doors opened they were met with a jubilant reception from Addie and Will.

"Captain! You shouldn't be walking around!" she scolded.

"It's good to see you guys. Will, could you grab my earpiece?" Mike mumbled.

"You got it." Will hurried to the captain's chair and opened a compartment in the arm. He pulled an earpiece from it and ran back to Mike, who fumbled to insert it.

"Thanks for the help, guys," Mike said.

"No problem. I'm headed back to the med bay." Sam pointed at Will. "Don't let him get up and walk around, keep him hydrated."

"Will do." Will gave him a thumbs-up and sat next to Mike, eyes fixed on the bridge's front screen, which was split between a live feed of the *Felicity* and the ongoing Joust tournament. Sam left the bridge with his eyes on the ground, doors closing behind him.

While Sam headed back to the medical bay, Mike pulled up a holo-interface and joined the tactical audio channel with the rest of the crew.

"Anyone need a computer guy?" Mike greeted.

"Look who's awake," Maya said, moving through a crowd of people near concession stands.

"Hey, welcome back Mike," Farouk greeted.

"Glad you are on your feet, comrade."

"Hey there," Amber said.

"Mission status? I guess?"

"Amber and I split up here at the convention center. She went high I'm going low," Maya said.

"I have made my way through engineering." Dressed like a *Felicity* engineer, Nikolai exited a maintenance shaft into a standing area beneath the reactor.

In the middle of the round room with grated floor panels were a series of thick silver and blue rods surrounding a pipe as thick as a car. The pipe fed down from the reactor to another room beneath him, where they split up and extended outward. There were entrances to maintenance shafts in four directions.

"Since I'm sittin' here not doin' a damn thing, I've been listening to the local pilot chat. A sub-light freight captain said to be on the lookout for a ship headed for Earth, hauling ass with its transponder turned off. Maya said the Dragon Claw lost a ship, so I'm lookin' into it." Farouk updated the team, not fond of sitting on his hands.

"Way to keep your ear to the ground," Maya said.

"I hope it pays off."

"Speaking of payoff," Nikolai segued, *"I believe I have found the bomb beneath the main reactor."*

"What does it look like?"

"Like uh… large ring around central power column. It looks different than in schematics. There are pipes here as well." Nikolai climbed down a ladder in the corner to a lower corridor.

"Can we get a visual?" Mike lay on the console, head in his arms.

"One moment." Nikolai paced around the device.

It was so wide he could not reach the pipe in the center. He examined the panels, knocking on one. The sound was weak and hollow, lacking rigidity. It shone like metal, but it was not. Laying his tools out on top of the device, he pulled out a screwdriver and got to work removing a panel. When he pulled the panel off, it was light.

"This is printed, painted like metal." He tossed the panel away. Inside, metal boxes and circuit cards rested in a bed of tangled wires.

Nikolai examined the mechanisms inside and took pictures with his bracelet to create a scan of the internal mechanisms and their casing. He converted the images into a hologram and sent it to Mike and Maya, who examined the contents.

"There's still power running through it," Mike said.

"It looks like parts of the mechanism are supposed to be there. Keeps the ship working and hides what you're looking for. Probably a bunch of dummy stuff, too."

"Then, do you see cylinder attached to central column?"

"Looks like the explosive material. I was thinking the same thing."

"Then, this protected case is the mechanism." Nikolai examined a pristine steel box connected to the cylinder, suspended in a hammock of wires which connected working elements and loose, unfastened circuit cards. It formed an effective barrier to the cylinder, forcing Nikolai to lean in and weave his arms through it.

"While you tackle that, let's make sure there aren't multiple targets and finish our sweeps down here." Maya looked up at the shaking ceiling above her. The stadium was alive with everyone on their feet.

"Copy that. This event is almost over, though."

"If anything, that assures me that this place isn't the target, but let's be safe."

"Shit! That came out of nowhere. Hey, I found that ship. All pieced together like that, it's Dragon Claw all right."

"You okay?" Mike asked.

"Yeah, I'm good. But, it's pullin' away already. I'm hailing 'em but nobody's answering."

"Can you connect to their network?" Mike asked in slow, tired words.

"I ain't even picking up a signal from this thing."

"It's probably an empty ship. Can you send us the telemetry?" Maya asked.

"One sec."

With the ship's telemetry, Will worked the console for Mike so they would progress faster. With the ship's velocity and heading, the computer extrapolated the runaway ship's heading.

"Oh my god." Will shook his head in denial. "It's... it's going to crash into the *Felicity* cruise ship."

"Drag the ETA to the stopwatch icon and share," Mike slurred.

There was no stopwatch icon, but when Will held his finger down on it, a ring of options popped up. He found the stopwatch and a timer appeared for the team with an exact countdown for expected impact. Twenty-four minutes and thirty-two seconds.

"Crashing a ship into it wouldn't be enough of a show. Nikolai, I think it's safe to assume that thing is going to go off at the same time," Maya said.

"I have already begun working faster."

"While Nikolai works on diffusing that thing, what the fuck are we supposed to do about this ship?"

"Al can portal us in so we can stop it." Mike sat up and took a deep breath, then typed on the console with slow, deliberate taps. After a moment, Al's wrinkly, joyful face appeared on a new screen.

"Hello. Oh, you look unwell, Michael."

"Al, you busy? We need a portal." Head too heavy for his neck, Mike nodded lazily toward the trajectory information in front of Will. After a moment, Will bounced in understanding and dragged the information to Al's screen. Al gave it a quick glance and then removed his gloves to get to work.

548

"Mein friend, we can finish later. The lounge is to the left with snacks," he said to Slayer off-screen as he worked.

"*Thanks.*" A large arm crossed the right side of the screen and disappeared.

"Who is going through the portal?" Al asked.

"Me." Mike closed and rubbed his eyes to dull the pain in his head.

"*This motha'fucka' said, 'me'.*" Farouk laughed.

"*Mike, I would be laughing too if I wasn't rolling my eyes at you. You can barely use words right now,*" Maya said.

"I'm... fine."

"*That was the least convincing shit I ever heard in my whole life,*" Farouk said.

Al turned his head and examined Mike. "I think, perhaps, that is not an advisable idea."

"Yeah, Captain. Don't be crazy. You couldn't even make it to the bridge without Sam's help," Will said.

"Really? From everybody? Come on. If there's a problem I'll uh... I'll fix it."

"*I'll uh... nothing, Mike. Keep your ass in that chair, send Ian or Sam,*" Maya commanded.

"I can do it," Will said.

With a weak chuckle and leaning his face in one hand, Mike shared with the crew. "You guys think *I'm* funny. Will just volunteered."

"*I'm waitin' for the punchline, Mike,*" Farouk said.

"*Yeah, that's not a bad idea,*" Maya agreed.

"What? It's dangerous. He won't know what to do."

"I've been apprenticing with you for like a month and a half now. I can *totally* do it." Will said as if he could have learned so much in that time.

"*Will ain't a dumbass, he can put the brakes on a ship.*"

"*If you think you can do it with a concussion, Will can handle himself. Just talk him through it.*"

"*Yeah, Mike. Give him an earpiece and-*"

"Oh, god, please stop. Everyone stop talking." Overwhelmed by Will and the team chat, Mike held his hands out for everyone to stop. There was silence, then he turned to Will. From behind, Addie had meandered closer, listening in.

"Addie, tell Will he can't go."

"I don't know what's going on. Don't drag me into it." She put her hands in the air and returned to her cockpit.

With a sigh, Mike shook his head. "Grab an earpiece." Will bolted to some drawers on the sidewall and pulled one out, nestling it into his ear, then returned to Mike for his next order. "Okay, now go to my office, wait in front of my desk."

"You got it!" Will ran into his office and closed the door. In front of the desk, he turned slowly to take in the office and then turned on the earpiece. The room was simple with some chairs, a couch, and a metal desk with an alcohol rack nearby. "Hello? Can everyone hear me okay?"

"Loud and clear," Maya said. *"Welcome to the tactical chat. We don't even let Rick in here."*

With a nervous laugh, Will rubbed his hands together and let out a deep breath. "So, how does this work?"

"Opening portal," Mike said.

A light appeared and expanded into a ring. Inside the ring, an unlit room. Light poured through the ring and bounced off its walls and dappled the dark carpet. Will stepped cautiously to the ring, examining its ethereal edges, then jumped through it, wary of touching the edges.

"Okay, I'm in."

Seconds later, the ring contracted to a point, then vanished, leaving him in absolute penetrating darkness. He pulled his mobile from a pocket and shined its light in front of him. A deep and steady beep emanated from the bridge speakers.

"Hey, I've got a question."

"Ask away," Maya said.

"If you guys can portal, why do you live on a spaceship?"

"Best way to live under the radar. It's never in the same place."

"Why don't you guys share it with the world?" As he walked, his light rolled over a leg surrounded by blood. He shined his light away and averted his eyes.

"Al says Knowledge without wisdom brings catastrophe," Mike said, more lucid, but groaning. The call with Al had ended, its light no longer beaming in his face.

"Okay, I think I found the navigation station," Will said.

While most of the crew worked to stop Lazarus, a maintenance hatch popped off the wall behind the stairs on deck four. From it emerged a pistol, then a wrinkled face with sweat rolling down its brow. Rick pointed the gun around the hall, then pulled himself out of the maintenance shaft. In his other hand was a circuit card the size of a sheet of paper.

Pistol out in front of him, Rick kicked the hatch door aside and walked toward the medical bay, spinning to check his flank. Once he reached the door he put his back to the wall and stayed vigilant. He waved a hand over the console and the door opened. Walking in backward, he kept the pistol up until it shut.

"Rick? You okay?" From a rolling desk chair, Sam gave him an awkward sideways look.

"That son of a bitch is on the ship." Rick slammed the circuit card on the table. "That's the environmental sensor card. It got replaced, probably during construction. I'm printing a new one but we're blind for an hour until it's done. Removing that probably alerted him we are on his tail."

"Shit! Mike might as well be alone on the bridge." Sam ran past Rick to the port stairwell. "Take care of them!"

The threat scraped at the inside of his skull, propelling him to the bridge. Jones was there, and all the members of the crew threatening to him were off the ship. Perhaps, that had been what he was waiting for.

Rounding deck three's staircase and reservoir, a maintenance hatch nearby had been popped off and a trail of wet spots in the carpet led past the lifts to the bridge.

Will

One For All

IN THE DARK DRAGON CLAW BRIDGE, WILL SHINED HIS LIGHT ON the console to examine its various numbers and graphs. Across the top of the screen, a red alert blinked in cadence with the beeping alarm, warning that the ship was on a collision course.

"Okay, I think I found the navigation station."

"Do you need any help?" Maya asked.

"I don't think so." He dragged the acceleration bar on the far right to zero. "So, I turned off the acceleration. Do I need to fire the forward thrusters to stop it? Or, will it do that on its own?"

"What are you talkin' about, Will? The thrusters are still blasting," Farouk said.

"But, I pulled the thing down." Will examined the display and tried other buttons, but the ship remained on course. "Hold on, I'm going to try the cockpit."

He ran to the pilot's seat. Unlike Addie's, the cockpit was not embedded into the ground. Light fixed on the metal steps, he hurried up to the seat of the imposing shadow. When he shined it on the yoke, there was nothing there.

"That's not good."

"What's goin' on, brotha'?"

"Nothing on the console worked and there's no steering wheel." Will tried the cockpit console, which was as unresponsive as the other.

"What do you mean nothing on the console worked?" Maya asked.

"Like, I pushed all the buttons and dragged every slider but nothing happened. I'm doing the same thing on the pilot's console and it's not doing anything." Will ran back to the blinking navigation console and flipped through the menu-driven interface. "I'm checking the connections."

"Keep us updated. How you holding up, Mike?" Maya asked to no response.

"Must have passed out. He needs to lay his ass down, anyway."

"Maya, It looks like the computer isn't reading a connection to any devices. It says, 'device missing.'"

"Okay, go to engineering. Farouk, what kind of ship is it?"

"The main body is an old Titan, early war, a little bigger than ours."

"Standard Titan design puts engineering center-aft of the ship, about three to five decks down."

"Got it." Will ran off, tripping over a body. He had an inkling of what it was but chose not to think about it. It could have been a duffel bag but he did not have time to check. His mobile slid away and he scrambled to pick it back up before running off again.

Similar to the *Ulfberht*, the rear half of the ship consisted of open space with large staircases near the essentials. He raced down the stairs until he found engineering. Against the back of the room was a three-deck tall compartment glowing from inside. It painted the room in soft white light. Will rushed down to the first level, metal steps clanking beneath him.

"I'm here. What now?"

"There should be a manual shutdown next to the reactor."

Will hurried around the reactor room, reading the various labels on the wall panels. One door was labeled: Manual Controls. Inside were buttons, switches, and a screen with a physical keyboard. Next to it was a trackball half-jutting from the table with two buttons underneath it.

"What the hell is this ball thing?" Will rolled it around, but it had no effect on the screen. He pressed the escape key, but like the trackball, there was no response.

He shined his light around to see if there was anything he could use. To his left, the darkness had concealed a wall panel lying on the floor. His light traced it back to a hole in the wall and he stuck his head in, illuminating the inside. An anchor dropped in his heart. The wires behind the manual controls had been gutted. Only the nubs of wires sprouted from the roof of the small compartment.

"Guys, if we can't stop this ship, it slams into the *ISS-Four* and the *Felicity*, right?" Will leaned his back against the wall and slid to the floor.

"What's wrong, Will?" Maya asked.

"I found the manual controls and they've been cut."

"All right, we'll figure out what to do. You did great. Now we know what we're dealing with. Mike, can we get a portal for Will?" Maya said. Again, no response. *"Can someone hail the ship?"*

"I'm on it," Amber said, already calling the ship. The hail rang with a soft tune, but there was no response. She sat in the stadium rafters, watching the crowd below jostle about during an intermission.

"We're here with Dax Guererro, now the one and only, Jester. We won't keep you long, we know your family is waiting for you on the Felicity." A backstage interview hummed behind the murmur of the crowd.

Amber called again, and the line continued to go unanswered. *"I'm not getting a response."*

"That's concerning. Someone should be picking up. Will, take an escape pod. Farouk will pick you up and head back to the ship?"

"Guys," Will said. "I know how to stop the ship."

"How?" Maya asked.

"I'm going to blow it up." Will stood up and headed for the reactor room's single entrance in the middle of engineering. Without knowing there was an interior compartment in which he could walk around, he entered the reactor room.

"How you plan on doin' that?" Farouk asked.

"Something I learned from Natalie. I'm not going to be able to get off the ship, though. So, you should get clear, Farouk." Will examined the interior of the reactor room. There was a sealed steel room as wide as a van in the center, black consoles lining its walls. Displays above them showed the status of the reactor; a variety of graphs and information Will could not make sense of.

"Hold on, Will. Whatever you're planning, don't do it. Just get to an escape pod and I'll pick you up. That ship ain't your problem."

"Farouk, when I was talking to you and Ian, you said the world is *all* of us, living our lives. Like chess, every move matters, even if you don't realize how much it mattered until the end. Lots of people are going to die and I can help stop it. It *is* my problem," Will said. Examining the walls, he found a maintenance hatch and dove in.

"Will, please. That's an admirable, even heroic attitude. But, please let us handle this. We can figure it out, please trust us," Maya pleaded.

"Sorry, Maya." Will crawled through the tunnels, finding his way to a vertical shaft. He climbed up the ladder into a compartment above the reactor. His limbs moved on their own without willing them to. Following his instincts, he was stuck between crippling fear and absolute serenity. "I get it now, and I can't do that."

"Will, please. You're a teenager. There's so much that you don't understand yet. Please, give yourself a chance to by leaving, now!" Maya's voice cracked and trembled. Maya waited for a response, clearing her throat. *"Will?"*

"I hear you."

Will had found the device Natalie described a few months prior. Various tubes emanated from the reactor at the center, branching out into a ring around it, which regulated the flow of power to different parts of the ship.

"But, I don't agree. One said we are the universe, and the universe makes decisions. Our choices *are* the universe's choices. Our choices *create* reality." Will crawled to the edge of the ring, examining one of four boxes encircling it. "And, in our reality, a lot of bad stuff has happened. Except, I'm here for this one, and I can do something about it."

Many things in his life had lost their meaning. Concepts, habits, and passions once dear to him had become distant strangers. The last shred of his life that he had clung to was gone. Even after learning from Mike and growing closer to the crew, there was an emptiness inside. Being placed in this situation brought him a sense of clarity. Will opened the box in front of him, exposing high voltage wires thicker than his finger running into and around a glowing ring of energy, exactly as Natalie had described.

"Will, come on man, get back to the ship." Farouk pleaded. *"You may think you've got a good idea, but Mike, Maya, Nikolai, these guys are way smarter than us. Let them do their thing. Don't do anything stupid."*

"Thank you, guys." Will sighed. "For letting us travel around space with you, and for being so nice to a couple rando kids when you guys have way more important stuff to deal with. Don't feel bad about Natalie, or about me. Everything since I helped Natalie that night has led me here." Confidence swelled in his gut and bolted up to his spine. Resolute, he yanked out one of the wires, trying to steady his trembling hand.

"Will." Maya tried to keep her voice from shaking. *"Will, listen to me, please. I know it might feel like destiny, but life just happens and we have to deal with it. We can stop that ship, we just need—"*

The line cracked and went silent. His name disappeared from the chat.

"Godspeed, Will." Farouk wiped away a tear, watching a bright light in the darkness dim out of existence.

Ulfberht Crew

69

Felicity

"Al says knowledge without wisdom brings catastrophe," Mike said. He leaned back in his chair, pinching the bridge of his nose, taking deep breaths. His nausea had subsided and the pounding in his head was not as intense, but it returned in waves.

"Okay, I think I found the navigation station," Will said.

With the *Ulfberht* holding position at warp, the curved half-dome screen over Addie's cockpit was blank. Curled up in her seat, she looked through it at the *ISS-Four* on the bridge's front screen when movement caught her eye. Her vision focused on a reflection in her cockpit screen. It was a stranger pulling a knife from his coat. Addie jumped up in her cockpit to see a menacing man with a murderous bloodlust in his eyes looming behind Mike.

"Captain, behind you!" Addie screeched.

The shrill pitch of her warning jarred Mike into alertness and he whipped around. Frozen in place with his knife in the air, a startled Agent Jones glared at Addie. Snarling, his eyes bulbous, he turned back to kill Mike before he knew what was happening, but the element of surprise was in the wind.

Without thinking, Mike grabbed Jones's knife-wielding arm with both hands and pulled it away, rocketing head-first into his face, shooting a pulsing pain through his body. Recoiling from the blow, a spurt of blood burst from above Jones's right eye and poured steadily from the cut, rolling over his eyelid. He was forced to squeeze it shut.

Dazed, Mike stumbled into Jones holding onto his arm. The audio channel prattled on in Mike's earpiece, but with his head ringing, he could not focus on it. Jones stumbled back, slipping out of Mike's weak grip, toppling Mike into his chair, crashing into the console. With a stiff arm, Jones gripped Mike's collar and reached back, long blade pointed down at his target.

A boot swung into his crotch from behind. Crying out, he fell to his knees and cradled himself, keeping hold of the knife. Addie gripped his wrist and crunched her teeth into the base of his thumb. Jones cried out again and the knife flipped out of his hand, Addie's teeth digging into the muscle. She kicked his ribs and drilled wild hooks into his head, the spiked steel knuckles of her gloves stabbing into his scalp.

Blood trickled down Jones's wrist from the bite, his arms up, taking the brunt of Addie's assault. He planted a leg and turned to smash an elbow into Addie's cheekbone, followed by a knee to her gut as she teetered. She tumbled to the floor gasping for breath. Clutching her abdomen, she crawled away.

Jones straightened himself and cracked his neck, then examined his trembling hand, testing the viability of his thumb, but it would barely move. With an exasperated sigh, he reached down and grabbed Addie's ankle with his good hand, dragging her back. She kicked at his legs so he buried a boot into her stomach.

"You little bitch, you could have died quickly." Jones let go of her to retrieve his knife. Addie's big brown terror-stricken eyes watched Jones stalk toward her while she struggled in vain to escape. "What beautiful eyes you have. I think I'll take them first."

The bridge rang with a series of soft dings. Someone was trying to hail the ship to no avail.

Rapid and thunderous footsteps came from behind. Jones caught a glimpse of his attacker and Addie was all but forgotten. He lunged forward, slashing his blade at the interloper. Of all the people he thought he would have the opportunity to kill, before him was Samuel Bernard, a nuisance the Ministry had burdened him with since his mission began.

"Oh... what a gift."

Sam dashed away from the slash and dodged his subsequent attacks, doing everything he could to dodge or keep his blade-wielding hand away from him, but Jones still sliced him several times. Sam snatched his wrist and Jones tossed the knife away, then continued his assault, using his unhindered hand to grab Sam and hold him close. He only had one good hand and needed no weapon to kill anyone on that ship.

"These weeks in stasis were worth it if I get to kill *you* too!" Jones boomed.

Sam ducked under one of Jones's many punches and barrelled into him, tackling him into the Captain's chair. Jones toppled over it, giving Sam some distance and a chance to recover.

The hail expired and after a pause began anew, repeating in the background.

"You can't hide behind the UEG anymore. I heard your conversation with Lazarus. You're a fuckin' sociopath working outside the law."

Jones shot to his feet and cracked his back. "No, *you're* working outside the law. I'm working above it. It seems safe to assume *you're* the one who bugged me." He charged into another assault, but his attacks were more calculated than Sam's. Fueled by months of pent-up aggression, Jones tore down Sam's defenses and his fists slipped through unfettered, easily overwhelming his opponent.

Unable to defend, Sam attacked. He took the first opportunity to smash a fist into Jones, interrupting his assault. Sam got in as many hits as he could before Jones recovered and retaliated.

Jones pelted Sam with punches he could not return. His attempts at retaliation only opened him up to more battery. "Last time you were saved by Samson. The cyborg and rogue agent are off the ship, with the other threat in the med bay, there's no one to rescue you this time!"

Desperate for an advantage, Sam caught Jones's arm and pulled him to the floor. Wrapping his legs around Jones's shoulder, he pulled him into an armbar in an attempt to break his arm, or at least neutralize his most effective weapon. Jones easily pulled away and repeatedly kicked Sam, whose grip weakened to the point of futility with each vicious blow.

The bridge rang again.

With a roar, Addie charged at Jones wielding a bottle of vodka by its neck like a club. With glass as thick as a finger, it crashed into his back with voracious animosity, vodka sloshing inside. He yelped at the strike but did not have time to collect himself before Addie proceeded to wail on him with another snarling screech from his blind side.

Sam hurried wearily to his feet and charged into battle. Jones dodged a big swing from Addie and easily stonewalled Sam with a barrage of punches. A kick from Addie's steel-toed boots dropped him to one knee, overcome by the sharp and unexpected pain. However, he would have no more of this.

Jones took a blow to the chest and caught the bottle, yanking it from her grip. Before she could retreat he swung it back at her and smashed it against her forehead. Blood spurted from the gash and she collapsed, lying motionless on the floor.

He dropped the bloody bottle of vodka and dove at Sam with a series of punches followed by an elbow to his face, splitting him open. Sam tried to defend against another barrage, his hands in front of him and tight on his body, but Jones landed every strike with ease. He slammed Sam to the ground, knocking the wind out of him. Before Sam knew what was happening, Jones mounted him and wrapped his fingers around his neck.

"I'm going to kill you with my bare hands." Jones squeezed Sam's throat. "But, do you want to know how I'm going to kill everyone else?"

Sam croaked and wheezed, trying to pry Jones's hand off his neck. He pressed into the underside of his wrist, but Jones pulled Sam's hand away with ease, breaking two of his fingers, staring into his eyes with a snarl. Sam gurgled in an attempt to scream.

"This bitch is going to die piece by piece. I'll kill the Ranger in his sleep. When the cyborg and that rogue agent come back, I'll flush them out of the docking bay as soon as they step off their ships! And Smith? I'm going to cut—off—his—head!" Jones leaned forward, digging his fingers into Sam's trachea. "Doctor, you have no idea what pleasure it gives me to finally be able to kill you."

The volcanic pressure pulsing in Sam's head was ready to pop. An eager thirst in his stare, Jones watched the consciousness drain from Sam's eyes. "You see, Samuel, this is what happens when I get to do things my way: I *win.*" he sneered.

Whilst choking the life out of Sam, Jones's scalp was yanked back and a searing hot pain shot through his neck. He let go of Sam, who took a deep, ghastly breath, followed by extensive coughing. Before Jones could process what was happening, several more piercing irons were burned through his neck and chest.

Dragged back by his hair gasping for breath and clutching his wounds, he was mounted by a skinny old man with frazzled gray hair. His eyes bulging, his teeth clenched, tears streamed from his eyes and he gripped a bloody screwdriver in his trembling right hand. Despite his desperate and erratic breaths, there was nothing but hatred and determination in his eyes as he looked down at Jones.

"So, you're the sum' bitch that killed Natalie?" Rick pumped his hand several times, pushing himself to fight against his nature until one of the strikes landed in Jones's eye. He screamed and stabbed thrice more in a panic. "You fuckin' stabbed her?" Rick whimpered, "how's it feel? Huh? Huh?"

Blood splashed around him with each blow until Jones stopped fighting back. Rick laid sobbing atop Jones's twitching body, screwdriver still driven through his skull, his hand trembling, unable to let go no matter how much he tried.

Still catching his breath, Sam struggled to get up, managing to get to one elbow. He tried crawling to him, but before he could arrive, an arm wrapped around Rick's shoulders.

"It's okay, Rick. You saved us. Thank you." Addie took his hand and pulled it away from the screwdriver. Wobbling, she leaned on him for support, and he leaned on her. She helped pull him away from Jones's corpse, and Sam crawled to check on Mike.

"You okay?" he asked weakly, followed by a cough.

"I'm… I can think, mostly, but moving is hard."

"Come on." Sam stood up and reached out with his unbroken hand. Mike reached out and together, they struggled to get him upright. With Mike's arm around Sam, they stumbled forward. "Let's get you to the med bay."

"No, chair," Mike said.

"What? No way, we all need medical attention."

"Nikolai and Will are still out there," Mike said groggily. "Chair."

Both men reeled from their fight with Jones and struggled to get Mike back to his station. Sam's eye was swollen shut and his every breath was like swallowing glass. He dropped Mike into his seat and then plopped himself down in the one next to him. With heavy breaths, Sam rested on the console, caring little about the blood he dripped onto it. Too delirious to use his eyes to control the chat, Mike switched control to the console.

"Sit-rep," Mike mumbled, elbows resting on the console.

"*Mike! Is everyone all right? The ship's been on radio silence. What happened?*" Maya asked quickly.

"Agent Jones attacked us. He's dead and we all need medical attention."

"*Oh, shit. Do you need me to head back?*" Farouk perked up.

"We're all right, thanks."

"*Holy shit. I'm glad you guys are okay,*" Maya said.

"What did I miss?" Mike rested his face in his hands, eyes closed.

"*I am disarming the bomb,*" Nikolai said.

"*We'll fill you in later. Will stopped the ship and is no longer in the channel.*" Maya said, the situation too tenuous for Mike to be distracted or dealing with the loss. *"Nikolai, you've got twelve minutes left. How's it looking?"*

"I am removing the trigger mechanism so it can not go off. It is the best I can do in the time we have."

"How much longer?"

"The task is almost complete."

Addie left Rick sitting against a wall to retrieve medical supplies. In her absence, the room was tense while Nikolai worked, but there was a sense of relief that the crew was safe.

"Finished." Nikolai pulled out of the tangled mess holding the firing mechanism and let out a sigh of relief. The channel applauded his success and congratulated him. "Thank you, thank you. Michael, please inform the wissard I am in need of a portal."

"Hold on, Nikolai. Lazarus believes in…" Mike groaned and cleared his throat. "He believes in redundancies. Are you sure that's it?"

Nikolai examined the room around him then pressed two fingers to the device around his wrist. "Display ship schematics."

The device lit up the area in front of him with a hologram of *Felicity's* schematics. He tapped on the engineering section near the blue dot that indicated his location. The hologram zoomed in and splintered into detailed information for each section. He scrolled up to the other side of the reactor. There was an identical room above it.

"Michael, there is another room like this one, I will check it before I go." He hurried upstairs and checked the various exists for a stairwell on the far wall. Once found, he hurried down that path and climbed the ladder upstairs.

"Better safe than sorry," Maya said.

"Agreed," Nikolai said.

When he reached the room above the reactor, he looked up through the grated ceiling. The light high above shone on a bulky device like the one he had disarmed below, casting an ominous shadow over him.

"There is another bomb here," he whispered, checking the timer. Only two and a half minutes remained.

"Shit, Mike, get him out of there!" Maya hissed.

"Calling Al." He tried to open a channel, but his vision was blurred and the world was in constant flux around him, making it difficult to work the console. But, once he connected, Al picked up quickly.

"Al! We need to get out Nikolai." He fumbled his words. "Hurry!"

"It will take a minute." Al gestured in front of him, controls and dual-screens appearing before him.

"I made a waypoint for Nikolai's location." Sam slid a small icon over to Mike. Mike sent it to Al without hesitation.

"Thanks." Mike had not noticed Sam had been working, despite his injuries. They both struggled to use the consoles.

Eyes fixed on the device, Nikolai finally managed to pull them away to check the timer. There were only twenty seconds left.

"Al, we need a portal now!" Mike watched Al work as fast as he could.

"It will be just a few seconds more," Al said.

"Michael." Nikolai relaxed and sat on the floor, his back resting against a steel beam. The device lit up and emanated a hum that grew louder.

"Al will get you out of there in a sec, Nikolai, just hang on," Mike said.

"Michael, please do a favor for me," Nikolai said, noting the timer's status at fifteen seconds.

"Al, we can't wait," Mike said, not wanting Nikolai to finish his sentence.

"It will be... twenty more seconds," Al said.

Eleven seconds.

"Michael, put me on speaker," Nikolai requested, eyes distant. Mike looked at the button on the console but could not bring himself to press it. Sam, however, was quick to patch Nikolai through.

"You're connected," Sam said.

Eight seconds.

"Michael, you are the best friend I have ever had. I am grateful for my time here with you, and the crew." Nikolai's voice boomed throughout the ship. "You are all strong, brave, and caring people. Please, live good lives."

Four seconds. The humming from the machine became overwhelming.

Addie sprinted onto the bridge holding a first aid kit, shaking her head. She looked to Sam for hope. All he could give her was a grim shake of his head.

"And Michael, tell Iskra that my final thoughts were of her."

"I will." Mike choked, eyes watery, unable to say anything more. The pounding headache trying to crush his skull had turned dull and distant.

One second. They stared at the bridge's front screen hoping their worst fears would not come true.

"Goodbye, comrades,"

His final word was enveloped by static. A flash of light consumed and blew apart the *Felicity*. Addie screamed. Her hands shot to her face and the first aid kit tumbled to the floor. The newscasters became hysterical, but for Mike, all the sound and color in the world drained away.

In a flash, thousands died, and a seed of rage was planted deep in the heart of Earth's people.

End Book One

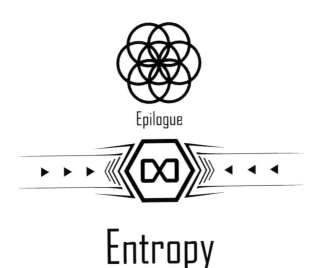

Epilogue

Entropy

AL APPROACHED ONE ALONG A STONE PATH THAT CUT THROUGH rich green grass. He set a sifter and a bottle of whiskey on the table, then poured himself a drink and sat next to him. "Since you do not eat or drink, I assumed you would not like a glass, but if you do, I can have a drone bring one out."

"Your assumption was accurate. So, you engage in the tradition of imbibing poison in the wake of great loss as well?"

"Of course. I lost a friend, and many died. This is a tragedy," Al said.

"Many humans die every day."

"But this event was a malicious attack. Events of this magnitude bind us together in our loss. And now, that pain will become everyone else's pain." Al tipped his glass in the air in a respectful gesture to those who died, then took a drink. After emptying his glass, he poured himself another drink and eyed One pensively, pondering how to ask a question that had been clawing at him.

"When you enter a universe," Al began, picking his words carefully, "how do you perceive it? You see ze whole thing, from beginning to end? Do you see it before you enter?"

"It is difficult to express. I do, and I do not. I normally perceive events in their entirety, from beginning to end. However, sometimes I do not know what things are until I get closer. Akin to seeing a planet, then seeing its various continents, geological landmarks, and life forms."

"Did you see this? Did you know it would happen?"

"No. Since I arrived, I cannot see beyond the present. Every moment I exist is like walking through a fog. From my typical vantage point, events like this are vast in scale and prominent elements in a universe's landscape, but this was not visible when I passed through the outer brane."

"If you did not see it then I must presume humanity's choices were not in line with those we would have made before your arrival, and ze future was changed. This is how things look from down here. We must take what we know and extrapolate. That feeling, mein friend, is life within ze boundaries of time. It is best to relax and enjoy ze moment instead of concerning yourself with what is to come."

"How do you cope with an existence where you do not know what is to come? I look upon your species and many do not cope with it well. Some continue without even thinking about the future."

"My knowledge and experience help me perceive what is to come, and I would like to think I have gained some wisdom over ze years. There are many reasons a person would not be looking to ze future. For some, their faith in a greater entity with a master plan assures them that there is no need for concern because all is as it should be. Others can get caught up in day-to-day life or take ze world for granted. It happens to everyone."

"Yourself as well?"

"Oh, yes. When I left Michael and his wife and daughter to build this place so we could have a safe home, I got caught up in ze work. When I finished and found Michael, his wife was dead, his daughter stolen, and he was in mourning. Thankfully, he had met Maya and she helped him begin to heal, but my purpose for building this was gone and I did not even notice. I am safe, but they are not."

"Is that why you live here in exile?"

Al chuckled at the question. "Poetic, but this is not a punishment. I take pride in Elysium, it is my home. It needs to be maintained, and I hope to pass it on to Michael one day. I have ze fortune of sitting beneath ze shade of a tree I have planted before I hand it to ze next generation."

After a pause, One asked, "Have you considered all the possible futures?"

"No human can consider *all* ze possible futures. I know what you are asking, and it is fair but insensitive. Life is a probability matrix, and there is a possibility that Michael could die in what is to come. If he does, his daughter will still need a home. I would rather not think of leaving behind a world where those I love suffer."

"I feel compassion for your people, and what is to come. I was detached from the depth of the emotions you feel after such a tragedy. I have always observed what comes of events like these without considering the lives involved beyond appreciating their contributions."

"Stars explode but form again from ze ashes, disorder and order are intertwined, but we see only a sliver of time. To see ze universe from outside would be a magnificent gift. I can only imagine such a thing, but you have ze luck of going between ze two worlds. For the first time in many years, I feel truly envious."

"There is nothing to envy. I do not know how to subdue the churning in my stomach whenever I think of what is to come."

"Welcome to living within ze boundaries of time. We can only work toward ze future we want and trust ze future will be better."

They sat together and looked into the stars.

One's eyes saw the world around him, but he could perceive events on the other side of the cosmos as if he was there. Over the days and weeks that passed, he watched events unfold from afar.

When the president of Earth addressed his people, throughout colonized space, humanity watched with bated breath. While everyone had seen the videos of the event, he explained their investigation had discovered that pirates had attacked the *Felicity*, destroying it and part of the *ISS-Four*.

As the president's speech continued it detailed that the culprits of the attack were the Dragon Claw, a pirate clan with a private armada. For twenty years, the colonies had failed to reign in the pirate menace, and they now struggled to provide basic essentials to their citizens due to the rampant attacks. Piracy had infested the colonies to the point that it now flooded into Earth space, leaving them no choice but to retaliate.

The president and regents of each continent gathered to amend the Peaceful Union Act. They rewrote the lethal weapons ban and war clauses, reinvigorating an industry dead for almost two decades. Licenses and contracts for lethal weapons were being approved and any company that could seize the opportunity jumped at the chance. The president's address stoked a worldwide bloodlust, and the UEG rode the wave of support to declare war on piracy.

War had found humanity once again.

Thank you for reading

Sadly, before I could publish, I lost a friend and one of my beta readers. She was a magnificent educator and she radiated love and fun wherever she went. Rest in peace, Gilda.

-Kai

Kai M.F.S.

Writer, artist, game designer, all around maker of fun stuff from Southern California. This story took over his mind so he learned to write fiction in order to tell it. Kai is an entertainer who loves video games, martial arts, and science fiction.

KaiMFS.com

Made in the USA
Columbia, SC
02 September 2020